W9-BMA-16

JUPITER:
27TH CENTURY

He was Hope Hubris: born into a grim life of slavery . . . until violence ripped his world apart, claiming his family and firing him with a hunger for vengeance.

Fueled by his own fury, he rose to triumph—obliterating his enemies and blazing a path of glory across the face of Jupiter. Military legend . . . people's champion, promising political candidate . . . he now awoke to find himself the prisoner of a nightmare that knew no past.

Other Books by
Piers Anthony

BIO OF A SPACE TYRANT
VOLUME 1: REFUGEE
VOLUME 2: MERCENARY

BATTLE CIRCLE

THE CLUSTER SERIES
CLUSTER
CHAINING THE LADY
KIRLIAN QUEST
THOUSANDSTAR
VISCOUS CIRCLE

MACROSCOPE
MUTE
OMNIVORE
ORN
OX

Coming Soon

BIO OF A SPACE TYRANT
VOLUME 4: EXECUTIVE

Avon Books are available at special quantity discounts for bulk purchases for sales promotions, premiums, fund raising or educational use. Special books, or book excerpts, can also be created to fit specific needs.

For details write or telephone the office of the Director of Special Markets, Avon Books, Dept. FP, 1790 Broadway, New York, New York 10019, 212-399-1357. *IN CANADA:* Director of Special Sales, Avon Books of Canada, Suite 210, 2061 McCowan Rd., Scarborough, Ontario M1S 3Y6, 416-293-9404.

BIO OF A SPACE TYRANT
VOLUME 3: POLITICIAN

PIERS ANTHONY

AVON
PUBLISHERS OF BARD, CAMELOT, DISCUS AND FLARE BOOKS

BIO OF A SPACE TYRANT VOLUME 3: POLITICIAN is
an original publication of Avon Books. This work has never
before appeared in book form. This work is a novel. Any
similarity to actual persons or events is purely coincidental.

AVON BOOKS
A division of
The Hearst Corporation
1790 Broadway
New York, New York 10019

Copyright © 1985 by Piers Anthony Jacob
Published by arrangement with the author
Library of Congress Catalog Card Number: 84-091247
ISBN: 0-380-89685-0

All rights reserved, which includes the right to reproduce
this book or portions thereof in any form whatsoever except
as provided by the U. S. Copyright Law. For information
address Kirby McCauley Ltd., 425 Park Avenue South,
New York, New York 10016.

First Avon Printing, May 1985

AVON TRADEMARK REG. U. S. PAT. OFF. AND IN
OTHER COUNTRIES, MARCA REGISTRADA, HECHO EN
U. S. A.

Printed in the U. S. A.

WFH 10 9 8 7 6 5 4 3 2 1

Contents

Editorial Preface

This is the third of five manuscripts to be published following the death of Hope Hubris, the so-called Tyrant of Jupiter, detailing his private impressions of his ascent through the political currents of the planet. The first manuscript covers his traumatic experience as a Hispanic refugee in space at age fifteen; the second covers the period of his enlistment in the Jupiter Navy. He has in all these narratives neglected or glossed over many of the technical details, such as hard-nosed quid-pro-quo bargaining or necessary political compromises or tedious research on issues and rivals. It is evident that his true interest was not in these things, though he was competent in all of them and always did what he needed to prevail. Fortunately, much of that material is available in the open record, while the purely personal aspect is not. It has been too easy for historians to forget that the Tyrant was in fact an intensely personal man, by no means arbitrary or cold-blooded in his dealings with others. This volume should help correct that misimpression, however else it may be faulted. It also clarifies the basis of such things as the "Sancho" situation, the mystery of "Dorian Gray," and the secret of how the Tyrant learned to speak Russian, and it offers hints of his nature that in retrospect make his tenure as the Tyrant less perplexing. Of course, no one realized, in the period that this manuscript covers, that he was destined to assume that power. He was merely a Hispanic politician.

H. M. H.

Chapter 1

SUB

I woke in squalor. The stench tried to choke me; I found myself trying to breathe only out, never in, but of course, that was futile.

Where was I? Darkness pressed in about me, absolute, impenetrable, horrifying. Slowly my disgust at the odor faded as my alarm at the gloom gained. Was I incarcerated in some deep subterranean cell, doomed never to see light again?

My panic gave way in turn to some common sense. Subterranean cells were rare, for in this age of space, mankind existed mostly in pressurized bubbles that orbited in interplanetary reaches or floated in planetary atmosphere or adhered to the surfaces of moons or fragments. Only in the last case was there any terrain to delve beneath—and that was generally used only for secure anchorage, being too precious to waste on mere people. If someone needed confinement it was easier to put him in a cage than to excavate a hole in a frozen moon. I was not even cold; the temperature was neutral. So, if I was buried it was in the bowel of some city or ship, and others of my kind were close by.

My mind focused on this problem, as I seemed to have nothing better to do at the moment, and it distracted me from the discomfort of my situation. If I assumed I was in a city—what city might that be?

Well, where had I last been? Again panic welled up. I could not remember! My past was blank. I had a general knowledge of solar geography but could not place myself within it. It was as if I did not exist.

Of course I existed, I reassured myself. I was here, wasn't I? Surely I had not formed spontaneously in the sludge of the Nile! I was an adult human being.

3

The Nile—that was on Planet Earth, the location of the origin of man. My kind had evolved there, learned to prevail over the restrictions of nature, and increased its population at the expense of other creatures and the natural environment until over five billion human beings crowded the single planet. Then the development of gravity shielding had enabled man to travel cheaply to other parts of the Solar System and to colonize them. It was simply a matter of building bubbles, which were giant spheres, hermetically sealed, pressurized to normal Earth-surface atmosphere, spun to generate centrifugal pseudogravity —simply termed gee—and stocked with necessary equipment and supplies. Then these bubbles were loaded with people and shielded from the effect of planetary gravity so that they floated free of the ground and, indeed, free of the atmosphere. If gravity diffusion is sufficient to reduce the effective weight of an object to one percent of its normal weight, a propulsive force of one percent will do the job of lifting that otherwise requires a hundred percent. That makes it relatively easy to escape the gravity well of a planet. Of course, mass, as contrasted to weight, is unchanged; acceleration in space still requires full force. But the enormous problem of planetary escape had been solved. Man utilized gravity shielding to spread explosively across the Solar System. He has not spread out into the wider galaxy because the shielding does not facilitate that; the ancient Einsteinian limits hold.

When the flow of gravitrons is focused instead of diffused, the effective weight of an object in that field of focus is increased. In this manner man was able to generate full Earth-gee in selected spots on the surfaces of smaller bodies, such as the moons of Jupiter. The city of Maraud, on Callisto, is an example; I had spent my childhood there. . . .

Callisto! I had just located myself on a body in the Solar System. My obscure past was beginning to clarify!

But my memory remained fogged. I had, as it were, spied Callisto peripherally; when my full mental gaze fixed on it, I could not perceive it. But at least I had gained something. Obviously I had been memory-washed. . . .

Memory-washed! Why should such a thing have happened to me? I was just a poor Hispanic serf who had lost his parents in space, and . . .

Lost my parents? Sudden sorrow swept over me. But again, as I focused it was gone. Memory-wash is like that; it blots out all recent experience, leaving only the early, and even that suffers depletion. The victim remembers the language, culture, schooling, and childhood, but not the events immediately preceding the wash. Only time could restore it all; months and years are required for the final details. Mem-wash is an electrochemical treatment that stuns rather than obliterates the key processes of recollection, but in the first few weeks it really makes little difference to the subject. He has been born again in innocence.

Such treatment is, of course, illegal. That meant that I was the victim of pirates or foreign agents, because ordinary people did not have the equipment or expertise for such a procedure. I must have done something or known something that—no, the wash is not a good interrogative technique, since it obliterates anything an interrogator might wish to know. So it wasn't any secret that my captor wanted of me.

What, then? It had to be something important but not anything ordinary. Had I learned something, such as a military secret, that had to be erased? Surely it would have been easier to kill me. Was I a criminal being reconditioned? That did not account for the filth I was mired in, for no legitimate rehabilitation institution would have permitted this. I was being deliberately degraded.

Well, in time I would remember. Meanwhile my best prospect seemed to be to figure out my present location, as that might offer some insight. I had started to do that before, but my mind had wandered, as a washed brain is apt to do. Suppose I was in a city? Maybe one of the bubble-cities of the Jupiter atmosphere, floating a current. If so, I should be able to tell my general location within it by my weight. A spinning sphere is not a perfect place to reside. Only a narrow band around the inside of the equator of the bubble can be set at gee; that is, precisely Earth gravity. Of course, this can be broadened by using a secant, cutting off a segment with a curved plane—um, I see that seems nonsensical. It's a plane running east-west but curved north-south or vice-versa; an effectively level band circling the inside of the bubble, really a cylinder. That cylinder can vastly increase the area of gee within the bubble, and all of the residential section of a city is on it. The heavy machinery is mostly below (i.e., farther from the center), occupying the region of gee-plus, while the gee-minus region above is left for air and light. So if I were in a cell in such a city, I would be normal weight only on that surface. In the upper section of a tall structure (one reaching in toward the bubble-center) I would weigh less, and down in the nether region I would weigh more. In a small bubble the divergence from gee is sharp; in a large one, slight. But it is detectable, for the human body is a finely tuned apparatus and quickly feels the effect of changed gee.

I concluded that I was at or very near gee, for my body felt normal in this respect despite my discomfort. I must have been here for several days, at least, for it was my own excrement that I squatted in. Each person's stink of refuse is different, and I knew my own. I had had time to feel any divergence from the Earth norm, and there seemed to be none.

If the excrement was my own, why had it so assaulted my nostrils as I woke? If I had been here for days, my nose should have been numb long since, as it was numbing now. Therefore I must have been away and then abruptly returned here—immediately after my memory-wash. Was that useful information? Perhaps not, but I would file it for reference.

The residential level of a city is not a place for private incarceration. For one thing gee-level is expensive real estate—about a dollar per square foot per month. That's just for the area, before charges for air, water, light, and services. Very few individuals would care to waste such area on excrement. Also, the smell, if it got out, would quickly attract the attention of a sanitation squad. And what if the prisoner banged on the wall? A secret operation could not remain secret long.

I was, therefore, probably not in an occupied city. However, there were agricultural bubbles with animals and manure. One of these might—

Light flared blindingly. I cowered away from it, clamping my eyes shut, covering them with soiled hands. A panel above had abruptly opened, illuminating my cell.

"Out, Hubris," a man's voice called. "Time for treatment."

Hubris! That was my name! I knew it, of course, yet had not thought of it. But what was this "treatment"? I distrusted that. Obviously I had already had the mem-wash treatment.

"Move it, Hubris," the voice snapped. I realize it isn't quite correct to personify the voice that way, but that was all I had to go on. It was masculine and unfamiliar.

No hand touched me. I suspected this was because I was naked and filthy, an untouchable. I pushed myself slowly to my feet, my eyes adjusting. My cell was small, a cube about four feet on a side. I had not tried to stand or stretch before; if I had done so I would have banged into the unseen limits.

As I got upright I felt light-headed. This could have been from the release from a cramped position, of course, but it could also signify a lessened gee. In that case this was no large city or agricultural sphere; it was a small bubble or a ship. Could I be aboard a naval vessel?

Goaded by the voice, I climbed out of the cell, into a passage. Yes, it was a ship, gee lessened in the walkway above the cells. I proceeded to a shower stall where I was efficiently hosed down. All water is recycled, so there is no waste in a liquid shower, though normally sonic cleaning is used instead. Obviously strenuous cleansing was required for me. In a moment I was free of filth. Then the sonics came on, prying free whatever contamination might remain.

Next, still naked, I was taken to a clean cell whose walls were padded. I was strapped into a padded chair. I did not like this at all, but it seemed pointless to resist until I knew more about my situation. If I broke and ran where could I run to on a ship in space?

The man who had seen to my preparation departed, and a new one entered the chamber. Evidently he was of greater authority. He fetched a small console that had buttons and dials. He twisted a dial and punched a button— and suddenly I was in pain. It felt as if my left foot were being crushed under an immense crate. I cried out and looked at it, for I could not jerk it away. There was nothing. Just the confining strap and the pain.

The man touched another button, and the agony shifted to my right foot, easing in my left. "That's a torture console!" I gasped, catching on.

The man did not respond. He touched another button, and the pain was in my right hand. Another, and the left hand. It felt as if my fingers were being pressed in a vice; in my mind's eye I almost saw the flesh splitting open and the blood bursting out. Yet I was not being touched.

"You don't need to do that!" I cried. "Just tell me what you want of me!"

The man ignored me. He changed the setting, and it was like being punched in the stomach. I gasped and fought for breath and tried to retch all at once, but only succeeded in drooling on myself.

"Why?" I rasped as the pain eased, but there was no answer.

The agony moved into my chest, and I thought I was having a heart attack. I strained at my bonds, unable even to scream. It felt like eternity but must have been only a few seconds.

Finally the torture struck my head. The brain feels no pain, but the blood vessels do. The pain blossomed in my skull like bursting arteries, and I sank into an agony of darkness.

I woke in my filthy cell, in more darkness. I did not know how long the interval had been; perhaps only a few minutes. Almost worse than the memory of the pain was the bafflement. Why had the torture been inflicted? I had offered no resistance, not even verbal retort, yet I had been tortured. In what way had I gone wrong? How could I avoid further pain? I did not know.

Why was I here? I did not know that, either. What was my position in life? That, too, was opaque. My captors seemed to be interested only in degradation and agony.

At least I now had a clearer notion where I was. Definitely a ship and not a civilian one. I had spent time in the Jupiter Navy, and . . .

There was another fragment of memory. The Navy! But that awareness, like the others, faded as I realized it. Now all I had was the memory of my recollection; it was as if someone had told me, "You were once in the Navy," without providing further detail, so that I had no context.

At any rate, I knew ships, and the little I had seen of this one was enough to narrow the possibilities considerably. It was a military vessel but not a standard one. It was too small to be a battleship, cruiser, or carrier; too big for a gunboat. It was silent; no motors hummed. That was peculiar. The only small ship designed for silence while in operation was—

A sub.

A sub was a very special type of ship. It was a military vessel dedicated to secrecy, to virtual invisibility in space. In the historic days, most naval vessels floated, on the surface of Earth's oceans of water (what a mind-staggering concept: all that water!), plainly visible, protecting themselves with armor and armament. Subs—actually, originally, submarines, being submersible in the fluid of the sea—were largely undetectable and so represented a formidable menace to surface ships. They carried torpedoes that could hole other vessels that never perceived the threat against them until too late, and later they carried missiles that even menaced land targets. This was especially true in the nuclear age of the twentieth century, about seven hundred years ago—how time flies!—and I suspect was one of the factors that spurred man's colonization of the Solar System. After all, what sensible person would care to reside on a planet whose cities were subject to obliteration by missiles launched elsewhere on that same planet? It's bad enough as it is now, when the threat of annihilation is merely interplanetary. Today we have greater warning.

Or *do* we? Today's subs are very similar to the ancient waterbound ones. In fact, any spaceship resembles the old submarine, in that it is tightly sealed against a hostile exterior environment. Then that environment was water under high pressure, always threatening to implode the vessel and crush everything inside to pulp. Today it is the vacuum of space, threatening, as it were, to suck everything out. In each case, the occupants cannot depart their ship without employing protective gear, and few care to go out, anyway. Modern subs are specifically similar to their ancestral vessels in that they still carry torpedoes and missiles and remain concealed in the depths of the environment.

How is this possible in bright open solar space? Oh, yes, it's always sunshine here; only on the limited backsides of planets does natural darkness occur. We become so accustomed to our structured cycles of day and night, patterned exactly after those of old Earth, that we tend to forget that it is not that way naturally. The murk of the ocean water concealed the ancients, but there is little murk for the moderns. The subs of either age make themselves physically quiet by damping down the sounds they generate and, when pressed, turning off all power and drifting "dead" in water or space. It is difficult to spot a small dead object in space, for space is immense. There may still be uncharted planetoids orbiting the sun. Consider how long it took for Earthly telescopes to identify our companion star, Nemesis. But in the vicinity of an inhabited planet a sub's mere silence is not sufficient, for the space there is constantly explored by radar. Nevertheless, subs often evade detection. To understand how this is possible, it is necessary to grasp the general nature of radar and similar systems.

Radar is simply an electronic signal broadcast into space. When it encounters an object, it bounces back to its source. A receiver notes that returning signal and calculates the distance by the time required for the signal to return. This is normally a reliable procedure, except when the region is crowded with a confusing number of objects, such as the particles of a planetary ring system. Even then, a properly programmed computer can identify all of the natural and "friendly" objects in the vicinity and highlight the suspicious ones. But the principle remains: The computer depends on the returning signals to spot the objects. If no signal returns the machine assumes that region of space is clear. This seems reasonable enough.

But suppose you could evade or divert the signal, so that it did not bounce back? Reflect it to the side instead of back? Or simply absorb it? That is what a sub does. It uses a special gravity shield to form a black-hole effect that absorbs all incoming energy, including the radar signals. That makes it effectively invisible to radar. Of course some care is necessary; if a sub passes between a person and the sun, it will show up as a dark blot. It also blots out the light of any star it occludes. Parties watching for subs are alert for this and pay close attention to what isn't visible, such as a particular star, as well as what is. Again, a programmed computer can constantly verify the positions of all light sources and signal alarm when any fail even momentarily. But a carefully maneuvered sub can avoid occluding any sufficiently bright stars while it floats near a planet and so remain invisible—up to a point. Close to a planet there are too many watching satellites, and the silhouette of the sub looms proportionately larger until concealment is impossible.

So most subs remain deep enough in space to hide but as close to the target planet as feasible, covering it with their deadly missiles. Jupiter subs surround Saturn, and Saturnine subs surround Jupiter. If war should break out the planet-to-planet missiles might well be intercepted before scoring, but sub-to-planet missiles could devastate any city on any planet. That is the true balance of terror. Subs, more than any other factor, contribute to the general feeling of insecurity on every planet; no one can be sure that his city would survive a third System war—and there is a general fear that such a war is inevitable. It makes planetary populations edgy, in much the way that a man threatened with arbitrary execution might be edgy. There are reasonably frequent flare-ups of protest and even violence scattered around the System, but no one has found a way to diffuse the threat. Perhaps one of the major appeals of the difficult life in the Belt is that the widely scattered settlements there would be most likely to survive a System war.

So I was in a sub. What was the significance of that? This was surely not a missile sub; those were too precious for the mere torturing of mem-washed captives. But escape from *any* sub was hopeless to the nth power. I couldn't flash a light out a porthole, for the signal-damping field would extinguish that. Theoretically I might surprise someone, grab a weapon, and take over the ship, but that sort of heroic is feasible only in fiction, and not the best fiction at that. In real life ships have safeguards, such as automatic sleep gas released into the air when unauthorized personnel step onto the bridge, and secret codes for the life systems support and drive computers. Only the regular personnel could operate this ship; I knew that without needing verification. It was one of the advantages of my Navy experience: I knew what wasn't practical. All I could do was try to steal a suit and escape the ship—and outside was only the void.

My presence here also meant that some military outfit was in charge, for civilians did not have subs of any kind and neither did pirates. Only governments. That meant I was the captive of a nation. Was I a hostage? Then why the mem-wash, degradation, and torture? That didn't seem to make a lot of sense. It would help if I could remember my position in life, but evidently they didn't want me to know it. Maybe I was some high military officer who knew something about an enemy nation's covert operations; they had kidnapped me and now were trying to erase that knowledge from my mind. Yet the torture wouldn't help do that. . . .

The panel opened again, blindingly. I clamped my eyes shut again. Something dropped beside me; then the panel closed.

I felt about me and found a soiled package. It was a loose net enclosing a hard loaf of bread and a soft plastic bottle of fluid. This was my meal, and it was already soiled with my own excrement.

I discovered I was ravenous. But how could I eat bread smeared with fecal matter? If I did it would only process through my system to become more excrement. Yet what choice did I have? If I did not eat I would starve.

I wiped off the bread as well as I could against my upper arm. In the darkness I couldn't see how well I was doing, but when I bit into it, I could tell that the job was incomplete; some refuse had been absorbed by the crust. I controlled my finicky reflex, uncertain how long it would be before I received anything more to eat. I drank the fluid; it seemed to be straight water.

As I finished the bread, I chewed down on something hard. Startled and pained, though the sensation was only a whisper of what I had felt during the torture session, I dropped my jaw reflexively without opening my mouth. The object jumped to my throat and I swallowed it before I could control myself. The thing tried to catch in my throat, scraping it; I had to gulp the last of my water to get it clear.

How had something like that, whatever it was, gotten into my bread? Were they trying to break my teeth? That didn't make much sense; they could break my teeth directly if they wanted to. Evidently they didn't want to; they preferred to torture me in various ways without physically injuring me. So this had to be poor quality control. Henceforth I would chew more carefully.

I tried to move about, to get more comfortable, but there was no comfortable position in the limited cell. I drifted off to sleep, steeped in my own manure.

It was hard to judge time in this eternal opacity. In due course I woke, feeling the urge of nature, and had no choice but to contribute to the refuse already all around me. Well, perhaps I could judge the passage of time by the level of organic matter. That indicated perhaps one more day, added to the several that had preceded my present awareness. I slept again.

More time passed, and the darkness remained, broken only by the periodic openings of the bright panel for food and, again, my removal for cleaning and a torture session. I feared and hated that pain, finding no rationale for it; apparently my captors simply wanted me to hurt. Hurt I did, though there was no mark on my body.

I had to do something to preserve my sanity, for the deprivation of comfort, light, and memory was getting to me, as it surely was supposed to. I explored my cell, discovering only blank walls. No help there, either physical or mental. I sank slowly into apathy.

Then I became aware of a presence. There was someone in the chamber with me! The panel had not opened, but somehow an entrance had been made.

"Who . . . ?" I asked.

A warm hand came to touch my arm. "Don't you remember me, Hope? I am Helse."

Helse! I remembered her but without context. I loved her.

I took her in my arms. I was covered with slop, while she was clean, but she did not protest. She moved her sleek body to accommodate me and spread her finely fleshed thighs to embrace me, and she was as naked as I, and the shape of man's desire. She leaned forward to kiss me, and her lips were honey and her breasts touched me with electrifying sensation. Suddenly I was in her, penetrating more deeply than I had thought possible, and my essence was pumping into her with an almost intolerable pleasure.

Then she was gone, and I was left spent, my substance dribbling into the muck. Helse had not been real; she had been a succubus, a phantom of my desire.

Yet I knew I had loved her in reality, once. Where and when and how had that been? What had become of her? What had become of *me?*

Dispirited, I tried again to remember my situation but could not. All I remembered was my distant past. I had grown up on Callisto, part of a family of five. Two sisters, one older, one younger, but I could not recall their names. Mem-wash does tend to eradicate specifics, such as names, more than generalities, such as being part of a family.

I wrestled with that, annoyed that my own family names should be lost. I was sure that if I could once catch a name, I would retain it. Helse had given me my own, Hope, though I seemed to have little hope at the moment. My father had been . . . surely my own surname should—ah, I had it! Major Hubris, who worked at the coffee plantation. My mother, his wife, Mrs. . . . Charity Hubris! And . . .

Suddenly I had it all, as if the memories had been accumulating in the course of the recent hours, awaiting this effort. We three children—Faith, Hope, and Spirit. We had had to leave Callisto and had suffered disaster.

Almost, I wished that memory had remained obscure. My father, my mother—brutally dead in space. My older sister raped. Our friends and associates perished. I alone had survived that terrible journey. No—some children had been taken as slaves perhaps. And my sisters had not died, that I knew of, but perhaps they might as well have. They had been taken aboard pirate ships. And my girl friend, my woman, my beloved Helse . . .

I screamed, but it did no good. Still I saw Helse's corpse. I had survived but at what price? My love had perished.

I banged my fist against the wall, trying to stifle the pain of memory; that was as bad in its fashion as the physical agony of the torture. But there was no escaping this horror. I sank back into the muck, my mind feeling as soiled as my body. The guilt of Helse's death lay on me.

Yet she had returned to me, here in this hole, to love me one more time. How much better her love had been than mine!

Finally I slept, dreamed, and woke in an agony of remorse. Whatever had happened after Helse died hardly mattered. If it had led me to this hole, well, here was my punishment, fitting enough. Helse had forgiven me, but I had not forgiven myself.

At some point the panel opened and another meal plopped down. Another six hours gone, perhaps. I ate, having no resistance, and chewed on another object. This time I fished it out of my mouth and felt it with my fingers. It was a sharp-edged fragment of metal, a rivet or nail. It must have been a similar object that I had swallowed before. I hoped it wasn't chewing up my insides, then realized that it didn't matter; what was a little more punishment to one who deserved it?

Yet the sharpness of it gave me a notion. Was it enough to scratch the metal wall? I could mark off meals, keeping track of time more precisely. . . .

Time? Why bother. I was here as long as my captors decreed. Better to write myself a message of consolation.

I propped myself up, slid my fingers along the wall to verify that it was smooth—and discovered that it wasn't. There were scratches already on it, perhaps made by a prior prisoner. Not large or obvious—of course, they were invisible in the pitch darkness—but clearly the handiwork of some person. I traced to the upper left and found the edge of the scratches, licking my fingertips to make them more sensitive, never mind what they tasted of. Could it be?

Yes! There was a number there. The figure 1. Next to it, the figure 2, and on, proceeding to the right, a continuing series. There were four lines of numbers, and when I had traced them all, this was the pattern:

```
1   2   1   14   4   15   14   27   8
15   16   5   29   27   1   12   12   25
5   27   23   8   15   27   5   14   20
5   18   27   8   5   18   5   28   27
```

I sat back and pondered. Obviously someone had used a pointed bit of metal, like the one I had recovered from the bread, to scratch this series. Why?

Why else? A message! In code, so the captors would not realize. A message to whomever followed. A camaraderie of prisoners, the first extending this tiny fragment of comfort to the next.

Code. Would the numbers simply stand for letters of the alphabet? That seemed too easy, but I tried it. Let 1 be A, 2 be B, 3 be C, and so on through. What was the result?

I worked it out, and was amazed at the confirmation and ease of translation. I had hit it right the first time. 27 was a space, 28 a period, 29 a comma. The message said: ABANDON HOPE, ALL YE WHO ENTER HERE.

My enthusiasm collapsed. This was no communication of encouragement—it was counsel for defeat! Who would do such a thing?

I pondered, still bemused at how readily I had unriddled the sequence. It was almost as if my thoughts were identical to those of the prior occupant. And the message itself, so simply coded—any guard could have translated it almost as readily as I had. This could hardly be expected to remain secret.

Then I suffered a new revelation: It was *supposed* to be easy! This was an open code, intended for the guards to decipher; therefore its message was spurious.

Yet what was the point? The captors had complete control, anyway; what did it matter whether they were fooled by a pseudosecret message?

I rolled it over in my mind. I was a creature of reason; I believed in cause and effect and in purpose in everything, however devious. If I assumed the prior prisoner had a mind like mine, then he certainly had had reason to plant that message. What would my reason be if I were to do such a thing?

Well, confusion. That is, I would try to fool the captors into believing I had capitulated, when in fact I had not. That way they might go easy on me. That was certainly a worthwhile effort.

Still, it wasn't enough. What other reason might there be?

A diversion. Like sleight of hand, an action of one type

that diverted attention from a more important action elsewhere.

What else could there be, here in the dark, in accumu-
lated excrement?

I mulled it over. Then, cautiously, I slid my hands along
the floor beneath me, under the slop.

Sure enough—there were scratches. A hidden message!
But these were neither letters nor numbers. They
seemed to be a pattern of boxes, like the border of embroi-
dery, some complete, some partial, some with dots or circles inside, some empty. What did it mean?

It meant a more sophisticated code, obviously. One that
would not yield readily to simple analysis. One the captors
could not decipher, assuming they became aware of it at
all. A double baffle: concealment where they would be
least likely to look, and an almost impossible code to crack!

Who would devise such a thing? Offhand I had just one
prospect: myself.

If I had been confined here and had known or suspected
that I was to be subjected to memory-wash, this was what I
would do. Leave a secret message to myself, to provide necessary information to confound my captors.

Well, had it been me? Quite possibly. As I explained, I
know the smell of my own refuse; some practical calcula-
tion based on the estimated quantity of material suggested
that I had spent about a week here before the mem-wash,
and my memory would have been with me then. I had
known or suspected what was coming, so it was only natural that I prepare for this post-wash period. My life and
welfare probably depended on it.

It *had* to be me; I had used a quote drawn from Dante's
Commedia that related most aptly to my situation: the
soul's entry to hell. It even included my name: Hope. I was
literally the Hope who had been abandoned. No one but me
would have thought to use that particular reference.

This conclusion was exhilarating. Now I had, as it were,
a companion in the cell whom I could trust absolutely: my
former self. One who might not have known the future, but
certainly knew the past, and would share it with me. Now
I could tackle the problem of my captivity with confidence.

Why had my captors waited a week to mem-wash me?
Not for psychological reasons, as the mem-wash would

wipe out any attitude I developed. Probably the sub had taken time to work its way free of the planetary environment without risking discovery, so they had waited to give me the treatment until they were certain things were secure. If they got caught early they could be charged only with abduction. So they had locked me into this secret hole and allowed my filth to accumulate so that it would have the appropriate psychological effect after the mem-wash. There was no problem about illness deriving from the filth, as there were no applicable agents of disease here. Certainly they were putting pressure on me by keeping me in a degrading situation except when they actively tortured me. The average person would soon break down under such treatment and do anything the captors wanted, just to get free of it.

Unfortunately for them I was not an average person. I had prepared for my humiliation and incarceration, giving my mind something compelling to occupy it. And, surely, some advice on how to deal with this situation.

Well and good. Now all I had to do was crack my own code. Doubtless I had learned its elements somewhere during the period of my life now washed out of memory. Or had I? Surely I would have anticipated that forgetting, so would have made it a point to draw from my early memories, giving myself a chance while keeping it difficult for any other person.

I felt again for the scratches—and realized that I might be under observation now, or at least monitored by recording. The cell was quite dark to me, but might not be so to my captors. That meant I should be careful how I approached the message below, so as not to give away its presence. Indeed, why had I hidden it so carefully, unless concealment were necessary? The "open" message on the wall suggested that I should at least *seem* to abandon hope. I had to seem to be sleeping or mulling fatalistically on my fate.

I reached up and retraced the message on the wall. I shook my head in obvious frustration. "But I don't even know what they want!" I muttered. "I *have* no hope, but they pay no attention!" It was easy to say; the isolation and degradation and torture sessions were intended to make me feel that way, and to an extent they did. The pattern was beginning to make sense.

I settled back with obvious resignation, one hand supporting my body partially upright. It was almost impossible to get comfortable here, physically, which was part of the point. Break a man down physically and you're on the way to breaking him down emotionally. The linkages are stronger than many people choose to realize. But I had experienced privation before; this really wasn't that bad.

My fingers slowly traced the scratches. I found where they began—I hoped. The first six were as follows:

ⴺ ⴺ ⴲ ⵝ ⵀ ⴺ

That was two ⴺ s, a ⴲ , a ⵀ , and two ⴲ s, one with an X in it. Probably orientation and the addition of an X made them different symbols, so only two were really the same: the first and sixth. What did they mean?

Now I remembered. My little sister Spirit and I had had a code game we had learned from a friend when we were children on Callisto. The letters of the alphabet were charted in grids, and segments of those grids became the representations of those letters. I think such games have been around for centuries. One grid had nine combinations, so that it translated into nine letters, in this manner:

The second grid had dots in the figures, for the next nine letters, and a third grid, with Xs in the figures, finished out the alphabet. A fairly easy translation had produced a marvelously hierographic rendition, fascinating us. We had had quite a fling with it, in English and in Spanish, when I was twelve and she was nine. Somehow it was usually Spirit I was closest to, rather than my older sister Faith. Spirit always joined me in childish pastimes while Faith found them—and us—beneath her. I had evidently drawn on that old code for this occasion.

For a moment I paused, savoring the strengthening memory of Spirit. What an engaging child she had been!

Not beautiful like her older sister but spunky, always full
of fight and humor, always there in my support. Some boys
have contempt for their little sisters; not me. Spirit had always been my complementary aspect, a girl who was a better friend than any boy had been. Where was she now? My
memory did not say, but surely she was looking out for me
as she always had.

If I had used that code, translation would be easy. I pic-
tured the grids in my mind; the pattern of them made visu-
alization feasible. ⊐ would be the second grid, fourth
section, or the thirteenth letter of the alphabet: M.   ⊐ was
in the first grid, the fourth square: D. And so on, spelling
the word MDGYBM.

I considered that, disappointed. Obviously that wasn't
it. Yet I was sure I was on the right track.

Well, perhaps a direct translation was too simple; the
captors could intercept it too readily. What else was there?

An indirect translation, of course. One that required an
additional key, that no other person had. Something I
carried in my head. A key phrase or sentence—that was
the way my mind worked.

Somewhere along the way I had learned about binary
codes—systems in which two elements were required to
encrypt and decrypt messages. One part might contain the
letters of the words, and the other part the mechanism for
putting those letters and words in proper order. That's an
oversimplification, but it suffices for now. If you have a
mere jumble or a simple listing of thirty As, five Bs, eight
Cs, ten Ds, one hundred and four Es, and so on, you are
hard-put to interpret the message. But if all you know is
the order, not the letters—one letter from the fifth group
followed by one from the sixth and so on—and the sample
is brief, you can't decipher it, either. I knew that the first
and sixth letters of this hieroglyphic message were the
same, but which letter might that be? It could be almost
anything. I needed both parts of the code, and all I had was
one. I had MDGYBM—how did it translate?

Where was the other part? It had to be accessible to me
or the exercise was pointless. I pondered awhile and concluded that it had to be in my head. Some key that only I
would know, that would survive a memory-wash. The
hieroglyphic code was an example: a person who lacked my

childhood experience with that code would not be able to make sense of those symbols. Even so, I had made only partial sense of them. The letters could be filled into that pattern in any order, and my sample wasn't large enough to analyze for any recurring pattern, not even if I translated all the characters on the floor.

Recurring pattern? There might not be any! Now another aspect of coding came back to me: the variable displacement. The first and sixth symbols might not stand for the same letter! There could be a translation key that said the first symbol stood for the tenth letter of the alphabet, and the second stood for the fifteenth. Yes, this was the way I would have done it. I could not remember when or where or from whom I had learned of this type of coding, but I remembered the fact of it. I definitely needed the key to that translation.

I pondered some more and was interrupted for another outside session. I was cleaned and conducted to the torture chamber, but this time they did not use the box. Instead a new man was there to ask questions. I knew that if my answers did not satisfy him they would use the pain-box again; that was a powerful inducement for me to provide acceptable answers.

"What is your name?" the man asked. He was moderately heavyset, with musculature remaining in the upper arms; he might have been an athlete in youth but was so no longer. There were old scars on his arms, neck, and face, including one that nicked his left ear; he had fought with blades and had a close call. Maybe he had been a pirate. I did not know his name and did not intend to inquire; I simply thought of him as Scar, for private convenience, and let it go at that. "Hope Hubris," I answered promptly enough.

"How do you know?"

"The guard called me Hubris, and then I remembered." Scar nodded. "What else do you remember?"

I shrugged. "My childhood on Callisto. We fled in a bootleg bubble, but my parents died—" I broke off, the memory hurting again.

"What do you remember after your arrival at Jupiter?"

I concentrated, but it wouldn't come. "I . . . don't think we ever got to Jupiter. They—they turned us away. Everyone died—"

"Where did you go then?"

Again I concentrated. "I . . . think to . . . to Leda. The Naval station. They—they let me stay because I was literate in English. Not all Hispanics are. Then . . ." I shook my head; it wouldn't come.

"You are not cooperating," Scar said. He nodded to the other man in the chamber, who picked up the pain-box.

"I don't remember!" I cried. "It—I need more time! I didn't remember even this much before!"

"Where did you work?" Scar demanded.

Yet again I concentrated. As in a fog, I perceived something. "I—the farm-bubbles—migrant labor!" I exclaimed. "The only work I could get at that age. I was . . . fifteen."

"And after that?"

"It's blank. I just don't know—"

The pain came on, deep in my abdomen, making me nauseous. It was as if my gut were rupturing. My hands became damp with cold sweat, and I started to shiver, though I was sweating.

"How do you feel?" Scar inquired as the agony abated.

"*Intoxicado!*" I gasped.

"You're not drunk," he snapped. "Don't try to play games with me, Hubris!"

"I—I spoke in Spanish, my mother tongue," I explained quickly. "It means nauseous. From the pain."

"Oh." Scar half-smiled. "That figures. We gave you a stone."

A stone. The effect of a gallstone or kidney stone. Such blockages could generate a certain nausea in addition to the pain at the site, whether the obstruction was real or phantom, as in this case. "But why?" I asked plaintively. "When you know I can't answer your questions?"

"Do you not remember joining the Jupiter Navy?" he asked.

"The Navy!" Suddenly I did remember—and, indeed, I had realized before that I must have been in it. "Yes, there was trouble among the immigrant workers, and I was drafted. . . ." I shook my head. "Basic training, I think. But it's misty."

"Try to clarify it," he suggested.

When I hesitated, the pain came on again, worse than before. This time I did retch, regurgitating on my body.

The pain eased. "Do you remember now?" Scar asked.
"I wish I could," I gasped.

He nodded, satisfied. He walked to a counter and picked up a cup of fluid. He brought it to me. "Drink this. It will make you feel better."

I didn't even question its nature. If they wanted to poison me they could do so anytime they chose. I took the cup with a shaking hand and brought it to my mouth and drank. It was some kind of beverage, pleasant enough, with a tangy aftertaste.

Then I was conducted back to my filthy cell and locked in. I was alone again, my new vomit only adding to the stench.

I returned to my reflections. Evidently my captors had merely been verifying the effect of the mem-wash. I had not been prevaricating; my direct memory beyond the migrant-labor period was hopelessly fogged. If they had mem-washed me to prevent me from testifying about some scandal of which I had had knowledge, this had been effective; certainly I could not remember it. Yet still it seemed simpler to kill me or to hold me incommunicado until the time for testimony was over. Evidently they wanted more from me than my silence.

Despite my isolation and physical discomfort, I experienced a burgeoning sense of well-being. Why was this? My suspicious mind wanted a reason.

That wasn't long in appearing. Obviously I had been drugged. That drink Scar had served me—not straight alcohol but something sinisterly potent.

Still, why? Why drug a helpless captive? That didn't make sense, unless . . .

Unless it was addictive. Hook a man on a drug, make him an addict, when you control the source of supply, and that man is yours. What had I fallen into?

I experienced rapid panic, then quelled it. The drug was making me emotionally unstable. Whatever was happening to me was happening, and I could not prevent it. They could dose me with the drug by force if I tried to resist; repeatedly, until the addiction was complete. I wasn't really worried, and though I knew this was probably false optimism sponsored by the drug and by my resignation to the situation, still I felt all right. For one thing I had a secret weapon: the coded message. Maybe that had the answer to my problem.

I concentrated on that. My mind seemed preternaturally sharp; my sensation of well-being seemed to extend into the brain tissues themselves. Was this a genuine enhancement of mental prowess or a hallucinogenic illusion? I tried multiplying numerical figures in my head and seemed to be facile at it. My more important challenge was to solve the riddle of the coded message. If the enhancement were real, this would be the best time to do it. If not—what did I have to lose?

ⴺⴺⴺⴺⴺⴺ —like a diminishing progression, one element of the figure deleted with each repetition. Then added again—no, that wasn't it. My original childhood chart did seem to be the likely key. Three grids could cover the alphabet, but what about spacing and punctuation? I checked further along the message and found some figures with little Os in them. So there was a fourth grid, making thirty-six representations. The alphabet, plus ten spots for other marks.

Then I had another notion. There was my alphabet—not in any direct ratio but in my head! A through Z and ten punctuation marks. There needed to be no symbol-letter connection; the symbols merely could be instructions on how to select the letters of the mental font. A simple displacement could do it, the symbols standing for numbers that showed how far to count for the proper letter:

And so on. The first, second, and third letter of the alphabet. So the message would be 13 4 7 25 11 13, translating to the corresponding . . .

Um, no. That was still a direct translation. It was pointless to interpose numbers if they only stood for letters. That was too easy to crack and needed no input from my unique experience.

Still, I felt that numbers were part of the answer. Displacement—not from a set alphabet but from a random one—*that* would be tough indeed to crack.

And, in my drugged brilliance I fathomed the next stage of the answer. That random alphabet—it didn't have to be an alphabet at all, just a series of starting points. P, Q, X, Y, Z—anything would do. Then the coded numbers could count off from those points. 13 4 7 25 11 13—count off thirteen from the first starting point, four from the second, seven from the third. Thirteen from the P would be off the end of the alphabet, into the punctuation. Did that make sense? Perhaps not, but that only meant that P wasn't the proper starting point; it was just my random guess. Find the correct starting points and the rest would follow.

How could I discover a random series of starting points? The answer was that I couldn't. So, they probably only *seemed* random. They could be represented by a key phrase or sentence—one that only I would devise. There was the true virtue of such a system: its personification. No one else could crack the code because no one else could think of my key sentence.

All well and good, but what was the sentence? I had no idea. Maybe too much of my memory had been washed, and the sentence was gone. Yet shouldn't I have anticipated that problem? I was an intelligent person, wasn't I? Surely I had allowed for it!

I pondered longer, but here at last I seemed to be balked. I was in a kind of hell, and part of that hell was my ignorance. What, in the period of my memory, would I have devised for my period of amnesia to recover?

Then I remembered the message on the wall: ABANDON HOPE, ALL YE WHO ENTER HERE. Could *that* be it? It would be just like me to plant the message of success under the noses of my captors, in the form of a message of defeat. Delicious irony!

I tried it. The first letter was A; count off thirteen, to N. Four from the second letter, B—it came to F. And so on, seven from A for H, twenty five from N—oops! That ran way off the alphabet. Well, skip that for now and go on to the next: eleven from D for O, and thirteen from O for punctuation. N F H ? O ? This couldn't be right, yet it had seemed like such a promising lead.

Wait—suppose the count started *at* the original letter, not next to it. That would change the displacement by one. I reviewed it in my mind, painstakingly recounting the letters. I had a good visual memory, but this was tricky to do. M E G ? N ? That was more like it. The final character could actually be a space, separating the word from the next; most words in the English language were short. The missing middle one . . .

Suddenly I had it. There were not thirty-six but thirty-seven characters in the original sentence, counting the space at the end. That might show how many there were in the alphabet/punctuation key. That brought the missing letter back around to A, and I knew that word.

MEGAN.

Chapter 2
NYORK

As gawky as any tourist, I looked at the large screen in the dayroom of the passenger ship. Spirit, beside me, was similarly fascinated. All the others watching were children. Normal adults, jaded by experience, were reading, sleeping, watching entertainment holos or indulging in other pursuits or appetites in private chambers.

Of course, the approach to mighty Jupiter required several hours if I disregard the fact that the entire journey from Leda was an approach. No one could sit and watch the orange Colossus constantly without losing the edge of excitement. But my sister and I tried!

We had never before been closer than the orbit of Amalthea, and that had been a bitter occasion: the Jupiter authorities had towed our refugee bubble back out to space rather than accept us as immigrants. That action had cost me my mother Charity, my fiancée Helse, and the rest of my companions. The mighty Colossus had not cared! I had been fifteen years old then, and Spirit had been twelve; now we were thirty and twenty-seven, our military careers abruptly behind us, and we were returning. How much better it would have been if we had made it the first time!

"Say, aren't you Captain Hubris, the Hero of the Belt?" a gangling Saxon boy abruptly inquired of me.

Startled by this recognition, I smiled. "I suppose I am."

"Gee! That's great!" he exclaimed, and wandered away, his attention span and interest exhausted.

The phenomenal bands of Jupiter fuzzed as we came close. We had first seen the planet as a kind of giant face, with white eyeballs crossing from west to east in the north, and the Red Spot gaping like a mouth in the south. Now we were spiraling down above the great equatorial band that was occupied by the United States of Jupiter, the most

27

powerful political entity in the Solar System. None of the giant city-bubbles was visible yet; they were on a plane at the five-bar level of atmospheric pressure; that is, five times the pressure of Earth's atmosphere at Earth's surface where the ambient temperature was a comfortable eighty degrees Fahrenheit, and clouds of water droplets precipitated from the gases there.

I should explain that there is no human development on the surface of Jupiter, or on any of the gas giant planets, for a number of reasons. First, there *is* no surface in the Earth sense, merely a series of somewhat arbitrary boundary levels, such as the translation from molecular to metallic hydrogen. We know hydrogen, which composes ninety percent of Jupiter's atmosphere, as a gas; but as the depth and pressure increase it becomes a kind of liquid and then a kind of solid, stripped of its electrons. The pressure of that metallic stage is about three million bars, and the temperature there is about ten thousand degrees Kelvin. These extremes would not be comfortable for human beings, to understate the matter significantly. Jupiter has been considered, historically, as a cold planet; in fact, it is a hot one. Had it been larger, the internal temperature might have triggered nuclear fusion, making a third star in our System. As it is, Jupiter has more mass than the combined mass of everything else in the Solar System, excluding Nemesis and the Sun itself. Not for nothing is Jupiter called the Colossus.

It is a colossus economically and politically, too. The Jupiter Navy, from which I had just been released, dominates space from the Belt almost to the orbit of Saturn, and the planet is the richest in resources of any in the System. The government of the United States of Jupiter hauls other governments about as arrogantly as the planet hauls other matter in the vicinity. The Jupiter standard of living is the highest in the System. This, of course, makes it the planet of choice for refugees throughout the System, refugees it repels with increasing determination that at times borders on savagery. Spirit and I were now being admitted—after a fifteen-year apprenticeship in the Jupiter Ecliptic region of space. We were now legal citizens of Jupiter, entitled to all prerogatives of citizenship, thanks to certain hard-nosed negotiations and the intercession of a special agency, QYV.

But it was not primarily the dream of sanctuary, power, or wealth that brought me here. It was Megan.

I had one true love at age fifteen, the refugee girl Helse, then sixteen. We were to marry, but she died in her wedding dress, so that I could live. There could be no complete love for me thereafter, until I encountered the one other woman my heart could accept: Megan. I had never met her, indeed had only seen her picture as she was at age sixteen, bearing a haunting similarity to Helse. It had been a false similarity, for the picture had been five years out of date; Helse had been only eleven when it was made. In addition, Megan was Saxon, while Helse was Hispanic. Those were, perhaps, the least of the differences between them, and this I have always known.

But man is not a rational creature, and the Latin temperament may be less stable than others, and I less stable and rational than most Latins. I say this with a certain bemused pride. Megan was the niece of a kindly old scientist who had helped Helse and me when we were desperate; my gratitude to him overflowed the boundaries of rationality and found a partial focus on his niece. When Helse died, that focus strengthened. I explain this objectively, but it has more power than that. Only through Megan could I recover any part of either Helse or the scientist—and I had to have that part. In Megan I might recreate my One True Love in her moment of greatest beauty and joy.

My eyesight blurred as I stared at the savage maelstrom that was the face of Jupiter. The turbulence between the bands was at once more vast and violent than any effort of man, and more measured and lovely in its slow motion. Huge and ruthless currents played across those fringes in their gargantuan rituals. Only the surface of that three-dimensional flux was visible, yet all of it would manifest in its own time and fashion. Nothing man could do would change this progression; we could only watch and wonder, trying to glimpse at least a fraction of our own ignorance of the phenomenon. Even so was my feeling for Megan, the woman I had never met. The submerged currents of my being had been progressing for fifteen years in their slow, but inevitable, pattern, and now they were bringing me to

her at last. A spectator might protest that it was foolish of
me to pursue such a dream so late, but the spectator could
not see the deeper imperatives that drove me, like the massive coriolis forces of Jupiter. Megan! As moth to candle, I
was coming to her.

In the long interim my sister Spirit had sustained me;
she was my strength in adversity, and my most intimate
companion and friend. Without her I could not have gotten
through. Spirit was the only one who truly understood. Oh,
there had been other women along the way, good women,
and I had interacted with them to the extent I was able.
But I had been able to leave any and all of them, as indeed
I was doing now. They had been wonderful, but they had
become part of my past.

Down we moved, following the planet around to the east,
matching its velocity of rotation. The giant bands alter-
nated colors; there were shades of blue, brown, and orange,
demarked by lines of black and yellow and spots both
bright and dark. In general the white spots were high-
pressure cells that had risen from the depths and were converting their heat to rotary motion, which motion was
greedily sucked at by the zonal jets. The zonal jets drew
their energy from the rising eddies they consumed, not
vice versa; the newcomers were consumed by the hungry,
established powers. There, too, perhaps, was a lesson for
me.

The white spots spun counterclockwise in the southern
hemisphere, and the cold low-pressure spots should have
spun clockwise, but the Great Red Spot, politically known
as the Nation of Redspot, was anticyclonic, spinning counterclockwise, too, and enduring eternally despite the hunger of the bands. Perhaps that was the example I should
follow: to maintain my own orientation, to endure regardless, even if others were destroyed by the environment.

We touched the thin fringe of atmosphere and glided
down toward our destination. I am of course contracting
this; in the hours of descent we paused to eat and eliminate
and sleep. But always we returned to view the tapestry of
the Colossus, mesmerized by it. The twenty-thousand-mile
broad orange band fuzzed farther, for we were technically
in it now, and the separate currents and spots of it fogged
out with proximity. We phased in more precisely to the ve-

locity of the band. Jupiter rotated a full turn in about ten hours, and the winds of this band moved faster than the planet by about two hundred miles per hour, and we exceeded that by about three hundred miles per hour so that we could use vanes to plane down through the thickening atmosphere.

We passed through the ammonia-ice clouds of the one-hundred-millibar level; now the ship shook as the atmosphere took hold. The screen showed only reddish haze; imagination had to fill in now. Then it cleared, the flight smoothed out, and vision cleared—until we encountered another layer, twenty miles below, this time of brownish clouds, and experienced more turbulence. Finally we came to the bluish layer, with gray and white clouds. We were at the water-precipitation level at last.

I looked down through a rift in that layer and suddenly saw a panorama of the whole of populated Jupiter—thousands of city-bubbles floating at the five-bar level, glowing like baubles in the band about the globe of Jupiter, a scintillating network of civilization ranged along the most extravagant geography extant. How paltry the land-bound cities of old Earth must have been, compared to this!

But it was illusion, a mere passing vision of the sort I am subject to. The bubbles were there, of course, but I could not see them. They were ranged one hundred, two hundred thousand miles around the planet, masked by the cloud layer; there was no way for anyone to see the entire array at one glance. Only in imagination, as I had done. But what a sight for the mind's eye!

Below us now, the view was relatively clear, but the sheer mass of the thickening atmosphere caused my gaze to fog out. There simply wasn't anything to see there! For a moment I felt uneasy, exposed, fearing a fall to the awesome depths of the planet. But, of course, no fall was possible; we were using gravity shielding now, as the planetary gee was over twice Earth-normal at this level.

Gravity shielding does not eliminate the force of gravity, of course, any more than a magnifying glass eliminates light, since gravity is really a deformation of space by matter, which cannot be negated. Shielding merely focuses or diffuses it, so that an object in that field is affected to a greater or lesser extent. The force of gravity is conveyed by gravitrons; when their normal pattern of flow is altered, so is their effect. Gravitrons influence everything, including others of their kind; that means that gravitrons can be used to deflect other gravitrons, at least temporarily. Then the gravitrons bend back, recovering their original configuration, like the resilient surface of a sponge, no permanent damage done. Gravity deflected for the moment, not negated: the breakthrough of the millennium.

The ship homed in on the metropolitan bubble of Nyork, one of the major cities of the Solar System. In the distance, as it floated beneath the cloud layer, it looked like a marble, then like a boulder, then like a planetoid. It floated beneath us, grandly rotating, a stream of tiny bubbles feeding into its nether hub, the local commuter traffic. We, as a shuttle ship from space, warranted the apex hub.

"It floats but it spins," Spirit murmured appreciatively.

I knew what she meant. One might have supposed that a floating city would not need centrifugal gee, as it would feel the planetary gee that was over twice Earth-normal. After all, the occupants of a boat floating on water experience full gee, and those of an airplane in flight, and those riding a balloon do, too. But the city-bubbles are, overall, more dense than water, while the Jupiter atmosphere at this level is about one-fifth the density of Earthly air. Such a bubble would plummet until it reached its level of density—down around the metallic-hydrogen translation zone. The overwhelming pressure would implode the bubbles long before they achieved that equilibrium. So they have to use gravity shielding to make them light enough to float in hydrogen gas, and therefore it is necessary to restore internal gee through rotation, exactly as in space. Only extremely diffuse bubbles could float naturally, and even those employ gee shielding to reduce their internal gee to Earth-norm or below. Gravity shielding is absolutely essential to man's existence in the wider Solar System. We might as well call this the age of the gee-shield, displacing the prior nuclear power age.

So the city floated and it spun. Nyork had a diameter of approximately eight thousand feet, or about one and a half miles. That was just about as big as any city got; larger bubbles were possible, but they lost cohesion and were unsafe. This one completed a full turn every six and a half minutes, which might seem slow, but that meant that its equator was traveling at about fifty miles an hour. That velocity was evident as we descended to it. Of course there was little velocity at the hub, which was why this was the point of access.

I had envisioned the cities glowing. That turned out to be false. Nyork had running lights and a beacon, but no portholes; it was basically an opaque shell, with the action all confined within. From a distance it would be no more than a dark hulk, hardly visible except in pulsar fashion, as the beacon swung brightly by. That really did not detract from its grandeur; what counts is usually what is inside, in cities as well as in men.

Tugships came out to latch on to us, and we landed, dropping vertically, the tugs employing maneuvering jets to effect contact. We descended into a circular hanger, and a panel slid over, sealing us in. The hanger was pressured in a moment, and we debarked, floating carefully out. It was all null-gee here in the hub.

We were guided along a tube-conduit to a transport chamber and elevator, where there was a routine bottleneck as the passengers had to wait their turns. I tried to look around, but there really wasn't much to see—just the machinery of baggage handling, refueling, supplies, and maintenance. I suppose it might have been much the same when a passenger ship docked at an oceanside city of old Earth; experienced travelers would not have craned their necks to glimpse the routine procedures of ship servicing. But Spirit and I had never been to Jupiter-planet before or to a city of this magnitude, and it was all wondrously new to us.

I could see that there were real advantages to handling baggage in free-fall; one little shove and it floated right across to its hamper. As it got to the edge of the chamber it seemed to curve. That was our perspective, of course; we were already at the edge, benefiting from the trace gee there, and thought of ourselves as fixed in place. Actually we were moving with the city's rotation while the baggage was going straight. I had seen the effect aboard ships, but here the scale was larger, making it seem like a novelty.

Then it was our turn for the elevator. We got in the cage, and it slid down the gradual curve of the bubble-shell. The cage was suspended by the top, so that as it moved outward from the pole region, it oriented to the increasing gee. The velocity was slow, but we knew why: If we were simply allowed to drop we would have fallen in an apparent spiral and crashed into something. Descent within a rotating frame is actually a matter of lateral acceleration, and it can be disastrous when uncontrolled.

After five or six minutes we stopped at a landing. We were now at full gee. We stepped out into the processing center. Most of the passengers were regular Nyork city residents with badges that let them pass without hindrance, but Spirit and I were first-time arrivals to this city and to this planet. We had to run the bureaucratic gantlet. We had to show our new citizenship papers and official releases from the Jupiter Navy and certificates of inoculation against sundry contagious maladies. It seemed that the planetary environment was not considered to be as sanitary as that of space.

"Where will you be establishing residence?" the official inquired.

I didn't know; for fifteen years in the Navy I had always gone where assigned. But Spirit was more practical about such details. "Ybor," she said. "In Sunshine."

"Ybor, Sunshine," he repeated, entering it in the proper sequence. "Nice country down there." He completed the entries and got a printout, which he handed to me. "This will clear things when you board that bubble. Now I suggest you freshen up for the ceremony."

"Ceremony?" I asked blankly.

He only smiled, perhaps assuming I was being coy.

We cleaned up and were conducted to another elevator that took us up to the top of the residential band. The general design of Nyork was standard; the apartments of the residents—one thousand cubic feet of space allotted per person, or a chamber ten feet on each side—were arranged in a cylinder within the bubble. The width of that residential band was four thousand feet, and the length of it about twenty-four thousand feet, theoretically providing space for 960,000 apartments per floor. Actually a lot of space was used for other purposes, such as hallways, public sanitary facilities, business and entertainment structures, storage, and the like, so that perhaps only four to five hundred thousand residential cells were there. Since there were twenty such floors on the strip, this put the total city capacity at eight to ten million people. Of course there could be more; in the slum sections large families crowded into cells meant for small ones, and some people had no established address. I knew this only from my childhood study of geography but was sure it remained true. At any rate, the rated capacity of the city was in the range of ten million, and there were a number of adjacent cities that swelled the metropolitan population to several times that figure. There were many people on Jupiter, as there were on Saturn, Uranus, and the lesser planets, such as Earth itself.

When we emerged at the top of the band, Spirit and I paused with renewed wonder. The entire center of the bubble, a space about a mile and a half across, was open, except for the mock-sun sphere in the center. By shielding our eyes from the concentrated brightness of that sun—for Earth-orbit radiation is twenty-seven times as intense as Jupiter-orbit radiation—we could look right across to the far side. There were a few fleecy clouds in the null-gee center, which made it appear as if we were peering down from above. Again I had seen similar effects before but never on this grand a scale. I simply stared, and so did Spirit.

"This way, please, Captain Hubris," someone said. Bemusedly I went where directed and found myself sitting in a strange, four-wheeled, open vehicle with a uniformed chauffeur in front.

"A car!" Spirit exclaimed beside me. "A genuine antique automobile!"

Now I recognized it. This was a replica of the kind of vehicle once used on old Earth for transportation. Of course this one lacked the pollutive combustion motor, but in other respects it seemed authentic.

A well-dressed man took the front seat. He turned momentarily to face us. "Welcome to Nyork, Captain Hubris and Commander Hubris," he said to us. "I am Mayor Jones." He reached back a chubby hand, and each of us took it in turn. "I hope you enjoy the parade."

"Parade?"

"We have to give you your hero's welcome to the city—

and to Jupiter, Captain," he explained. "Just smile and wave every so often; it's a necessary event."

"But—"

"You are the bold officer who cleaned up the Belt, so long a blemish on the fair face of the System," he explained. "We of Jupiter want to demonstrate that we really appreciate that."

I shrugged, knowing that he gave me too much credit. I had been with a fine organization at the Belt, and even so, it had been a chancy thing, with necessary compromises and consequences. "That's over now."

The car started moving. "Well, Captain, we folk of Empire State just want you to know we're proud of you. Nyork has a sizable Hispanic element, in case you should want to settle here. The way you handled the refugee-robbing pirates of the Juclip did not go unnoticed! We're really glad to see a genuine Hispanic hero!"

A Hispanic hero. That was evidently what made me novel in this Saxon culture. Somehow I was not completely pleased. I knew without looking at her that Spirit shared my reserve.

"Why, you could run for President right now," the mayor continued exuberantly. "You'd pick up all the hero votes and the minorities votes, too, and that's a potent political base!"

I laughed as if this were humor, but Spirit gave me a significant nudge. An entry into politics had already been urged on me by a party whose knowledge of the situation was thorough. That was why I planned to settle in Sunshine; it had been targeted as the best locale for the rise of a Hispanic politician.

The car moved into a parklike region where deciduous trees lined the drive, and there were extended reaches of green lawn. Indeed, it would have been easy to believe that this was Earth itself, had it not been for the concave curve of the terrain. There was evidently an abiding longing in man for the things of Earth, evinced in the emulations of that planet that showed whenever feasible. Some of it was practical, such as the day-night cycle and standard gee, for the tides of man's chemistry could not be changed in mere centuries; but much of it was simple nostalgia for the old planet. I could not deride this; I felt it myself.

Then we came to the parade area. Crowds of people lined the road, waving and cheering as we came among them. Confetti flew up as they threw handfuls toward us.

"Wave, sir, wave!" the mayor muttered tersely.

I raised my right arm somewhat awkwardly and essayed a motion, not sure it was really me the crowd watched.

The noise jumped in magnitude. The crowd became frenzied. Then a chant began: "Hubris! Hubris! Hubris!"

I felt an odd surge in my chest, as if falling suddenly in love. They really *were* cheering me! I waved more vigorously, and the noise increased as if I were orchestrating it.

We continued along the winding road, passing a golf course and a small lake and a series of statues, and everywhere the people were crowded close and cheering. To my amazement the throng seemed to be getting thicker. But I realized that this probably represented a change of pace for the average citizen, a chance to go to the park and relax; I was merely the pretext. Any other man in my position would have received the same reception; it was really an impersonal thing.

Yet it certainly didn't *seem* impersonal! As I looked I could see men smiling at me, and women blowing kisses. All the time the beat of "Hubris, Hubris!" continued. It was intoxicating.

The mayor turned to speak to us again, his voice barely audible above the noise of the crowd. "Hang on to your hat, Captain! We're coming to the Hispanic district."

Sure enough, the complexion of the crowd changed, the paleness of Saxon visages giving way to the more swarthy Hispanics. The mass of people was thicker yet; now a cordon of helmeted policemen held it back, and even so it surged close to the car. The chant became monstrous. *"Hubris! Hubris!"* The car was pelted by flowers. I was impressed; decorative plants were expensive, even if they were imitation. Spirit picked up several that fell inside the car and made a bouquet that she set in her hair, and there was a deafening roar of approval. She made another, her nine fingers nimble enough, and put it in my hair, and the response was a storm tide that swept the policemen back until they collided with the car itself. Hands reached through the cordon, trying to touch the car or us. The mayor was beaming, but he looked nervous. I could appreciate why; it would be easy for people to be crushed by the moving car.

There was a siren. More police were coming, reinforcements. But the throng was so thick that the new police could not get through. Slowly we forged on—as it were, alone—plowing through a mass of humanity as if it were indeed a viscous pool.

A body hurtled over the cordon and fell onto the car. It was a woman, a girl—a teenage Hispanic maiden in a pretty summer dress. I tried to help her get upright, taking hold of her shoulders, fearing she had been injured, but she rolled right into me. "Hubris, I love you," she cried in Spanish, and flung her arms about me.

A Saxon policeman climbed onto the car, and it shifted with his weight. "Shit," he exclaimed, grabbing at the maid. "Get out of there, girl!" He hauled at her sleeve, but it tore, leaving her arm and part of her torso bare. He repeated his expletive, which happens to be a Saxon term for excrement, and grabbed again, tearing away more.

"Why don't you take it all, gringo!" the girl cried, and began snatching off her clothing and throwing it at him. I think she was wearing one of those paper garments that are intended for single use before disposal.

Spirit interceded. "Let her stay, officer," she urged the policeman. "She will be no trouble, I'm sure." She put her arms around the girl protectively.

Sweating, the mayor grunted acquiescence, and the policeman got off the car, disgruntled. The girl took her seat between Spirit and me, smiling.

An observation saucer floated low above us, its holo lens orienting. I realized that a picture of our carful would make the day's news: two visiting heroes, one half-naked girl, one red-faced mayor. I had to smile to myself.

The crowd pulled back a little, as if satisfied with this intrusion, and our forward progress resumed at moderate speed. "This is getting out of hand," the mayor yelled over the continuous chanting. "Got to cut it short before somebody gets hurt."

But there was no way to cut it short, for the crowd blocked all potential exits. Every time the chauffeur tried to turn the car, the people surged in to block it off. We had to continue forward.

"I don't like this," the mayor muttered. "They're too hyper! Could be trouble in the blue-collar district."

"Oh, go jump out a lock!" the girl snapped in Spanish.

The mayor's neck reddened. Obviously he did not understand the language, but he understood the tone.

"You do not like the mayor?" I asked the girl in Spanish.

"He's a Saxon pig," she exclaimed. "Always poor services for our slums, graft for the rich white politicos." Then, realizing she had my attention, she snuggled closer to me. "Hero Hubris, why don't you stay here in Nyork and become mayor, and I will be your mistress!"

I was so surprised that I choked. The girl was obviously under the age of consent by a year or two, though her anatomy was fully formed. It had never occurred to me that such a person would proposition me in this fashion. But Spirit had better control. "My brother had already arranged to settle in Ybor, in Sunshine. He will get married."

"Married!" the girl cried, clutching me.

"He is not for you," Spirit said. "You would be too much woman for him. He is thirty years old."

"Thirty," the girl repeated, shocked that anyone could be such an age. Then she reconsidered. "Still, a married man needs a mistress, too, and May-December liaisons can work out. Sometimes an older man can be very considerate and not too demanding—"

"And he has been long in space," Spirit continued, keeping her face straight. "The radiation—"

"The radiation!" The girl glanced down at my crotch as if expecting to see crawling gangrene. It was a superstition that mysterious rays of space made men impotent or worse. She released her grip on me, her ardor chilled. "Poor man!"

Now we came to the blue-collar district, and the crowd changed complexion again. The chanting finally faded, and the spectators stood relatively quiet.

"Damn," the mayor said. "Looks like trouble."

The car accelerated, but that only seemed to trigger the response of the crowd. Now it was definitely ugly. "You spics—you take our jobs!" a man bellowed.

The girl let loose a torrent of Spanish expletives at him. She was evidently a fishwife of the old school.

Now the crowd started a new chant: "Jobs! Jobs! Jobs! Jobs!"

I had known there was an employment problem in the civilian sector, for some of my associates in the Navy had joined in order to obtain better work and job security. But this put a new and more personal face on it. The Hispanics blamed the Saxon management for poor services, and the Saxons blamed the Hispanics for taking employment away from them. I doubted this was true, but it was evident that the belief was widespread here.

Something flew through the air and crashed into the car. It was a brick.

"Damn!" the mayor swore. "They've been at the monuments again. Those are glazed decorative bricks. Cost the city a fortune!" He seemed more indignant at the vandalism than concerned about personal safety. "Damned agitators from outside, stirring up trouble!"

More bricks flew, denting the car. Now it looked serious. The people were surging closer, shaking their fists, cursing. For the first time I was aware of personal danger. These men were angry, and I had become the focus of their rage. There was no more justice in this than in the adulation of the Hispanics; I was merely a symbol. But they might very well kill me if they could. The police cordon had disappeared, overrun by the crowd.

The mayor nudged the chauffeur. "Call the riot police," he snapped. "Tell them to lob a gas grenade here!"

But as the chauffeur started to make the call, a brick smashed down the antenna. Suddenly we were unable to call out.

"Try to bull through them," the mayor cried in desperation. "They're really out for blood this time!"

"This time?" Spirit asked. "You have had similar riots?"

"It's the recession. Lot of local unemployment. Hard feelings. We rounded up the known troublemakers, but we must've missed some."

So things were not entirely rosy on Jupiter! Indeed, the man who had started this aggression was now barring the progress of the car with his body, buttressed by a dozen cohorts. He was shouting and gesturing toward us. It looked bad.

"Crowd control procedure," I said. "Cover me, Spirit."

She reached into her blouse and brought out a pencil-laser pistol. "Covered."

"Hey, you aren't supposed to be armed," the mayor protested. "Weapons are banned in—"

Spirit pointed the laser at his nose and he stopped talking.

I jumped out of the car and ran ahead. For a moment no one realized what I was doing; then a worker pointed at me and shouted.

But by that time I had reached the leader. I caught him by the right arm, spun him around, and applied a submission lock. "Walk quietly with me," I told him.

"Hey, what the—" he started, then cut off as I abruptly tightened the lock, putting him in pain. He was a big, muscular man, much larger than I, but he had never had combat training and was helpless in my grip.

"You can't do that!" another man cried, reaching for me.

From the car, a beam from Spirit's laser burned a hole in his shirt and stung his chest. It was only a momentary flash, just enough to make him jump. Jump he did, falling back, staring at the car.

"We're from the Navy, remember? We know how to shoot," I told him. "That was just a warning. Stand clear."

The others stood clear, realizing that we did indeed know how to conduct ourselves in a fighting situation, and that the presence of the weapon made us far from helpless. Most folk, even those in an enraged mob, are rendered uncertain when abruptly faced with superior will and power. We were exploiting that uncertainty, not giving them time to regroup.

A kind of hush descended on the crowd as I marched the labor leader to the car. Spirit's gaze remained on the crowd, not on me, and she fired again, stinging the hand of a man who was getting ready to throw another brick. She had acute reflexes and perfect marksmanship; with that confidence I was able to concentrate on my own job. I got the leader into the car.

"Sit there," I told him, indicating the seat I had vacated. "Put your arm around the young lady."

"That spic?" he demanded angrily. "I wouldn't touch her with—"

Spirit's laser tube swung around to bear on his nose.

"Uh, yeah, sure," he said, disgruntled. He took the seat and moved his left arm.

"Keep your filthy Saxon hands to yourself!" the girl snapped in Spanish.

"Suffer yourself to be touched by this man," I told her in the same language. "We want to show the crowd how tolerant their leader is."

Her eyes widened as she caught on. She smiled sweetly. "Come here, you Saxon tub of sewage," she said in dulcet Spanish tones. "Put your big fat stinking white paw on me, snotface." I have of course cleaned up her actual terminology somewhat.

Like the mayor, the leader couldn't understand the words but knew he was being mocked. "Listen, slut, I'd as soon hang that meat of yours up with the other pigs," he muttered, his gaze flicking across her bared breast.

I perched on the side of the car. "Say what you will, both of you, but keep smiling." I smiled, too, and waved to the crowd, and so did Spirit, but she did not conceal her laser weapon, still pointed at the leader's head.

The mayor forced a smile of his own. "Very good," he muttered fatalistically.

The car moved on, and the crowd reluctantly parted. We had taken a hostage and deprived the opposition of its leader; the riot was fizzling out.

The mayor nodded. "By damn, it's working," he said. Then he stood up, faced the crowd, and gestured expansively. "Hubris! Hubris!" he cried. "Hubris! Hubris! Hubris!"

After a moment some in the crowd picked up the cadence. "Hubris! Hubris!" Soon all were chanting. We continued to smile and wave, and the labor leader continued to embrace the Latin girl. The parade had resumed.

"Because you have been kind enough to join us," I said to the labor leader while I continued to watch the crowd, "and to help pacify the throng by your generous gesture of tolerance, I believe you should be rewarded." Spirit was watching the crowd on the other side, knowing I would alert her if anything needed her attention on my side. We both knew that we could not relax until we were beyond this section of the city.

"You mean I can let go of this Spanish sass?"

"Not yet," I said.

"God, my wife's going to kill me!"

"Tell your wife the truth: There was a laser at your head. It was duress."

"Yeah," he agreed, glancing again at the breast. It was a well-formed one, young and perky. "I'd never touch anything like that if there weren't a weapon on me."

Another camera-saucer floated near. "But there *is* a weapon on you, isn't there, you Saxon slob," the girl said in English, delighted. And, as the saucer-lens took it all in, she twisted about, plastered her anatomy against him, grabbed his head in both her hands, and kissed him wetly on the mouth.

"Gross," he muttered, but he did not seem totally displeased.

"What is it you desire most?" I asked.

He had to crack an honest smile. "You had to ask that right now, didn't you?"

"I mean you collectively—the workers in the street."

"No secret there, Navy boy. We want jobs."

I turned to the mayor, who was still woodenly beaming for crowd and camera. "Why don't you have jobs?"

"The recession," the mayor said. "Nyork's been hit bad. Twenty-five percent of our industrial capacity's dormant. Companies closed down, moved out. We passed preferential tax measures, allocated choice real estate, upgraded our educational program, and still can't get enough new business in to stop the slide. So it just gets worse, and the unemployment and welfare rolls are murdering us."

"We don't want welfare, we want jobs!" the leader exclaimed.

"So do we," the girl said.

"You? You've got *our* jobs!"

"Dishwashing? Maid work? Street cleaning?" she asked derisively. "My brother's a competent mechanic, and he's out of work, too. We don't like welfare any better than you do."

"Nobody likes welfare," the mayor said. "Especially the taxpayer who has to pay for it. But the jobs just aren't there."

"Where *are* the jobs?" I asked. I have a talent for reading people and knew that these people—labor leader, girl, and mayor—were speaking honestly now.

"Mostly down south, where you're going, and west. The companies get this will-o'-the-wisp gleam in their corporate eyes and take off for greener pastures. By the time they learn it's illusion, they're stuck. They'd be better off right here in Nyork, if they only knew it."

"Then someone should tell them," I said.

"We've been trying. We run ads, we make reports—it just doesn't register."

"Ads and reports are impersonal," I said. "Suppose two people like this man and this woman's brother—trained, competent workers who really do want to work—suppose they went to prospective companies and laid it on the line? Would that influence them to return?"

The mayor shrugged. "It couldn't do worse than we've done."

"Why not try it, then? Appoint a select committee of workers—Saxon, Black, Hispanic—and pay them to go out and brace those companies. Arm them with the best information you've got, so they can really make their case. You can be sure they'll put their hearts into it, because they really do want those jobs. If there's any way to get through, to make those company execs appreciate the excellent company climate you have here, they'll do it. All you need is to get their attention, get them to take you seriously; then wonderful things might follow."

The mayor frowned. "That's not standard procedure—"

"To hell with standard procedure!" the girl exclaimed. "My brother needs a job! He's got a silver tongue when he's hungry!"

"Don't we all," the labor leader agreed.

"You'd do it?" she asked him. "You'd go with my brother, to—"

"I'd go to hell with the devil for jobs for me and my crew," he said.

"You know, you don't seem so bad, for a Saxon cesspool."

He glanced once more at her anatomy. "I could say the same about a 'Spanic pig, but my wife—"

"Remember that laser," she said, and kissed him again, more lingeringly than before. She was young, but she had evidently had some practice.

I looked at the mayor. "Will you do it?"

He spread his hands. "I may be a fool, but it won't be the first time. I'll set up the committee and give it a year. If it produces—"

"It'll produce!" the leader and girl said together.

"Know something, Captain?" the mayor said to me. "You're a born politician."

"It's a necessary skill for a Hispanic officer," I said.

The parade continued, and it seemed happier now.

Chapter 3

YBOR

We took an airplane from the state of Empire to the state of Sunshine. We had never been in one of these before, so we were fascinated all over again. The shuttle ship had not been the same, though it had planed down into the atmosphere. This vehicle had huge projecting wings on either side that planed much more emphatically against the Jupiter atmosphere as the craft jetted forward at relatively high velocity. That, and an assist from the gee-shield, enabled this heavier-than-gas vehicle to fly. We got clear of the city, rising above the water-cloud layer, then looped around and accelerated roughly southward at gee for ten minutes. That got us up to about twenty-eight thousand miles per hour velocity, at which point we coasted. The lift provided by the wings was so great at this speed that the pilot turned down the gee-shield to forty percent, so that we experienced approximately normal Earth-gee as a fraction of Jupiter's own greater gravity. Thus we did not have to suffer through a meal in free-fall, which was a blessing.

The meal was somewhat casually served, plunked down on small trays before us, but the stewardesses were shapely, so I was satisfied. Spirit seemed less satisfied but put up with it. As with the shuttle descent, the other passengers were plainly bored with the ride; obviously the meal was mostly to give them something to do. Some snoozed after eating, some read magazines, and some watched the little flat-screen video images set into the backs of the seats before them. Curious, I turned ours on and discovered a news report in progress, showing my own parade of the day before. "Welcome, hero," Spirit murmured, nudging me.

I looked out the window-porthole. The plane was racing over the nether clouds, so that I could see monstrous cloud

47

shapes passing like armies. Close clouds fascinated me; they did not exist in space or on airless moons. It was dusk at the moment at this part of Jupiter; though I could not see the direct rays of the sun, I did see the relative brightness of the cloud surface below us and the faint glow of the cloud layer above. We were zooming between the two, a sandwich of clouds, and the experience was moderately surrealistic. I could imagine us traveling forever in this limbo, traversing the vast entirety of Jupiter, never roosting, never resting. The notion had a certain muted appeal.

Then, all too soon, we were warned to fasten our seat belts, and the deceleration and descent commenced. The airplane simply turned around and accelerated backward in the manner of a spaceship, its wings reoriented appropriately. I dare say this particular maneuver would not have been feasible in the days of the primitive aircraft of old Earth, which were strictly one-way affairs, but, of course, technology has advanced in half a millennium. For that matter our cruising velocity would have been well beyond escape velocity on Earth. But Jupiter's escape velocity is quintuple that of Earth's, so we were in no danger of flying free. I used to wonder how the escape velocity could be quintuple when the gee was only two and a half times Earth's, until I realized that the total size of Jupiter's gravity well is much larger than Earth's; size does make a difference.

We dropped through the turbulence of the cloud layer and homed in on the city of Ybor. This bubble seemed small, only half Nyork's diameter and perhaps only an eighth the population, but it was still a big city. There was nothing like this out on the moons!

Landing was routine, with similar procedure as for the shuttle. Soon Spirit and I were ensconced at a downtown hotel.

There is no need to detail the details of our settling in. We elected not to reside in Ybor itself, as most of our lives had been spent in space, and even our planetary residence—technically the large moons of Jupiter shouldn't be called planets, but we do think of them that way—had been in a smaller dome than this. We simply felt more comfortable in small vessels. So we checked the ads and explored the region, renting a tiny bubble-car to travel to the various addresses. For Ybor, like Nyork and the other major cities of North Jupiter, did not exist in solitude; it was the center of a metropolitan collection of bubbles of varying sizes. There was constant local traffic to and from Ybor's nether port, and we joined it.

Our car was only ten feet in diameter, with harnesses for five riders. Its thick hull was translucent so that we could see in every direction. It had a powerful fan that collected atmosphere from around the bubble and blasted it behind, propelling the bubble forward. There was also a compressor that operated when the fan was idle, so that gas could be ejected with much greater force for emergency use. The fan and compressor were powered by oxygen; that is, the oxygen combined with the ambient hydrogen for combustion, yielding water. The oxygen had been processed originally from water, as there is virtually no free oxygen in the Jupiter atmosphere. It is not entirely coincidence that the occupied level is right where water precipitates.

I suppose I should clarify something here. If oxygen is the source of our power, and it requires energy to obtain it, whence comes the power to produce it? The answer is CT—contra-terrene matter, popularly called antimatter or null-matter—the same thing that powers the ships of the Navy. Rods of null-iron are merged with rods of terrene iron, converting into total energy: that is what powers our civilization. Iron is used because it can be handled magnetically; it is of course impossible to handle contra-terrene matter safely any other way. Even with magnets it's tricky; special attract-repulse circuits are necessary to prevent the CT from flying into the magnets themselves and blowing up the entire installation. So CT power is no small-bubble matter; only major cities and military vessels use it directly, with scattered exceptions. CT merging is used to generate electricity, which is then used for most other purposes, including the production of oxygen, which is then the fuel of choice for small motors, such as this one in the car-bubble.

And where does the CT iron come from? Well, much of the best iron comes from Mars, which was thought to be a barren desert-planet until the Moslem sheikhs discovered a huge natural cache of the power-metal. Oh, there is iron elsewhere; the rocky fragments in the vicinity of the major planets have it, and Jupiter and Saturn are major producers of it. But the iron of Mars is of high quality and easy to mine, and the Martian reserves are huge; this is the source of choice. That gives Mars economic leverage disproportionate to its physical or political importance as a planet. The pure terrene iron is processed in special gravity laboratories sponsored by Jupiter, Saturn, or Uranus, popularly called Black Hole Labs; the actual mechanism is beyond my understanding, but basically a rod of terrene iron is subjected to such gravitational stress that it inverts, becoming CT iron. Thus gravity-shielding technology is the ultimate source of civilized power. This, again, is no small-bubble operation; only the major planets can handle it. Thus a small planet like Mars has the leverage of the raw material, while a large planet like Jupiter has the leverage of Black Hole technology. It leads to interesting economic interactions.

Yet power does not derive from nothing, either politically or physically. What is the ultimate source of this chain? Opinions differ; it seems that either it is the literal destruction of matter, which might have a deleterious consequence for our universe in the course of a few billion years, or it is the gravity well of the major planets, which might eventually render them into minor planets. Assuredly the human species will be long departed before anything like this occurs.

At any rate we fanned along the highway, and it was another novel experience. The route was actually a jet of atmosphere, one of the myriad that twist along in the eddy-currents of the levels of the gale that is the Jupiter environment. Here at the southern edge of the equatorial band the turbulence was greater than at most places, but actually it wasn't obvious; it simply meant that there were some currents that moved faster than the average, and some that moved slower, and some that twisted around like serpents. They flexed constantly, but the change in position was usually only a few feet per day, and any given jet tended to return to its original position after a few days. This made car-bubble traffic convenient; it was only a matter of blowing one's bubble into the appropriate current, then riding the current to one's destination. It wasn't fast but it conserved energy.

The channels were bounded by glowing netting, so it was impossible to get lost in the wider atmosphere. Cars thronged this one, virtually touching each other. Brightly colored police bubbles tried to keep order, but there weren't enough of them. Private bubbles jockeyed endlessly for position, narrowly avoiding collisions. I became nervous; this was entirely too crowded!

We passed an intersection. The two jets of atmosphere passed each other skew, not actually touching, but the netting connected so that bubbles could move from one to the other. They did so in a tangled three-dimensional cloverleaf pattern.

We maneuvered from jet to jet, Spirit studying the map on the car's little vid-screen while I watched the other bubbles and sought to avoid the collisions that their reckless motions threatened. The cars were of all colors, and of course had transparent domes, so that I was reminded of the strings of glistening soap bubbles we blew as children. The scene was really rather pretty when viewed that way: lines of bright spheres against the backdrop of the layer of clouds.

After a brief trip that seemed much longer, we reached the suburb-bubble we sought. This was Pineleaf, a private development. Its radius was only one hundred feet, and its apartment cells were all on one level, so that its comfortable capacity was three hundred people. The volume of a sphere varies by the cube of its radius, so the little ones suffer. Ten one-hundred-foot spheres do not equal the capacity of one one-thousand-foot sphere. Far from it! It took a thousand of those little spheres to match the big one. That was one reason most people lived in the big ones: rents were cheaper. But our Navy retirement pensions put us in an income bracket that permitted upper-middle-class residence, and that meant a little bubble.

Even so, we were surprised as we blew up to it. "It's smaller than a spaceship," Spirit remarked.

Of course the larger ships of the Jupiter Navy were of entirely different construction, but I shared her impression. Residential developments were supposed to be larger than ships.

We approached the entrance and locked on to an admission port. We opened the hatch and climbed through, into the receiving chamber of the bubble. We gave the suited attendant our car key, and he climbed into our vehicle and sealed it off. He would take it to one of the parking hooks, secure it, and return to this office; that was why he was suited. We were in atmosphere, but the pressure was five bars; we might as well have been under water. The attendant's suit was braced for the pressure; we, as civilians, wore no protective gear. This, too, was a little eerie to one accustomed to the rigors of space duty, but I knew we would get used to it. Civilian ways are not military ways, after all; it was our job to adapt. When we were ready to leave, another attendant would bring our car around to the south pole egress for us.

"Oops," Spirit murmured. "I think we should have tipped him."

I had heard of that. Tipping was a pernicious custom that centuries of consumer dissatisfaction had not succeeded in eradicating. Employees of establishments expected to be paid token sums for performing their offices, the implication being that if such graft were not forthcoming, damage to the visitor's property might result. But this, too, was part of civilian life.

Inside the bubble the construction was typical but simpler than that of the big cities. There was not only an open lift for the descent to the residential cylinder, but also steps and a simple slide. We took the slide. It was banked to compensate for centrifugal acceleration; objects do not fall in an apparent straight line within a spinning sphere, as I have mentioned. This bubble completed its revolution in ten seconds, so we were picking up a lot more lateral motion than vertical. Regardless, we slid down like children, and for an instant I felt as if I were fifteen again, and Spirit twelve. Even at that age, she had been some girl!

"Do you still have your finger-whip?" I asked her as we came to rest at the base.

"I can get one," she replied, laughing. The finger-whip had been a juvenile weapon, a length of nearly invisible line weighted at the end, which attached to one of her fingers. When someone attacked her, she could sling that line at his face with devastating effect. It requires skill to use such a whip well, and she had had that skill. Today, the same coordination manifested in her deadly accurate aim with a laser-pistol.

We made our way to the registration office, which was beside a tiny park. Perhaps back on old Earth plants had been taken for granted, but here at Jupiter the semblance of nature was prized. A flower garden, a bit of lawn, some trimmed bushes, a dwarf pine tree, the smell of green, growing things—it was indeed precious. The moment we stood in that park, all four hundred square feet of it, we wanted to live here. Surely the proprietors of the Pineleaf subdivision had set up the park there for that very reason, to sweep prospective renters off their emotional feet so that they would not balk at the price. We knew that, yet we felt its impact. Man is a feeling creature more than a rational one.

We rented an apartment of two cells. It had sanitary and cooking facilities, two beds, closet space, and a picture window looking up into the central air space of the bubble, which made it seem roomier. The feeling of elbow room is also important to the human animal, even when we know it is illusory.

We performed the routines of settling in, getting our phone number listed, mailbox assigned, learning the peculiarities of this particular bubble, meeting our neighbors, and so on. There was just a hint of reserve in some cases, which I suspect was the covert objection of Saxons to having Hispanics in their midst. Theoretically Jupiter is an amalgamated society, free from interculture friction, but in practice it falls short, as we had seen in Nyork. Well, I hoped to do something about that, in due course. For now, we just wanted to get along.

The routine was not completely without event. After our first night we emerged to discover the words *Spic Go Home* crudely lettered on our door. We made no complaint but simply got out cloths and detergent and went to work scrubbing the door clean. A neighbor lady, a retired Saxon, heard the activity, came out, perceived the situation, and spoke up. "That's vandalism! I'll complain to the management!"

"No need, Señora," Spirit said, thus deliberately emphasizing our Hispanic nature. "It is a small thing."

"So is burning crosses," the woman snapped. "I want you to know that this is a decent neighborhood; we don't condone such behavior here. I shall see that it doesn't happen again."

We introduced ourselves. She was Mrs. Croft, a widow, and after she had helped us clean up the door she invited us in for tea. In our presence she called the management and described without emphasis what had occurred.

"I will apologize to them immediately," the manager said. "That man is Captain Hubris, the hero of the Belt; we are honored to have him here, and I am shocked that he should be treated this way here at Pineleaf!"

Mrs. Croft terminated the call and turned to me. "You did not tell me you were a hero," she reproved me gently.

"I am a civilian now," I said. "Does it make a difference?"

She laughed. "Of course not." Then she reconsidered. "Not to me, at any rate; I am not concerned with military matters. But perhaps the manager . . ."

We nodded. There were different types of prejudice, negative and positive. The manager might not think much of Hispanics, but he evidently did appreciate war heroes. We had not told him about my Belt connection; he must have recognized me from the news holos. It seemed that the positive more than balanced the negative, in this case. A poor, unfamous Hispanic might have triggered a different response. This, too, was part of the reality of civilian life.

That was about all there was to the episode, and there was no repetition. But I think it correctly signaled the situation. Prejudice, racism, and unprovoked hate do exist in our society, though normally they are masked; they do their mischief in darkness. But they are more than compensated by the elements of openness, tolerance, and fairness that manifest in light. The forces of bigotry, however directed, are an evil that must be constantly curbed, but they can never be completely eradicated. I suspect they are part of the makeup of the species of man. There must be some survival potential in them, as there evidently is in the similar percentage of individuals who are left-handed, homosexual, or who have rare blood types. Nature does not encourage deviance capriciously; she always has reason, though we may not comprehend it, and we try to interfere at our peril. Actually it is dangerous to trust strangers too readily, and bigotry may be the logical extension of that natural caution, just as war is the extreme example of competitive spirit.

Once settled in, we proceeded to our next task: the location of Megan. One might suppose that my sister would have little interest in helping me pursue a woman, but Spirit has always been my left hand. We could justify this quest in practical terms: Megan was perhaps the most knowledgeable person, politically, in the society of Jupiter who was not already committed to some other program. If I wished to enter politics with some chance of success, here was the advice that would be most useful. So I had been assured by an outfit in a position to know. It was indeed my intent to pursue a political career.

The fact that Megan was the one woman remaining in the Solar System whom I could love was secondary—or so I told myself. After all, I had known of Megan's existence for fifteen years and only now was following it up. But I can't honestly assess my own emotions; my talent is assessing the natures of others, not myself. This is part of the reason I need Spirit with me. She backstops me, she understands me. She is my hidden strength in ways that others need not understand. Without Spirit I am so far diminished as to be hardly worthwhile, and perhaps it is best that others *not* appreciate that. The symbolism in our names is to an extent valid: I have the aspirations, the hope, while she has the courage, the spirit.

I put in a call to a code I had memorized. The letter Q appeared on the screen. "This is Hope Hubris," I said.

I should say something about the entity I called. The Q stands for QYV, pronounced "Kife," a secret organization I encountered first through Helse. She was a courier; that is, a person who carried something for QYV. She had those letters tattooed on her body at an intimate site. I lost Helse; technically I killed her. Speculation on that is futile; I did what I did and cannot now undo it, however much I wish I could. The point is, all I was able to retain of her was the key she carried for Kife, and finally I traded that key for a way out of a serious situation in the Navy. Part of that deal was Megan.

In a moment the screen lighted with a silent schematic

of what I recognized as our own Pineleaf apartment complex, with one apartment briefly highlighted. Then it faded out, and the connection broke.

I looked at Spirit. "Here?"

"Are you surprised?"

"Yes. I thought they'd just arrange to print out the data—"

"She's a woman, Hope."

I laughed. "She's interested in my career, not my body!"

"So am I."

That gave me pause. Spirit was my closest relative, companion, and friend. Had she not been my sister I might have married her. There was nothing about each other that we did not know—as well as we cared to. She understood me perhaps better than I understood myself, in part because she was able to view me not only from the affinity of blood and culture and experience, but also from the vantage of the opposite sex. Even as children, when I had been the protector of our older sister Faith, Spirit had been my protector. There was little I would not do for her—and nothing she would not do for me. She never opposed me, but she was still my guardian, in more than the physical sense. If she likened the woman of QYV, Reba, to herself, she surely had reason.

It is true that I have a way with women. I believe it derives in part from my talent, for women do crave understanding, and in part from my own great need and hunger for them. There is not a woman I wouldn't take were she willing and the circumstances right. But, of course, circumstances are seldom right; the constraints of society are pervasive and powerful. Yet I had never thought of Reba in that way before. She was, after all, about fifty years old, no impulsive young thing.

"But it is to locate Megan that I need Kife," I said.

"You haven't located her yet."

Therefore I was not yet committed. I saw the point. I had shared intimacies with a woman a week in the Navy; it wasn't as if I had any diffidence about sex. Still, I seemed to be developing it. "I don't suppose you'd care to accompany me?"

Spirit just looked at me: answer enough. She supported me ultimately, which meant she had to absent herself from certain key occasions. Once I located Megan, I would not be dealing with any other woman on any except a professional basis. In that sense, it had to be now—for what Reba might have in mind.

I sighed inside. "Well, I have something to give her, anyway." I searched out the manuscript I had written, which detailed my military experience. I knew that Reba would take the best possible care of it.

I walked to the indicated apartment and touched my forefinger to the recognition panel. It opened and I stepped inside.

A completely unfamiliar woman met me inside. She was about my own age, dark-skinned, heavyset in a muscular way, and with flaming red, curly hair. That would be chemically colored, of course; women had been dissatisfied with their natural coloration from the nascence of the species.

I looked again and realized it was Reba. She had changed enormously in the months since I had seen her last, but now the underlying traits were manifesting. "A disguise," I said. "You folk travel anonymously."

"We do," she agreed as we sat on her couch. "I am trusting your discretion."

"The last time I saw you, you were a portly fifty with iron-gray hair. I mistook your age completely."

"Thank you."

She was certainly excellent at appearances. Despite my ability to read people, I could not now judge her true age. It was more than a matter of dress and makeup; her entire bearing had changed. She was indeed a professional. "You knew I was about to contact you, and you knew where I would be when I did."

"Your progress is my business."

"I had supposed your interest in me would decline, once you got what you wanted."

"We wanted an object. By the time we got it we had become interested in the bearer."

"In what way?"

"You are immune from addiction. You have a talent for dealing with people. You are extraordinarily motivated and intelligent. We are interested in such folk."

"You have not answered," I said.

She smiled. "You are beautiful," she said seriously, acknowledging my reading of her. "You are a prospect for power. You may have assumed that your talent is merely in comprehending the people you meet, but it is more than that. You also project, causing people to react to you more actively and positively than is normal. Men respect you and women love you. That is why you are potentially our next president."

"President!" I exclaimed, startled.

"With your talent, your sister's nerve, and proper guidance, you have a real chance—if you are lucky."

"Who provides the guidance? Kife?"

"No. We merely watch. We are not permitted to interfere with the domestic situation."

"Then what are you doing here?"

She smiled. "As I said, I trust your discretion."

"You have it."

"We are active primarily off-planet, and primarily as an intelligence network. But we do have to protect our agents and our secrets, and there are risks on-planet, too."

"That is, you have broadened your scope," I said. "And your employer does not necessarily know to what extent."

She shrugged, not denying it. "Administrations change and lose track of prior directives. Organizations have an instinct for self-preservation, much as living creatures do. Abrupt changes in policy can interfere with the continuity of our own efforts—such as that to abolish the drug trade."

"I have observed how you go about that," I said dryly.

She smiled more warmly, evidently enjoying this minor fencing. "Changes in our personnel become problematic, too. I was not the one who tried to addict you, and I never approved of that effort."

She was telling the truth. "Still, you can be as unscrupulous as the next when you approve an effort."

"Yes. But I believe your purposes now coincide with mine."

"Let's see if I have this straight. You think I might get to be president—and do you some good in that office?"

"If you feel you owe us some favors," she agreed.

"So we are bargaining. You will help get me there if I will help you when I get there."

"This would, of course, be an unenforceable agreement."

But we both knew it would be honored. "Yet you can't do anything actively, on-planet."

"Except provide key information—when requested. Exposure of our role would destroy it."

I shook my head, the enormity of it sinking in. "I had thought to go into politics, perhaps achieving a position of power. But *president?*"

"It will take time, of course," she said. "And it is by no means certain. But that should be your objective."

"And you personally—what is your interest?"

"I am the agent on your case. My power within our organization will be affected by yours. As president you could, for example, designate me to be head of Kife."

"Or I could fire you."

"Or abolish the organization," she agreed. "We take a calculated risk."

Still, she was reaching for the prize. She could get fired for exceeding her authority, or she could reach the top of her ladder. Through me. She had the nerve to carry it through.

"Then your interest in me is commercial rather than personal," I said.

She spread her hands. "Naturally I cannot deceive you in this, Hope Hubris. I am affected by you in the normal manner. But your sister is not the only woman with discipline."

Indeed not! Reba's will was steel, though she normally avoided showing it. "So you did not bring me here for any personal dalliance."

She grimaced, looking down at herself. "Alas, no. You can do better than this."

I was intrigued. "Can I? What woman is more intelligent or competent than you?" For, despite her matter-of-fact attitude, the power of her mind fairly radiated, and that had its own appeal. I had known beautiful women in the past; in fact, I still missed my last Navy bride, Roulette, the most stunning creature of the spaceways, but none approached Reba in intellect.

"Understand this, Hubris," she said. "I was never an attractive female, not even in the bloom of youth. I learned to survive by using my mind and will and by extirpating illusions. I do not deceive myself that you could not have your way with me at this moment or that it would not be the high point of my emotional life—*or* that you have any such inclination. I admit the temptation to discover whether such inclination could be roused . . ." She paused and made a motion with her torso that abruptly accentuated the salient aspects of her body from breast to thigh. "But I am satisfied to know you vicariously and to share part of your power when it comes. Think of me as a business associate."

She was correct; she had stripped herself of illusions. But that motion, slight as it had been, had stirred an immediate response in me. She could certainly rouse the male inclination when she chose. "Do I really have reason to want to be president?" I asked, returning to business.

"Yes. It is the only way you will have power to achieve your design to eliminate piracy of all types from the System."

She was surely right. I knew that pirates did not merely swagger about aboard spaceships; they could wear business suits on Jupiter, too. "But will Jupiter accept a Hispanic in that office?"

"That will be your hurdle," she agreed. "Historically, no naturalized citizen could assume that office, even the purest Saxon, but today it is open to any citizen—in theory. In practice no woman or obvious minority member has done it. You will encounter racist opposition from the outset, both overt and covert. But the more serious threat is from the pirates themselves—such as the drug runners—when they discover your intent. All politicians express themselves against organized crime, but few are truly serious. You are. See to your own security, Hubris."

I shrugged, unworried. "When someone takes a shot at me, I'll take steps to prevent recurrence. I have faced threats before." I lifted my case. "You will want this."

She got up and fetched a similar case. "And you want this."

We exchanged cases. They looked identical; she had seen even to this detail. Then I leaned down and kissed her.

She stood unmoving, accepting it. On the holo shows female intelligence agents are invariably young and voluptuous, therefore a real pleasure to pursue. Reba had to live with reality—but for that moment, perhaps, she dreamed.

Then I returned to my apartment, and Spirit opened the case. It was filled with computer printouts and fax clippings relating to Megan.

Was Reba jealous of Megan, the woman I had never met? Or did her vicarious fulfillment encompass this, too? I concluded that I would prefer not to know.

We got to it. Megan, it turned out, had a considerable history. In her youth she had been a singer; in fact, she had been a musical star. Then she had entered politics and run for Congress. She had served three terms as congresswoman, then run for senator—and had the misfortune to run against another congressman who was completely unscrupulous. Megan was a liberal, concerned with human values and the alleviation of poverty and oppression on the planet, and her political record reflected this. Her opponent, an aggressive man named Tocsin, was a creature of the affluent special interests. He promptly denounced her as "soft on Saturnism," that being the dirtiest political accusation it was possible to make. Theoretically the government of Saturn represented the comrades of the working class; actually it was a leftist dictatorship that suppressed the working class as ruthlessly as did any other system. Megan certainly had not supported that; she believed in human rights. But Tocsin hammered away at it, equating social conscience with Saturnism and therefore making Megan appear to be, if not a traitor to her planet, at least something of a fellow traveler. It was a scurrilous tactic, an open smear campaign—but it worked. Tocsin won the election. Megan, appalled that such innuendo and misrepresentation could deceive the majority of the voters, retired from public life. She had supposed that competence, experience, and goodwill should carry the day; she had been brutally disabused.

"That woman was raped," Spirit murmured.

I knew what she meant. I felt anger that Megan should have been abused like this, though there was nothing I could do about it, two years after the event.

Megan was now thirty-six years old—six years my senior. That hardly mattered to me. Helse had been my senior, too. Megan had been beautiful; in fact, this literature quoted a remark that she was *"The* ten most beautiful women of Jupiter." An interesting description! Today, she remained a most handsome woman, said to have a dramatic presence. I had no difficulty picturing her in my mind as Helse, as she would have been, had she lived to her thirties. Yet appearance was only part of it. The more I learned about Megan, the more I knew QYV had read me correctly; this was the woman I could love.

Megan lived in the glittering huge city-bubble of Langel, in the state of Golden—over a hundred thousand miles around the planet from Ybor. She was a pedigreed Saxon while I was a mere Hispanic refugee and discharged military man, recently enfranchised. She was a glorious dream, and I, a mundane reality. I had never met her, and she had surely never heard of me.

Nevertheless, I intended to marry her.

Chapter 4

MEGAN

Of course there were a few details to attend to first. I had to arrange to meet Megan. I tried to call her, but her phone was unlisted, and the phone company declined even to admit she had a number. I would have more respect for such companies if they elected to tell the truth about such things; institutional lying is as bad as individual lying. I sent her a letter, but it was returned refused. She was evidently reclusive and not interested in being contacted by strangers. After her political humiliation I couldn't blame her, but I was not to be denied.

We took an airplane to Golden. This time we were suitably blasé about the experience; it was, after all, our second such trip. We checked in at a hotel in Langel, rented an autobubble, and blew out to the suburb where Megan resided.

She lived in a very restricted neighborhood: a spoke village. This was not a bubble but a framework like a spoked wheel, turning in the atmosphere. Sixteen spokes radiated from its hub, each tipped with a minibubble about thirty feet in diameter; completely separate individual residences. Access was via hub and spoke; we had to park in the low-gee center and enter the airlock and formally check in.

The hub-guard was meticulous in verifying our identities. Did we have an appointment? No? Well, he would call the condo owner and pass us through if she cleared us. Otherwise we would have to depart. He was very polite but very firm. I knew from my reading of him that he was not bluffing; it was his mission to protect the privacy of the residents, and he was dedicated to it.

He buzzed Megan's unit, got an answer, and frowned. "I am sorry, sir. She does not care to see you."

"Please," I said. "This is important! At least let me speak to her on the com."

"As you wish, sir." He regarded it as a challenge to maintain absolute courtesy in the face of persistent intruders. He buzzed her again. "The visitor wishes to address you via this unit, ma'am. Will you accede?"

This time we heard her voice, though we could not see her face in the dark screen. "I do not talk with strangers, Mr. Bruce. Thank you."

He looked up again. "She declines, sir. Please depart now."

Desperately I cast about for some lever of acquaintance. I knew that once I talked with her I could impress her with my sincerity, but first I had to get her attention. What could I say to a woman who refused to listen?

"She was a singer," Spirit murmured.

I grasped at that straw. "Tell her Captain Hubris will sing her his song!" I exclaimed. "She need only listen, then I will go. Surely she will grant this much to one who has crossed the planet to meet her."

Mr. Bruce, plainly impatient with this nonsense, nevertheless buzzed her once more. "Ma'am, he is insistent. He promises to depart if you will listen to his song." There was a pause, then he repeated, "Captain Hubris." He was evidently answering her query. "He says he has crossed the planet to meet you. There is a woman with him." He paused again. Then he glanced at me. "Sing your song, sir." At this point his emotions were mixed. It was obvious that he did not approve of this, but it did offer relief from the dullness of the routine; he would be able to regale associates with the story of the intruder who insisted on singing to a resident who didn't want to see him.

I sang my song. In the Navy I had required every person in my command to master one song, the song that identified him or her. This one was my own: *Worried Man Blues.*

It takes a worried man to sing a worried song
It takes a worried man to sing a worried song
It takes a worried man to sing a worried song
I'm worried now, but I won't be worried long.

I sang all the verses and refrains without response. Had she disconnected? Was she listening? I could only hope. Hope was very much my name now.

When I stopped, the guard listened to the com, then looked up once more. "Who is the woman with you, Captain?"

"My sister, Spirit Hubris."

"Does she also sing?"

For answer Spirit sang her song:

I know where I'm going, and I know who's going with me;
I know who I love, but the dear knows who I'll marry.

When she stopped, we heard Megan's voice clearly. "Miss Hubris, you love your brother, don't you?"

"I do," Spirit agreed.

"I will see them, Mr. Bruce."

"As you wish, ma'am," the man agreed gruffly. He was startled by this abrupt reversal.

We took the shaft down, riding the lift within the spoke, feeling the twisting gee increase as we descended, exactly as if we were in a city-bubble. There was a landing at the bottom, and a door. We knocked on it. It opened; we entered and found ourselves at the top of a flight of archaic stairs. We stepped down these and arrived at the residential floor of an old-fashioned apartment. There were pretty pictures of operatic scenes on the walls, and there was deep, plush carpeting on the floor. To one side was a mini mock piano, the kind that was electronic but was crafted to resemble the historical article. In the center stood the regal figure of Megan.

I remembered her picture, made when she was sixteen. Now she was twenty years older, but the beauty of her youth had not paled; it had matured. The more recent pictures in the material QYV had given me had suggested it; life confirmed it.

"It is not often I am visited by military personnel," she remarked.

"Retired," I said. "We are civilians now."

"Do sit down."

We settled into stuffed chairs. This could almost have

been a room in Victorian England of Earth, some seven or eight hundred years ago.

"So you knew Uncle Mason," she said.

"Only briefly," I said, surprised. Evidently we were not complete strangers to her. Perhaps the scientist had mentioned the episode before he died. "I was with . . . Helse. She . . . looked like you."

"Of course," Megan said, as if it could have been no other way. She had that certain presence that facilitated this. "But that was some time ago."

"It's still true," I said, gazing at her. Indeed it was true, in my vision. The sight of Megan was casting a spell over me, as I had known it would.

"Where did you learn your song?"

"Among the migrant harvesters," I said. "I spent a year with the pickers, going from one agricultural bubble to another. The migrants took me in, and I remember their ways."

"You still identify with the working class?"

"I do."

She nodded. As a politician she had sponsored social legislation; she was a friend of the working class, though she had never been part of it herself.

"Yet you achieved a certain notoriety as an officer in the Navy, I believe."

"I helped make peace between the migrants and the farmers," I said defensively.

"Indeed you did," she agreed. "At one stroke you forged a settlement and set a precedent none of the rest of us had been able to arrange in years."

I was surprised again. "You . . . were watching that?"

She laughed, her animation making her steadily more lovely. "My dear Captain, it was the headline of the day! I knew that you would be going far."

I was trying to read her as we conversed, but it was difficult because my own burgeoning emotion got in the way. I had known that she was beautiful and intelligent and motivated; now I had the confirmation, and it was like color holography compared to a black-and-white still picture. Megan was, indeed, all the woman I had ever desired on every level. My talent was rapidly being blunted, and I had to depend on relatively obvious signals. She was relaxing, beginning to enjoy herself—and it was evident that my record was no stranger to her. "You were aware of me before then," I said.

"Uncle Mason had mentioned you," she said, confirming my supposition. "He said it was like seeing me again, as I had been in my youth . . . that girl with you. I was then in my early twenties."

Spirit made a half-humorous sigh of nostalgia: the notion that a woman in her twenties was beyond her prime. Megan responded with a smile, and it was evident that the two women were coming to like each other.

"Then when you showed up at Chiron," Megan continued, "which I know was a very ticklish situation, I recognized you. Naturally I was curious. But I hardly thought you were aware of *me*. You caught me quite by surprise, coming here like this. Perhaps I should have realized that a military man normally takes direct action."

"But if you recognized my name why did you refuse my letter?"

"Did you write? I'm so sorry. I refuse all mail from strangers because of the hate mail."

"Hate mail?" Spirit asked, surprised.

"Let's hope you never have occasion to understand about that," Megan said. "I knew I had no acquaintances in Ybor. I'm afraid I didn't really look at the name."

"But you recognized it when it was announced just now," I persisted. "Yet you refused to see me."

"Captain Hubris, I have put that life behind me," she said firmly. "I knew the moment I heard your name that you were here on a political errand. I shall not suffer myself to be dragged into that mire again." She grimaced in a fetching manner. "Then you sang, and it was a song of the working class. . . ."

"But you were wronged!" I protested. "You should not let one bad experience deprive you of your career!"

"Didn't you, Captain?" she asked.

I had to smile ruefully. I had just lost an extremely promising military career because of political machinations within the Navy. "But I have retired only from the Navy, not the fray," I said. "I had already done most of what I could do in space. Now I want to see what I can do planetside in the political arena. I need your help."

She frowned. "Setting aside for the moment the fact that I have absolutely no intention of getting involved, what makes you suppose that a discredited former congressperson has anything to offer you in that arena?"

"First," I said seriously, "I know next to nothing about planetary politics and will surely fail badly if I don't have competent guidance from the outset. Second, you have had the experience I lack, and you are not otherwise engaged at the moment. You can guide me as well as any person can, and I hope you will. It will be a full-time occupation."

"My dear man, whatever makes you suppose I would do such a thing?"

"I'm sure you are loyal to your principles and your family. Therefore—"

"But we are not related!"

"Not yet," I murmured.

She looked at me directly, and I warmed to the glory of her gaze. "What are you trying to say, Captain?"

"I want to marry you, Megan."

Her mouth actually dropped open. "Have you any idea what you're saying?"

"You are the only living woman I can love," I said.

She was stunned but rallied quickly. "Because I once resembled your childhood sweetheart? Surely you know better than that!"

"It is not precisely a logical thing," I said carefully. "I have had three pseudowives in the Navy, and they were all excellent women in any capacity you might care to define, but I did not truly love them. They were worthy of love without question, and I think they loved me, but for me there was a certain barrier, so that while perhaps at times I thought I loved, in retrospect I know it was not so. I can love no one except Helse—and you. This is the way I am structured."

Megan looked at Spirit. "You are his sister, and you love him more than any other. What do you make of this?"

Spirit shook her head. "I'm not sure you would understand."

"I suspect I had *better* understand! Describe to me his nature as you appreciate it."

Spirit dropped her gaze, frowning.

"Tell her, Spirit," I said.

She sighed. "Hope Hubris is a specially talented person. He reads people. He is like a polygraph, a device to record and interpret the physical reactions of people he talks with. He knows when they are tense, when they are easy, when they hurt or are happy, when they are truthful and when lying. He uses his insight to handle them, to cause them to go his way without their realizing this. He—"

"You are describing the consummate politician," Megan exclaimed.

"So we understand," Spirit agreed. "But that's not what I'm addressing at the moment. Hope . . . is loved by others because he understands them so well, in his fashion. The men who work with him are fanatically loyal, and the women love him, though they know he can not truly return their love. But he—his talent perhaps makes him inherently cynical, emotionally, on the deep level. On the surface he is ready to love, but below he knows better, so he can not. Except for his first love, Helse. She initiated him into manhood, and there was no cynicism there. But having given his love to her, he could not then give it elsewhere—with one exception.

"He was with Helse when he saw your picture, which so resembled her. She saw it, too, and your Uncle Mason helped them both; helped our whole bubble to survive when he really didn't have to. Mason was a generous man, and we owe our lives to him and will never forget the debt we owe him. He is dead now, so we can never repay him directly. But you are his kin. He loved you as his niece, and he helped Helse, perhaps because she seemed to resemble you. In Hope's emotion there is a connection, and I cannot say it is a wrong one. His happiest time with Helse was also with your uncle. So the cynicism of his talent does not apply; it is preempted by the love he bears, which has no other place to go. You are the symbol of his onetime happiness; he believes, emotionally, that he can recreate his love of Helse only through you."

Megan dabbed at her forehead with a dainty handkerchief, as if becoming faint from overexertion. "But he doesn't even know me."

"He doesn't need to," Spirit said. "This has nothing to do with knowledge. It has to do with faith."

Faith . . . Coincidentally, the name of our older sister,

lost among pirates. The most beautiful member of our family.

Megan shook her head. "You were right. I don't understand."

"I think you do," Spirit said.

For answer Megan quoted from a poem by Edgar Allan Poe:

I was a child and *she* was a child,
  In this kingdom by the sea:
But we loved with a love that was more than love—
  I and my Annabel Lee

That time at the scientific station on Io—a kingdom by the sea. Helse and I, children, with love that was more than love. How aptly it fitted! Megan *did* understand, and I had to have her.

"It is also true that I need your expertise in politics," I said. "So there is a practical foundation. Marry me and it will make sense."

Megan dabbed again. "Captain, this is not the way!" she protested. "This is not your Navy! This is civilian life! You have to consider the needs and feelings of others. You can't just toss aside wives as they become inconvenient."

"Here marriage is permanent," I agreed.

"And not entered into capriciously."

"This is not caprice," I said. "You are the perfect diamond I have finally found. The last fifteen years of my life have developed toward this union."

"Well, the last fifteen years of *my* life have not," she said with some asperity. She was a trifle angry now, and this, too, became her.

I understood her increasingly well, but understanding is not always the same as management. Megan was no creature of casual influence. I was at a loss about how to approach her.

So I turned it over to Spirit again. "Convince her," I told my sister.

Spirit smiled as if she had expected this, which was true. She focused on Megan and took a breath.

"Surely you—his sister—are not going to play John Alden in his presence!" Megan exclaimed indignantly.

I had to reach far back into the recesses of my memory to place that reference. Megan's literary background, so readily applicable, was another delight. John Alden was the name of a man who was required to plead for the favor of a young woman, in the name of another man who lacked the social courage to propose to her himself. Unfortunately John Alden was enamored of the woman himself, as she understood. She at length interrupted him with the inquiry, "Why don't you speak for yourself, John?" I hesitate to conjecture the implications of that reference in this present situation.

At any rate Spirit took it in stride. "Megan—may I call you that?—I must argue that your life has indeed developed toward this union. You are a fine person, an outstanding political figure, and a lovely woman, though my brother would have come for you had you been otherwise. You deserve better than what the maelstrom of Jupiter politics has given you. You deserve to wield power, for you do know how to use it, and you have a social conscience unrivaled in the contemporary scene. You did not lose your last campaign because you were inadequate but because you were superior. You refused to stoop to the tactics your opponent used. As with money, the bad drove out the good, and you lost your place in the public eye, while your opponent flourishes like a weed. But whatever the politics, the bad remains bad and the good remains good, and this my brother understands."

Megan spread her hands. "He seems to be not the only one who understands. You certainly know how to make a person listen." I could tell she was alert for the kicker; she was sure that Spirit was flattering her for a purpose. As indeed she was.

"As a practical result, that man Tocsin now holds the office that should have been yours," Spirit continued. "He will use it merely as a steppingstone to higher office. You would have served your constituency loyally and well; his only real interest is himself. You cannot view his victory as merely a loss for you; it is a loss for the State of Golden and very likely for the United States of Jupiter as well. When you lost, you retired to a comfortable private life; those whom you should have served cannot do the same. They must endure the machinations of the callous and perhaps evil man who played upon their ignorance and baser motives. You owe it to those people to return to the political arena and defend the causes you know are—"

"No!" Megan cried, wincing as if in physical pain. "I will never again expose myself to that—"

"There is another avenue," Spirit said. "Naturally you do not wish to become another target for completely unscrupulous opportunists. But you need not be the target; you have only to advise him who is ready to be the target, to guide him so that—"

"I would not foist on another person the contumely I would not bear myself!"

"He can be properly prepared to counter it," Spirit continued. "My brother is not a delicate flower; he has survived the most brutal situation any person can experience."

"As have you," Megan put in.

"He is a cutting knife. Had he run against Tocsin, knowing what you know now, he would have found a way to impale that ugly man on his own spit. As an officer in the Navy my brother demonstrated his capacity to—"

"*You* were his chief of staff," Megan put in.

"—prevail in difficult situations. He has courage and ability; all he needs is competent guidance and advice. He has always accepted the best advice. This is what you can provide."

"If I ran my last campaign over, knowing what I now know, I still would not be able to handle the scurrilous slanders that man hurled at me!" Megan exclaimed. "I don't see how any ethical person could. How could an inexperienced—"

"My brother is excellent at delegating tasks and yielding to necessity," Spirit said. "If he does not know the proper course he will consult with someone who does, and consider the alternatives with an open mind. This is how he won battles in the Navy, both physical and diplomatic."

Megan nodded. "Do you mean to say it was not Hope Hubris who devised that farm-bubble compromise that so benefited the workers?"

"He presented it, but he did not devise it alone. His staff worked it out. Because he had the most competent personnel it was feasible to assemble, and he implemented their program . . .''

Megan nodded again, seeing the confirmation of her conjecture. She did have a good grasp of the realities of organization. "I really wasn't good at selecting a staff. I can appreciate that better in retrospect. Oh, they were fine people, individually, but the dynamics—"

"My brother is matchless at this," Spirit said with conviction.

Megan shook herself, as if fighting free of a morass she was unwittingly stepping into. "Still, it is presumptuous—a preposterous leap to assume that if Captain Hubris needs my advice I must marry him!"

Spirit smiled. "You are no common staff member, Megan. A staff member may be hired and fired at the whim of the employer. An independent consultant may be ignored. But a spouse is permanent. Marry him and you have power over him—not only legally, but also because he will listen to you first, last, and always. That is important for the realization of your programs. Through him you can implement them all."

"You tempt me most foolishly," Megan said. "You offer me a reward for a service to be rendered, as you would a biscuit to a performing dog. This is not the manner in which I bargain. I will sell myself neither for money nor for a program; that is prostitution."

"It is not selling so much as coming to terms with the situation," Spirit said. "It is the political way. One must deal for what one wants, and compromise, and indulge in the quid pro quo. There is no stigma in this; it is true in more subtle fashion for all of life. An honest compromise can benefit all parties, like a good contract."

"True," Megan agreed. I could tell she was intrigued by this discussion; she had been reclusive for two years and had had enough isolation. "But one does not bargain with marriage."

"Oh, but one does!" Spirit said. "Historically that was standard. Kingdoms formed alliances by intermarriage. It fostered cooperation and helped prevent wars between them. If one marriage prevented one war, surely it was worthwhile."

"Are you suggesting that we are at war?" Megan inquired with a wry flash of humor.

Spirit smiled. "Not exactly. But the importance of a liaison remains. It is better to have direct input into a force than to allow it to proceed randomly. A spaceship would not be useful without a pilot. My brother is going into politics, and he will be a considerable force because he has, as you pointed out, the ideal attributes for this business. He will seek advice where he can find it. The question you must ask yourself is whether you will exert your considerable influence on him as he rises, insuring that your ethics govern his campaigning and his actions in office, or whether you will turn him loose to seek other influences and go another course."

"Well, I hardly think that my input would make any significant difference! The planet is large, and no single person affects more than a tiny bit of it."

"So thought the pirates of the Belt," Spirit replied.

"Touché!" Megan agreed. "I confess I cheered with the majority when their power was destroyed, though I oppose war on principle. I do have, as it were, some weakness of the flesh. But politics is not a matter of sending a fleet of ships to—"

Spirit stared her in the eye. "When my brother becomes President of the United States of Jupiter, where will you be?"

Again Megan's jaw dropped. "President! You can't possibly be serious!"

"I am serious," I said. "I have things to do that can only be done from the top. I hope to do them with your help and guidance, but I will do them any way I can. I think I can be a much more effective force for good on this planet if you are with me, but if I cannot have you with me I will still do what I can."

Megan just looked at me, amazed. "You—you could become another Tocsin, or worse!"

"Not if you are with me."

"As the saying goes," Spirit murmured, "if you can't beat them join them."

"A literal political marriage!" Megan exclaimed. "Just like that!"

"But I will love you," I reminded her. "And I hope you will love me."

She looked at me as if considering how to set me straight without hurting my feelings too seriously. But she was flattered, too. The insidious worm of political desire was gnawing at her, after being quiescent for two years. No person gets into politics indifferently; the lure of power is always there, and it never truly abates. She had been badly hurt, but she could not truly stay away. I offered her a place in what we hoped would be the most spectacular campaign of the times: the rise of a Hispanic refugee to the top position of the planet. I knew she would struggle against it, thrashing like a fish on the hook, but she could not in the end decline. Spirit had found the correct approach for me to win Megan.

And so it was. It took several months, and in that time Megan's nemesis, Tocsin, was elected vice-president of the U.S. of J. Perhaps that fact affected her as much as any. She knew that a creature like Tocsin could not be allowed to have his way completely unopposed. Probably she did not see me as the ideal opposing candidate, and certainly she did not think in terms of vengeance; she was too nice a person for that. But she did perceive the need and did feel responsible, for she had provided the springboard for Tocsin's leap to prominence. She had to reenter the fray, however painful it might be on the personal level, and I proffered the vehicle. She accepted me, perhaps, as a necessary evil, as she might have accepted an aggressive attack dog as a companion when walking through a dangerous neighborhood. She hardly approved of all I stood for but recognized my place in the larger scheme and accepted what had to be. She did it with that certain grace and even éclat that so endeared her to me; though the decision was difficult for her, in no way did she suggest that there was anything offensive about me personally. Megan had style.

We worked it out very like a contract. She would marry me but would neither live with me nor be intimate with me. She would be my political consultant and would have veto power over any appointment to my staff. We might have disagreements, but neither of us would express these publicly. She would introduce me to her political contacts

and teach me and/or Spirit all she could about the funda-
mentals and strategies of politics.

We were married in a civil ceremony in the State of
Golden. Megan permitted me to kiss her once, chastely.
Then Spirit and I caught a flight back to Sunshine. It was
not an auspicious beginning, but I was well satisfied.
Megan was mine—legally—and I was sure she would in
due course be mine in reality.

Chapter 5

DORIAN GRAY

They brought me into the painful light again and cleaned me up for another interview. "Do you remember any more?" the interrogator inquired.

Did I remember more? Most of my first year on the planet of Jupiter had suddenly been revealed to me. Now I knew that it was the arena of politics I had entered after my departure from the Navy. It had all been triggered by the key word MEGAN. Somehow I had prepared myself to respond in that manner to that key word, when I understood that it *was* a key, much as a computer will respond to the touch on a particular button only when programmed to do so. But this new memory I surely had to conceal from my captors, for it was well within the range they believed they had erased.

"Some more," I said guardedly, glancing at the pain-box.

"Your military service."

Oh. I concentrated on that. "Yes, I went through basic training. There was a girl, Juana—I shared quarters with her. She was a Hispanic refugee, like me. A very nice, very pretty young woman. But I had to leave her, when . . ." I found that the tremendous volume of experience triggered by the word *Megan* was an isolated thing; my military experience remained at the prior pace of recovery. Except that, as if it were a glimpse into the future, I knew I had married more than once and left the service with the rank of captain. I just had no memory of how I had achieved it. Perhaps there was a key term to evoke that experience. But it seemed that my prior self had not wished me to have that information at this stage, and I had to trust the judgment of that self. Thus my Navy memories were returning at the normal crawl permitted by recovery from the mem-wash; it would probably take months to cover the fifteen years or so I had evidently spent there.

"You like women?" Scar asked.

I was somewhat taken aback by this seeming camaraderie. "Yes," I answered.

"How do you feel?"

I considered that. "Low," I concluded.

"Nauseous?"

"No. Just low." The malaise had developed slowly, so that only now did I realize I had it.

"Try this," he said, bringing me another cup of the beverage he had given me before.

I drank it without protest. I knew he would torture me with the pain-box if I did not, but also I welcomed this distraction from the subject of my returning memories. In a moment I began to feel better, physically. "Yes, good," I said. "What is it?"

He shrugged. "Merely an upper. You will have all you want, if you cooperate with us."

"But I don't know what you want of me," I said plaintively.

"Merely your cooperation," he said. "A positive attitude. With that, all else is possible."

Just as I had endeavored to gain the positive attitude of Megan. This man evidently wanted a lot more of me than I would ordinarily give. But this was not the time to arouse his suspicion. "Anything you want," I agreed.

"First, a lesson-session," he said.

He brought me simple gray clothing—shirt, trousers, slippers—and I donned it, relieved that the pain-box had not been invoked. I felt much better now; clothing has a strong psychological effect. But, of course, the drug contributed considerably, though the high did not seem to be as strong as it had been before. Maybe they had given me a weaker dose. I didn't like getting drugged, but I still didn't see any point in resisting. They would do with my body as they wished. And there was something from my Megan memory—a reference to my supposed immunity to addiction. Could that be true?

We entered a separate chamber where there was a tiny library of books and two easy chairs. I was told to sit down.

It was a luxury to inhabit such a chair after the hard and filthy floor of my dark cell.

"Do you remember how the present political order came about?" the man asked me, taking the other chair. It was easy to imagine that we were merely two acquaintances indulging in a postprandial conversation. But I had not forgotten the dark cell or the pain-box—nor was I intended to. This was a technique I recognized: the carrot and the stick.

I focused on the question. "The—the nations of Earth laid claim to the properties of the Solar System, in accordance with their representations on the mother planet," I said, as my early education came back to me. "When the gee-shield made System colonization feasible, there was an agreement in the old United Nations, now called the United Planets. They tried to do it very fairly, so there would be no war in space." I paused to smile, and Scar smiled with me. We both knew that there were as many wars in space as there had been on Earth, so that this aspect of the compromise had been a foolish dream. Man had exported his nature with his technology. "The nations of old Europe took the planet Uranus, with its moons and rings, and set up governments like those they had on Earth, along with their individual languages and cultures. The Asian nations took over Saturn, with its more spectacular moons and rings, and the American nations got the big prize, Jupiter. The Africans got the hot planets, Mercury and Venus. Of course, the pattern isn't perfect, but in a general way it is true that the contemporary political Solar System resembles the planet of prediaspora Earth, but on a larger scale. The languages, the cultures, even the histories conform to a remarkable extent. The two Solar wars—"

"Do you approve of war as an instrument of political policy?"

That brought me up short. "I don't really know," I confessed. "I suppose it depends on the situation. Certainly there have been unjust or foolish wars, and war is certainly one of the most dangerous and costly ways to settle differences. But when the Deutsch Reich of Uranus set out to conquer that planet and Saturn, too, what was there to do but make war to stop it?"

"You believe in the existing order, then?"

"Well, I'm not sure about that. As long as the existing order tolerates piracy in space—"

"The pirates are gone," he said. "You had a hand in that, Hubris."

"I did?" Almost, I remembered it directly, instead of as the memory of a statement made in the time of my introduction to life on Jupiter. *Hero of the Belt!* "I'm glad. They had to be extirpated."

"By lawful means," he said.

"Certainly." What was he getting at? Did this have something to do with my confinement here? Could I have broken the law and required rather special rehabilitation? No, that did not seem likely.

"The existing government of Jupiter is working to solve the problems of the day," he said. "Do you believe that?"

I shrugged. "I don't know. I don't remember the current government. That is, which party is in power, or who is President now. When I was a refugee in space, the government seemed to have no interest in dealing with the problems of refugees or the eradication of piracy. But that was . . . I think it must have been some time ago. Maybe it's better now. Certainly the Jupiter system of government is a good one, perhaps the best in a flawed Solar System. But—"

"That's enough," he said, and terminated the interview.

I was not returned to my dark and stinking cell. Instead I was conducted to a larger, brighter one, with a conventional hammock and a lavatory facility. What an improvement! Evidently I had pleased my captors, and this was my reward.

What had I said to please them? I had only described the contemporary Solar System, which was familiar to all school children, and expressed my support for the type of government Jupiter possessed, with my reservations for specific practices. Why should that deserve reward?

Had I become a revolutionist, trying to overthrow the system? If so, I could hardly protest my fate. But this treatment seemed overly harsh and secretive—and why should anyone bother to rehabilitate a revolutionary?

At any rate, I did appreciate my improved quarters and

would try to continue pleasing my captors. Clean, clothed, comfortable—what more could I ask?

Freedom, I answered myself mentally. But I knew that wish was useless.

Apart from that, I lacked entertainment. There were no books, no holo units, not even any old-fashioned board games. And no one with whom to play them.

Ah, there was the crux! Companionship! It was hard to be continually alone.

Still, I knew when I was relatively well off. I lay on the hammock and contemplated the patterns in the paint on the ceiling of the chamber and slept.

I dreamed of Annabel Lee, who had lived in a kingdom by the sea:

And this maiden she lived with no other thought
  Than to love and be loved by me.

My memory of Helse, of course. Every so often she visited me, though she was long dead, and I always appreciated it.

In due course a meal was brought. This time it was on a tray, and there was variety: some sort of juice, mashed protein mix, and a pastry. Royal treatment indeed—all because I had expressed support for the present order?

I finished, used the lavatory, and sat on the hammock. Now that my lot had improved, I was bored. My feeling of malaise was returning. Why should this be?

I thought about it, and the answer came: The drug they had given me to drink was wearing off. I was suffering withdrawal. So much for being immune!

Restlessly I paced the cell, trying to abate the discomfort. It wasn't actually extreme, but something prompted me to make a show. They were trying to addict me, to make me malleable; suppose they realized that the effect was uncomfortable but not truly compulsive? If my immunity was working partially, it was better to persuade them otherwise.

Soon Scar appeared. "What is your problem, Hubris?"

"That drink," I said. "Could I have another—now?"

He smiled. "Indeed." He departed and returned in a moment with the drink. I took it and gulped it down eagerly. Point made.

I was left alone again. The euphoria of the drug took me, more mildly than before, so that instead of enjoying it I remained bored. Apparently my immunity was a slowly developing thing, cutting down the highs and lows with greater facility as time went on. Good enough; I had caught the hint in time to conceal the nature of my resistance to the drug.

I explored my cell. It was about eight feet by twelve feet, with a ceiling of eight feet. That was palatial, for a sub. The hammock was at one end, the lavatory section at the other, the door in the middle. The walls were featureless, and I didn't dare scratch them, knowing that my marks would immediately be apparent. No secret codes here.

There was a glassy window in the door, really a narrow slit that sufficed only to allow the captor to observe the captive. All I could see from inside the cell was a segment of the access passage, and the door to the opposite cell, with its own vision slit. Not much to entertain me there.

Yet I looked. In fact, I stared, having nothing to do. I oriented on that opposite portal as if it were my gateway to escape.

I don't know how long I remained there, staring. Certainly my vision fogged, and perhaps I slept. But abruptly I spied an eye in the opposite slit. There was another prisoner there.

This transformed my awareness. I had company. Oh, I couldn't talk with him or shake his hand or even see him clearly; the window allowed little more than one eye and a vertical slice of face to show through. But he was a fellow captive, and that made up for the inadequacy of appearance.

He saw me, too, for his eye locked gazes with mine, and then he winked. I winked back. We had established communication. Oh, no words, no written message, but communication nonetheless. It was enormously gratifying to have a companion in isolation, as it were, even without words.

Then a guard came, and we had to get away from the window slits. But the guard only turned out the lights—for night—and departed. We were alone again.

I returned to my hammock, as there was nothing to be seen in the dark. But the lingering effect of the drug kept me hyped up. Now that I knew I had company I could not be satisfied with ignorance. I had to know more about him. Why was he here? Had he been memory-washed, confined in filth, and tortured? Did he know anything about our captors or our prospects for release? It didn't matter what the answers were; I simply had to know.

I considered the door. My prior cell had had a sliding panel that bolted tightly in place; no hope for escape. But this one had a regular door catch, the kind that was slanted on one side and slid into place because of a spring. Child's play to force that open. Why the superior mechanisms of recent centuries had not been employed was a mystery; I conjectured that this vessel had begun its career as a yacht, with deliberately archaic furnishings and mechanisms as a signal of status, and later converted into a sub. At any rate, this was a major break for me, as my military training had schooled me in lock-picking, among other things. All I needed was a bit of wire or metal.

Well, I had left my rivet in the other cell—and, anyway, I wasn't sure that was suitable for this. It was too small. What else offered?

I checked my new clothing. It was soft, without buttons or stays. I might have used an eating utensil, but that was gone with the meal tray.

I got up to find the sanitary unit in the darkness—what a blessing that was, in contrast to my prior circumstance!— and as I used it I realized that this could be the answer. The unit was standard for spacecraft: a tube leading away into a central processing apparatus, a moderate suction conveying solids and liquids there. In free-fall it tended to be more complicated, and primitive ships required separate facilities for solid and liquid wastes. But evidently this ship maintained centrifugal gee steadily enough to warrant more conventional facilities. The toilet was sealed by an airtight panel; the unit was flushed when a lever was operated to slide the panel momentarily aside, allowing the gee and suction to draw the refuse down.

Sure enough, I was able to unscrew part of the connecting rod and detach it. I had my instrument!

I paused. Was I under observation, here in the cell?

Well, I might be, but if I was, why did my captors need to lock me in? Probably they could monitor me but didn't bother unless there seemed to be immediate reason. There might be a continuing holo-tape of activity within this cell, but it would be a boring job reviewing that tape. After a while the clerk in charge would get slack and leave it to the computer. The behavior patterns of human beings were so strange as to defy computer analysis, however, so probably this action of mine would not be called out as either an attempt to escape or an attempt to commit suicide.

At any rate, if I allowed the fear of observation to restrain me, I was captive indeed! I would take my action and discover what the consequence was. Some risk had to be taken, in order to gain. I used the thin rod to jam open the door latch, then pulled the door in to me. It swung on armored hinges, proof against any tampering except what I had done. Designers tend to overlook the obvious.

I peeked out into the dark hall. I saw nothing, of course— and trusted that no one could see me. Infrared light could do it, but again, why bother when the doors were locked? I started to step out and paused again. What about an alarm?

Again, why use a lock, if a laser alarm system was in place? It could be done and should be done, but probably wasn't. I decided to risk it.

I moved into the hall. Nothing happened. That did not necessarily mean there was no alarm; it could be silent, a light blinking elsewhere in the ship. If so, I would soon be in trouble.

I waited. Nothing happened. Apparently my captors were asleep, and there was no alarm. I deemed that to be criminally careless. Maybe they just weren't worried, knowing that I could not escape from the sub no matter how cunning I might be. Captors do tend to underestimate the potentials of captives, perhaps assuming that natural selection accounts for the roles.

Meanwhile, I felt deliriously free. Certainly I remained trapped in the sub and subject to the will of my captors, but I had achieved a measure of independence they had not granted me. I was, to this limited extent, master of my destiny. That did great things for my self-esteem.

I did not bother to walk down the passage; I knew the cell block was sealed off by airlock, not simple gates. If I broke that I would really be testing my luck. I closed my door, then went instead to the cell door opposite mine. I knocked.

There was no response. I knocked again, not loudly, sure that the inmate heard me. He would be wondering what was happening, assuming that it was a guard, puzzled because the lights had not been turned on.

I knocked a third time. At last there was a response—a hesitant return knock. I tapped on the window, then used my rod to work the latch. In a moment the door swung open.

"Make no sound," I whispered. "I'm from the other cell. I used the bar on the sanitary fixture to jimmy the lock."

After a moment a hand touched mine. Fingers caught me, drawing me in. I went and quietly closed the door behind me. If any guard made a spot check all would seem to be in order. He would have to turn on the lights and peer into the cells to discover that I had moved.

"This is folly," my fellow-prisoner said, alarmed.

I froze in surprise. Those words showed me two things. First, my companion was Hispanic, like me, for they had been spoken in Spanish. Second, my companion was female.

"A woman?" I asked in Spanish. I realized that I had not been able to see enough of the face through the two window slits to identify gender; I had merely assumed male. I myself had missed an obvious alternative.

"All my life," she agreed. "What I can remember of it."

"Memory-washed?"

"Yes. You?"

"The same."

We paused, there in the darkness. After a moment she said, "What if they catch you here?"

"What can they do to me that they haven't already?"

"But you must go back to your cell soon, so they don't know."

"Why?"

"Because if they catch you, they'll see that we never meet again."

There was that. To be effectively deprived of company

now that I had found it—that would be torture indeed. "Soon," I agreed. There was risk, but I had to get to know her better.

"I—hardly know you," she said. "I can't see you at all. May I . . . may I touch you? Your face, so I can recognize you?"

"Touch me anywhere," I said generously. I had not considered what I might do after reaching my fellow captive and remained surprised that it was a woman.

She stepped close, so that I inhaled the special female atmosphere of her, which was not a matter of perfume, for she wore none. She reached up her hands to find my head and face. The darkness remained impenetrable; I could not see any part of her. On a planetary surface, I understand, darkness is seldom absolute, because of the diffusion of light in the atmosphere. But here in the closed cell of a ship, there was none at all. It was as if I were back in my degradation cell—except that there was no woman there.

Her hands stroked lightly over my forehead, eyes, and nose, then down to my mouth. Her touch was ticklish on my lips. There was something ineffably sensual about it, causing me to become sexually aroused. "Oh, you're bearded," she said.

"They gave me no way to shave," I explained apologetically, though I had not thought of the matter before. "It's all right," she said quickly. "I was just surprised." Her fingers traveled on down across my face and to my neck and shoulders and arms. This, too, aroused me; I hoped she wouldn't go farther down, lest I suffer embarrassment. "I suppose I know you now," she said.

"Do I get to check you similarly?" I asked.

"I suppose so." I could tell she was smiling.

She stood for me while I ran my fingers over her face. I was not used to this and may have poked her in the eye, but she did not complain. Despite my ineptitude, I became aware of one thing: These were extremely comely features.

"What's your name?" I asked as my hands passed across her firm young chin and her smooth neck.

She shook her head, not answering. Because I was touching her, I could read her to some extent. My question caused her to tighten; she knew her name but did not feel free to tell me.

"Then I will name you," I decided as my hands continued down. No, I did not handle her torso, though the temptation was there; I checked her shoulders and arms, as she had mine. "Dorian Gray."

"Who?" she asked. She was relaxing now, a hurdle evidently having been negotiated. That was interesting; I had expected her to become tense as my hands reached hers, as the further exploration might be more intimate than she liked.

"The one whose face I cannot see," I explained. "It's a historical or literary reference."

"Oh." She shrugged. "You'd better go back to your cell now."

"But I don't know anything about you," I protested. "Why are you here? Have they—?"

"I don't know why I'm here," she said. "The mem-wash, remember? Yes, they used the pain-box on me, but they didn't ask me any questions, they just made me hurt. I don't know what they want of me."

"Any lesson-sessions?"

"They showed me how to bake bread. I knew it was for prisoners, so I slipped some rivets into it, so maybe they could use them. I don't know."

"*You* put those rivets in?" I asked. "I chewed on one!"

"I didn't know how else to do it. Did you get any use of it?"

"I thought of using it to scratch a message on the wall, but there was already a message there."

"Oh? What did it say?"

"Well, it was in code. It took me a while to figure it out, but, of course, I had plenty of time and few distractions. Then it turned out to be only advice not to hope."

She laughed. "How can you, of all people, abandon hope? It's your name!"

"It may be good advice, anyway. This is a sub, a ship hidden in space. It's impossible to escape."

"But there has to be hope," she said.

I shrugged. "Maybe so. I haven't found it yet."

"Now you'd really better go. A guard could come anytime."

She was correct, of course. I used my bar to jimmy the door again, exited, and got back into my own cell. I restored the bar to the toilet fixture, then lay on my hammock. It had been quite a little adventure; soon I would learn whether I had gotten away with it.

Nothing happened. Gradually I relaxed. It seemed that our cells were not being monitored.

But sleep did not come. Something was bothering me, and as the first nervousness abated, that secondary concern loomed larger. What was it?

First, my excursion had been too easy. There *should* have been an alarm of some sort. This was a modern sub, whatever kind of yacht it might have been before conversion; the modernity had to do with the technology of concealment, not of vessel construction. They wouldn't be primitive about observation procedures, external or internal. My captors had to know when I left the cell. Why hadn't they pounced on me?

Second, there was something about my dialogue with Dorian Gray. I had noticed it on one level of attention while conversing with her on another. In a moment I had it: We had not exchanged names. I had asked her, and she hadn't answered, so I had named her myself. I had not told her mine. Yet she had known it. How?

Oh, there could be explanations. A guard could have told her. She could have been a captive longer than I, or at least longer than the time since my mem-wash. She could have sent me a rivet before my wash, enabling me to scratch my message to myself. She could have seen my name written on a cell door or something. But I doubted it. For one thing, she had not been telling the truth. I had been touching her when she told of her own mem-wash and pain-box treatment, and her body reactions had suggested that she was lying or, at any rate, not telling the whole truth.

Third, the facility with which I had escaped the cell. A latch that could be jimmied, a rod available to do it. It was almost as if my captors had wanted me to escape.

To get out, thinking myself unobserved, and meet my fellow captive, who just happened to be a lovely young Hispanic woman who had helped me make messages to myself? Perhaps I would have believed that, if I had remained mem-washed to the extent my captors believed me to be. But my secret message to myself—the one *not* intended for my captors to read—had triggered the recollection of a major sequence, and that substantially modified my out-look. For one thing, I now remembered my association with Megan, the woman I loved. That canceled any romantic interest I might have had in a mysterious young woman.

If this had been set up for me, what course did my captors plan? It fell into place readily enough. Their program was threefold. First, they washed out my memories and tortured me, making me vulnerable to change. Second, they addicted me to a drug, making me dependent on them for gratification. And, third, they meant to literally seduce me from my prior associations. They wanted me to cleave to my fellow captive, to know her and love her, so that I would be emotionally compromised before my memory of Megan returned.

But my message to myself had foiled the wash, and my body was throwing off or muting the addiction, and now I knew the true face of Dorian Gray. How aptly I had named her. She was no fellow captive; she was an enemy agent planted to complete my corruption.

But this insight did not ameliorate my situation. Why was I here? How could I prevail? I did not yet know enough of my real life to grasp why I had been taken captive. Probably I was a politician; that was what I had been headed for when my vision memory ended. Had I become important enough to be worth eliminating? But they hadn't killed me; they were trying to change me. If I were a figure in a powerful office, that might make sense, but surely my absence would be noted. So I still didn't have that answer.

There was also a problem about the woman. Now I knew her to be a spy or agent, but how could I safely reject her? If I did, my captors might suspect that their program was not working. Then they would try something else, and that other thing might be more effective. Suppose they lobotomized me? I would not be able to recover from that. Or they might simply give it up as a bad job, kill me, and start over with some more amenable captive.

No, I could not afford to show my captors the extent of their failure. Which meant I could not turn down the offering they were making in the person of Dorian. I had to play the part of a fish securely hooked, three ways. If that meant loving Dorian, I would love her—with my body only.

Forgive me, Megan! I thought fervently. I was not at all sure she would. I was of the new school, pragmatic, doing what I had to do. She was of the old school; there were some compromises she would not make. Of course, my memory did not take me as far as intimacy with Megan; we had married, but there had been no certainty that there would be anything more than the formality. It was possible that we had existed for the duration in that mock marriage and that I was free to dally wherever else I wished. But I doubted it.

Perhaps I was making a mistake. But at the moment this seemed to be the reasonable compromise. Only if I fooled my captors completely could I hope to survive—and for me, survival was my first priority.

At last I slept, ill at ease. Recognition of the realities of one's situation does not necessarily make for a feeling of well-being.

In the morning the lights came on, and food arrived. I begged another drink of the drug, and it was granted. At this point I really had no physical need of the drink; it had become pure charade.

I was taken for another lesson-session. This one was about general economics and the advantages of a stable industrial system, and I was happy to agree. For one thing, this represented my best route to knowledge of what my captors really wanted of me. Evidently they were satisfied with my progress, for when I was returned to my cell, I was given a book to read. It was an instructive tome on the subject we had been discussing, written in English, excellent as far as it went but biased toward a conservative, authoritarian outlook. I perused it with interest; after all, *any* book was far, far better than none. But I assimilated it cynically. Some points were valid; others were not.

At night the lights went out again, and I knew my captors would be expecting me to stray and would be suspicious if I did not pay a call on Dorian Gray. So I had to do it, but with misgivings, for I suspected the art she would practice on me.

I was not disappointed. I still could not see her, but she touched my face to identify me—as if there could be any other man in this cell block!—and required me to do the same to her. Logically this was nonsensical, but esthetically it reminded me how well-formed her features were. This time she insisted on getting better acquainted, passing her hands down along my torso, and, of course, I had to do the same for her. She was young and voluptuous; on the proverbial scale of ten, she was overqualified.

My captors had not merely made corruption possible for me; they had made it compelling. Even knowing what I did, thanks to my Megan memory flash, I felt the temptation to do . . . what I would have to do. I had somehow believed I might play along by rote, my true face averted; now I knew I would have to answer to my wife not only for my body, but also for my mind.

But not yet. These things took time, and I intended to take all the time I could that was consistent with my situation and my presumed situation. First Dorian and I had to get to know each other.

We sat together in her hammock and talked in whispers, exchanging histories. I told her of my upbringing on Callisto, of my two sisters, and of the problem that had led to our abrupt departure to the peripheral society of the Jupiter Ecliptic—the Juclip—my year as a migrant worker in the agricultural belt, and my entry into the Jupiter Navy at age sixteen. "I don't know how long I remained in the Navy," I concluded. "Maybe I'm still there." That was a lie, but I could not tell her of my Megan memory, which put a cap on my military experience. "I don't even know how old I am, but I suspect I am twice your age."

She laughed. "But I don't know my age, either. Maybe I'm middle-aged."

It was my turn to laugh. "If so, you will go down in history as possessing the secret of eternal youth. Your body is twenty."

"You are an expert in bodies, Don Hope?" she inquired archly.

"I don't know," I admitted. "But I am certainly capable of appreciating what I encounter."

She took my hand, drew me to her, and kissed me. There was a certain fragrance about her, perhaps this time enhanced by some perfume, and her hair was like a velvet curtain. I was sure that she was experienced at this; her every motion and mannerism was completely seductive.

Oh, yes, she knew what she was doing. But she, too, was constrained by her role; she had a part to play, and she had to play it well enough to deceive me. So we were deceiving each other.

She was, she said, a refugee from the Communist colony of Ganymede. She had been born five years after that revolution occurred and the leftist premier assumed power, but her parents had never accepted the new order. (I should clarify that revolutions, like elections, occurred frequently in the System, as they had on old Earth; Ganymede had changed governments and types of government many times following its colonization. Each change was welcomed by some and detested by some, and there was generally a certain attendant unpleasantness.) Her family had been especially concerned about her schooling, not wanting her to be indoctrinated into the Communist ideology. So they had joined the bubble-lift of 2640, which was their first opportunity to flee the planet, and came to Jupiter.

I was startled. 2640? That was six years, no, eight years after my most recent memory. I had had the (mis)fortune to be born at the turn of the century, so that my age always matched the date. I had, as well as I could reconstruct it, served in the Jupiter Navy from 2616 to 2630. I would have been forty years old at the time of the bubble-lift that Dorian Gray spoke of, and that was evidently some time in the past.

"I was but fifteen then," Dorian said. "Much of my education was already behind me, but I had resisted the indoctrination. Of course, I had to learn English and adjust to the Saxon culture, and it was hard at first, but I did complete my schooling, and . . ." She paused. "And I don't remember."

So she remained memory-blocked from the time she was seventeen to the present, according to her story. She was lying, but only about the mem-wash; her dates were otherwise accurate, according to her body signals. I judged her to be about twenty-two, which would make the present date 2047, and my own age forty-seven, with an error factor of as much as three years. I was older than I had feared. I was indeed over twice her age, and a great deal more of my own history remained forgotten. She had perhaps given me more valuable information than she knew.

If I was forty-seven years old, with about fifteen missing following my Navy career, what had I done in that anonymous time? It must have been something to make me worthy of being captured and mem-washed and trapped by drugs and sex. They wanted to have a firm hold on me, to change my way of thinking. What could possibly be worth the trouble they were taking?

"You are silent," Dorian murmured.

I started. "Sorry. I was thinking."

"I would offer two cents for your thoughts, if I had any money."

I considered quickly. There seemed to be no reason I couldn't tell her my thoughts this time. "With your help I have now calculated my age as between forty-five and fifty, and I wonder what I have been doing in all the missing years since I was sixteen, to warrant being here."

"That's a good thought," she said, unsurprised by my age; she had known it. "There must be good reason. Did you work in some sensitive military job where a seemingly minor decision could make a big difference?"

"I wish I knew," I said.

"Maybe you knew too much about something in the Hispanic sphere."

"Maybe. I just don't remember."

"I don't, either, though I suppose less of my life is missing than yours. It must be pretty important."

"It must be," I agreed. "Perhaps if you reviewed the major System events that occurred during your life, which falls in the period of my life that has been washed out, I could remember—"

She put her hand on mine. "Hope, since you came to me yesterday, I've been thinking about you so much. I was alone—no one to meet except my torturers—and suddenly I saw your face across the hall—part of your face—and then I touched you. You gave me something to live for just by existing. In one day it's as if I've known you all my life."

I knew she was playing a part, and I noted how adroitly she had diverted my suggestion about catching up on System events; but she played that part very well. I had had in mind obtaining some information from her, not only to try to trigger more of my memory, but also to account for any slip I might make about the period I did remember, such as

Tocsin's rise in politics. Obviously Dorian was under orders to tell me nothing of this period. I had to admire the finesse with which she distracted me; it would have been easy to believe she was sincere. Now I knew it would be hard to come up with some excellent reason to distract her forthcoming physical advances very long. This trap was closing on me. "I think time dilates in a situation like this," I said.

She nudged closer. "I don't even know whether I'm married," she said. "But I don't think so, though I'm not a virgin. I feel so close to you, though we are of different ages."

That was my cue to confess that I didn't know my own marital state and to deny that age made a difference. She had let me know the state of her availability. I had to think fast. "I—I think I was married, in the Navy. I remember a girl I shared residence with. Her name was Juana."

"Hispanic?"

"Yes. She was a really nice girl."

"But those service liaisons are impermanent," she pointed out. "Only for the duration of an assignment."

"True. So I suppose it didn't endure." I tensed, as if just thinking of something. "Maybe I'm involved in some sexual scandal!"

She laughed. "No, it's not that!"

"You know?"

She retreated hastily. "I overheard once . . . about a prisoner who was a politician. I think it must have been you."

"So it's something political!"

"I suppose so." I knew she regretted her slip. Now I knew that she knew why I was here. Could I get that information from her? Surely not by asking for it. But perhaps if I turned the ploy and seduced *her* emotions. . . .

But that would take careful management. First, I had to show some mettle of my own. "I'll ask them," I said.

"Don't do that!" she exclaimed in genuine alarm. "They'll torture you!"

They probably would. "Well, maybe I'll just argue with them and force them to show what they really want of me."

"I don't like this," she said. "You are flirting with real trouble."

"Some things just have to be done. I'll tell you what I find out."

"Can't I talk you out of this folly?" she asked, moving very close to me.

"If I could be talked out of folly," I said firmly, "I probably wouldn't be here."

To that she had to agree. "Be careful, Hope. I don't want anything to happen to you."

And with that we separated, for too long a stay was risky. The seduction was forgotten for now. The ironic thing was, she was now genuinely concerned for me. She had her mission, but she was coming to respect me as a person.

Next day I implemented my decision. I had more than one reason for my course. I wanted to impress Dorian with my character, to reassure her that I trusted her. Of course, she would tell my captors, so they would be prepared, but they would not give her away. They, too, would know that I trusted her, and that she was doing her job. This trust and reinforcement of positions was important in a project like this. But also, I wanted to be punished by being returned to my original cell. I was sure they wouldn't leave me there long, for that would interfere with Dorian's subversion of my emotion. They would incarcerate me just long enough to bring home to me the consequence of my unreasonableness.

We were discussing taxation. My textbook recommended the so-called flat tax, a concept that had existed for centuries, perhaps for millennia, but somehow had not become established. It consisted of a personal deduction for each person in a family, certain necessary business deductions, and a set percentage of taxation on the remainder of earned income. It was quite simple.

"What's wrong with the present system?" I demanded. "It's worked well enough for centuries, hasn't it?"

Scar demurred. "It has bumbled along for centuries. There are three serious flaws in it. First, its immense complexity, which forces every taxpayer to spend interminable time merely calculating what he owes and requires many to seek some kind of professional help to draw up the required forms. Second, its loopholes, which enable clever or unscrupulous people to escape without paying their proper share, thus shifting the burden of payment to others. Third, its graduated stages, so that the person who earns more pays a larger percentage of his income to the government. That discourages initiative and penalizes the hardest or most efficient workers."

"It's not complex for the average wage earner," I countered. *"He* has no loopholes. It's only fair that he pay the lowest rate; he barely has enough to survive on as it is. When I was with the migrant workers—"

"He would be no worse off with a simple flat tax," Scar pointed out. "In fact he would benefit by—"

"No!" I exclaimed unreasonably. "The old system's good enough for me. I won't listen to anything else!"

He looked at me and sighed. "I'm sorry to hear you say that."

The session was over. I was conducted to my dark, filthy original cell, which had been saved unchanged. The smell almost gagged me as the hatch slid open. This was my punishment for being recalcitrant, and I knew that if my attitude did not improve, I would face more sessions with the pain-box and deprivation of the drug-beverage. Two of those were real punishments, and the third I would have to honor as if it were equally effective. Oh, yes, it was easy to reconsider my position with my self-interest so obviously in the balance.

But now I was where, ironically, I wanted to be. I needed more information, and this was where I could get it. I squatted in the grime and supported myself with my hands, and slowly I slid my fingers under the muck, feeling out the next set of symbols. I had an irrational fear that the scratches would be gone, but they were there: ⏋ which meant 7, counted off from the N in ABANDON, or T. ⨼ , which was 19, counted off from the space following ABANDON, or H. ⊓ meaning 8, counted from the H in HOPE—oh, the new significance of my name!—or O. ⊐ , 4, from the O, or R. ⦀ , 34, from P, or L. ⨽ , 1 from E, which, of course, was the same letter, E. ⦀ , 34 again, this time from the comma following HOPE. I wrestled with that and decided that most likely the order of punctuation in the font was space, period, comma; on that basis it came to Y.   ⌐ , 1, which was a space, translating itself into itself, a space. I had my word.

I assembled the letters mentally, so that I could appreciate them as the word, so that my second memory-vision could commence:

THORLEY.

Chapter 6

THORLEY

I quickly learned how naive I had been about politics. I had thought I would simply pick an office, run for it, and win it. Megan disabused me: rarely could a newcomer to politics pluck the office of his choice from the electorate. The great majority came up through the grass roots, building their constituencies before emerging as serious contenders for the favor of the voters.

What were these grass roots? She sent me into the turf to find out. The process reminded me of Basic Training in the Navy, though the education was not physical.

I had to join a citizen's activity organization and do my homework. This was the Good Government Group, better known as GGG, or Triple-Gee, or 3-G, whose stated purpose was to accelerate the existing government into conformity with the needs of the citizens. The present government, GGG said, was seriously out of phase, and hardly represented its constituency at any level. The result was corruption, inefficiency, and despoilation. A monthly national publication, *Gee Whiz*, pinpointed specifics on the planetary scene, and a state publication, *Sun-Gee*, covered the local issues. Everything was covered: the nefarious influence of special interests; the ongoing weapons development race; sloppy accounting practices by the government; the Saturn hot line that was supposed to keep interplanetary communications open in times of crisis; the perennial Balanced Budget Amendment; controversial subsidies for agricultural interests; wasteful use of chauffeured autobubbles by bureaucrats; tax reform; the campaign for the G-1 Space Bomber that threatened to bankrupt the planet before it was produced; the question of monopolistic mail service; an attempt to enable Congress to overturn Supreme Court decisions; protection of the atmospheric environment; the Equal Opportunity drive; pros and cons of subsidized bubble-housing; the revised Planetary Voting Rights Act; another routine administration scandal; the problem of continuing monetary inflation; unemployment; neglect of the elderly; restrictive construction codes; prison reform; retirement reform; the activities of the Jupiter Medical Association; the Jupiter Weapons Association; the ethics of drafting citizens into the Navy; athletes making commercials; huge cost overruns on military contracts; a bill to subsidize private schools; the problem of organized crime; a survey on the ages of members of Congress; research for new applications of contra-terrene matter; an antidrug campaign; city-bubble pollution; ways to prevent interplanetary war, or at least postpone it. There seemed to be an endless array of issues, and Megan assured me that most of them had been around for centuries in one form or another without any real resolutions. "But how can I make sense of all this?" I asked plaintively. "We were never faced with such matters in the Navy."

"You have led a sheltered life," she replied grimly. I found that statement ironic, but, of course, I knew what she meant. I had been exposed to the problems of survival in space but not to the problems of planetary political interaction. "This is the cesspool of civilian life. Keep reading and thinking, and it will start to fall into place. You must acquire a sensible grasp of every significant issue, for the one you do not master will become your Achilles' heel. It has happened many times to politicians before you. A single ignorant statement can finish you."

"Like a pinhole leak in a space suit," I murmured.

"Meanwhile, focus on one particular issue, the one you feel is most important, and learn what you can about that. Become active in that one area, become expert if you can—and when you are satisfied that your position is correct, you will be ready to tackle the next issue."

"But there are hundreds of important issues," I protested. "I'll never have time to master them all!"

"Now you perhaps appreciate why public officials occasionally make ignorant statements or do foolish things," she said. "The perfect candidate knows everything about everything."

"But in the Navy my staff—"

"True. And you will have a political staff, too, and use it similarly. But first you must grasp the basics yourself."

I delved back into the myriad issues, and so did Spirit, as if we were two students in school, seeking the one I could deem most important. It was a headache, for they were *all* important in one devious way or another.

Meanwhile, our limited activity had not gone unnoticed. The political columnist for a local newspaper was a man who signed himself simply "Thorley." Between elections he was evidently short of material, so minor things warranted comment.

"Guess who's coming to town," Thorley wrote conversationally, showing by this signal that this was not a subject to be taken too seriously. "Remember the darling of the bleeding-heart set in Golden, Megan? It seems she married the gallant of the Jupiter Navy, Captain Hubris, a man some years her junior. Rumor has it that one of them has political pretensions."

"That's insulting," I said angrily. "What right does he have to—"

"We are, or were, public figures," she said. "Our names are in the common domain, his to play with at will. He tosses them about as a canine tosses a rag doll, entertaining himself. You will have to get used to this sort of thing if you wish to survive in politics. Words become as heated and effective as lasers. Perhaps you can better appreciate, now, why I was not eager to return to the arena myself."

I took her hand, which was as much of a gesture as I felt free to make at this stage of our marriage. She was exactly the woman I needed her to be. "I confess that the political knives are more devious than the military ones, but I will master them."

"I rather fear you will," she agreed. "Just remember that *any* publicity is generally good news."

"Bleeding-heart set?" Spirit grumbled, unappeased.

"Those who favor liberal social legislation to alleviate the ills of society," Megan explained. "Conservatives generally hold such ideals in contempt. I certainly qualify as a bleeding heart. I'm not sure about you."

"Social *reform*," I said. "I've already seen enough to know that there is an immense mountain of reform required. If that makes me a bleeding-heart . . . well, I may arrange to make some other hearts bleed before I'm through."

"There speaks the military mind," she said, smiling. She was, of course, against militarism, but she was coming to understand me, so she smiled to signal that she was not condemning me personally. She was very diplomatic in little ways like that, and I appreciated it. If I had not been programmed to love her, I would have found myself falling in love with her now. Helse had been my ideal love, in that kingdom by the sea, but now I understood that Megan was to Helse as a nova is to a star. "Just keep in mind that though Thorley is at the opposite end of the political spectrum, he is a competent journalist and an honest man."

"You would find good in the devil himself," I charged her, also smiling.

"That might be a slight exaggeration. But Thorley is no devil. His beliefs may be wrong-headed by my definitions, but he is no demagogue. He will not compromise his principles, and that is to be respected."

"I see no principle here!" I snapped, staring at the item. But I knew it was useless to talk back to a piece of paper.

Gradually the underlying currents came clear. Politicians as a class were not noted for their integrity, but they ran true to form in certain ways. All of them were interested in money, because they required huge amounts of it to publicize themselves, and publicity was the lifeblood of politics. All had to solicit money from their constituents, but none ever had enough. This was not greed, it was the breath of political life. The politician who spent the most to promote himself usually prevailed, when the contest was in other respects even. Of course, it was seldom even; the incumbent always had an enormous advantage, because he was already known to the electorate, and his office generated natural publicity. To unseat an incumbent, a challenger needed to spend much more money, but the incumbent had much readier access to the sources of money.

"How can any challenger ever prevail?" I asked as I contemplated the statistics.

"Now you can see why some campaigns get dirty," Megan responded.

Of course. Dirt was relatively cheap. A little money

could purchase a lot of dirt and muddy the waters so that the dirt-slinger might have a better chance. Obviously this was a strategy that Megan's nemesis Tocsin had mastered. I liked Tocsin less as I got to know his ways, but my understanding was growing. It was like guerrilla fighting on backworld settlements; the government had overwhelming resources, so the opposition had to resort to stealth and terrorism. It wasn't *nice*, but it evened the odds somewhat. Politics followed similar rules, but the evidences were more subtle. Tocsin had not fired a laser into Megan's back during their campaign in Golden; he had circulated a bogus description of her positions on issues, the paper tinted a delicate pink. This was, for complex and irrelevant reasons, the color associated with the Saturnists. Thus he had implied that she was a traitor to Jupiter. A laser in the back would have been cleaner.

The main supplier of money was the community of special interests. This amounted to institutionalized bribery. The small-arm laser manufacturers contributed to candidates who promised to prevent any legislation restricting the manufacture or distribution or sale or use of handlasers. The agricultural interests contributed to those who believed in higher price supports for vegetable bubbles. The military-industrial complex contributed to those who argued for a strong planetary defense. Special interests abounded, and the aggregate of their contributions to politicians was huge. Evidently it was cost-effective, for by means of contributions of thousands of dollars, they could reap legislation that returned them millions. Out of those millions in profits came the contributions to subsequent campaigns, and those contributions were tax-deductible. The common taxpayer always ended up paying for it.

Some politicians tried to be honest: they turned down special-interest money. They generally lost their elections. Thus victory went to the ones who were most freely for sale. It was open, legally sanctioned corruption, causing the entire government to be corrupt, because it was hard to get really clean government from those who became members of it only by committing themselves to minority interests for money.

I concluded that this must be the fundamental evil of the system: the pervasive influence of special-interest money on the governmental process. Stop that flow of money, and much of the inherent corruption would lose its motivation. Some campaigns had solved the problem by providing for public funding; the campaign for the highest office, the Presidency, was that way. But those for Congress were privately funded, and the purchase of elective offices was chronic.

Campaign finance reform—there was my special project. That was the starting place, for the government and for me. I familiarized myself with it. I commented on it in Triple-Gee meetings. I made contact with and developed associations with those who had a similar concern. I became known as a campaign finance reform activist. There were tax-reform activists and racial-integration activists and defense-freeze activists and education-upgrade activists; in this I was one of the crowd. But I was learning about the political system.

That system was worth learning about, from the grass-roots vantage. Structurally, the States of North Jupiter were collections of floating bubbles in the currents of the mighty atmosphere, linked by systems of physical travel and networks of communications. It was a mighty and amazing system of colonization, impressive in its concept, execution, and technology. But the social politics comprised a similar network, as intricate in its fashion as the physical one. In fact, it was a seething cauldron of special interests—the fount from which the moneyed interests drew. In the circles I moved in, the people tended to be active and liberal, politically, but I perceived that there were equivalent circles of opposite persuasion. It was all part of the mix. Jupiter truly was a melting pot of political dissension, which most of us agreed was one of its great strengths.

Columnist Thorley had another comment in print: "Captain Hubris, he who tightened the Belt, has been delving into the arcane lore of Campaign Finance (his caps, not mine). Could he be interested in something of the sort himself? Stranger things have been known to occur in the murky bypaths of the liberal establishment."

I was improving; it took me only five minutes to get my temper back under control. I even managed, after Megan's strenuous urging, to refrain from buzzing out a nasty rejoinder about the murky *conservative* bypaths of the wealthy.

Time passed. I don't mean to imply that what I have summarized occurred in a day or a week. I was three years in the undercurrents of the social maelstrom. I assumed the chairmanship of a committee to monitor the campaign finances of the elected representatives of our locale. Theoretically all campaign finances were open; in practice we had to struggle to get our hands on some of the records, which were treated like classified material and kept from the ordinary citizen. We managed to get printouts of the lists of all their contributors, and we checked the names and amounts against the requirements of the law. We did not discover any significant violations, but the patterns of contributions emerged.

One office holder was known to favor increased price supports for milk, which was, in space, an inefficient industry. Foliage had to be grown, fed to cows, and thus converted to milk, when the original foliage would have fed many more people than the milk did. The dairy industry contributed strongly to that office holder, and his position became even more favorable to that industry, despite the expense to the government. He preached economy, but he did not practice it in such cases. I saw how a number of employees of a particular farm-bubble gave identical and significant gifts of money, though they were themselves low-paid. How could they afford this? Why didn't they use the money for their families? Megan explained it: "Their employer is making one large gift. Since that amount violates the legal limit for an individual, he splits it up into legal-sized segments and donates them in the names of his employees. The recipient understands and knows whom to thank."

"But why should the employees agree to this?" I asked. "Wouldn't they rather have the money themselves?"

"Would they rather lose their jobs?" she asked in return. Then I understood. I had, after all, once been a migrant laborer; I remembered the problem of earning a living. I saw, now, that the law limiting the size of individual contributions was being circumvented. Still, it was better than nothing.

Tri-Gee decided to make a planetary campaign about

the campaign finance issue, coordinated with other civic-minded groups. I got to work on the liaison. I went from group to group, asking them to join with Tri-Gee in sponsoring a public presentation on the subject. This turned out to be another education for me. Some organizations welcomed such a joining of forces; others did not. One example of each will suffice: the Female Electors Membership, whose acronym was, of course, FEM, supported the effort instantly and lent attention, time, and money freely; in fact, they became the mainstay of it. In contrast the Legal Arts Wing—LAW—whose interest was in representing necessary but sometimes unpopular causes that could not otherwise afford to take their cases to court, and who had run full-page newsfax ads condemning the abuses of political payoffs, hardly gave me the time of day, and refused to participate.

"I don't understand," I complained privately to Megan.

"They prefer to do their projects alone," she explained.

"But by joining with others they could make much more progress!"

"And lose control. Some groups are jealous of their prerogatives."

There was the lesson. Even among civic groups, there were rivalries and imperatives. The members of the grass roots had their own turfs to defend. They would do good work alone, but their sense of individual identity and control was more important than their impact on the issues. If this meant that their efforts did not win the day, then so be it. Better to lose the battle alone than to win and have to share the credit.

But in fairness I must admit that once I had been the route and had thrown my effort into the program of promotion for the cause and had seen how the end result differed from what I had envisioned, I was frustrated. My input had been diluted by the consensus of others, and it seemed to me that the resulting program had been less effective than it should have been. But I was no dictator and had had to go along.

In addition, FEM cut me and Tri-Gee dead the moment its interest had been served, and so did some of the other organizations. I had naively supposed that all of us were working selflessly for a common cause; I found that each was serving its own cause. I could not protest openly because the job *had* been done and the other organizations had contributed, but I resolved that next time I would keep it within my own organization, GGG. LAW's somewhat insular attitude now made more sense, though I still did not like it.

Megan only nodded. She understood. "Even the most bleeding of hearts becomes a trifle cynical," she observed.

"You knew I would discover this," I accused her.

"I knew you had to experience it for yourself, as every politician must. As I did. It truly is a jungle."

It truly was. Not good, not evil, just a tangle from which it was difficult to extract anything truly enduring or worthwhile. An anarchy of good intentions and insufficient compromise. I was further disappointed because, although we had put on a good program in the name of a score of civic organizations, I had perceived that the attendance had been composed of members of the sponsoring groups. It had looked fine, with rousing speeches and applause; but, in fact, we had been talking to ourselves. Only those already committed to campaign finance reform had bothered to attend. The larger public remained indifferent. What, then, had we really accomplished?

"Damn it, I have wasted my time!" I exploded.

"By no means," Megan assured me. "You have been learning the grass-roots realities and making valuable contacts. You are now recognized as a concerned citizen; you have a base. Now you are ready to run for office."

For a moment I was taken aback. Of course, I would run for office. That was why I had started all this. My involvement in the campaign finance reform effort had absorbed my attention completely. Certainly I had not tried to curry favor with prospective voters; my only interest had been in the issue.

Megan took my hand and kissed me gently on the cheek. "You may have done better than you know, Hope," she said. "It is time."

I should clarify that our marriage remained one of convenience, and I honored the understanding we had made at the outset. But I loved Megan, as I had always known I would. She was a truly lovely individual, outside and inside, the perfect woman. Now I was thirty-three and she was thirty-nine; we were not children. But it was as if there was a radiance about her, to my eyes. At first she had commuted, in a manner, between Golden and Sunshine, but after a year she had joined me permanently, sharing my apartment while Spirit took another. Megan had not been married before, and acclimatized to it slowly. She never acted precipitously. For a year she had slept in a separate bedroom. Then she had shared mine, in a separate bed. There is a distinction between love and sex, and I had known from the outset that Megan was a creature of the former, not the latter. I had never seen her unclothed, and she had not seen me. It was enough to have her presence.

Oh, we did interact. We went out to entertainment functions together and to restaurants and civic meetings, where I discovered she was much better known than I in these circles. Who was I but a former military hero whose fame had been eclipsed by the following week's sports headline? She had been an office holder. I'm sure our associates assumed that our marriage was more intimate than it was.

At the same time she gravitated steadily toward me, as if her gee-shield were being damped. When she understood that I really was honoring our pact, she became more relaxed. She would kiss me at odd moments, as if doing something naughty. I neither solicited nor extended such intimacies; one might have thought that my interest in her was casual. It was not, and she knew it; all that Spirit had said about my orientation toward Megan was true. We were not children, and this was no kingdom by the sea, but I did indeed love her with a love that was more than love. I knew that if I forced her, however subtly, in any way, I would lose her. She had to come to me. It was as if she were a delicate flower that would wilt if touched by human hand, if plucked before its time. I did not even look at her inappropriately; the look of a man can be an aggressive thing. Those who had known me as a Navy man might have found that hard to believe, but only Spirit had been with me in the Navy and she understood.

Megan and I had been married three years, together two, and sharing the bedroom one. I knew that her respect and fondness for me had been growing. Megan took time to travel her way, but she was not coy. A month before, she had let me see her in her slip, and she remained a fair figure of a woman; I had of course given no overt signal of awareness, but she had known I was aware. I knew that, to her, physical nudity was tantamount to sexual contact, indeed was a form of it. Her gradual onset of familiarity was no striptease but a measured silent statement of her sentiment. So now, when she said, "It is time," I knew it was no casual thing. That statement was fraught with commitment.

"I love you in whatever way you would be loved," I said carefully.

"I know that, Hope." She looked about the room, as if searching for something, but it was nothing physical she sought. "I believe we are entering your area of expertise."

My expertise being, in the symbolism that existed between us, sexual. I had served in the Navy; I had made love and/or sex frequently, and to a number of different women over the years, in accordance with the military mandate. I knew what I was doing, in that respect, far better than I did in politics, despite her tutelage. By the same token I knew that Megan was afraid; she had no experience in the physical aspect of love.

I never wanted to cause her the slightest discomfort of any kind. There are those who ridicule what they call the Madonna complex, the attitude of a man toward a woman he deems to be untouchably perfect. This is not precisely the way I viewed Megan, but there might be a parallel. "There is no need."

She smiled tremulously. "You have been extraordinarily patient, Hope. I thought at first—forgive me—that you would tire of a sterile marriage and take a mistress. It has taken me time to believe that a handsome and talented man like you could actually love an older woman. Yet I see that it is so."

"It is so," I agreed.

Again she looked about, and again found nothing to fix on. "I am not good at this, Hope, but I have been impressed by your—your dedication to the cause that you have chosen. I have come to appreciate the qualities that you have. So let me just say, I am ready to be yours. Do with me what you will."

But she didn't mean it, quite. What she really meant

was that she was ready for me to take the initiative in our private relationship. It was a most significant turning point.

I did so—cautiously. For the first time since our ceremony of marriage, I kissed her at my behest, rather than hers. I touched her lips with mine. I held her for a moment, savoring her, and let her go. "Sing for me," I told her.

Surprised but relieved, she went to her piano and played and sang an operatic aria. She was, of course, a very fine singer, a former professional, and I had always been enraptured by her melodies. When she finished, I joined her, singing a folk song. We made a duet, and it was very sweet. And that, for now, was as far as it went. It was as far as it could go without impinging on her nature.

The state of Sunshine had a unicameral legislature. In the archaic days on Earth, most states had had divided assemblies, but over the centuries these had given way to the more efficient single-house situations. It was time, Megan decided, for me to run for state senator, in my local district.

"First, you'll need an executive secretary," Megan said. "She must be as competent, intelligent, and loyal as it is possible to obtain in today's inferior market. You can use your talent to select her; it may take a while."

"Just to type letters?" I asked.

"I said *executive* secretary. She will become your right hand and be empowered to act for you in routine matters."

"But Spirit already—"

"You cannot fire your sister," she said, a trifle firmly.

Oh. Well, I had married Megan to set me straight on the political scene; now she was doing it. We went in search of a secretary.

First we checked the employment agencies, public and private. There were competent women, but they lacked the intelligence Megan required. There were intelligent ones, but they lacked the capacity for loyalty that I required.

"Are you sure I need such a fancy secretary?" I asked.

"I'm sure. She will be with you throughout your career; she must have the potential to rise with you."

"Maybe a male secretary."

"No." Megan was conservative about such things, oddly enough. "We'll check the schools."

We checked the schools. Still nothing perfect. I wondered whether Megan was concerned about my getting a very young, impressionable, pretty girl who was desperate to hold her position and therefore ripe for sexual advantage, but that did not seem to be the case; she knew exactly what we wanted and refused to settle for less.

After the trade schools we tried the colleges and then the high schools. There we discovered Shelia.

"Sheila?" Megan asked.

"Shelia," the girl repeated firmly. "My father never could spell very well, but he made sure I could. By that time it was too late to correct the name."

Megan was looking at the girl's record while I looked at the girl, judging her with my talent. Shelia was coming across with an intensity I had not observed in other interviewees, despite her youth. She was seventeen, in her last year of regular schooling, and she had extraordinary nerve and drive. I could tell by the way Megan was nodding that the school record was excellent. This was the one we wanted—except for one thing.

Shelia was a cripple. She was confined to a wheelchair. It was all in her records: an attempted shakedown of her family, and when her father refused to pay, they had beaten her to cow him, and when she was unconscious, they had beaten him. Contemporary medicine had saved her life to this extent, but not his. The criminals had been caught, but the damage had been done. Shelia would never walk again. Only her indomitable will had carried her through, but even that could not make her employable in any exotic capacity.

Did we want to be saddled with a wheelchair wherever we went? Most employers would not hesitate to say no. Yet we knew Shelia was ideal in the other respects, and both Megan and I had sympathy for those whom life had wronged. Had Shelia not been crippled, she could have obtained a much better job; she was actually overqualified for the position I offered. So we hired her, as of graduation, which was to be a few months hence.

In retrospect I consider this to have been one of the best decisions I have ever made. Shelia, when she came to us, was a very quick study and a dedicated worker. Soon she had a clearer notion of my campaign strategy than I did. I had supposed she would be relatively immobile, but she wheeled about as rapidly as any normal person would have walked. In fact, it took only a few days before I lost any awareness of the distinction; Shelia was normal in my office and soon became indispensable.

I ran for state senator. Immediately I discovered the value of my grass-roots years. I knew, personally, just about every person who was anyone of distinction in the Ybor area. That did not necessarily mean that they all supported me, but it helped considerably. They knew what I stood for: campaign finance reform. Some were curious how I would finance my *own* campaign. Would I set a good example and lose the election, or would I succumb to the lure of easy money and become a creature of the special interests? Their curiosity encouraged them to welcome me to their various meetings so that I could address them. I was an effective speaker, and the audiences were generally friendly. Oh, yes, Megan had seen to it that I was properly prepared.

I set the good example. I accepted contributions from the public and refused those of the special interests. Consequently I ran a lean campaign. Spirit was my campaign manager, Shelia my secretary/treasurer, and Megan my strategist. Of these, only Shelia was paid, and not enough for the job she was doing. Fortunately Spirit had served in a similar capacity in the Navy and was good at it, and Megan's political experience guided us safely past shoals we might otherwise have foundered on.

I had two potent things going for me in this region: I was a hero; and I was Hispanic. My Navy record has been quiescent but now revived, like a holofilm taken from storage. It gave me instant name-recognition, and my origin brought me firm support from the very sizable Hispanic community.

I had, however, one overwhelming liability: I was running against an incumbent.

I really don't care to dwell on the tedium of campaigning. I went everywhere, talked to any group that invited me, no matter how small—and some were very small!—and challenged my opponent to a debate. Naturally he refused. It was a clean campaign, because I would not stoop to dirty tactics, and my opponent saw no reason to. The polls showed him comfortably ahead from the outset. No matter how hard I struggled, I could not close the ten-percentage-point gap that separated us. The incumbent was no prize; he was a conservative, self-interested man who was beloved of the local special interests and well financed by them. Though I could roundly criticize his record, I could not get enough publicity to give myself credibility in the eyes of the majority of the electorate.

Thorley summarized my situation succinctly. "Hope Hubris constituency: Belt 20. Hispanic 20. Total 35." That is, despite a twenty percent support by the Hispanic community, and twenty percent because of my reputation as a former Navy officer, my total was only thirty-five percent, against the forty-five percent plurality the incumbent enjoyed. Thorley was having fun with the mathematics; there was a five percent overlap between the two groups. This suggested that I had no support at all from the broader Saxon community. It wasn't quite that bad but almost.

"It is usually necessary to lose one election, just to get sufficient name recognition for the next," Megan remarked. No one expected me to win, not even us.

My ire focused again on Thorley. "I'm about ready to do something about that guy," I muttered. "I'd like to debate *him* before an audience."

"Great idea!" Shelia agreed enthusiastically. Remember, she was barely eighteen.

But Spirit cocked her head. "You know, I wonder—?"

Megan nodded. "That would be truly novel. We really have nothing to lose at this point."

So I made the ludicrous gesture of challenging Thorley to a public debate, since I couldn't get the incumbent to share the stage with me. I expected either to be ignored or to become the target of a scathingly clever column.

But he accepted.

Bemused, we worked it out. "He must find this campaign as dull as I do," I said. "This will at least put us both on the map of oddities."

"True," Megan agreed. "But do not take it lightly. Now

we shall find out what you are made of. Debates are treacherous."

"Like single combat," Spirit said.

I was certainly ready to test my verbal mettle against that of the journalist. Would he try to argue against campaign finance reform? That would be foolish.

I prepared carefully but reminded myself that this was not a major office I was running for. State senators were relatively little fish, virtually unranked on the planetary scene. I was running mainly for experience, which I surely needed, and to increase my recognition factor.

The occasion was surprisingly well attended. The hall was filled and not just with Hispanics. It seemed that quite a number of people were curious about this—or perhaps they, too, had nothing better to do at the moment.

Thorley showed up on schedule. He was a handsome man about my own age, a fair Saxon, slightly heavyset, with a magnificently modulated voice. He shook my hand in a cordial manner and settled into the comfortable chair assigned to him as if he had been there all his life.

We chatted in the few minutes before the formal program, and I have to confess I liked him. I had expected a sneering, supercilious snob, despite Megan's assessment; I was disabused. Thorley was remarkably genial and likable, and soon my talent verified that he was indeed absolutely honest. Evidently the jibes he put into print were an affectation for the benefit of his readership. In person he was not like that.

"I feared I would be late," he remarked with a momentary slant of one eyebrow to signal that this was a minor personal crisis. "Thomas was not quite ready to come in."

"Thomas?" Spirit asked. "I thought you were childless."

Thorley grinned infectiously. "Naturally your camp has done its homework on the opposition, but perhaps imperfectly. Thomas is our resident of the feline persuasion."

Spirit had to smile in return, touching her forehead with her four-fingered hand as if jogging loose a short circuit. "Oh, a male cat. We did not have pets in the Navy."

"The Navy remains unforgivingly backward in certain social respects," he said. "Cats are admirably independent, but in this instance, with my wife visiting Hidalgo to cover for a discomfited relative, the burden of supervision falls on me. Regulations"—here he made a fleeting grimace to show his disapproval of regulations as a class of human endeavor—"require the confinement of nonhuman associates when the persons concerned are absent from the immediate vicinity." I am rendering this as well as I can; the nuances of facial and vocal expression that he employed made even so small a matter as a stray tomcat seem like a significant experience. The man had phenomenal personal magnetism. I realized that I was in for more of a debate than I had anticipated, for Thorley could move an audience.

"Well, in a couple of hours you'll be back to let him out again," I said.

"I surely had better be," he agreed. "Thomas is inclined to express his ire against the furniture when neglected, as any reasonable person would." That fierce individualism manifested in almost every sentence he uttered, yet now it became charming.

It was time for the debate. There was no holo-news coverage, but I had my recorder and Thorley had his, so that neither could later misquote what might be said here. His newsfax had sent a still-picture photographer, at least. This was such a minor event on the political scale—a debate between a novice about to lose his first election and a columnist for a secondary newsfax—that we had no elaborate trappings. No moderator, no formal rules; it was discussion format. I knew that could be awkward, but it could also be the most natural and effective. We had agreed to alternate in asking each other questions, with verbal interplay increasing after the initial answers. We flipped a coin, and he won the right to pose the first question.

Megan and Spirit moved to either side of the small stage, while Shelia merged her chair with the front row of the audience and took notes. I suspect most people didn't realize that she was my secretary; she resembled a curious visitor.

"I understand that you, Captain Hubris, in accordance with many of the liberal folly, are opposed to capital punishment," Thorley said, his attitude and his language hardening dramatically as he got down to business. I felt as if a laser-cannon were abruptly orienting on me.

"I am," I agreed, knowing what was coming.

"Yet you are, or were, a prominent military man," he continued. "You could have been responsible for the deaths of hundreds of living people—"

"Thousands," I agreed tersely.

"How do you reconcile this with your present stand opposing the execution of criminals?"

Fortunately I was prepared for this one; Megan had anticipated it from the outset of our association. "The two situations are not comparable," I said carefully. I knew I was speaking more for the record than for him; Thorley surely knew what the nature of my answer had to be, and this was merely a warm-up question. "As a military man, I was under orders; when killing was required, I performed my duty. I never enjoyed that aspect of it, but the Navy did not express interest in my personal opinions." I smiled, Thorley smiled with me, and there was a ripple of humor through the audience. Everyone knew how strictly and impersonally discipline was kept in the Navy. "There is also a distinction between the violence of combat and the measured, deliberate destruction of human life that legal execution is. If a man fires his weapon at me and I fire back and kill him, that is one thing; but if that man is strapped to a chair, helpless, that is another. To my mind, the first case is defense; the second is murder."

"Well and fairly spoken," Thorley said smoothly. "But can we be sure there is a true distinction between the cases? The man fires at you, and your return fire kills him; granted, that is necessary defense. But the man who fires at an innocent little child, callously murders her, and is then brought to justice . . . is your return fire not justified? It is true that return fire is delayed longer, perhaps months instead of a split second, but the only distinction I perceive is that the first criminal failed to kill while the second succeeded. How can you favor the second?"

It was getting rougher! "I don't favor the criminal," I protested. "I oppose premeditated killing—his *and* mine. I do not believe that a second killing vindicates the first—"

"I did not suggest that it does, Captain. The second killing *punishes* the first."

"Granted. But in what way does punishment help the victim of the first crime? It may instead be better to rehabilitate the criminal, so that he can try to make up for—"

"My dear Captain, he can not restore the life he took!"

"Yes. But killing him won't restore it, either."

"But it will deter others from doing the same thing, and that may save the lives of many other innocent folk."

"There's no conclusive evidence that executions actually deter others from—"

"You prefer to set a killer free to do it again?"

"No! I want him punished. But that doesn't mean I should kill him."

"You propose to support him indefinitely at taxpayer expense?"

There was a trap. No taxpayer liked the notion of having his money used to benefit a criminal. "No. I want to put him to work to make up, to whatever extent possible, for the wrong he has done."

Thorley cocked his head. "And what type of work is that, pray?"

And there he had me. "I'm sure suitable work can be found. . . ."

He tilted his head farther, in elegant theatrical doubt. "The effort might better be spent finding work instead for the law-abiding unemployed." There was a murmur of agreement from the audience, not excluding the Hispanic contingent. The Hispanic level of unemployment was higher than the Saxon. Thorley had scored against me, with my own people. He could hardly have maneuvered me more neatly into that trap. The irony was that I was sure I had the better case, but my opponent had succeeded in obfuscating it. Had this been a physical trial, I would have been in the position of having a better weapon, but losing because I had not been able to use it effectively.

We moved on to the next question. "I understand that you conservatives oppose big government on principle," I began.

"Indeed," he agreed. "We regard bureaucratic intervention as fundamentally malevolent."

Damn his finesse of expression! He somehow seemed more convincing than I did, even when I was posing my question to him. But I plowed on: "A government is like a person: it has many components, many systems of operation, but it is necessary for the efficient management of society in much the way the brain is necessary for the proper functioning of the person. Without a brain the person soon dies; without government mankind dies. To oppose government is like opposing a person's brain. Do you really prefer anarchy?"

Thorley smiled in the feline way he had. He was enjoying this. "I confess the temptation, especially when I see our headlong progress toward the other extreme. Certainly I would choose anarchy over tyranny. But I do not actually demean government per se. I merely feel that *too much* government, like a bloated stomach, is inimical to human progress. We do not need Big Brother to tell us how and when to comb our hair or pick our teeth, and certainly we do not need a swollen bureaucracy to process the permissions for same in quintuplicate, charging the inordinate expense to the taxpayers. In short, that government is best which governs least."

"But only the government can alleviate some of the problems of the planet; they are too vast in scale for disorganized individuals to solve."

"That strikes me as a beautiful rationale for tyranny. I believe, in contrast, that only *free men* can solve the problems *caused* by ineffective government that meddles in everything and understands nothing."

"I've seen what completely free men do!" I retorted. "They are called pirates, and they prey on helpless refugees!"

The Hispanic contingent applauded, but they were efficiently undercut by Thorley's reply. "I would apply the death penalty to piracy. Would you?"

He was tying me in knots! I glanced about, and saw Megan nodding; she had known I would discover this problem. It was one more thing I was having to learn the hard way. But still I fought. "I would send the government's Navy after them."

That recovered some territory for me, for indeed I had done so. Still, I knew I was getting the worst of this debate.

With the next question, Thorley came at me like a heat-seeking missile. "It has been said that a free press is the best guarantee of honest government. Where do you stand on that?"

This was another difficult one. I supported freedom of the press, but as a military man I appreciated the need for secrecy in certain cases, and I had practiced censorship of the news during my campaign in the Belt. He would surely make much of that. I would have to qualify my answer carefully.

Before I spoke, there was a commotion in the audience. A burly Saxon man was striding forward, brandishing a portable industrial laser unit, the kind used to spot-weld steel beams. I had seen them in use when ship repairs were being made in space; they were dangerous in inexpert hands.

"You spics are stealing our jobs!" the man bawled. "We don't need none of you in office!" He brought his laser to bear on me and pulled the trigger.

I was already flying out of my chair, the recoil sending it toppling backward, my military reflexes operating. Spirit, too, was diving away. But I saw, as if it were in slow motion, that Megan did not understand. She was standing stock-still, gazing at the worker.

The first bolt seared into the floor where my chair had been. I veered around to charge the man from the side, and Spirit moved in from his other side. But it would take us seconds to reach him. Already he was striding up past Thorley.

The Saxon worker's face fastened on Megan. "And we don't need no spic-lovers, neither!" he cried, and swung the laser to bear on her.

"Get out of there, Megan!" I cried, but still she stood. Maybe she didn't believe she could actually be a physical target; it was foreign to all her experience.

The man pulled the trigger just as Thorley launched himself from his chair. The deadly beam sizzled out and was muffled by Thorley's body. Steam spread out, and in a moment the horrible odor of fried flesh developed.

In another moment I reached the scene. As Thorley fell to the floor I got my hands on the worker's arm. I locked it in, neutralizing the laser, and ducked down to haul him over my shoulder in a judo throw, *Ippon seoi nage.* He rolled over me and landed hard on the floor beyond, the air whooshing out of his body. The laser tool fell free. The man had the fight knocked out of him; he would be no further trouble even if no bones were broken.

I kneeled beside Thorley. He was curled up in agony, trying to grip his left leg. The laser beam had seared into his thigh. I saw at a glance that it was not a lethal wound but was certainly a hellishly painful one. It could cost him his leg if a key nerve had been burned out.

There were more urgent things to do at this moment, as the hall erupted into pandemonium. Thorley needed immediate medical attention, we needed the police to take charge of the murderous worker, and I had to get Megan away from this place before she went into shock. But for the moment all that was closed out, pushed back into the background of my awareness. It was as if only the two of us existed.

"Thorley," I said. "Why did you intercede?"

His pain-glazed eyes focused briefly on me. "I don't believe," he gasped, "in assassination. Not even of liberals."

I had to smile grimly. "How can I repay you?"

"Just . . . keep the press . . . free," he whispered, and passed out.

"Always!" I swore to his unconscious body.

Then the planet resumed its motion. Things were happening all around us. I looked up and saw Spirit, who was bringing heavy bandages, knowing that prompt attention to the wound was essential. All officers in the Navy had paramedic training; she knew what to do.

"Spirit," I said. "Take care of this man."

She nodded. She worked efficiently, cutting away his burned trouser leg, applying the bandages to the seared flesh. No cauterization was required; laser wounds are already cauterized. It was only necessary to protect the surrounding flesh.

When the medics came for him with the stretcher, Spirit went with them. "His cat!" I called after her, and she nodded again. Thorley would be in competent hands.

I put my arm around Megan, who was shivering with reaction. She had never seen physical violence like this before; it was a shock that could send her into trauma. I had to take care of her.

Chapter 7

SENATOR

I can't say that it makes much logical sense, but that was the turning point of the campaign. Photographs appeared on the front page of the newspaper: the angry worker charging out of the audience; Spirit and I jumping out of the way; Megan standing astonished; Thorley intercepting the laser beam; the worker flying over my shoulder; Spirit bandaging Thorley. The photographer, a professional in his own specialty, had gotten it all, in marvelously clear pictures. No written story was even needed. It was obvious that Spirit and I had acted with dispatch, but that Megan and at least one of us would have been caught by that laser if Thorley hadn't acted.

Thorley was a hero, but I got the votes. Perhaps it was sympathy for my close call. Maybe the voters thought that anyone worth assassinating was worth electing. Most likely, it was merely the impact of notoriety. I won the election by a comfortable margin, unseating the incumbent, who really had had nothing to do with any of this. He was a victim of peculiar circumstances. Of such flukes is politics made. But I felt little sympathy for him. Had he done the decent thing and agreed to debate me, none of this might have occurred.

The event made national news, because I was a former Navy hero and also one of the few Hispanics to win office anywhere. Thorley got less press on the national scene, but there was no question about the enhancement the event brought him. He was now newsworthy in his own right, the conservative who had risked his life to save that of the liberal he was debating. He became the symbol of the saying "I disagree with what you say, but I will defend to the death your right to say it." He was promoted and became a popular local speaker after his recovery.

Spirit was away from me much of the time, in the first days after the event, seeing to it that Thorley was taken care of. She arranged for his cat to be cared for, his plants watered, and she made sure his hospitalization was expedient. He was confined only briefly before going home. His insurance did not cover the cost of a registered nurse, but Spirit arranged for that, too, while his wife remained absent. A competent Hispanic boy stayed with him, handling his routine. Thorley was not generally kind to Hispanics as a class, in print, but he had no personal animus. It was that he felt too many of them were illegal immigrants from Redspot, where they forged across the sparsely guarded border, and too many did not bother to learn English, complicating things, and too many of their children were burdening the school system. But it seemed that he had no trouble accepting a Hispanic male nurse and houseboy. Certainly he never expressed objection.

"Whom did you appoint?" I asked Spirit when I saw her again.

"Sancho," she said.

I was taken aback. Sancho was a very special person, who lacked legal status on Jupiter. "Are you sure that's wise?"

She grimaced. "It's necessary. We can afford him."

It was true that our finances were limited, and Sancho was as cheap as it was possible to get. I shrugged, refusing to interfere. "He can certainly do the job—if no one suspects."

"No one will."

"*Thorley* will! That man is no fool!"

"Thorley knows," she said, meeting my gaze.

I made a motion as of washing my hands. "It is your affair, Spirit."

She smiled obscurely. We did not speak of that matter again.

Megan, stunned by the violence, soon recovered. "I can appreciate the advantage of military reflexes," she remarked. "You and your sister moved like lightning while I stood dazed."

"But it was Thorley who saved you," I reminded her. "He's no military man."

"True. I must call and thank him."

"After he recovers," I suggested, knowing that she would indeed call.

"After he recovers," she agreed. "But I do understand correctly that you have arranged for an illegal immigrant to care for him in the interim?"

"Not exactly," I said. I explained about Sancho, for I kept no secrets from her.

She pursed her lips and nodded thoughtfully. "Certainly it is not my prerogative to interfere." Then, after a moment: "Hope, I am especially vulnerable right now. I wonder whether you—" She did not finish.

She was speaking her special language again. We had replaced our twin beds with a double bed and slept holding hands, but it had not gone beyond that. Now she was suggesting that it should.

It did seem to be time. Gently I led her to that bed, turned out the lights, and took off her clothes and mine. I did not handle her; she was not yet ready for that. I lay on the bed with her and took her in my arms and kissed her, and slowly and delicately made love to her for the first time. It was not anything spectacular in the physical sense; my overwhelming concern was that I not hurt her in any way. I had to climax; she expected that of me, to show that the experience was genuine. But I did not attempt to bring her to climax; that would come another time. It was enough for her to have completed the act without trauma. In that I believe we were successful.

Perhaps it seems I was indifferent to her satisfaction. In fairness to myself I must say that this was not so. I cared very much for her need, but on this occasion that need was not for sexual gratification. It was for that minimal degree of interaction that qualified as complete consummation of our marriage. She was too disturbed to enjoy it physically, and would, ironically, have felt guilty if she *had* enjoyed it. In her archaic lexicon of romance, which she knew to be dated but which remained in her deepest nature, sex was a thing the cultured woman submitted to as an unfortunate necessity, never for pleasure. Her sole satisfaction was supposed to be in the satisfaction of her man and in the effort to beget offspring. Megan was beyond the latter stage, having had the decycling treatment before I came to her, so only the former remained. Now she had tolerated my ul-

timate familiarity; the worst was over, and in the future
she should be able to relax and participate more fully. I
looked forward to that occasion. I remembered how it had
been with Juana, my first Navy roommate; a wonderful
woman but never comfortable with the sexual act. The
Navy had required performance of male and female, so she
had obliged—in much the way Megan had. A man who
judges a woman solely by her sexual performance is a fool.

When it was done, Megan kissed me more in relief than
in passion. "Thank you, Hope," she murmured. "You are
very understanding."

"I love you," I said. This had nothing to do with sex, and
she knew it. She took my hand again and squeezed it, and I
brought her fingers to my lips and kissed them. In this gesture I was perhaps being more intimate than I had been
before, because I was showing genuine affection. The body
of any woman may be taken by guile or force but never her
love.

"Would you mind very much if I cried?" she inquired.

"I would consider it an honor."

She set her head against my shoulder and sobbed, delicately, for several minutes. I stroked her hair. After a time
she fell asleep. I thought of Helse, my first love, and knew
that however different these two women were in most matters, they were similar in this: Love, and the expression of
it, came hard to them. Helse had had absolutely no trouble
physically but had been unable for a long time to tell me
that she loved me; Megan had not done it yet. That was
part of what caused me to love each of them—make of that
what you will.

I do learn from experience. I had supposed that I had put
physical violence behind me when I left the Navy, but obviously that was not the case. I believed that Spirit and I
could take care of ourselves, but when a laser was as apt to
be trained on Megan as on us, I got nervous. So I set about
hiring a bodyguard. "Find me some candidates," I told
Shelia. "Winnow them down to the probables and let me
know."

"Got it, boss," she said. Shelia still looked young and
frail in her wheelchair, but that was deceptive. She had
kept her head during the assassination-attempt crisis and

had summoned the police and ambulance, though the experience must have brought most unpleasant associations to her. Now she was glad to get on this assignment.

"We could use a gofer, too," Megan said.

"A gofer?"

"Gofer. A person to run errands," she explained.

"Got it, Megan," Shelia said.

"Why do you call her by name and not me?" I inquired.

"The distaff hath its privileges," Shelia replied, and went to her communications.

The gofer was easy to find: Shelia sent the first applicant on to me. She was a Black woman named Ebony, about thirty, without distinguishing features.

"That name—isn't it unkind?" I asked, nonplussed.

"Nickname that stuck," she explained, evidently used to this. "In the flux of the reintegration of schools I got shipped to a mostly Saxon nursery school, and I was twice as dark as anyone else there, so they called me Ebony, and I stayed with it."

"You are aware that this is a rather simple, low-paying job?" I inquired. "You will simply run errands for others?"

"That's what I'm good at," she said.

I found no fault with her; she was honest and interested in doing a good job, simple as that job might be. She had accurately assessed her prospects and capabilities and knew that she would never be a top executive or policymaker; she was good at following simple directions and satisfied to do that all her life. What she wanted most was the security of a regular job, one that she understood.

There really wasn't any problem; I hired her.

The other was more complicated. For a bodyguard I needed a man I could trust with my life, and that was not a casual thing. It wasn't just a matter of skill *or* trust; I had to be sure that he knew how to ferret out the threats before they materialized, and distinguish real from false. We found a number of highly trained martial artists, but some were unprincipled and others were unsubtle. For a politician needs not only to protect himself physically but also to protect his image. If my bodyguard attacked a man who turned out to be innocent, my career could suffer. Discretion and finesse were vital. Far better to nullify a killer by applying a subtle come-along grip and marching him quietly to the police than to have a blazing brawl that might damage bystanders. I had known people in the Navy who qualified, but this was not the Navy. So the search continued, fruitlessly.

One day a young Mongol woman called for an appointment, wishing to talk to me personally. She said she sought employment and was qualified. Shelia tried to explain that we already had hired our gofer, and in any event there was a language handicap, for the woman was a refugee from Saturn and spoke English poorly. But she would not take no for an answer; she believed that everything would be all right if she could just meet me directly.

At last Shelia buzzed me. "Senator, if you could make a few minutes for Miss Coral—" She knew I could, as she maintained an iron grip on my schedule; at the moment I was researching a routine piece of legislation, doing my homework before deciding my position. She knew I had a way with people, and this was called for now.

So Coral was admitted to my private office. I could tell immediately that she was far more potent as a person than she looked; her motions were precise and her expression sure. She was a petite, black-haired, olive-skinned woman whose figure, while not voluptuous, was remarkably apt; she could be a beauty of her race—or any race—if she wished. But she did not wish; her simple trousers and long-sleeved jacket deemphasized her attributes, and her hair was cut almost masculinely short.

"Coral," I said, wishing to feel her out before committing myself to any further impressions. "That is not a Saturnine name."

"Name—translation," she said, her words accented. "Pretty snake—poison."

"The coral snake," I agreed. "Loveliest and most deadly reptile in the zoo."

"Yes. For job."

Suddenly it clicked. She meant the bodyguard! I had never thought of a woman, but of course, it was possible. "You know martial arts?"

She nodded curtly.

I kept a rubber knife in my desk, a memento of Navy days. I brought it out, flexed it to show its nature, and circled my desk. Suddenly I charged her, knife stabbing.

She caught my arm in an aikido hold that caused me to pause and drop the knife. So I closed my left hand into a fist and moved it toward her pert Oriental nose. Her free hand intercepted mine, deflected it, and her fingers seemed only to touch my forearm. Suddenly my arm was numb.

I was now standing behind her, one arm trapped, the other numb. I raised a knee, slowly, as if to ram her in the back. She twisted around, caught my standing foot with her own, and laid me gently on the floor.

It wasn't just the fact that she had countered my moves; it was the way she had done it. I had made my moves deliberately, inviting the appropriate counters. I am versed in judo, aikido, and karate, and can tell the competence of an opponent almost immediately. Coral was black-belt level in any of these and, despite her smaller size, could probably have taken me in an honest match.

But I needed more than this. I got up and returned to my desk, flexing my arm to restore sensation while she remained where she was. "Suppose that door," I said, gesturing to one across the room, "is a man with drawn laser, about to shoot."

Coral's arm hardly seemed to move, but something flashed through the air and smacked into the door at head level. It hung there, a bright little metal star, one point lodged in the door. "Shuriken," she said.

"Shuriken," I agreed. It was one of the throwing-knife type weapons of the ancient Earthly ninjas, or secret warriors.

"But if I want merely to disarm, not to hurt—"

Her arm moved again. This time a little whirling thing flew, with extended weighted threads. It wrapped around the shuriken and carried it to the floor, entangled.

Impressive indeed! "Suppose we suspect a concealed ambush, in a crowd, and want no disturbance?"

Coral smiled. "You buy X ray, computer, red-beam?"

The so-called X rays were no longer used, being hazardous to human tissues, but I knew what she meant: a device that used radiation in radarlike fashion, with computerized image-tracking. We had such equipment in the Navy, to locate all metals in the vicinity and distinguish what belonged from what did not. In this fashion the metal compo-

nents of a laser pistol could be distinguished from those of
a news camera, even if the laser parts were built into the
camera. Once a weapon was identified, it could be neutral-
ized in several ways, such as the use of a spot-infra-red
heater that would cause the metal of the weapon—and no
other metal—to heat until too hot to handle, or to melt.

"Will you swear loyalty to me and mine?" I asked.

She nodded, knowing she had the job. The code of the bu-
shido under which she had been trained made such a commitment absolute; having so sworn, she would dedicate
her career to my service.

I had my bodyguard and, to my surprise, an all-female
team. It was of course not long before the media remarked
on this, both positively and negatively, but I had not done
it for either sexist or social reason; it just happened. I always did get along well with women.

There followed a flurry of work. The state of Sunshine
was growing rapidly in population, which complicated
things, and that growth was comprised in part by the influx of conservative middle-class Saxons from the industrial north and in part by the influx of poor Hispanics from
the politically and economically desperate south. The
problems increased logarithmically as the two elements
merged. Merged—like fire and water! Mine was one of the
two districts where the most solid collisions occurred, for
Ybor was a city with a significant Hispanic base, while
nearby was Pete, a resort and retirement city. It hardly
helped that both groups, whatever else they might have
left behind, brought their cultural prejudices with them
undiminished. I was Hispanic, so I got hate mail from the
Saxon bigots and also love letters from the militant Hispanics that were just as awkward, because they expected
me to solve all problems instantly. The truth is, a state
senator has very little real power. He can not reduce a person's planetary income tax or sales tax or property tax,
and even in the in-between region of state taxes, he's only
one of a hundred senators. Sunshine had fifty somewhat
arbitrarily defined districts, crafted to be equal in population, each electing two senators on a staggered basis: an
election every two years for a four-year term. As one of the
most junior senators, I was at the bottom of the totem in

just about every respect and had no effective leverage in the State Senate. In addition, that Senate was in session only two months of each year, its agenda determined by the governor and Senate leaders, and it related to things like the regulation of intrastate commerce, insurance, and educational requirements. There was another sore spot. Recently a state literacy requirement had been restored, in the form of a standardized test for all high school students. They had to make a certain minimum score or be denied graduation, and any county school system with too low an average would be penalized. Since many Hispanics spoke English poorly, and some spoke it not at all, they were at a serious disadvantage and scored in the lower percentiles of this test. Not only was this unfair but also it annoyed all parties: those who scored low, those who blamed the Hispanics for pulling down the county averages, and the school administrators who were caught in the middle. But I couldn't even get the matter on the agenda for reconsideration. Not as a fledgling senator, Hispanic at that. So I simply could not do very much for my constituents, whatever their culture. The office I had won seemed a lot less effective from the inside than it had from the outside.

I did the best I could. I was allowed a small staff, and the budget for that just about covered the salaries of Shelia, Ebony, and Coral, who had to pitch in to help answer my mail. Soon the letters I dictated became so repetitious and familiar that Shelia rigged the word processor for standard statements and simply brought me the printouts to sign. It was impersonal, which bothered me, but how personal can you get when trying to explain to a constituent that you have very little control over interplanetary relations or the price of imported vehicle-bubbles? In those rare cases where I really could do something positive, such as sending my autographed picture to a grade-school civics class, I did give them my personal attention. But all this was another learning experience, as Megan had warned me it would be. I now understood why the bureaucracy tended to become impersonal. My attitudes toward government were changing as my knowledge of it increased. In these practical matters my philosophy became almost indistinguishable from that of the most conservative of senators, and indeed I found myself making friends with exactly such folk, because they understood my situation as perfectly as I understood theirs. It became increasingly easy to indulge in the quid-pro-quo bartering I had, as an outsider, condemned: I'll give you your tax break for the citrus beverages if you'll give me mine for disabled Hispanics. We were, after all, friends, but we did have our separate constituencies, and this was perhaps the only way to do any good at all for the people we represented.

"Am I being corrupted by power?" I asked Megan in some distress. "I am doing the very things I once condemned."

"You are not being corrupted as long as you retain your ideals and strive to achieve them," she reassured me. "What you are doing now is coming to terms with the realities of government. It is a somewhat debasing process, but necessary, like cleaning up after a sick animal. I had to do it when I was in office. Do the best you can and broaden your base of acquaintance, but never lose sight of your ideals."

There was the formula, of course. I knew that the moment I started accepting money or privilege for special-interest legislation, I would be on the road to corruption. I swore to myself never to do that.

Meanwhile I had another problem: earning my living. My Navy stipend halted when I won election, for I was now employed, and there were laws against so-called "double-dipping" that had been passed by reformers like me. Spirit had elected not to take any paid position in my office, so her pension remained, but I was not seeing much of her at present. I knew she could take care of herself and would return the moment I truly needed her; I was not concerned. But the job of state senator was part-time, and the pay was not enough to sustain a family in the manner a public family needed to be sustained. So I had to moonlight: that is, get another job. The term dates from centuries past, when people worked on Planet Earth and the light of Earth's relatively huge moon shone down at night. The term doesn't apply well in the present situation but remains because of its usefulness as a concept. There was nothing illegal in getting other work; it was standard and open practice, justified on the basis of not soaking the suffering taxpayers unnecessarily. I agreed with the principle, but how was

I to hold a full-time job without shortchanging my constituents? There was a lot less glamor in holding office than I had fancied.

Megan again had the answer: I would become a consultant. "Use your talent, Hope," she told me. "There is a great need for expert advice on the employment of key people in industry, and you need to establish statewide contacts beyond the legislature."

"Statewide contacts?"

"For the time when you run for governor."

Oh. She had never lost sight of the stages of my political career, however embroiled I might be in the problems of the moment. I had married her, theoretically, for that, and she was delivering. The fact that I loved her was presumed to be secondary.

I knew now that the political program that Spirit and I had envisioned before we went to Megan would never have worked. We had asked Megan whether she wished to be a part of my drive toward the presidency, but I now know that without Megan there could never have been such a drive. Megan, of course, had known it from the outset but had joined me, anyway.

"Why did you do it?" I asked her.

She understood me. "Your sister was persuasive."

"But our program was hopelessly naive. We had no notion of the nature or magnitude of the task."

"It was her love for you that was persuasive," she clarified. "I suspected that if a woman of her caliber could love you, then perhaps you were worthy of it."

"But she's my sister. We Hispanics are very close—"

"She is more than your sister. Do you not have another sister?"

I nodded soberly. "Faith, my senior by three years. But she is gone, perhaps dead."

"But when you were with her, were you as close to her as to Spirit?"

"No," I admitted. "Spirit has always been like part of me."

"She is a very special woman, and I would do more for her than perhaps you appreciate. She is strong where I am weak, but I sought to understand what she saw in you, and I think I have not been mistaken in the effort."

"I don't think I understand," I said.

She kissed me. "Of course you don't, Hope. But we shall make you president."

And so I became Hubris Consultations, Inc. Here, Megan's national contacts helped. She spoke to friends of old, who spoke to other friends, and some fairly large companies began soliciting my advice. I knew they were doing it mainly as a favor to Megan, but I responded seriously. I traveled to home offices and interviewed personnel and prospective personnel. I was quickly able to perceive who was competent and who was not, and who was motivated and who was not, and who was honest and who was not, and I made my recommendations accordingly. In one case I had to tell the man who solicited me as consultant that he himself was not fitted for the job he held. "You are honest and trying hard, but the sustained tension is destroying you," I said. "Thoughts of suicide are coming to you, and your family is suffering. I recommend that you step aside, accept a non-decision-making position, and relax. It may save your life."

He stared at me. "You have read me like an open book!" he exclaimed. "But it's an executive rat race! How can I ease up without being destroyed?"

I showed him the company chart of responsibility. "Promote this man to your present position," I said. "He is hard-driving and competent—and he never forgets an affront or a favor. Do him this big favor, and trust him to protect you in the future. I believe you will be secure."

He frowned. "But what of this man?" he asked, pointing to another name on the chart.

"He is embezzling from the company. Fire him."

"How can you possibly know such a thing? You've only been here two days."

"It is my private skill. I can read the guilt in a person. Verify the facts in your own fashion. Have a surprise audit made now."

"I will," he agreed. "Though it tears me up to do it—"

"That is why you must step down."

"But if you're wrong—"

I was not wrong. Within a week the personnel changes I had recommended were made, and news spread through the business community. My business picked up. This was something I was good at. My financial concern was over; I was starting to get some fat fees. My income rose, and I entered a higher tax bracket. I began to understand why wealthy folk objected to the graduated bracket system. Through my own effort and skill I had made my business a success; the government had contributed nothing. Why should the government take a larger cut?

In the second year of my office, something quite different and significant happened. A baby appeared. Spirit had been away on separate business for some time, but she returned to consult privately with Megan, and Megan consulted privately with me. It seemed that Sancho had obtained this newborn infant from a mother who could not keep her, as the mother was single and the father was married. The child was a Saxon/Hispanic cross, difficult to place. What was to be done?

"Hope, you know I cannot bear a child," Megan said.

"You decided long ago never to bring a child into this System," I agreed. "I understand that and accept it."

"I want to adopt this one."

I knew her well, but this surprised me. "Are you sure?"

"Completely sure."

My wife was a generous woman, but it had not occurred to me that she would be generous in this way. "Why this one?"

She looked at me as if I were hopelessly naive. "Hope, you know why."

"But you know what people will say. That baby is Hispanic!"

"And Saxon," she said. "Hope, I never wanted to be a mother, but now I do. For this one baby."

Amazed and gratified and more than slightly discomfited, I acceded. We undertook the necessary paperwork and the foundling became ours. We named her Hopie Megan, because we wanted her to be ours as completely as she could be, in name as well as in law. We became a full family.

It took me some time to adjust to the idea of being a father, but Megan seemed to know what to do. She handled the feeding and changed the diapers and whatever else was required; I was permitted to hold the little thing for a few minutes at a time, and that was about it. Still, my outlook changed significantly, for now there was someone to follow me. When I aged and passed on, she would remain, and perhaps remember me fondly. That made the prospect of eventual extinction less objectionable.

Trouble cropped up on the political front. A court decision struck down the system of districts on which the last election had been based and required redistricting with a more equitable division of population. The districts were supposed to be even, within a couple of percentage points, but they were not. The bubbles of Ami, Ybor, and Pete had grown much more rapidly than the state's average, and now my district was a good twenty percent overpopulated. The state legislature had to redraw the lines.

The lines were redrawn in a heated sequence, but in the process I was gerrymandered out of my district. What had been mine was now split between two new districts and incorporated parts of what had been in other districts. My four-year term was cut to two years, and I was forced to run again, for a new four-year term.

They hadn't had to do it that way, but I was short on tenure and had little clout, and I was Hispanic, which was sufficient reason to make me the odd man out. I seethed at the injustice of it, but I had no choice; if I didn't run again, in a district that excluded half my natural constituency, I wouldn't have my office at all.

I ran again. Thorley's caustic pen followed my progress. If we had respect for each other—and we did now—it didn't manifest in public. He pilloried my positions as "bleeding-heart liberal" and "knee-jerk Hispanic" as I suspect they were.

But I was an incumbent now, of a sort. I had a constituency and notoriety and name recognition, and I had learned some things about campaigning. I did not bother to appeal to the Hispanics; I knew, with necessary cynicism, that they were in my pocket. Instead I campaigned for the support of the Saxons, and I had treated them fairly, too, in my tenure. I had mastered my positions and was ready to argue any one of them effectively. Never again would an opponent catch me flat-footed in debate, in the manner Thorley had. Thorley had really done me a favor by showing me my vulnerability.

I had the advantage, so my opponent challenged me to a debate. Here was a direct test of my attitude: It would be to my advantage to decline, but in so doing, I would be turning my back on my ideal of fair campaigning. I didn't even need to consult with Megan; I knew where she stood. I accepted—and destroyed him on stage. Thorley commented wryly on the ethics of mismatches but concluded that I had evidently benefited from competent instruction. I still did not accept special-interest contributions, so my campaign was lean but honest. I picked up several media endorsements, including that of Thorley's own newsfax; it concluded that there was something to be said for having a token Hispanic in the Senate.

I won the special election handily, pulling in almost as great a percentage of the Saxon contingent as the Hispanic, and a fair proportion of the Black vote, too. It seemed that women noted my recent adoption of a foundling and also favored my all-female staff. I had become the candidate of all the people.

Now I had a bit of standing in the State Senate. I was no longer the most junior member; several new ones had appeared around the state, from other new districts, and several old ones had been gerrymandered out. My standing was greater because I had overcome the gerrymander; a number of senators were sympathetic. I introduced a revised literacy bill designed to give Hispanics a fair chance —not a gift but a fair hearing—but I also pushed for reform of the graft-ridden highway-construction funding apparatus. The surveying and netting of the shifting atmospheric currents was assigned to major contractors on the basis of competitive bids, but the process was notoriously corrupt. I lost my Hispanic bill, but my drive at the construction irregularities stirred up so much commotion that a certain measure of reform eventually passed. Even Thorley grudgingly admitted it: "More should have been done, but Senator Hubris's half-loaf is better than none. Too bad a competent conservative didn't initiate this one."

Meanwhile, at home, little Hopie was a surprising joy. Megan, who had no more planned on motherhood—at age forty-one—than I had planned on fatherhood, discovered that she liked it. She believed in woman's rights, and so did I, but she claimed with some justice that I was only marginally competent at important things like formula mixing, midnight feedings and lullaby singing, so she reserved those privileges mostly for herself. All mothers, it seems, are good at singing to babies, but Megan was professional; I tended to listen with much the same rapture that the baby did. To my mind no one ever sang anything as well as Megan did. But I was permitted to bounce the baby on my knee; it seemed that men were considered minimally competent for that sort of thing. As a result it was mostly playtime I spent with my daughter, which had the perhaps ironic effect of causing her always to be happy to see me. She would chortle and hug me with her fat little arms and sometimes burp milk over my suit. Who says men can't burp babies? All it takes is a good, clean suit. We got along famously. I could hardly imagine how I had gotten along all these years without a baby.

Not all my crises were political. Periodically the state of Sunshine suffers fierce storms that rise from the fluxes between planetary bands and drift to intersect settled regions. They seldom, if ever, penetrate to the central section of the equatorial band, but Sunshine is at the southern fringe and can be ravaged. Of course, storms vary in size and intensity; any day, anywhere, there can be fleeting perturbations that cause rain to drive against bubbles. Technically Redspot is a giant storm, so big and stable that it has assumed the status of a band and is occupied in much the same manner. The citizens of Redspot fancy red-hot peppers and sauces and trace their genealogies back to the ancient Earth country of Mexico. Big stable storms aren't our problem; we know their paths and can handle them. But little spinoff storms that happen to plow through our territory can be terrors.

I learned about this the hard way. Remember, I was not raised planetside; there are no storms on airless Callisto and none of this kind in space. I had heard about them, but that's not the same.

"Storm watch," Megan announced, viewing the news while she fed Hopie her bottle.

"Watch?"

"It could strike this area within thirty-six hours."

"It can't hurt this bubble, can it? A little rain?"

She didn't comment. She just tracked the weather reports.

Next day it was a storm warning. "It could strike within a day," Megan said worriedly. "I think we had better take refuge in Ybor." She sounded genuinely concerned, so I humored her. We packed the auto-bubble for overnight, checked out of Pineleaf, and blew out to the highway leading to Ybor.

I began to appreciate Megan's concern. Bubbles jammed the route, and the netting was twisting slowly like a giant python. The current of wind was irregular, as if disturbed by some unseen force. The cloud layer above was thick and restless, forming goblin-faces that glared momentarily before dissipating. Tendrils of cloud descended, with spinoff cloudlets. Occasional flashes of lightning illuminated large patches of cloud. It was indeed ominous.

I drove while Megan held little Hopie in her arms. The baby evidently picked up the tension, for she began to cry and would not be pacified. But we were stuck for the drive, however long it took. The traffic was slow, and I watched nervously as other bubbles crowded closer to ours. The velocity of the highway current changed, causing the bubbles to jam in closer yet. I saw one bubble try to pass on the outside; it bounced off the net and struck another bubble. Suddenly there was a mayday call on the emergency channel: "Collision—crack in hull—need immediate repair!"

A police vehicle answered. "All units occupied. A repair unit will be with you in fifteen minutes."

"Can't wait fifteen minutes," the damaged vehicle replied. "That crack is creeping!"

"We're tied up with four separate accidents and a hole in the net," the police replied. "Get to you soon's we can."

"Four separate accidents," Megan said, appalled. "And a hole in the net! That means a car crashed through and is lost."

For the reaches of the Jupiter atmosphere were so vast and turbulent that any bubble going out of control off the highway was very likely to disappear into the swirl. It might be rescued if its radio-beacon operated, but the chances diminished when the police were already fully occupied. This was ugly.

We moved on, trying to ignore the repeated pleas for

faster service by the stricken bubble; there was nothing we could do. Hopie bawled more loudly, adding to our tension. "There just aren't enough traffic police for a situation like this," I said. "After the last budget cut—"

"It's leaking!" the stricken vehicle cried.

"Emergency vehicle now being dispatched," the police reported. "What magnitude leak?"

There was no answer. We knew what that meant: Once the leak had started, it had widened, and suddenly the bubble had been filled with hydrogen at five times Earth-normal pressure. We didn't care to think about what that would do to unprotected occupants.

We blew on, and finally we reached the giant bubble of Ybor. The wait to enter was interminable, and Hopie cried incessantly. I felt as if I were in a space battle, only more helpless.

Inside, we had to pay a ruinous price for a hotel accommodation; naturally prices had been jacked up for this emergency. I smoldered. Gouging those who came here for safety reminded me of pirates preying on refugees. "There should be a law," I muttered. But then I thought of Thorley, raising his eyebrow eloquently as if to inquire, "A law for every little detail of human existence?" and I knew I could not defend that position. The free market had to be given play, even when elements of that market abused the situation.

We thought we were now safe from the storm, but we were wrong. We watched on holovision as the approach was recorded. Small bubbles were rocking like chips on a wave of liquid, and large ones were being shoved from their normal positions. The city-bubble of neighboring Pete was struck first. We watched with awe as the cloud layer broke up, dropped down, and enveloped that bubble, lightning radiating. A report from within showed debris scattered across the central park. "Tremendous vibration," the announcer was saying. "Spin is affected; we're precessing as the winds fight our rotation. Gee is down, and power is low. But the hull is tight. Repeat: The hull is tight."

It was a necessary reassurance, for if the hull leaked, the whole city could be afflicted with five-bar hydrogen atmosphere, exactly as the stricken car had been. That would mean hundreds of thousands of deaths.

The holo switched to another locale. "One of the suburbs is moving out of control!" the announcer exclaimed. "It's starting to drop. Power seems to be out—" Then, with open horror: "The gee-shield's failed!"

We watched, appalled, as that small bubble, about the size of Pineleaf, started its fall. Nothing anybody could do could save it now as it spiraled down into the immense and deadly gravity well of the planet. All its occupants were doomed to implosion and pressure extinction.

Megan cut off the holo. "Oh, I wish I had stayed in Golden!" she cried, distraught. I did not argue; at this moment I wished I had stayed in space. The deep dread of the crushing pressure of Jupiter tormented me. How was it that puny man had dared to try to tame the Lord of Planets?

There was a shudder through the city. The walls creaked. We were encountering the high winds. Suddenly it was much easier to believe that the hull of the city-bubble could crack and leak, or that the gee-shield could fail. I felt claustrophobic. How much better it was on a moon or planetoid, where gravity was so slight it had to be enhanced.

The power flickered, causing us both to start. "Oh, Hope, I'm afraid!" Megan cried.

So was I. But I had a job to do. "It's just turbulence," I said reassuringly. "Nothing to worry about." But neither of us believed that, and neither did little Hopie; she was squalling with nerve-racking penetration.

I simply didn't know how to cope with this. In the Navy all personnel were trained and tough, knowing death was part of combat. But this was civilian life. I hated to see Megan like this; suddenly she was looking very much her age. Violence terrified her, and all my skill of analysis was useless in the face of the storm.

"Let me take Hopie," I said gruffly. Wordlessly Megan gave up the baby and huddled alone on the bed. I paced around the room, holding the screaming baby, no better at comforting her than I had been with Megan. Seldom had I felt this inadequate.

Then the door alarm sounded. "Not more bad news," I breathed, and went to answer it.

It was Spirit. "I would have come sooner, but the traffic—" Then she saw our situation. She reached out her arms, and I handed Hopie to her. "You take care of your wife," she said, holding Hopie close.

I went to Megan and took her shivering body in my arms. "Spirit is here," I said, as if that made everything all right.

Megan sat up, listening. "Hopie—"

Hopie had stopped screaming. "She's with Spirit," I explained. "Now relax."

"Yes . . ." she agreed, relaxing.

Spirit was supporting Hopie close to her bosom and singing her a lullaby. Why hadn't I thought of that? Of course, that was the way to soothe a baby, as Megan had done so often before. I had forgotten my common sense in the pressure of the moment. My sister had retained hers and acted on it, as she had during combat situations as a refugee and in the Navy. We were indeed in combat now, the foe being the raging storm. Our weapons were not ships and lasers but understanding and song.

"Sleep, my child, and peace attend thee," Spirit sang, "all through the night."

Megan heard. Suddenly she became animated. She sat up and joined in, her fine voice filling the room. "Guardian angels God will send thee, all through the night."

I joined in, too. Soon we were singing other songs, including our Navy identity songs. How clearly I remember Spirit singing "I know who I love, but the dear knows who I'll marry," while the baby slept blissfully. I realized at that moment what I had not chosen to understand before, that Spirit *had* found love—and could not marry. She had been as fortunate in love as I had been but not in marriage.

And so we spent the tense night, Megan with me on the bed, Spirit with the baby on the chair. Perhaps it was my imagination, but the force of the storm seemed to abate after Spirit arrived, and we knew things were getting better. Maybe it was just that when Hopie's crying stopped, things seemed more positive. Maybe it was that Spirit has always been my mainstay in crisis of any kind; she really is stronger than I am, in ways she seldom cares to show. It is a secret between us, this aspect of our relationship.

In the morning Spirit looked tired but relieved. She gave the baby back to Megan and went her way. I doubted that she had had much sleep, but she could handle that, too. We cleaned up, ate a quick breakfast, and checked out, nervously eager to get back to Pineleaf.

The press of traffic was much less, but the highway was just as grim: defunct bubbles littered the route. We did not pause to peer into any, knowing there could be nothing inside we would want to see. A devastating battle had been fought here, the carnage no less awful because the enemy had been the weather. About halfway along we encountered a wrecker-bubble hooking on to a car; the cleanup was commencing. Soon all would be as before, except for the relatives of the casualties.

The Pineleaf bubble was intact. "We could have stayed here," I said, aggrieved. Megan didn't answer, but the little grim lines deepened on her face. No, we couldn't have stayed here; she had had to have the security of a major bubble. Pineleaf's survival was mere chance; a gust could have swept it away.

Our apartment was in a shambles; this bubble had evidently received a worse shaking than had Ybor. It would not have been at all comfortable here, physically or psychologically. In my mind I saw the other suburb-bubble plummeting to its ghastly doom, and I shuddered. Jupiter was a monster!

But the storm was past, and we had survived. That was what counted. Now I would have to see what I could do as a state senator to alleviate the problems of those who had suffered more than we had. At least I had a notion how they felt.

In the last year of my four-year term Megan discussed strategy with me for my next effort. "You are now forty, which is coming into prime time for a politician, and you have good, solid credits and a loyal constituency. It is time for your first try for governor."

"My first try?"

"You will lose," she said matter-of-factly. "Your support statewide is too thin. But you can make a creditable showing, and that will prepare you for the second try, which should be more successful."

"I would distrust a commander who planned to lose the first battle, to gain experience for the second."

"Fortunately, few political campaigns are run by military men." She kissed me warmly. Over the years our relationship had ripened, and our love had become correspondingly strong. I had always known I would love her but had not been certain she would love me. That concern had abated. Though her love had been glacially slow in its development, it had also been glacially certain. It had flowered at last with something less than volcanic force—metaphor-mix permitting—but persisted like hardened lava. There are those who suppose that a woman in her forties is not worthwhile as a love object, that her form and fire are gone. The truth is that a literate, feeling, competent woman is never past her prime. There is, to put it colloquially, one hell of a lot more to a woman than sex appeal, but in Megan I had that, too. She was, indeed *the* ten most beautiful women, and well worth the wait.

It was more complicated, running for governor, than it had been running for the relatively minor office of state senator. Technically I was running for the nomination for governor, because Sunshine is essentially a one-party state on the local level. The Ybor bay region had two parties, but that was atypical. If I could get the nomination the election would follow almost automatically. I needed a lot more campaign money, and I needed significant endorsements, and I had to do an extraordinary amount of campaigning. I could no longer speak to PTA meetings and impromptu gatherings in parks; I had to travel fast and far and with an entourage. I needed my staff with me, and I did not want to be dependent on commercial carriers to get me to my appointments on time.

"A campaign car," Megan said. "It may seem a trifle quaint today, but it is feasible and it makes sense."

"A what?" I asked blankly.

"In the old days politicians campaigned from trains," she explained. "It was convenient and cheap and it got the job done."

"I'm game," I said.

Spirit returned to be my campaign manager for this effort. Megan remained as my strategist, preferring to take no overt part, but she consulted frequently with Spirit. My secretary Shelia knew exactly how much money we had to work with and where our contacts were. My bodyguard and my gofer were drafted again to handle the details of campaigning; this was the way it had to be, for a lean campaign. Together, these five women decided where I should go and how I should spend my time. It was reminiscent of my time as captain in the Navy, when women had mostly run my show.

I should explain that a train, in the Jupiter atmosphere, is not the same as the archaic vehicles that roamed old Earth on metal rails but does have its affinities. Indeed, those affinities were deliberately strengthened by the transport companies, who played upon the vested nostalgia of our culture. A train is a chain of transport bubbles linked by means of special flexible airlocks and towed by a tug. It takes relatively long for such a string of beads to accelerate to effective velocity, but a good deal of freight can be transported in that manner cheaply. There are special train routes established between major cities, marked by glowing buoys, and the trains have the right of way over any other vehicles that may intrude on such routes, because the trains are unable to halt or maneuver rapidly. It can be quite comfortable aboard a train, however; in fact, train travel was once considered to be the ultimate in luxury. I was intrigued.

What we could afford, it turned out, was a rental unit. This was an old dining car converted to residence after being retired from active duty and now used mainly for novelty occasions. It was shaped like a cylinder rounded off at the ends, so as to be aerodynamic; that was important for any vehicle traveling rapidly in atmosphere. It was so narrow I was sure rotation would be unfeasible; how would it provide gee?

The answer was obvious: It used natural planetary gee. Its gravity shield deflected approximately sixty percent of Jupiter's gravitrons, leaving enough to provide precisely Earth-normal gee. What prevented the car from plummeting down toward compression and destruction? The buoyancy of the other cars in the train. Inanimate freight required no weight and was easier to handle in free-fall, so

full gee-shielding was used in them. It was the same principle as dirigibles, or passenger balloons that once floated
in old Earth's atmosphere; the relatively large volume of
diffuse balloon provided buoyancy to offset the small volume of dense payload, and so the whole was suspended sta-
bly. Only the freight cars were not gaseous; they were
absolutely solidly filled, with the gee-shielding making
them as light as balloons. I remember a minor historical
note about the buoyancy of lead-filled balloons on Earth
that did not float well. Today, of course, lead balloons readily float, with null-gee.

There is another intriguing parallel to the old times of
Earth: the railroad discovered that freight was more lucrative and easier to handle than people, as it did not complain about delays and didn't even require oxygen to
breathe. It could simply be loaded, sealed, and shipped.
But the railroads were subsidized by the government, because of the great expense in starting up, so were expected
to cater to public need. As a result, they served that need
nominally but with increasing ungraciousness, trying to
discourage voluntary passengers. The prices of tickets
moved up; delays were so common that trains hardly ever
arrived at their destinations on time, and personnel were
discourteous. But such was the society's romance with the
concept of trains that it took many decades for the companies to discourage a significant fraction of their passenger
market. Even today, there were those who, contrary to all
common sense, insisted on using this form of transport. I,
it seemed, had become one of these.

The car, inside, was reasonably sumptuous. There was
room for our family and several staff members. Spirit saw
to the room assignments, and Megan kept Hopie out of
mischief. There were cabins for Shelia, Ebony, and Coral. I
was, in a manner of speaking, just along for the ride.

Of course we had to align our timetable with that of the
railroad. That was awkward, because the freight trains
were not scheduled with political campaigns in mind, or,
indeed, with any living folk in mind. But it was cheap. The
cheapest possible way for a party our size to travel the
state, in style.

We worked it out. We set up a campaign route that
meshed with convenient freight-train schedules. We hooked

on to the first freight train, paid the rental, and headed for a date with Ami, across the state.

The start was slow, as the distant engine cranked up. It was an old-fashioned chemical burner that spewed its exhaust into the atmosphere, leaving a trail of smoke that slowly dissipated behind. We watched from the old-fashioned observation windows; since the car did not spin, such apertures were feasible. We saw the buoys flashing by for a while, faster and faster as the train slowly accelerated, until they were pretty much of a blur, and the route seemed almost enclosed in the fashion of the netted highways. But this soon got boring, even for little Hopie, and we turned our attention back inside. Travel really wasn't all that exciting, not when the surroundings were largely featureless.

In Ami I encountered something new, unfamiliar, and disturbing. Several men in the audience periodically yelled terse objections to my points. They were not reasoned refutations, merely opposition, such as "Says who!" or "That's bull!" They put me off my verbal stride.

I got through by ignoring the gibes, but I was disturbed. After the speech I consulted with Spirit and Megan.

"It's heckling," Megan explained. "Every politician suffers it eventually. It's a sign of success."

"Success! They were interfering with my speech!"

Spirit was more practical. "I gather this is a tactic of the opposition?"

"Of course," Megan said. "Such men are for hire, relatively cheap. But a candidate who is sure of success does not bother with such a minor tactic."

"I still don't like it," I said. "How can I stop it?"

"Let me consider," Spirit said.

Megan glanced at her. "I don't think I want to know what you are going to come up with," she murmured.

My next address was in Kyst, the southernmost bubble of the band. We drove down through a long highway that was a scenic wonder. It followed the five-bar contour, but the dynamics of the planet and the fringe of the band caused the cloud cover to dip, so that first it loomed low, then intersected the route, so that special fog-cutting buoys were necessary. It was like an eerie tunnel through foam that seemed always about to stifle out. As usual,

Spirit and I gawked, while the Jupiter natives of our party ignored it. Little Hopie, now a pert four years old, sat in my lap and shared my enthusiasm; she liked traveling. She was a charming child, and increasingly people were remarking how much she resembled me. We had not made a secret of the fact that she was adopted but did not advertise it, either, so most people assumed she was ours by blood rather than by choice. That hardly bothered me.

The clouds dropped below the highway, so it was like emerging from some nether realm to the surface. The light was stronger here, and because there was a fracture zone in the next cloud layer above, some halfway direct light came down. To an Earth person all this would have seemed shrouded in gloom but bright enough. As we rose somewhat above the cloud surface the light touching it sharpened the fringe so that it resembled an enormous mountain slope. Rifts in it seemed like reaches of dark water, as I explained to Hopie while Megan smiled tolerantly. Thus we were, in our innocent and childlike fancy, driving along a narrow length of land, or a series of islands, bright fragments surrounded by the enormous silent sea. But, of course, I am a dreamer, and perhaps it was wrong for me to infect the child with that virus. On the other hand, I thought wryly, maybe it was in her genes: a fascination for the kingdom by the sea.

Kyst was a delight, seemingly perched on the last major cloud-isle of the series, overlooking the southern reaches of the planet. Some distance farther along, I knew, was the giant Redspot, but here nothing like that showed. Jupiter is big, and thousands of miles can separate adjacent territories. We had traveled at quite high velocity, our autobubble boosted by special jets, but still the drive had taken several hours.

The hecklers had also made the trip. I had two speeches scheduled here, on consecutive days, and the hecklers were present in force at the first. News must have spread that I was not apt at dealing with them, and so they swarmed like the proverbial stinging flies. I suffered through, not daring to take any overt notice of them, for fear I would be drawn into a type of exchange I could not profit from. But my audience became increasingly restless as their interference went unchecked.

However, I saw the personnel of my staff quietly taking pictures of the culprits, so I knew Spirit was working on something. Ebony was stalking each one with her camera. That reassured me.

After the program Spirit explained, "Now we know exactly who they are. As they enter next time we'll touch them with mustard-six. You will have the activator at your podium."

Slowly I smiled. Mustard-six was the colloquial name for a rather special, if minor, preparation used in Navy training drills. It burned like fire when activated by a particular electronic signal but was otherwise quiescent. It was considered a nuisance device, not a dangerous one, as it lost its effect only after a few seconds of activation, but no victim ever forgot those seconds! I remembered it from my time in officer training school; I had had to infiltrate a mock enemy position, and every time I blundered into an activation zone, I regretted it. "Just remember," the training officer had reminded us. "In real action those errors will cost you more than burns. Then the antipersonnel agents will be real." The lesson had been effective.

I proceeded with my address on the following day. Soon the heckling commenced. I gave it a few minutes, so that every individual heckler had his chance to sound off and the audience had opportunity to appreciate what was going on. Then I said, "I would like to take an impromptu survey. Will all those who harbor un-Jupiterian sentiments please rise and make yourselves known?" Then I switched on the mustard-six activator.

Six hecklers leaped out of their chairs, exclaiming loudly.

I turned off the juice after a one-second jolt. The hecklers were abruptly free of discomfort. They stood bemused, not understanding what had happened, as the other members of the audience chuckled.

"Thank you," I said graciously. "I am glad to know your true nature. I happen to support Jupiter myself; indeed, I chose to be a naturalized citizen of this great planet. But tastes do differ, and you certainly have a right to follow your own beliefs. It's a free planet! I hope someday you will come to respect it as I do."

The audience applauded patriotically. Sheepishly the

hecklers resumed their seats, and I resumed my speech. My audience was now somewhat more responsive.

After a while the heckling resumed. They had been paid to do a job. I paused. "Is there by chance any person here whose mother was a baboon?" I inquired, and hit the switch.

Again the six hecklers jumped up, cursing. I cut the current after two seconds, and they quieted. "Thank you," I repeated. "I'd go to meet your mothers at the zoo, but I'm afraid they wouldn't vote for me." The audience laughed.

Later in the speech the heckling began again. Once more I paused. "Do any here support my opponent for election?"

"Oh, no!" a heckler cried, just before I activated the mustard. Again they all danced out of their chairs, to the delighted laughter of the audience.

I didn't have much further trouble with heckling, on that day or during the rest of the campaign. Little Hopie amused herself by doing an imitation of a heckler cutting the mustard. The episode made minor planetary news. "Hecklers," Thorley remarked wryly, "had better not mess with Navy heroes. If only the complex problems of government could be similarly addressed." Naturally the implication was that my solutions were simplistic.

That was perhaps my high point of the campaign. I lose my taste for remembering the rest of it, so I'll just say that it was not yet the season for Hispanic candidates on the statewide level. I made a good effort, but I lacked the finances for a saturation campaign, while my opponent seemed to have, literally, millions of dollars to spend. The special interests fairly poured money into his coffers. Had significant campaign finance reform been instituted . . . but perhaps that is sour grapes. I saw that as long as the special interests could put their favored candidates into office, the system would not be reformed.

So I lost the nomination, as Megan had foretold, but it was a creditable loss, a respectable showing. I had gotten my name known to the electorate.

Now, however, I was out of a job, for I had not been able to run for another term as state senator, an office I could readily have retained, otherwise. It was not permitted for candidates to run for two different offices simultaneously, and I don't fault that regulation. It had been put in by reformers, but again I had come to understand the other side of it. When good office holders are required to give up their offices in order to gamble on higher offices, good men are going to be lost.

Megan assured me that my political career was not over, just on hold, and I was sure she was right. She had always been right hitherto. But still it smarted. I could so readily have won, had I only accepted enough special-interest money to finance a broader campaign.

Chapter 8

SEDUCTION

They let me out of my stinking cell the next morning. After I had cleaned and dressed Scar talked to me again. "Have you had occasion to reconsider your position, Hubris?"

I certainly had, though not in the manner he supposed. I had, in my fashion, just spent six years as a Sunshine state senator and lost my bid to be governor. I now knew my life to age forty. I had learned political finesse. "Yes. I can see now that my position was in error," I said. "The flat tax would represent an improvement over the present system."

I could have been lying, but he was satisfied. Evidently he knew that I would not take a position I did not support, and indeed it was true: I now believed in the flat tax. I had seen the abuses of the present system of taxation and knew that the tax code needed to be drastically simplified and the nefarious loopholes eliminated. The flat tax would do that. I did not regard it as ideal, for it did tend to benefit the wealthy and penalize the poor, but it remained a fairer system.

"Actually, I have been reconsidering, too," Scar said.

That startled me. I looked at him inquiringly.

"What I am wondering now is whether *any* system of taxation can be fair," he said. It was as if he were a friend arguing a rhetorical case, figuring out his own position. "What, after all, is the definition of theft?"

"Theft? Taking something of value from a person or institution without his consent."

"So if I take money from you, without your consent, I am stealing it?"

"Yes," I agreed, uncertain where this was leading.

151

"If I point a weapon at you and require that you hand me money—"

"Yes, that's still a form of theft," I agreed. "Armed robbery."

"Even though I do it openly and you actually hand me the money?"

"Yes, because it's involuntary. I don't want to give you the money, but I'm afraid you'll hurt me if I don't."

"Suppose I don't actually point a weapon," he said. "Suppose I merely suggest that something unpleasant will happen to you if you do not pay?"

"Yes, that's still theft, if the threat is unequivocal."

"Such as confining you in a dark, noisome cell."

Again I was startled. "Yes."

He smiled. "I am not a hypocrite, Hubris. I have robbed you of your freedom, and I am coercing you to part with something you value. I am a thief. But I believe I am acting in a good cause."

"The ends do not justify the means!" I exclaimed.

"Don't they? Suppose I proved to you that the cause I serve is the worthiest possible cause and benefits the whole planet of Jupiter, while all it costs is the temporary inconvenience of one person. Doesn't that justify it?"

"I hardly believe that your cause can really—"

"But, for the sake of rhetoric assume this is true. Then is theft justified?"

I pondered and could not answer.

He smiled again. "Now back to the taxes. If I have a world of good works to perform with the money, does it justify my taking it from you in the form of involuntary taxes?"

"But that's not the same," I protested. "Taxes are a requirement of citizenship!"

"And if you don't pay them you may lose your citizenship—and become a refugee or a prisoner."

I had been a refugee and was now a prisoner. My family had rebelled against an unfair aspect of Callisto society, and it was evident that I had in some way crossed a powerful opponent later in my life. The parallel had power. "I don't know."

"Obviously I do believe that the ends justify the means," he said. "Actually it's a matter of proportion. I see the greatest good for the greatest number and am prepared to sacrifice the few for the benefit of the many. You may feel otherwise, and perhaps I would, too, in your situation. But the position is worthy of consideration."

"Perhaps if I knew what your cause is," I said.

"All in good time, Hubris. I am not trying to hurt you or humiliate you; all I want is your serious consideration of the points I raise. I did not punish you last night for differing with me but for refusing to hold a meaningful dialogue. Give me your serious attention, even in opposition, and your existence here will be comfortable enough."

"But you tortured me before ever inquiring about my attitude," I protested.

"That was necessary to demonstrate my power over you. To prove to you at the outset that I can and will do what I deem necessary to gain your attention. It is not enough merely to speak to you; I had to make you believe absolutely. Just as one learns by hard experience to treat electric current with respect, you learned about me. You do not need to grovel; just deal with me on my terms, as you would a natural force."

That concluded the session. I had to admit that, given the present situation, what he said made sense.

Other books awaited me in my cell, on the subjects of taxation and law enforcement. I read them; I had nothing else to do at the moment. Obviously I was being reeducated, but even with my extra memories of my political life on Jupiter, I couldn't grasp the thrust of it. Of course, a lot could have happened in the intervening five or ten years. I might not be in politics at all anymore.

That evening I visited Dorian Gray again, knowing it was expected of me. The irony was that though I knew this was part of the larger trap my captors had laid for me, and that I had to seem to fall into it, I felt its power nonetheless. Knowledge is not necessarily a perfect defense. I was alone so much of the time that *any* human contact was valuable, even the interview with Scar. Dorian also happened to be a woman, which made the appeal that much stranger, and she was a lovely one. Yes, I remembered Megan, and loved her and longed for her, but she was far away, while Dorian was here. I know this seems fickle, a confirmation of the evil women are apt to believe of men, that men love only what is in reach, isn't scratching and biting, and is fair and fully formed, and that men have no lasting commitment beyond sexual gratification. Like many myths, this one has some substance; men are indeed sexual creatures and feel the attraction of nearby women in the manner a body in space feels that of a proximate planet. I was sexually vulnerable now; a part of me wanted to fall into the trap. Thus my pretense was apt to become real. *Forgive me, Megan!* I prayed in silence again, but I had no assurance that she would.

Dorian did not make it easy. Rather, she made it too easy. She embraced me and kissed me the moment I arrived. "Oh, Hope," she breathed. "I missed you. When you didn't come last night, I thought . . ."

A further irony: she meant it. She was an actress playing a part, yet she did care. The best actors *do* care. Perhaps she used the ancient Stanislavski method, trying truly to experience her role, but it seemed like more than that. With her, too, the role was to a certain extent becoming reality. Yet she had to know her true face, too, as I knew mine.

"I did what I said I would," I said. "I talked back. So I got dumped back in the smell-cell for a night. I don't think I'll do that again."

"I was afraid they'd do worse to you," she said.

"I won't talk back to them soon again," I said ruefully. "I had forgotten how bad that cell is." Which was, of course, a lie of sorts, for the benefit of the recorders. Scar must never suspect that I *wanted* to visit that cell from time to time, so as to catch up on my recent history. The truth was, I had hardly been aware of the smell; I had in effect been transported to Jupiter.

"I did tell you not to do it," she reminded me, as she held me tight. "Oh, Hope, if anything had happened to you . . ."

Why was she so eager to get so close, so fast? I enjoyed the feel of her flesh, but I distrusted this. Was there a time limit on my treatment, so that the seduction had to be accomplished early? That could work to my advantage. So I demurred. "I mustn't take advantage of you," I said gallantly.

She realized that she was moving too fast and eased off. "Come, sit and talk. It's been so lonely."

That suited me. My talent was tuning in on her, adapting to the dark. I was used to visual contact, as perhaps my captors knew, but now I was tuning in on her touch.

We sat together in her hammock and talked. The hammock tended to wedge my left hip and her right hip together, and our corresponding shoulders. That suited her because she wanted to seduce me, and in the darkness touch was her main asset. It suited me, too, because I wanted to read her with my talent, and touch was my main asset, too. And it suited us both because we had to keep our heads close together, to whisper, so that we would not be overheard, theoretically. Actually, modern auditory pickup devices are so sensitive that they can monitor a heartbeat from a quarter mile's distance, so that was illusion; if our captors were listening, as they surely were, they were hearing everything. If they were not listening, it was because they trusted Dorian to inform them of anything significant. But human reflexes die hard; we whispered.

I told her what little more I remembered of my experience in the Jupiter Navy, taking advanced training, winning an accelerated promotion to private first class—the enlisted men having army-style rank, while the officers had Navy-style rank, in the merger of the old separate services—and rooming with lovely Juana, who was also Hispanic.

"I'm Hispanic," Dorian reminded me in Spanish.

"And lovely," I agreed. "I have never seen you, but I know I would be smitten by your beauty in an instant."

"Thank you," she said. Women like to be reminded that they are beautiful.

"But I don't understand why you should have any interest in an older man like me."

"There *is* no other man," she said. This was of course true on the surface, and untrue beneath, and I read both reactions in her. But there was another current of reaction that cut across these like a solar wind. I was looking for some weakness in her, some human aspect I might exploit, and suddenly I had a hint of where to look.

"Surely you have known other men," I said, holding her hand in mine lightly, so as to pick up any quiver of tension passing through the fingers.

"No," she said, but her fingers gave her the lie.

"Now I have been candid with you," I chided her. "I told you of Juana. Won't you tell me of your first love?"

"You didn't love Juana," she retorted accurately, but again that tension rippled through her hand. Oh, yes, she had loved.

"Perhaps not," I agreed. "My true love was Helse. But she died. . . ." This time it was my own hand the tremor shook. "And life continued for me. Juana was a good and lovely girl, and what I felt for her was as close to love as I was capable of feeling. I think—I can't quite remember—that there were others, but she was the first in the Navy, and I will always treasure the memory."

"I—I suppose there could have been, in the period of wash," she said. "Maybe in due course I'll remember."

She was lying. She remembered now. This was her point of vulnerability. I regretted having to do it, but I knew I had to. I had to get hold of her vulnerability and turn it to my advantage.

But not openly. If the captors knew what I was doing, they would remove Dorian and mem-wash me back to coordinate zero. I had to do it covertly, and this was a challenge.

Fortunately the scratches in the hell-cell had given me the clue. I needed an open code as a starting base, and a closed one for the real action. Our overt conversation and gradual seduction would serve for the first, and our physical contact could be adapted for the second.

I took her hand more firmly. "I want to understand you, Dorian Gray," I said. "Maybe if I had understood Helse better, I could have prevented her death. I never want to make the mistake of incomprehension again. I am desperately lonely in my cell, and I do not know when or why I may be tortured or killed, and I would cleave to you in a moment, if I felt I knew you well enough so that you would not dissipate in my arms like mist. You must be real to me; I must *know* you." As I emphasized the word I squeezed her hand, not hard enough to show on whatever nightlight scanner was watching us but enough so that Dorian was definitely aware of it.

She was moved; I felt the tremor pass through the whole

of her body. "You're not just a—a body, are you?" she asked. "You value the mind, the—"

"The essence," I agreed, squeezing her hand again. "But do I know your essence, Dorian?" This time I squeezed twice: two quick pulses.

She was startled. Obviously I *didn't* really know her, and in the common code of one for yes and two for no, I had answered my question.

She fumbled for words, realizing that something special was going on. "I—what can I tell you, that—"

"Only the truth, Dorian," I said, squeezing once.

Which I knew she could not do. "Why don't we just lie down and relax, Hope," she suggested after a moment. "Here, close, in the hammock, and I'll try to tell you anything you want to know."

The seduction ploy again. She hoped to use her body to distract me from this odd approach. She certainly had the body to do it.

"All right," I agreed. That surprised her; she hadn't expected me to capitulate so readily.

We worked our way around and managed to get into the hammock together, face to face, my arms around her body and hers around mine. The hammock pressed us close, and her thigh, belly, and breast were warm against my body.

My right arm was the upper one. I slid my hand down along her back to her left buttock and cupped it familiarly through her skirt. "What is your name?" I asked.

"Why, Dorian Gray," she said with a shake of amusement.

I squeezed her buttock twice.

She tensed, realizing that I was denying her answer, rather than being familiar in the physical sense. I suspect it might be a shock to any beautiful woman to discover that a man is more interested in her mind than her body, for whatever reason. "Does my name really matter?"

"Yes," I said, and squeezed her firm flesh twice.

Again she tensed, but this time only in the buttock. The feel of that was interesting. "What are you up to, Hope?"

"I think I'm seducing you," I said, and squeezed once.

"Well, two can play at that game." She moved her left hand to my right buttock and squeezed.

I smiled. "Oh? Then try this." I moved my hand, finding

the band in her prison skirt, and slid my fingers inside. I found the silk-smooth surface of her panties. "No one can see what I do." And I squeezed once.

She laughed again, playing the strange game. She undid my trousers and reached inside. The flesh she found was not that of the buttock. She took hold and squeezed. "What do you think of that?"

"No effect," I said, squeezing her buttock twice. Indeed it was a lie, for in her grasp my flesh was rapidly changing. I knew she was an agent of my captors, serving their purpose, but she was indeed a luscious item of the flesh. That was what made this so difficult emotionally: I had to keep my inner feelings apart from my outer ones, while causing her inner and outer emotions to merge. That might not be easy to do.

She hesitated. She had expected the hand signals to stop once real progress toward a sexual act was made. "What do you want?"

"I want *you,*" I said with a single squeeze.

"Well, just let me take off my clothes."

I squeezed twice.

"I don't understand!" Her confusion was understandable, for she held in her hand the proof that I desired her body.

I found her face and kissed her lips—and squeezed her silken buttock twice again.

Yet again she tensed, which caused me some discomfort because of the position of her hand. She started to protest, but I stifled it with the continuing kiss. Then I repeated, "I want you." One squeeze.

She lay still, analyzing, trying to figure out what I was getting at. She squeezed my hard anatomy once, as if it were a question, and I squeezed her soft bun twice in negation. She laughed silently. "You are very firm. You want . . . more than my body?"

"Yes." And my squeeze agreed.

"You want my love as well?"

"Yes." But I did not squeeze.

She hesitated. Then, "You can have it." But then she squeezed my flesh painfully hard, twice.

It was my turn to tense and pause, for different reasons. I was in physical discomfort and mental turmoil. Overtly she was offering me everything; why should she deny it privately? (I really did not intend that pun.) It was her assignment to seduce me and win my love; surely she would have better success if she convinced me she loved me. She was acting against her own best interest.

Or—she was telling me the truth for the first time. That this really was only an assignment and that her secret heart was not in it. In that case I was making genuine progress.

"I'll settle for what you offer," I said with one squeeze. She squeezed once in response, more gently.

We had established communication. We talked, and while she denied it verbally, by the squeeze route I learned that she had not been mem-washed. I had already known that, of course, but now she confessed it. She was indeed on assignment to seduce me. Why? Because my captors knew I was married and they wanted me to be sexually compromised, emotionally, too, if it could be done. Why was she cooperating? That was a longer story, harder to gather because the key words could not be spoken. To maintain the pretense of sexual seduction, we had to get undressed and proceed toward the physical culmination, but our true attention was elsewhere.

In the course of our secret dialogue the pretense became reality, and we did complete the act. I felt guilty, even as my fluid pumped into her body, because of my memory of Megan, but I knew it was necessary. I felt worse because it turned out to be so thoroughly pleasant; Dorian was good at her trade and almost made me believe that she liked doing this.

I wanted to know more about her, but I had been too long away from my cell and had to return. "My fate is in your hands," I told her openly. "If you report what I have done here, they will wash everything away."

"I'm guilty, too," she replied. But she knew what I meant: I had told her that I knew she was an agent, which was supposed to be a secret from me. She had admitted it, which was a forbidden action for her. She could turn me in, but that would implicate her, too. I was gambling that she would keep my faith and report merely that she had succeeded in seducing me, which the spy pickup would confirm.

We parted, but I was restless the remainder of the night. I realized that she might have played along in order to win my secret confidence, the better to betray me more thoroughly in the end. She could report on this matter without penalty to herself. She would have done her job and shown my captors an aspect of my capabilities they had not suspected. Still, I did not think she would; her secret responses had been true. My talent suggested that I had reached her on a personal level and compromised her mission to that extent.

If nothing happened in the next day I was probably right. My captors would have no reason to continue in their present program once they knew that I was not being truly compromised.

The day passed routinely, with further discussion/indoctrination. My captors did know I was sneaking out of my cell at night but evidently believed that their agent had the situation in hand.

Night came again, and I had not been punished. My gamble seemed to have paid off.

I returned to Dorian Gray, and we proceeded to fondle each other again, leaving our clothing on so that it was more complicated and therefore slower. Also, the clothing concealed the squeezings on bare buttocks, so that we could communicate more freely. I discovered that it was more stimulating to touch and be touched inside clothing than it was naked; perhaps it was the suggestion of illicit discovery that enhanced the effect. It got to the point where the game overtook me, and I almost raped her in my urgency to complete the position before spewing on the clothing. She found that very funny; it was a special victory for her, though the entangled clothing had to have been uncomfortable for her.

Meanwhile I learned the essence of her situation. Dorian, a beautiful young woman just coming out of her teens, had found employment with a Jupiter government office, but instead of routine office work, she had found herself on assignment to seduce a diplomat from Ganymede. She was offered such a bonus for success that she couldn't refuse. So she had done it. The man had been easy to seduce; she had simply moved in with him and served as his sexual plaything. Heedless of consequences, she soon found herself pregnant. She thought that would end the affair, but it didn't; the man was pleased to have his virility demonstrated and kept her with him through the birth of the baby. There was no question of marriage; he wasn't interested, and neither was she. They were a satisfied, unofficial family.

Then, abruptly, he was gone—with the baby. Whether he had somehow learned of her assignment to spy on him or simply had his own assignment changed, she didn't know. He had said nothing to her, perhaps because she would never have given up her infant son. The loss devastated her, but Ganymede was the last place she could go, as she was a refugee from it. She appealed to her employer, who promised to recover her baby for her if she would undertake another assignment. So she had, knowing nothing about it—and here she was.

Why had she confided all this to me? If I betrayed her she would surely never recover her baby. She hadn't had to tell me; I could tell when she was lying, but I couldn't make her tell me anything she really wanted to hide. She was cooperating—too well.

"Why?" I asked her, by squeezing that word in an unrelated sentence. "Why . . . tell . . . me?" Such questioning was slow, but we were used to that. We had already made sex, rushed and awkward as it had turned out, and were theoretically relaxing in the aftermath, still glued together in the hammock. We no longer had to use our hands directly for signaling; we could use any part of the body to nudge.

"I . . . know . . . of . . . you," she answered. And then she made her pitch, coming so swiftly into my camp that even with my talent I was suspicious of her motive. And she asked me: If she helped me, would I help her recover her son?

I needed her help, but I wasn't sure how I could ever help her in that way. But I agreed that if it ever did become possible, I would do what I could to restore her son to her.

It was time for me to read another key word and see what memory it evoked. That, added to the information I had from Dorian, could complete the background I needed to deal with my situation. But I wasn't sure how to get back to my old cell. I had balked at the indoctrination once, had been punished, and had "learned my lesson"; it would not be in character for me to balk again. I was sure my captors were planning something for me, and I had to act before that happened—but how?

If I didn't misbehave how could I get to that cell? Could Dorian help? But she wasn't supposed to know me personally; theoretically she was just a prisoner in another cell whose eye I could see in the opposite window, no more. She *did* know me—rather intimately—and the captors knew it. But none of us could admit that to the others. There seemed to be no avenue there.

Could I sneak in? No, I had checked out the bulkheads at the end of the passage, and they were tight. I could not pass them. It was a foolish notion, anyway. I had to be *sent* there.

I wrestled with it but saw no better device than another balk on the indoctrination program. I didn't want to do that; it would ruin my credibility with Dorian. But what choice did I have? I had to have the next key term.

I procrastinated, unable to make the decision. And abruptly I was returned to that cell, no reason stated. It was exactly where I wanted to be, but I distrusted the mechanism. Why had they so conveniently put me there? Did they know what I was up to? I had not mentioned the code terms to Dorian Gray; as far as I knew I had not in any way betrayed that most vital secret.

I had to assume that they did not know, that this was no elaborate trap. In any event I needed that key term, as I did not have enough information without it. If they were watching me, so be it; better to risk giving away my secret than to lose the game by default.

I felt in the muck for the symbols, translating each tediously as I got it. I was up to ALL in the open key: ABANDON HOPE, *ALL* YE WHO ENTER HERE. A was the fifteenth spot, and the symbol in that location was ⌐ . That translated, appropriately, to the number 7. Seven characters from the letter A was the letter G. The next symbol, ⊏ , was 27, and that far beyond L counted off to A. Then ∟ , 3, readily converting to N. ⌐ was 36, or after a horrendous mental count from the space following ALL, Y. And ⊓ , 26, going from Y to M. And ⌟ , 1, translating to itself, E. ⊏ , 15, from the space following E, becoming

D. ⊔ , 20, from the W in WHO, E. And ⊔ , 20 again, this time from H, counting off to the space. My word was finished.

GANYMEDE.

Chapter 9

GANYMEDE

Politics works in devious ways. My losing campaign for governor of Sunshine attracted the notice of the president of U.S.J., who was of my party. I received a call from New Wash, inviting me and my family to visit the White Dome for a private conference.

Megan's eyes gleamed. "This could be important, Hope. It means he is considering you for an appointment."

If she thought it was important it probably was. I hastened to accept the invitation and to make the required appearance before the president.

President Kenson was gracious. He was a tall Saxon, in his fifties—height seems to be an asset in a candidate—with a lovely wife. He had been in office two years, having turned back Tocsin's determined effort to move from the vice-presidency to the presidency. Naturally Tocsin had tried to portray Kenson as incompetent, soft on Saturnism, ultraliberal, filthy rich, and other political crimes. Only the fourth had been true, and hard-nosed use of the leverage of that wealth had enabled Kenson to turn the tables and defeat Tocsin in a very close campaign. Megan had been glad to see it. It was not that she favored Kenson in all things—no truly clean person achieved this high an office, she claimed—but she knew what a disaster Tocsin would have been. But whatever else he was or was not, Kenson had immense personal magnetism. This was another necessary attribute for a politician, of course; I just had not encountered it at this magnitude before. My talent was blunted because of my tendency to like this man; emotion always interferes with judgment.

Hopie ran around the halls, enchanted by the complex that was the White Dome. "They're darling when they're little," the president remarked, smiling. Then he glanced at Megan. "And beautiful when grown." Fight it as I might, I found my appreciation for this man magnifying. He was like a power source, radiating competence and goodwill. I knew he had a mean streak and was a ruthless political gut-fighter when campaigning, but none of that showed now.

Kenson was a charming host but also an efficient one. Very shortly I found myself closeted with him and talking business. He had evidently sized me up as rapidly as I had him, and, of course, he had done his homework on my background. "Hope, we are opening a new embassy," he said. "It's a critical one, and delicate; it must be handled correctly. I believe you are the man for the position."

"An ambassador, sir?" I asked, not crediting it. I had supposed he was considering me for some bureaucratic position without much significance, so as to be able to lay claim to some support from the Hispanic community. Of course, some embassies were quite minor; it depended on the planet.

"Ganymede," he said.

If he had intended to floor me he had succeeded. Communist Ganymede was the current sore spot of the Jupiter sphere of space. "Gany? But—"

"But we have had no diplomatic relations with that satellite since the revolution," he said. "However, that is changing; I would much rather be in touch with my enemy than out of touch; it's safer. But the identity of the ambassador is critical. He must have stature, competence, caution, and courage." He smiled, and again that incandescent camaraderie manifested. "It is amazing how few politicians fit that description."

No understatement! "I—"

"I do not deny that this post has been turned down by more than one nominee," he continued, as if this were a personal communication that only I was privileged to hear. "They are afraid; not for their persons but for their reputations. The far right will seek to blacken anyone who goes to Ganymede. Success in this position may appear as damning as failure. But there is no more important spot at the moment, and I believe you can handle it. After all, you cleaned up the Belt."

"Yes, I—"

He clapped me heartily on the shoulder. "Excellent! I'll set the wheels turning." He winked. "Nice device, that mustard-six. I remember it from my own training in the Navy. I kept smirking when I thought about it, and I was in a strategy session at the time. I probably made a fool of myself." He did a little jump, as of someone feeling a sudden burn.

I had to smile. I hadn't realized that news of that episode had reached this far. "I—"

"It's really good to have a man of your caliber aboard, Ambassador Hubris!"

In this manner I became Jupiter's representative at Ganymede. The president had been too diplomatic to mention my two outstanding qualifications for the office: I spoke Spanish fluently, and I was unemployed, politically. I remained bemused by the proficiency with which he had dazzled me into acceptance; when he smiled at me, I would have accepted appointment to the post of Assistant Slop Inspector. He had a talent for personnel management that I envied. I would have to study it, with the hope of making it my own.

Megan understood. "I was sure you would like Kenson," she murmured. "His talent is the complement of your own. You understand people; he manages them."

"He managed me," I confessed. "I really don't know if I should have accepted the post or even if I *did* accept it. Ganymede . . . I mean—"

"You had no choice," she said, "from the moment his eye fixed on you. I confess I had hoped for something less controversial, but . . ." She shrugged.

I stared at her. "You had a hand in this."

"Not really," she demurred.

"You are too modest. What did you—"

"I merely mentioned to one of my friends that it would be unfortunate to allow such a talented person to lie fallow for any length of time."

And that friend had had the ear of the president. He had done it for Megan, not for me. That angered me. "I—"

She turned to me, her head cocked slightly sidewise, her eyes wide, in her fashion challenging me to make something of it. My ire melted; I could not oppose anything she wanted for me. "Thank you, Megan," I said humbly.

She only smiled, faintly, and I felt rewarded. I had married her, I claimed, to forward my political career; she was certainly doing that.

The announcement of the resumption of diplomatic relations with Ganymede generated a furor in Jupiter. There were angry editorials in the media and cries of "Impeach the President!" from the conservatives. They were serious, too, which shows how foolish they were. Somehow there always seemed to be greater outrage when an attempt was made to encourage communication and peace, than when the effort fomented confusion and war. I came in for my share, but I was sheltered by the competent mantle of presidential favor. It was assumed that as a defeated candidate for office I had been desperate for any political appointment, so was not really to blame. Perhaps there was truth in that.

Then there was an especially violent eruption on Io, generating a spectacular visual effect, and the fickle attention of the public eye shifted to that.

Spirit remained on Jupiter to caretake my consultancy firm. That had turned out to be such a good business that we couldn't afford to close it down; we had hired a young man who had some of my talent, and used him for preliminary work. Many cases could be handled by the application of common sense, and when a difficult one developed, he would arrange for me to interview by vid-phone. This wasn't ideal, but we believed it would suffice.

I took Megan and Hopie with me, of course. Megan wasn't easy about the matter, but she didn't want to send me in alone or give any public impression of doubt. She bore, after all, a certain responsibility.

Thorley's comment didn't help: "The liberal set may be about to experience the end product of their naiveté." Naturally he considered liberalism to be three-quarters of the way toward Communism and liked to imply that the true liberal would be a Communist if he only had the courage of his convictions. That sort of insinuation could work both ways, of course; the conservatives were sometimes equated with the dictatorship of the Sixth Reich, this century's incarnation of the historical Nazi party. With no more justice.

I had been ten years on Jupiter, after fifteen in space; I

experienced a panoply of nostalgic impressions as the chartered shuttle ship jetted outward to rendezvous with Ganymede. Gany was physically the largest moon in the Solar System, popularly called a planet to distinguish it and the other giants—Io, Europa, and Callisto orbiting Jupiter, Titan orbiting Saturn, Triton about Neptune, and, of course, Earth's Luna—from the myriad bits and pieces that drifted everywhere. Basically a body was called a planet if gravity-shielding could bring its settlements to normal Earth gee. Pluto, technically a planet, was marginal because of its small size, but it didn't matter; only research stations were there. Old Earth had had a similar problem with the definition of islands and continents.

We never saw Io, but as we passed the vicinity of its orbit I shivered; it was there that my mother had died, aground in the sea of sulfur storms that was Io's hell-face. It was there that I had first seen the picture of Megan. Rationally I doubted the significance in that juxtaposition of events, but emotionally it was one of the guideposts of my life. Megan, too, seemed absorbed, and I knew she was thinking of her Uncle Mason, the scientist, a good man. On that we emphatically agreed.

Then she put her hand on mine. I turned to face her and saw her eyes shining with tears. Then her face blurred, and I knew my own tears were flowing. In that moment I saw her as the beautiful girl of sixteen whose picture I had glimpsed, and my love for that girl expanded from my protected inner heart to encompass my whole body and being, and hers.

"Mush stuff!" Hopie protested, and I realized I was kissing Megan. I brought the little girl up to share our embrace.

A gunship came out to meet us and escort us to the planet. If there had been protests to the establishment of the Jupiter Embassy at this end, none was in evidence. We tuned in the Gany newscast, which showed a massive crowd cheering the opening of the embassy compound.

I knew better. Spirit and Shelia had done some spot research for me, and the news was not good. The premier of Ganymede was a temperamental fanatic, a natural orator, devoted to his family and capable of lasering to death a companion without notice. He had forced out his predecessor, then executed him on a trumped-up charge. A minor bloodbath had followed, as supporters of the prior regime had been systematically eliminated. But over the years, as he had come to terms with the realities of his planet's situation, he had become more moderate. Ganymede was dependent on Saturn for its weapons and most of its technical equipment. Gany's major cash crop, sugar, was boycotted by Jupiter. Saturn bought the sugar but didn't need it, which put Gany in an inferior position. Saturn made various demands, and these were increasingly onerous as Gany's economic situation deteriorated. Gany was locked into the Saturn orbit economically, but socially it was no mutual admiration society. This opening of a Jupiter Embassy, in fact, was being done at Saturn's behest, in exchange for a similar one Saturn was opening with the Rings. The Saturn Rings had been taken over by the last vestige of a former government of South Saturn, driven out by the present one, and represented every bit as much aggravation to Saturn as Gany did to Jupiter. So it was a major exchange deal, promising to significantly ease interplanetary tensions. Jupiter had pressured the Rings to accept the Saturnine presence, as Saturn had pressured Gany to accept Jupiter's. Therefore the Gany premier deeply resented it, as did his counterpart of the Rings. He didn't like being told what to do, even if it did make sense on the larger scale. *He* should have been the one to decide to reopen diplomatic relations with Jupiter—had he wanted to. I understood his position.

Now Gany would be exchanging ambassadors, setting up its own embassy on Jupiter. This would, of course, be another outlet for Saturn's activities in New Wash. All the personnel of the Gany Embassy would be hand picked by Saturn, and all would be Saturnine agents. There would be no contacts between Jupiter and Gany not sanctioned by Saturn. It was, in short, a sham, just as the exchange of embassies between Saturn and the Rings would be. All the key parties understood this; only the ordinary people were ignorant, as perhaps they deserved to be. But it *was* a potential avenue to peace, so was perhaps justified.

Naturally I was expected to keep my opinions to myself. But it had occurred to me that I just might make the contact genuine. That was the real challenge of my position that President Kenson also had not mentioned, consummate politician that he was. He had in effect thrown me into the lion's den, giving me opportunity to tame the lions and so increase my power—or to be destroyed by them. Double or nothing. Megan was right: a man did not achieve high position if his hands were entirely clean; he had to know how to scheme and flatter and put a fancy face on ugly business. Kenson was obviously a master at this— and I was learning much. The System powers were playing a devious strategic game, and it was difficult for the underlings to grasp the full significance of the position of each pawn. But somehow I was not completely satisfied to be a pawn.

We arrived at the dome-city of Vana with due fanfare. The premier himself was on hand at the old docking port, stepping forward to shake my hand vigorously and put an arm around my shoulders in a display of public camaraderie. Then the cameras were turned off and the premier departed, hardly bothering to notice me further. I knew why; he did not like being a pawn, either, and he hoped to encourage me to leave as soon as possible. It had to be my choice, though; nothing that could be traced to any failure on his part. He wanted to be able to express sincere public regret at my decision to vacate. The situation reminded me of that of the railroad companies' treatment of their passengers.

We were conducted to the embassy compound. It was an old fortress, later converted to a prison, converted again to diplomatic use. The back wall was notched by the burns of laser beams: prisoners had been executed here. I hoped Megan would not recognize its nature but feared she did, for she hurried Hopie on past the wall.

The main building was a warren of tiny cells, and in some there were manacles attached to wall mountings. In one there were white bones. Very little effort had been made to conceal the prior use of this place. The campaign of private discouragement was definitely on.

We had a small household and office staff—Shelia, Ebony, and Coral—but were expected to hire locals for most of the maintenance work. This turned out to be an awkward chore. Megan did not speak Spanish, and it seemed that none of the eligible employees spoke English. In addition, they were a slovenly bunch, by no coincidence completely unsuited for the kinds of work we required. We needed a governess for Hopie, as this was the diplomatic style; the Vana employment service sent us five candidates, all of whom were middle-aged males. I called in and explained the problem, and they promised to locate some more suitable candidates. But somehow nothing happened. This was typical; it seemed that the city of Vana was very short of English-speaking cooks, maids, and handymen. We had to make do for the time being without local employees, which made a bad impression.

The power was erratic, tending to fade out at the most awkward times, such as when Megan was trying to cook in the antiquated kitchen. Even the gee wavered, making our stomachs unsettled. At times there were piercing noises of adjacent construction. In addition, it was difficult to go out into the city freely; we immediately picked up an entourage of grim-looking men carrying laser rifles. "For your security, señor," one explained when I inquired, but somehow they seemed more menacing than protective. We made a household rule: Not one of us went out without being accompanied by Coral, who could demolish half a dozen men in about as many seconds if the need arose. She carried an amazing arsenal of assorted weapons, none of which showed. What did show was her comely figure, so that few Ganys believed she was dangerous, though they knew her function.

In addition, we suffered an immediate flood of defectors, who claimed to be fleeing political oppression and who demanded sanctuary. Now, this is a legitimate function of an embassy. It is considered planetary ground of its sponsoring planet, and very few powers ever violate that privilege. But I knew even before I interviewed these people that they were impostors sent by the Gany government to make my position untenable. We lacked the facilities to care for this mass of a hundred or so people, and they were not about to make our job easy. We would become a zoo, with the animal gates open.

Quick and firm action had to be taken, but I knew the local authorities would not cooperate. So I arranged for a stiff test of motive. I placed an interplanetary call to a person I knew. Theoretically the call was private; actually I knew it was monitored by the locals. The call was to the Jupiter Naval Base at Leda, routed through the Jupiter base on Ganymede, Tanamo. As an ambassador I had the authority to make such calls, and as a retired Navy man I knew whom to reach. There was a six-second delay each way, because of the distance; thus there were twelve-second pauses in the dialogue.

"Ambassador Hope Hubris to Captain Emerald Mondy," my opening went. There was a delay of a good minute while the Navy ran her down; then her face appeared on my screen. Emerald was a decade older than I remembered her; she was my own age, but somehow I thought of her as I had known her personally, unaged. At forty-one she was not the lithe and angular creature she had been; her brown face had filled out, but she retained the slightly rebellious expression I remembered. She had once been my wife; we had separated for tactical rather than emotional reasons, as was often the case in the Navy. Of course she remembered me well; no doubt she had kept track of my political progress over the years. Her words alluded mischievously to the time of our intimate association. "What can I do for you, Ambassador, that wouldn't gripe your spouse and mine?"

"You can contact Rue for me and ask her to approve immigration of approximately one hundred defectors seeking political asylum from Ganymede," I said. "If the Belt will take them, then I'd like a transport ship dispatched here to pick them up."

Emerald considered, after the transmission pause. "I'm sure the Belt will take them," she said. "The Belt is always short of men. I will start the scutwork and have a ship dispatched in forty-eight hours. But, you know, Ambassador, it's not exactly cushy living in the Belt, especially for untrained recruits. How many speak English or French?"

"None," I responded. "They'll just have to learn. Thank you, Emerald; give my respects to Rue."

"I won't give her those," she replied with mock severity. "She's still hot for you, Captain, and she's only thirty, you know. Lot of juice left in her."

I smiled as the connection ended. Emerald had always been a blunt speaker. She was also a strategic genius, which was why I had married her. She had risen in the Navy much as I had risen in politics, in fits and starts, but I was sure she had not yet seen her apex. She was sure to become the first female admiral of this century. Rue, on the other hand, was not in the Navy. That name was short for Roulette, for she had been in a pirate band that ran big-time gambling. She had been my final wife in space, the most stunningly beautiful woman, physically, I had ever known, fiery of hair and temperament. At age thirty, she would indeed still be lovely. She was now the wife of Admiral Phist and was the Belt's liaison to Jupiter. I had excellent connections in these women.

Next, I spoke to the refugees assembled in our compound. "You will all be pleased to know," I informed them in Spanish, "that I have arranged for your expeditious emigration to the Belt, where you will find gainful employment at the prevailing wages. Of course you will have to learn one of their languages, and it will take some time to learn the ways of the sparse planetoids, but you will be forever free of Ganymede, so I know you will find it worthwhile. The transport ship will dock at Tanamo in two days, and you will be given clearance to board it there."

My announcement was greeted in silence. I left them to their thoughts.

Within a day all of them were gone.

My bluff had worked. Genuine defectors would have accepted the deal; provocateurs on the Gany payroll could not afford to. There had never been any ship dispatched; Emerald had played along with me, knowing that I knew it could not be done that way. Only direct presidential authorization could have moved out those defectors that promptly. But those who had monitored my message had not realized that, and certainly the pseudo-defectors hadn't.

Emerald was a good woman. I trust it in no way diminishes Megan if I confess that there are times when I remember my Navy wives and associates with pleasant nostalgia. We understood each other in ways that only personnel of the Navy would understand.

But I had solved only one problem; others remained. When Hopie screamed at night, and we rushed into her room to discover a rat scrambling away from the light, I decided it was time to take action. Rats—in a planetary dome? That could hardly be by chance. Those creatures had to have been bred elsewhere and placed there. Hopie moved into our bedroom, and I pondered morosely.

By morning I had worked out a program. "Megan, I want you to learn to sing some songs in Spanish," I said. "Can you do this quickly?"

She knew I was up to something, and such was her distress at the situation that she did not question it. "If you tell me how to pronounce the words."

I went to the local library with Coral and did some research. At first there were objections, but I showed my credentials and charmed the library clerk, and she helped me locate what I needed and copy it. I could not be denied access to the library, and, of course, I was not regarded as very important in the practical sense; this gave me the freedom I needed.

Megan had no trouble learning the songs; she had been a professional singer, after all, and still possessed a remarkable voice. I was trusting that the premier did not know that.

I called him. Naturally I got through only to the barrier office. I announced that the Jupiter ambassador was coming that evening to pay a social call on the premier, and bringing his family to meet the premier's family. I cut off before the functionary could protest.

And so, self-invited, we called on the premier. Even a sham ambassador has some leverage; I could make a most unkind headline that would arouse both Jupiter and Saturn, if openly snubbed. After the matter of the defectors, the premier knew that I would do just that. He, of course, had known I was bluffing about the shipment to the Belt but, had he intervened, it would have tipped his hand. Perhaps at that point he had begun to appreciate the quality of the opposition. Also, I knew the premier would be intrigued by my temerity in visiting and would be braced for my complaints about the embassy facilities. He would look for an opportunity to further humiliate me, if he could do so without directly soiling his hands. I intended to provide him that opportunity.

Everything was very proper as we arrived. There would be no open show of animosity here. The premier was cere-

monially garbed, and his wife accompanied him to the door
to greet us. I sized her up immediately: she was a decent
woman, in awe of her husband but closely guarded in her
heart. I knew she had suffered things she could not utter.

We were treated to a fine meal, and the premier was
genial, though he watched me carefully. He wanted me to
make my move before he made his. We conversed in Spanish, leaving Megan out of it. I had warned her that it would
be this way, and she bore it with grace.

As the meal ended I said, as if casually, "But where is
your son? I understood you had a son."

The premier almost glowered but caught himself. Now
he knew I knew, and his anger intensified. "He is indis-
posed, Ambassador."

"But I promised my little girl she could meet your son,"
I exclaimed innocently. "She will be most disappointed—"
My words were polite, but my stare advised him that I in-
tended to have my way in this.

The premier's teeth showed in what was barely a smile.
His wife had generally remained out of public view, and
his son was never exhibited. There was good reason for
this; it was an extremely sensitive matter. Natives of
Gany had been executed for acting less brashly than I was
now, but the mantle of Jupiter protected me no matter how
obnoxious I became.

"Fetch Raul!" the premier snapped at his wife as we adjourned to the parlor. Surely he was picturing me against
the execution wall and aiming the laser himself.

She brought Raul. He was a boy of about ten, thin and
small, and he walked mechanically, only when urged.
When released, he stood by himself before the room's piano
and twisted his fingers in front of his face, tuning out the
rest of the planet. He was, as I had known, autistic—the secret shame of the family. By my insistence on seeing him I
had let the premier know I could tacitly blackmail him, for
the Jupiter press was not censored in the manner of the
Gany press. I could demand better service at the embassy
and get it now.

"Go meet Raul," I told Hopie. I had warned her privately what to expect. She was only five but pretty savvy
for the age, perhaps possessed of some talent similar to
mine. I knew Raul was harmless if treated diffidently,

though the wrong approach could provoke a savage tantrum. The premier was so tense, he was having trouble maintaining his composure.

"You know, my wife sings," I remarked. "She's really quite good. Would you like to hear her?"

The premier had little interest in music, but his wife did. He grasped at this straw, to divert attention from the autistic child. "Yes, yes," he agreed gruffly. "Let her sing."

"Perhaps your wife will play," I said, indicating the piano. It was one of the electronic ones, similar to Megan's own, set on a table so as to emulate the style of the mechanical pianos that had existed on old Earth.

"No, no, Señor Ambassador," she protested, blushing. She was not expert; she practiced to divert herself and knew she would only embarrass us all.

"Then perhaps if my wife could accompany herself—"

"Yes, yes," she agreed quickly. She spoke in Spanish, but her intent was evident to all.

Megan sat at the piano, near Raul, who ignored her and the world of normal folk. He contemplated his moving fingers with total fascination. Megan checked the piano to be sure it was in tune, adjusted it, and began.

First she played and sang an operatic selection in English. The premier understood the language but did not deign to acknowledge, and his wife could not follow the words at all though she obviously appreciated the music. Thus this selection was to an extent lost on its limited audience. But I watched Raul, using my talent, and confirmed what I had suspected. His fingers slowed slightly, as if part of the music were reaching his mind.

"Now," I murmured to Megan.

She began the first of the Spanish songs I had had her learn. It was a pretty one, popular with children, very quick and light, with a catchy refrain. She sang it well—probably better than it had ever been sung on Gany before, for there was no singer of her stature here. The room filled with sound, and Hopie began moving to the beat, as a child will. "Oh, lovely," the premier's wife breathed in Spanish.

I took the premier's elbow unobtrusively. He stiffened, furious at this familiarity; he touched others freely in public but did not like others touching him. "Raul," I murmured.

He looked at his son and saw the boy's gaze turning to Megan. The restless fingers paused, and the expression of complete indifference was shifting to one of faint interest.

"He hears!" the premier whispered, awed.

Megan finished the song, and the boy froze again. His gaze became blank. Whatever current had passed through him had been turned off.

She started the next, another pretty one with a strong Latin beat, and again Raul responded. He began to move, ever so slightly, to the music, copying Hopie. There was no question that the song reached him.

The third song Megan played and sang was the planetary anthem of Ganymede. The premier, startled, stood to attention, and his son copied him, standing straight but not tuned out. There were tears running down the face of the boy's mother.

When Megan finished that one, she smiled at Raul, and he smiled back. "A miracle!" the premier's wife exclaimed.

"Sometimes music helps," I said. "The right music, sung with proper feeling. One cannot expect too much, but . . ."

That was the turning point. The premier's stifled rage was replaced by an opposite emotion. Thereafter we were welcome at his home, Megan especially. She worked with the premier's wife to discover what music would reach the boy most effectively. And by a seeming coincidence, a number of quite qualified people showed up to work at the embassy. The sinister men of the street disappeared. We had no further significant difficulties of any kind.

As time passed I came to know the premier better. He was a ruthless and, at times, violent man, but he was in an environment that required such qualities. He did have firm principles, and he was trying to improve the lot of his planet. Gradually we spoke more candidly to each other, as he recognized that it was not my purpose to judge him, humiliate him, or to work against his interests. I had, after all, been as ruthless as he, in the course of my prior military career. It was my purpose to improve relations between Jupiter and Ganymede.

"How would it be," I inquired musingly, "if we arranged to find something to do?"

His eyes narrowed appreciatively. "What do you have in mind, *Señor?*"

"Suppose we were to commence negotiations for the resumption of sugar purchases by Jupiter, the orderly transfer of Tanamo to Ganymede suzerainty before the lease expires, that sort of thing?"

His eyes fairly popped. "You would do that?"

Tanamo was a major Jupiter Naval base situated on Gany, the one I had invoked for the mock defector shipment. It operated under a long-term lease arranged before the revolution that had changed the nature of Gany's government. Tanamo's presence was perhaps the leading sore spot of the present Gany regime. But there was no way Gany could take over the base without provoking war with Jupiter, and that was not to be contemplated. That lease would terminate in another decade, but it was not known whether Jupiter would give up the base even then. Treaties are honored by governments only when it suits their convenience, and Jupiter's interplanetary record in this respect was no better than Saturn's, no matter what the school texts might claim.

"Sometimes capitalistic and communistic purposes coincide," I said. "I would like to facilitate peace in our time in the Solar System, naturally—"

"Naturally," he agreed dryly.

"And the elimination of trouble spots should help," I continued. "It is possible that the position of the premier who arranged for the resumption of territorial integrity—"

"And the reputation of the ambassador involved—" he added.

We looked at each other, smiling. We both could profit.

"Of course, there is always a certain quid pro quo," I said. "Ganymede has been accused, perhaps erroneously, of fomenting revolution elsewhere in the Jupiter sphere, and of serving as a supply conduit for Saturn arms."

He nodded. "Were this the case, it might be that it would not be entirely under the control of the local authorities," he pointed out. "There might be debts to pay. . . ."

"Granted. Yet perhaps a dialogue with the appropriate party . . ."

"Perhaps a dialogue," he agreed.

"And some have claimed—naturally I do not personally credit this—that there are political prisoners who might safely be released: intellectuals, misled youths, ill folk."

"If, perhaps, an initiative were made."

I nodded. We had an understanding.

And so it was that I, in the dutiful performance of my office, relayed to my government the Gany petition for early consideration of the transfer of Tanamo and other matters.

And the antimatter, as the saying goes, hit the matter.

I received a close-coded message from President Kenson: "What the hell are you doing, Hubris?" But the lure of progress toward genuine peace was too strong; the president had to permit the initiative. When the furor raged, he had to support it. When Congress passed a resolution of condemnation, Kenson had to assert his position by appointing a Jupiter/Gany committee to explore matters. And I received an invitation to visit the Saturn Embassy on Ganymede.

The man I met was one Mikhail Khukov, a captain in the Saturn Navy. I knew the moment I saw him that he was a meteor. That is, a man with the background, intelligence, and drive to blaze to the top, if not assassinated on the way. Saturnine politics, I knew, were played in true hard-ball style; one small error of judgment could render a person dead, figuratively or literally. This one intended to make no mistakes, yet he was also a creature of calculated risks. His type had to be.

He shook my hand, western-style. Technically the Solar System has no east or west, but the terms derive from antiquity: Jupiter is west, Saturn is east, and all else is indeterminate. "So glad to meet you at last, Captain," he said in English. "I have admired your conduct of the matter of the Belt."

"I regret I am not acquainted with your own record."

"Nor would you wish to be, Comrade Capitalist," he said heartily, dismissing the subject. "So you lit a fire under the tail of your own president."

"Well, I was sure he would support an initiative for peace."

"Don't we all—in our fashions. Exactly what concessions do you seek?"

"Naturally I would not interfere with existing negotiations—"

He laughed. "You have the power, Hubris! Do you not know it when you see it?"

I had to smile. "I had thought to conceal my observation." For he did indeed have a talent similar to mine; the genius of judging people. He was reading me even as I was reading him. We were in a contest of skills—a contest that had no discernible object other than understanding, and no reckoning of points. We could not deceive each other.

"We can do each other much good—or ill," he said.

"Have we reason to do ill?"

"I see none, when we allow for certain distinctions in our situations."

Such as his murderous political environment. In his situation I, too, would have had to kill or be killed. His was basically a pirate government. I did not necessarily approve, but I understood.

"Do you play pool, Captain?" he inquired.

"Does a black hole squeeze?"

"It has been long since I have matched against my own rank." I was no longer a captain, technically, but there was indeed a kind of interplanetary camaraderie of rank: a lieutenant competed against other lieutenants, and a commander against other commanders. Every unit had its ladder of proficiency, but at the level of captain or above, there were few to compete against. Evidently it was similar in the Saturn Navy.

We adjourned to the embassy pool room. The table and equipment were top-line, as that of such establishments tended to be. I had not played regularly since leaving the Navy, but such skill is never truly lost; I knew I could, after wearing off the rust, give a creditable account of myself. But the point was not really to win; it was to match against one's own rank in as varied and exotic a manner as possible.

We played. I do not remember who won; I think we split games. He was out of shape, too; Saturnine officers are not given undue leisure. It was fun; I realized again that I missed the Navy, and this was like being back in it. While we played, we continued to measure each other. I judged Khukov's talent to be less than mine, but he was a harder man; he had the kind of backbone that my sister Spirit had, so he used his powers more effectively than I did. Essentially I won over people, who then served my interests loyally; he served his interests directly.

"Perhaps we could exchange favors," he said.

I had known he was working up to something; he saw in me a way to magnify his power in some way. "Perhaps."

"I speak no Spanish, yet I must deal with those who do. I distrust interpreters."

I could appreciate why. Ganymede was an often unwilling partner to Saturn; if he used a native interpreter, his words might suffer more than was comfortable, and there could be much he missed. That could be dangerous. "You might learn the language," I suggested, realizing what he wanted of me.

"There might come a time when you found it advantageous to comprehend Russian," he said. "You will in due course be dealing on that level."

"I'm only a minor ambassador!" I protested, intrigued.

"And I'm only a Navy officer, on inclement duty. But sometimes it is possible, how do you put it, to make of a sow's ear a silken purse?"

There could indeed be advantage to knowing Russian. He read in me the same ambition I read in him: to achieve the ultimate seat of power. The odds were against either of us making it, but careful preparation and special skills could help. I nodded, interested but not committed.

"But one reservation," he said. "I prefer that such ability not be known."

Again I nodded. A man could learn a lot, if those about him believed he did not understand their language. Such secret understanding could on occasion make a life-and-death difference. "I have no need to advertise such a skill as the speaking of Russian, either," I said.

We shook hands, trusting each other as no two people lacking our avenue of understanding could. This was not a matter of friendship or even of compatibility; our loyalties and philosophies were diametrically opposed. But in this we were united, as two panthers might unite to preserve a favored hunting ground.

Thus it was that over the course of the next year I taught Khukov to speak Spanish with very little accent—he was an apt study—and he taught me to speak Russian with, I trust, similar finesse. Neither of us told any other party of this deal. Nominally we were playing pool and discussing ambassadorial matters. We never became friends—a too-complete understanding is no better for friendship than a too-complete familiarity is for romance—but we knew that neither would betray the other.

Meanwhile, Megan had not sat idle in the Jupiter Embassy. She set about learning Spanish herself, openly, and encouraged Hopie to do the same. Indeed, Hopie entered the local school system as she came of age. We had faced the choice of private tutoring, which seemed affected and expensive; or sending her to the Navy Dependent School at Tanamo, which Megan would not hear of for several reasons, such as her aversion to military commitment and her refusal to separate our child from our family; or letting her go to a Gany school. That course seemed simple enough, and Hopie was welcomed there. The original alienation shown by the population had entirely disappeared.

But after a year our course seemed less certain.

The schools of Gany are not for simple education. It is the revolutionary philosophy that political education is fundamental; that a person cannot function as a responsible citizen if his political attitudes are wrong. For example, he cannot be a truly selfless team member if his philosophy is one of self-interest. He can not budget his money wisely if he is dedicated to immediate gratification at any cost. It is *attitude* that is critical—and so the Gany schools educate for that as thoroughly as for the literary and technical and social skills.

Hopie was a bright child and a pleasant one. She got along well in school, as she mastered Spanish, made friends, and learned the lessons well. When she began debating the liabilities of capitalism at home, Megan grew uneasy. When Hopie challenged some of the Jupiter versions of history, such as the manner the so-called Mid-Jupe Canal was arranged, Megan became angry. And when the child began praising the dedication of Saturn to System peace, Megan had had enough. "I shall not suffer my child to become a Saturnist!" she exclaimed.

I tried to reason with her, pointing out that the child did

understand that there were different ways to view every issue and that the Gany school espoused merely one view, not the ultimate truth. But Megan replied that even a little bit of brainwashing was too much. In this we had our first significant disagreement, for I was unworried by propaganda, knowing it to be a standard tool and a two-edged one, while Megan simply could not tolerate it for the child. I tried to point out that there was indeed a question about the Mid-Jupe Canal, but that only upset her further. We had come up against a Saxon/Hispanic schism that was best left buried.

In the end Megan took Hopie back to Jupiter, while I remained on Ganymede. I had a post to fill and things to do here that were too important to leave; I simply could not yet return to Jupiter. And so we separated, and it hurt me deeply, and Megan, too, but we were helpless in the circumstance. It had never occurred to me that anything could drive us apart, least of all our child, but for this occasion it was true.

Shelia and Ebony and Coral expressed their condolences and seemed to regret the situation as much as I did; but all three had suffered their own privations during schooling, and understood. None of them attempted to console me directly, for a reason they presumed I would not understand: All three of them were too strongly attracted to me to risk it. This effect on women is one of the liabilities of my talent. I appreciated their discretion.

The premier expressed regret but did not interfere. "Women have their own perceptions, which men must tolerate," he said. "Raul will miss her." But Raul was now making progress independently, now that the channel had been opened; his mother was singing to him and doing well. The premier was a busy man, not given to much concern about the private problems of others.

Khukov understood. "My wife—when I joined the Party . . ." He shrugged. I had not known he was married, and it seemed that was no longer the case. Only a few citizens of Saturn actually join the Party, of course—those who are seriously interested in government and power. Evidently Khukov's wife had wanted a different kind of life.

"This is new to me," I confessed in Russian. "And painful."

"Ah, yes," he agreed in Spanish. "There is no pain like it. But you and I, we must sacrifice all else in the pursuit of our destinies."

"I love Megan," I said. "I will never give her up."

"It will not be by your choice," he said with the wisdom of experience.

I also received a note from Thorley. "Methinks I judged your wife too harshly." Naturally he approved of the direct expression of opposition to the Communist indoctrination but had evidently supposed that Megan did not. I appreciated his interest; it reminded me that though he and I still opposed each other philosophically, we retained a kind of friendship personally.

The committee on the sugar and Tanamo issues was hopelessly deadlocked. The problems were these: the sugar market that had once been Ganymede's had been apportioned among several other Latin countries on and off Jupiter; they raised a howl of protest at the notion of losing those shares. Sugar was their major source of income; without that market some of them would quickly bankrupt. The Tanamo transfer was opposed by the Jupiter administration itself, though President Kenson remained publicly noncommittal so as not to undercut my position. The base could not be allowed to fall under Saturnine control.

These two objections blocked the other parts of the negotiation. Neither Saturn nor Ganymede would agree to halt the export of arms and subversion to nations of the Jupiter sphere unless Tanamo were yielded, and the premier was adamant about regaining the sugar trade in return for whatever prisoners he might release. The barriers were, ironically, with the Jupiter side, rather than the Gany side. Megan's protestations to the contrary, there was some merit in the Gany political indoctrination. Not a lot, but some. A contrary political view was a serious matter here; this was something few of the folk on Jupiter could appreciate, because of their much greater freedom to adopt any political configuration they chose, or none.

"Those bureaucrats will never lift out of the mire," Khukov said to me. "It is time for us to finish what we started." He had been instrumental in getting Saturn's acquiescence to the negotiations, and I knew that failure would reflect adversely on him where it counted: in the Party.

"Can either of us accomplish what they can not?" I asked.

"If we can not we do not deserve the power we reach for!" He gestured with his pool cue. "Let me make you a little challenge, señor, to test our mettle as captains against each other. I will take one issue, you the other. Let us see who is the better politician."

"Agreed," I said. "Shall we play for the choice of issues?"

"Indeed! Tanamo and sugar, winner's choice."

So we played, and he won; he could beat me in pool when he chose. "Sugar," he said, smiling grimly.

I sighed. "You took the sweet one, Comrade!" But we both knew that both issues were intractable, and that both of us were more likely to fail than to succeed. But we both had much to gain by success.

Khukov put in a word to Saturn, and I to Jupiter. The essence of each was that he wished to arbitrate the sugar issue, and I the Tanamo issue, in nonbinding fashion. We would make recommendations for the governments of Ganymede and Jupiter to approve. Saturn, theoretically having no direct interest in either case, would stand aside. Of course, Saturn hoped to gain a naval base and lose the liability of the sugar trade if we succeeded, and to lose nothing if we failed; it was easy for Saturn to be gracious.

"What the hell are you up to this time, Hubris?" President Kenson demanded privately after summoning me to New Wash for an emergency conference.

"Sir, isn't the cessation of the shipment of Saturnine arms to our sphere via Ganymede worth the discontinuance of a Naval base whose maintenance on a hostile planet is costing us more than we like? Haven't we been looking for a graceful way to cut our losses—just as Saturn wants to cut its sugar losses?"

He pondered. "Why should we assume those sugar losses—which are more than monetary—ourselves?"

"No need," I said. "If you don't like the proposal Captain Khukov makes, turn it down."

He stroked his chin. "Yes, of course. But I do not want to

be forced to turn down *your* proposal. That would look bad. But we can't risk that base going to Saturn."

"It won't, sir. It will be useless to Saturn."

"Hubris, you were a Navy man. So was I. You've got to know better than that."

"Sir, I was in longer than you were. As a Navy man I know what I am talking about. Let me explain."

"Captain, you had better," he said grimly. He quirked a smile. "Show me your power."

He had invoked the old Navy challenge. I obliged. His jaw dropped. "I didn't know that!"

"Few civilians do, sir, and few officers without the need to know. That's why the bureaucrats on the negotiation team are stymied. As a commander in battle I had to know."

"Let me check this out, Hubris." He reached for his phone.

In moments he had confirmation from our own military staff. "Idiots!" he swore, referring to those on the committee who had not researched this information. Then he turned to me. "I think you're a damned genius, Hubris. You're due for promotion. I can give you an embassy that will thrill your wife."

"Thank you, sir, but I prefer to make my own way."

"Oh?"

"I plan to run for governor of Sunshine again."

He squinted at me. "Exactly where are you headed, Hubris?"

I glanced around his office meaningfully.

"Oho! You've already caught that virus!" He had won reelection handily the year before and could not run again; the nomination would be open. "Well, I'll not interfere. Certainly you'll have my support for governor. Go to it, Captain!" He shook my hand and dimissed me. He didn't take my ambition seriously; he was patronizing me. But his magnetism was such that I appreciated even that. And his support for my upcoming gubernatorial race would be invaluable.

The trip to Jupiter enabled me to stop by Ybor, consult with Spirit, and spend a night with Megan. She confessed that she missed me, and that, having become accustomed to family life, she felt distinctly awkward without it, though she did have Hopie. She was most affectionate, and the night was a delight. It was also wonderful for me to see Hopie again. I hoped to return to Jupiter in a few months, and now I felt more urgent than ever about it. Perhaps separation does make the heart grow fonder—or maybe it simply forces a person to realize what he is missing.

"I have a gift for you," the premier informed me by phone. "Are you free to come here tonight?"

The ambassador could hardly *not* be free to visit the premier at his behest, but I knew it was more than that. "Certainly," I agreed. "But it is not necessary to promise me any gift. In fact, my position requires that I decline all—"

"This one you can not decline," he said smugly. "It is my thanks for what you did for Raul."

"But I was glad to—"

"A woman."

This grew more awkward by the moment. "Premier, I am a married man!"

He smiled on the screen, full of some secret. "This one you will take into your house, I am sure. She is in need of rehabilitation. I will expect you tonight." He cut off, leaving me in a quandary. What would Megan think if such a woman even came near the embassy? Yet I could not openly insult the premier by failing to make the appearance.

I pondered. There had been something about his attitude. On the one hand, he enjoyed serving me as I had served him on the first occasion, forcing the social visit and the display of his autistic child. But there was more. The premier knew I loved Megan and knew she had returned to Jupiter because of the child, not because of any marital falling-out. He was a family man himself, and no supporter of adultery. He really believed I would be pleasantly surprised. Maybe he had found a superior cook for the embassy, though we had no problem there. Still . . .

"Would you like one of us to chaperon you?" Shelia inquired mischievously.

"Go spin your wheels by the Wall!" I retorted. We had become so acclimatized to our residence that the dread execution wall had become a thing of humor.

"I'll go find a blindfold," she said contritely, and rolled her chair away.

It was a minor exchange, but it served to remind me how well off I was. Shelia could never walk or dance, so probably would never marry, though she was physically capable of conceiving and bearing a baby. Her tragedy was mountainous compared to mine, yet she always appeared cheerful and was certainly competent. Here I was chafing because my wife was away for a few months, and I might have to deal with a new cook.

Still not entirely at ease, I made the required appearance.

There was a woman there, all right. She seemed to be in her mid-forties, perhaps older, and not in the best of health. I could tell by her bones that she had once been beautiful, but physical and emotional toil had broken her down. Rehabilitation? What she needed was some joy of existence.

She looked at me. Slowly her eyes widened. "Hope?"

Then I recognized her. "Faith!" I cried, stepping forward to take her in my arms, my eyes stinging with tears.

For this was my older sister, whom I had not seen in more than a quarter of a century. She had been taken away by pirates when I was fifteen, and I had not been sure she was even alive, and had been afraid to inquire. In retrospect I condemn this cowardice of mine. I might have rescued her from many years of drudgery had I searched her out. But, of course, it was more complicated than that; it was not merely the fact of losing her, but the manner of it that had caused me to tune her out of my life as if she were already dead.

I took her back to the embassy, of course. The premier smiled as we left, putting his arm around the shoulder of his son, who was much improved. "*Now* I think we are even," he said. Surely he was correct; he had returned a lost family member to me, in exchange for the one I had helped return to him. Such private obligations can be very important to Hispanics and perhaps to others, too.

I introduced Faith to my staff, and they welcomed her. I think they were as relieved and gratified as I at the way this had turned out. I did not try to pry into my sister's history, for it was nothing she was eager to share in any detail, but I did pick up an approximation.

Faith had volunteered herself to become the plaything of a ship of men, in order to prevent them from robbing and raping the other women of our refugee bubble. It had been a gallant sacrifice on her part but had not been successful. I had to advise her, as gently as I could, of the fate of the rest of the refugees. As far as I knew, only she and Spirit and I survived. At age eighteen Faith had been a stunning beauty, with fair hair and a form that caught every eye; in fact, it had been that form that precipitated the problem that led to our flight from Callisto, for men would not leave her alone. She had gone to the ship from our bubble, and it seemed she had been passed from man to man and from ship to ship to ship for some time—some years—until that life took its toll on her beauty. Finally she had been traded to a Europan merchant ship for supplies, and in due course carried to the home port, where she had become the creature of the dome. As she lost her sexual appeal she had had to do other chores, becoming a workwoman, maid, or cook—whatever was required. In short, she had been reduced to a peasant woman, and so she remained. All the expense our father had put into Faith's education had been wasted, as had Faith's phenomenal initial beauty. But she had survived, when a woman of more pride would have been cast out. She had earned a reasonably secure place by tutoring children of the better families in English. "I became very good at that," she said wryly. "It was certainly better work than . . ." She shrugged.

"I will take you with me to Jupiter," I told her. "Spirit is there."

"Spirit!" she exclaimed. "I remember her as a child of twelve, with a finger-whip!"

"She still has a whip," I said, smiling. "But she is no longer a child. She is a woman of forty, her face is scarred where she was burned by a drive unit, and she is without a finger." Spirit had never sought corrective surgery for either condition. It made no difference to me, but it may have been one reason she never married on Jupiter. Yet in the Navy Spirit had proven her ability to capture any man she chose, so I really don't know.

"What could I do at Jupiter?" Faith asked wearily. "My life is past."

"I will find something," I promised. "You will never suffer privation again."

She smiled. "You were my protector, then." She meant when we were teenagers. Indeed, it had been my job to shield her from unwelcome attentions—a job at which I had signally failed. Perhaps it had been, in part, that guilt that had prevented me from seeking her. The premier had done for me what I should have done for myself.

I became her protector again, trying to make up for that long neglect. I arranged for the paperwork to grant her entry to Jupiter as a resident alien, for she lacked the citizenship Spirit and I had obtained via the Navy. I saw that she was fed well and that she did not feel threatened. Well, in that I may be overstating the case; it was my tight little staff that did the job; they adopted her as they would a foundling. And, like a late-blooming flower, she became healthier and more cheerful, beginning to suggest the creature she once had been.

As yet I had no notion as to what position I would find for her at Jupiter. Well, she could become part of my staff until a suitable situation offered. Spirit would surely have input. Faith was bilingual, and that was a genuine advantage in the state of Sunshine. In fact, there was a shortage of bilingual teachers, but I wasn't sure she would be interested in that type of employment, now that she was free of bondage. Surely she had memories that were best forgotten.

Meanwhile, it was good to have her with me. She helped fill the gap in my life made by the absence of Spirit, Megan, and Hopie. Women have always been important to me; I relate well to them and suffer in their absence, especially when they are my kin.

I had the essence of my solution to the Tanamo problem already, but Khukov took three months to study the sugar issue, researching every aspect, talking with all parties, including representatives of the Jupiter business community involved in the handling and processing of the commodity and the Latin nations now providing it. He was hampered by having to use an interpreter, for he concealed his new knowledge of Spanish. Perhaps he was taking his time for that reason: to offer no clue to any other party that he had means to grasp the essence much more rapidly than was evident. But he researched in English, too; he even asked to talk with the chief procurement officer of the Jupiter Navy. I suspect he learned much more about the Navy than he did about sugar. But I kept my counsel and even helped him by introducing him to Admiral Phist, my friend and the husband of my former wife Roulette.

"Beware of that Saturnine," Phist advised me privately after the interview, which took place physically at Tanamo. "He is one sharp officer. He reminds me oddly of someone—" I met his gaze. Suddenly he laughed. "Of course!" Then he sobered. "But that makes him doubly dangerous."

"Not if I get where I'm going," I said. "I understand him."

Phist shook his head. "You know I'll serve you loyally if you do, and I'm not the only one. The careers of the officers in your unit did not end when you resigned from the Navy."

Phist typically understated things. I was sure my friends in the Navy now had a good deal more power than showed. "Give my regards to your wife."

"Rue is a good woman," he said seriously. "It is unfortunate that she and I both love others."

"Still?" I asked, surprised.

"Still. But we do have a good marriage."

"I'm glad to hear it." I found myself flattered, for myself and for Spirit, for we had been the prior spouses of both parties of that marriage. Navy associations were something that civilians did not understand. Civilians tend to think that sexual fidelity is the most important aspect of a marriage; those in military service know that the heart can travel an independent course. I shook hands with Phist and departed.

At last Khukov was ready. We set it up for an interplanetary broadcast: two proposals to be presented sequentially. Of course, the concerned governments would not rule on them immediately, but it would be a fine show. If our proposals failed, the issues would die—and with them the hopes of two captains for advancement.

Khukov presented his proposal first. In essence, it was this: Do not interfere with existing sugar quotas at all. Let the Jupiter government purchase a set quantity of sugar from Ganymede at a set price and use it for the Navy. Not necessarily for its own consumption, though there was an enormous demand for sugar to use in reconstituted foods and beverages. For trade elsewhere in the System. "The problem of hunger is endemic," he concluded. "The food exists but cannot be economically distributed to the needy. The Jupiter Navy, however, makes routine training missions everywhere. Cost of transport on such a mission would be minimal." He smiled. "The trainees could think of the cargo as weapons. It would be a fairly simple matter to trade sugar at far-flung posts for raw materials, equipment, labor, or information, at a net saving to the Navy. Sugar is, in fact, currency in space; it becomes quite precious in regions where all food has to be imported. I believe the supply officers of the Jupiter Navy will verify that this is true."

And I, as a former officer, knew it was true. Sugar was used on isolated outposts to make potable alcohol, among other things, and that greatly enhanced its practical value. If the Navy had a lot of sugar to trade it could make a lot of good trades. Whether this could be done at a profit was uncertain, but certainly the initial cost of the sugar would be largely offset by such use, and morale would improve.

"In return for the reopening of a valued market and the economic stability this would contribute to the planet of Ganymede," Khukov continued, "and as a simple gesture of amity, certain personnel will be permitted to emigrate in a disciplined manner. The list of names is too long for me to present on this occasion, but it will be released to the media. Here are a few examples." And he read a dozen names, all of which, I knew, were of notorious political prisoners that Jupiter had tried without success to get released before. It was more than a "gesture of amity"; it was a striking counter-offer. The impact of those names would affect Jupiter society like the detonation of a black hole: the seemingly impossible abruptly made real. I knew then that President Kenson could not afford to turn down this offer; Khukov had sweetened the pot too much. The sugar trade would resume.

Now it was my turn. "If Jupiter vacates the Naval base at Tanamo, neither Ganymede nor Saturn will feel further need to supply military equipment to powers in the Jupiter sphere," I said, knowing that this was a concession Jupiter was desperate for. "There has been some concern that the base might be abused, but this is needless. The equipment there is military, not civilian, and is therefore locked against unauthorized use. To use any of it, from the largest space dock to the smallest water dispenser, one must have the proper key. Without that key the entire base is little more than a metal monument. It is, of course, mined; use of an incorrect key or an attempt to force the equipment will trigger detonation."

I paused to glance at my audience, though there was only the holo-camera. "One might suppose that the keys can merely be passed on to the new personnel. This is not the case. Each key is a magnetic pattern, a portion of which is tuned to the specific individual authorized to use it; if any other person attempts to use that key, it is inoperative. Key and operator go together, and naturally the key-keepers are carefully selected and trained. When a keeper changes, a new key has to be made, and the lock revamped to accommodate the new pattern. This adjustment is complex; in fact, it requires the presence of very sophisticated equipment. Such equipment exists only at Jupiter and Saturn; no one else can change the locks or keys. The equipment must be brought to the base along with specially trained personnel for this delicate operation."

I paused again. I wanted to be sure this got through to the average viewer. I had had to get special permission to reveal this information, and I wanted to do it exactly right. "Obviously the base will have to be operated by its present key personnel, regardless of the sovereignty of the facility. I'm sure suitable arrangements can be made. Now let's suppose that some power like Saturn wishes to change the locks and keys and personnel, for its own purposes. Do you suppose the present personnel will acquiesce? Will they operate the gates to admit and facilitate the equipment and personnel employed to effect their replacement? The lock-changing equipment is bulky; it can be transported only by a sizable vessel, and Ganymede lacks port facilities elsewhere to accommodate such vessels." Once more I paused. "In short, the little pig is not about to open the door to let in the wolf—or the bear."

That was the essence. Saturn could not change those locks covertly. Jupiter personnel would operate the base for the benefit of Ganymede alone, and facilitate its use as a commercial port for the shipment of sugar and such. I believed that my proposal would be approved, disappointing as it might be to Saturn; it was definitely advantageous for Ganymede.

Khukov came to me and shook my hand. "I rather thought it would be that," he said in English. "May all our problems admit of such ready solutions."

Thereafter he returned to Saturn, his job done, and I made plans for Jupiter and reunion with my family. I could not claim I had enjoyed all of my experience on Gany, but certainly it had provided me more than it cost me, including a planetary spotlight that would enhance my future as a politician. For one thing it had returned to me my long-lost sister—an event more significant for my peace of mind than I had allowed myself to believe before the event.

Chapter 10
CONFESSION

Now I knew I could help Dorian Gray; a simple personal request to the premier of Ganymede would produce that baby in hours. Dorian must have known this; that was why she had been so ready to enlist my aid. My captors might not choose to honor their promise, but I, Hope Hubris, the former ambassador to Ganymede, would certainly honor *my* promise. I had become a better bet for Dorian's purpose than my captors were. Suddenly it all fell into place, and I believed I could trust her. True, she might be covering all bases, ready to collect from my captors if they prevailed, and from me if I prevailed, but she would probably elect to go with me if she could. That was a comfort to me, because I suspected I would have to tell her more of my memories than I had hitherto, if I was to make further progress. And I did have to make progress, for I didn't know how much time I had or what my captors really wanted of me. I only knew I had to thwart their plans, and I couldn't do that if I didn't know enough.

In due course I was released from the cell, cleaned up, and taken to Scar. "If I may inquire," I said cautiously, "in what way did I transgress this time? I had not intended to."

"You play the innocent with me?" Scar demanded curtly. "Confess your crime and I'll let it go without further ado."

Was he fishing for something? I gave him the minimum, hoping that was what he wanted. "Then you found out how I escaped my cell at night."

He nodded. "How long did you think you could fool us about that, Hubris?"

Of course, he had known about it all along, so this was merely a pretext. But I had to play it through, relieved

197

that my true secrets had not been exposed. There was no evidence that Dorian had betrayed me; certainly they would not have punished me openly if she had, for that would have given her away. Why had Scar chosen this time to brace me with this?

"I didn't tell you because I knew you'd stop it," I said with genuine regret. It was not for the discovery but because now he would surely have to cut off my contact with Dorian, to maintain appearances, and I did indeed value that contact. "My only female companionship. I hoped she wouldn't turn me in."

"She didn't," he said.

"Don't punish her!" I exclaimed with suitable feeling. "She didn't start it! I used a plumbing rod to jimmy the doors—it was so hard to be alone."

"Evidently she felt the same way," he said grimly. "We put her back in the stink-cell too, but she hasn't talked."

"Let her out!" I pleaded. "I won't do it anymore. Maybe she didn't dare say anything for fear I'd get out again and attack her!"

"You seem quite interested in the slut's welfare," he remarked with satisfaction.

"She's no slut!" I protested, showing exactly that commitment he wished.

"You like her so well?"

I spread my hands as if caught in an awkward admission. "She . . . gave me comfort."

"Considerably more than comfort!" he exclaimed with righteous indignation.

"Please, just tell me what you want, and I'll give you no trouble. Only don't hurt her anymore."

Scar grimaced, but he was well pleased. I was giving every evidence of the very sort of attachment he had wanted. It seemed that the woman was now an excellent lever on me.

"I'll do better than that," he decided. "I'll put you in a cell together, as long as you both cooperate completely."

I gaped, showing my amazement at his generosity. He had, indeed, surprised me. This was definitely the carrot instead of the stick. I had been careful to maintain the pretense of increasing addiction to the beverage-drug, so now he believed he had another excellent lever on me.

Dorian Gray was moved into my cell, and the plumbing was fixed so that escape from the cell was no longer possible. Now we had light and saw each other for the first time.

She was exactly as beautiful as I had judged. Her hair was jet-black and hung in gently curving hanks to her armpits. Her face was elfin, but her body was as finely formed as any could be without requiring an entry to starlet career. Surely she had no need of this sort of employment. But, of course, folk of either sex can be foolish in their teens and get themselves trapped in situations that greater experience would have enabled them to avoid. Dorian, by her own account, had been as foolish as any.

"They found out," I said somewhat awkwardly. "So they put us together, but if either of us fail to cooperate with their program completely—"

"I know," she agreed. Then she moved to me, and I took her in my arms. "I did not tell on you; I don't know how they found out." She raised her lips to kiss me, and her tongue darted through to caress mine, twice. Of course, she knew how they knew; we were being watched now!

We undressed and squeezed into my hammock, not turning off the light. Actually we couldn't; the day/night switching was automatic. That didn't bother me; it was a treat to handle her body when I could see it.

"That pit-cell was awful; I hated it in there again," she told me as she signaled "no." I understood; she was supposed to be their agent, hiding the truth from me. She would hardly be punished for doing what she was supposed to do. Naturally she had been reporting on our encounters all along—up to a point. Now she was supposed to make me believe she had suffered, to intensify my sympathy and feeling for her.

I responded as I was supposed to. "I dread the thought of your being put in there because of me! After this, anything they ask you to do, do without question; it's the only way."

"The only way," she agreed, kissing me again and tonguing me twice.

As we proceeded toward the love act, discovering it to be a new experience in the light, she informed me by words and signals what had really happened. There had been a sudden visit by an officer not in the know about the program here, so that they had had to scramble to make things appear routine. I had been dumped out of sight, and she had been put in a uniform and put to work again in the galley. After the officer left things had returned to normal, except that they had had to cobble up a pretext for my apparent punishment. It seemed to have worked out all right. Scar had tricked me into confessing, so that he did not have to reveal his connivance. It had also shown how effectively Dorian had hooked me; Scar was pleased with her.

"But you know," she said in un-talk. "You *are* married, Hope. When your memory catches up—"

"I know," I agreed in the same way.

"You know?"

I had decided to tell her part of my secret, because I was sure I would need her help to return to the smell-cell, and I wanted to be sure she remained in good repute as a spy. "I discovered a key term that triggered a segment of my lost memory: how I married Megan."

"A key term?" She was genuinely surprised. "You knew—before you made love to me?"

"I knew. I, too, am a professional."

She was abruptly angry. "How *could* you!" I was lucky she hadn't bitten me instead of tonguing me!

"I love her. I would do anything to return to her, just as you would do to recover your baby."

She considered that, shaken. "I suppose turnabout is fair. But you will help me if you can?"

"Yes. And now I know I can—if I get free of this captivity."

"Then I will do whatever you ask of me."

We continued on to the culmination, for such coded discourse took time, and there was only so much seemingly idle dialogue we could indulge in without arousing suspicion. Then we slept.

I had implied that I had no real feeling for Dorian, but that was not true. I was doing what I was doing with her because I had to, but I did enjoy it on its own level. It was becoming more difficult to reconcile this with my memories.

Next day I went through the routine indoctrination and performed well. Next night I talked further with Dorian, not making love but spending the night in her embrace. I told her that she would have to betray my secret: my keyed memory.

I cupped her ear with my hands and whispered directly into that enclosure: nonsense syllables that would seem to the recording mike like not-quite-distinguishable information. I was officially telling her my secret, and my captors, when they reviewed this portion of the record, would be desperate to know what it was. She would tell them and thus prove herself to be even more useful to them. But she had yet to find out exactly where I had seen the key term, though the implication was that it was in this cell.

In return I needed to know exactly what my captors really wanted of me. She would have to ask them, in the guise of discovering how dangerous my returning memories might be to their objective. If she could get me that information I might have a chance to counter it.

She made her report—and suddenly I was back in the hole. This time I knew why: They were going over my regular cell with as fine a brush as possible. They were desperate to find and eliminate anything that would cause my memories to return prematurely. That confirmed a suspicion I had. Their mission for me involved something recent, and if I remembered that thing I would probably be able to counter it.

Why didn't they simply mem-wash me again? That, too, was now clear: they didn't have time. I needed to have a substantial portion of my memories so that I could function without obvious incapacity—without the key memory that would give me too much information. They were fine-tuning me for their purpose.

As much by luck as by planning, I had a tool to counter their program. I had the memory-evoking key terms.

I felt under the muck for the scratches, finding my place. I had gotten to the H in WHO before; now I had to resume there. WHO ENTER HERE. The symbol for the O-space was a square, □ . That was the number 5. Count off five in the mental alphabet, O, P, Q, R, S—the first letter was S. The next symbol was ⌊⚬ , 12 from the space after O. That took me through the punctuation portion and back to the beginning of the alphabet, A. Then ⌐⟩ , 16, counting from the E, to T. And ⊓ , 8 from the N, to U. Then ⌐⚬ , 36 from the T—simply count back 2, for R. ⌟ , 10 from the E, or N. And ⌟ , again, 10 from the R, taking me to the end of the letters, the space, making the end.

The word was SATURN.

Chapter 11

PARDON

I returned to Jupiter a hero, again. This time my campaign for governor brought larger crowds than before. I was better known because of my prior campaign and my Gany success, and, of course, many people remembered my reputation from the Navy. In the interim the current governor had fouled things up in the usual manner, catering too openly to the special interests who had gotten him into office. He was running for reelection, so had the power of incumbency, but he was not otherwise a strong candidate. He saw me draw ahead of him in the polls, so he went the dirty route: smearing me as a Hispanic, a dealer with Saturnists, and a killer of hundreds. All true, of course, but it backfired, because the Sunshine electorate understood the circumstances and objected to the smear attempt. Angry Hispanics started a registration drive and added many thousands of voters; on election day their weight was felt in Ami and especially in Ybor. I won, not by any landslide, but comfortably enough, and I still had not succumbed to the lure of special-interest money.

As governor I had a lot more power and a lot more responsibility, and things were more complicated than they had been when I had been a senator. From the outset I received threatening letters from anti-Hispanic bigots who called me un-Jupiterian, by what logic I am uncertain. To my way of thinking the bigots are the un-Jupiterian ones. Coral had to keep alert, and she did intercept a letter bomb.

I started immediately, setting up committees to formulate the reforms I had in mind. But I discovered that I could not simply institute a program and implement it; I had to reckon with the legislature and the bureaucracy. Resistance to any change I initiated was indirect but massive—a political coriolis force that blunted every effort. As an officer in the Navy I had become accustomed to determining policy for my unit, giving the necessary orders, and seeing them carried out. Here, none of it was straightforward. After my first year in office I considered what I had accomplished in the way of monetary reform, improved education, prison reform, and suppression of the burgeoning trade in illicit drugs, and shook my head in frustration. Hardly anything seemed to have changed. The present system simply wasn't geared for change of any kind; it was like wading through molasses. Certainly I had made thrusts in all these areas and hoped that success would come, but it had not yet manifested itself.

As governor I also received a good deal of mail. Most of it Shelia handled, summarizing it efficiently for me, but some required my personal attention. Sometimes seemingly minor things developed into major ones. One example was the missive from Mrs. Burton:

Dear Governor Hubris:
I am seventy-four years old, a widow, in pretty good health. My stipend isn't really enough, and, anyway, I'd rather be a productive citizen. I am a competent stage technician, conversant with most technical equipment currently in use for broadcasts, and my record is good. But no one will hire me because of my age. Governor, I call this age discrimination, and I wish you would do something about it. A lot of us older people are ready, willing, and able to contribute to the economy—if you will let us.

I pondered for about three seconds. "Shelia, draft up a policy memo for signature: There shall be no discrimination in Sunshine on account of age. Anybody who can pass the tests and perform the job shall be considered on an equal basis, beginning with Mrs. Burton. We'll make an example of her; if she's as competent as she says she is I'll hire her myself."

In two days we had Mrs. Burton in my office. She was a large, heavyset woman of grandmotherly aspect; her hair was gray, her skin mottled, and her hands gnarled. But she checked out personally, and she did know her stuff; we used her to set up the stage for any public addresses I made, and my performance did improve as the result of her expertise. Now the sonic pickup was always aimed and tuned correctly, so that my voice sounded authoritative, and the light always brought out my best profile. The lectern was the right height for me and the seat comfortable. I felt quite at home in a setting that she had worked on, and that was worth a lot.

She became a kind of handywoman on the off days, seeing to the repair of furniture and furnishings. I liked to relax on occasion by reading old-fashioned books, the kind where you turn the pages by hand, but they tended to pile up awkwardly near my chair or desk. Mrs. Burton constructed a little bookcase that solved the problem.

Hopie took to her right away, adopting her as a grandmother figure. It would be an exaggeration to suggest that I could not have functioned without Mrs. Burton, but certainly she earned her keep and was a worthwhile associate.

But for every letter that worked out positively, there were a number that did not. I simply was unable to solve the personal and economic problems of every person in the state.

Rather than detail the tedious minutiae of my frustrated efforts, I'll concentrate instead on the matters in which I was successful. Perhaps this is my human vanity manifesting itself, but success did not necessarily assuage my vanity. Early in my tenure trouble broke out in the Ami area. Here there was a large number of immigrants from Ganymede who had arrived over the course of the past twenty years as the economic situation of Gany worsened. They had formed a fairly cohesive community of their own, which was taking hold and doing well, but in the eyes of the Saxon majority they were shiftless louts. Since the police were mostly Saxons, some law enforcement seemed to have racial undertones.

On this occasion the precipitant was bilingual education. The sizable Hispanic minority wished to have school classes taught in Spanish as well as English, so that the children who spoke no English would not be at a disadvantage. The school system had refused, once more, and so another riot had broken out. These events made the headlines periodically. The police tended to be heavy-handed. Sometimes there were serious confrontations, with deaths occurring.

I, as the newly elected Hispanic governor, felt more than ordinary responsibility, because it was partly because of my election that the Hispanic community had made the issue at this time. The people felt that a Hispanic governor should set all things right for Hispanics. But my margin of victory had come from enlightened Saxons, who had taken the gamble that I would be evenhanded, not partisan, while having a mollifying effect on the minority elements. I did not want to disappoint them.

Politically I could not give the Hispanics what they wanted, even if it had been in my power as governor to declare it as fiat. In addition, I believed they were wrong. Thus the Hispanics didn't have, in me, the ally they supposed. How great would be their sense of betrayal when they discovered this?

I tackled the matter directly, as I wanted the rioting stopped. It was my impression that there was a rising tide of violence throughout Jupiter, as the economic situation slowly constricted; I hoped to ameliorate it in Sunshine. I made arrangements to appear in the center of the rioting district in the heart of the Hispanic section of Ami, in the park above their apartments. Technicians and Mrs. Burton set up an amplification system, and the event was announced on the Hispanic news service. It was short notice—only hours—because I wanted to stop the riot *now*, not after several days and much damage. Knowing the problem with the local police, whether genuine or perceived—expectations can be self-fulfilling—I asked the mayor of Ami to keep the police away. It would be just my party present: myself, Spirit, and Faith. My staff remained in Hassee, Hopie was in school, and Megan remained to supervise her; I couldn't take my family everywhere I went as governor. I wasn't worried about violence; a Hispanic governor was the one person these people would not hurt.

"I have a job for you," I told Faith as we traveled. "A teaching job, teaching English to Hispanics, but not as you have known it. For this you will be paid by the state of Sunshine—I have cleared this with the appropriate authorities—and you must assume administrative authority."

"Teaching English I can do," she said. "But I've never—"

"You will be assigned a competent staff," I said. "All you will have to do is verify that applicants are truly bilingual and that they are able to teach children or adults without antagonizing them."

"But don't you have professionals to do that sort of thing? You can't just put another relative on the state payroll. That's nepotism!"

"In this case it must be a relative," I said. "You must be in charge, no one else. You will see."

She shrugged. "You always knew what you were doing better than I did," she said. "I hope you know this time."

"He does," Spirit said.

Despite the short notice, the crowd was enormous. They were really interested in this, expecting good news. Well, I had to do what I had to do.

"All I ask is that you give me a fair hearing," I began, speaking in Spanish. "The same kind of hearing you want for yourselves. I have not come to tell you what you want to hear. I have come to tell you the truth. Listen to me and try to understand, for I do have your interests at heart, and not just because I happen to be of your number."

They were quiet, for never before had a governor come to talk to them directly, let alone in Spanish. Now they *knew* I was one of them. There was a holo news crew, but I knew that not much would go out on the national tapes; only Hispanics would understand it, unless they used subtitles or a translation. The Hispanic Network crew was there, though, and they would certainly broadcast it.

"You want your schools to be bilingual," I continued. "So your children will not be penalized for being what they are. But this is folly." There was a stir, but I moved on. "Listen to me! I am a refugee myself; only I and my two sisters survived our bubble-trip to Jupiter. It took two of us fifteen years to get citizenship, and the third doesn't have it yet." I indicated Faith. "She's a resident alien, like many of you. We know, we understand! But my child is in a Saxon school with Saxon teachers; she has no classes in Spanish. When she was in Ganymede, her classes were all in Spanish, because that is the language there, as perhaps you remember." There was a murmur of mirth; of course they remembered. "She had to learn, to become bilingual herself. Now she's back in Jupiter, and English is the language, so she speaks it."

I bore down on my point. "When in Rome, you do as the Romans do; you don't try to make the Romans learn your language, you learn theirs. If you don't care to do that, you don't stay in Rome. Now you live on Jupiter, which resembles Rome in certain ways. Certainly it is as strong and arrogant as Rome was." There was an understanding laugh. "You want to make a good life here, of course. But it will not be given to you on a platter; you have to earn it. In fact, you may have to wrest it from reluctant hands, as I had to." There was another laugh; they were with me. I was playing this crowd the way I play an individual, reading it as I spoke, tuning in on its affinities. "This is the planet of free enterprise; you are entitled to what you can get. As long as you stay within the law. As long as you pay your taxes." I grimaced and was rewarded by another laugh. "But to do this *you must speak Jupiter's language!* It is the only way to break your bonds of ignorance and isolation and make it in this society."

Now there was a muttering. I overrode it. "Listen to me! If you had schools taught in Spanish, do you know what this would lead to? It would lead to the ghetto! You would be locked into your closed society and your children would be locked in because you did not speak the language of opportunity. You would have in the end a completely separate school system. Do you know what that means? Do you? The Blacks can tell you. It means inferior schools that lock your children into an inferior place in the society. The Blacks fought for integration, to share the Saxon schools. You must fight for it, too! You must make them educate you exactly the same as Saxon children are educated—the same standards, the same teachers, the same language—so that when your children go out to compete for the best jobs, no Saxon is better qualified than they are. Only then will your children be able to achieve a better place in Jupiter than you have now." I paused. "How many votes do you think I would have gotten for governor if I had campaigned in Spanish?"

There was another ripple of laughter. They knew I would have lost again, if I hadn't courted the Saxon vote. That helped make my point. "You can't persuade a man of anything unless you speak his language. Don't let yourselves be ghettoized," I concluded. "Insist on your right to learn English so that the entire spectrum of opportunity available in Jupiter is yours. You know your children will never learn English well if they can have their classes in Spanish. They wouldn't go to school at all if they didn't have to. You can't afford to have their education governed by that. It isn't easy, but it has to be done—so that every child will have the same opportunity I have had. To hold office, even to become governor!"

"But we don't have good teachers for English!" someone protested.

"That we can remedy," I said. "My sister Faith will help you learn English."

They were silent, not quite understanding this. But I acted, seizing the moment. I stepped forward to where a woman stood with her little boy of about six. "*Señora,* my child is not here," I said in Spanish. "May I borrow yours? For only a few minutes?"

She gazed at me nervously. "What will you do, Don Hope?"

"I will teach him English," I explained. I knew, somehow, that this child spoke no English, and neither did his mother; it was the nature of this audience. "My sister and I will teach him."

Reluctantly she turned the child's hand over to mine. "What is your name, *señor?*" I asked him formally.

"Pedro," he replied shyly.

"Very well, Pedro. Come here by the pickup. You know what it is?"

He shook his head in negation.

"It is what makes my voice loud," I explained. "Listen." I leaned toward the pickup and said "Loud." And the word blasted from the speakers around the park: *Fuerte!*

The boy stepped back, impressed, looking around. The crowd waited and watched, curious to learn what I was up to.

"Now, Pedro," I said, reassuring him with a smile as I read his willingness to respond. "I will teach you a word in

English. It is the word for what you need to survive in the society of Jupiter, to help yourself and your mother. You want to help your mother?"

"*Si,*" he agreed.

"The word is *power,*" I said, pronouncing it carefully in English. "Pow-er."

"¿Pow'r?"

"POW-er."

"Powr," he mumbled.

"Ah, but you must say it as if you mean it," I told him. "Loud. *Power!*"

"Pow'r," he said with greater volume, recovering the second syllable.

"Here where they can hear you," I said, guiding him to the pickup.

"*Pow'r!*" he cried, getting into the feel of it, and this time the speakers roared it back, startling him again.

"Yes, that's your voice," I told him. "Say it again. Make them answer you."

"*Pow'r! Pow'r!*" he cried gleefully into the amplification.

I gestured to the crowd. "Power! Power!" they called back, catching on. Many of them may not have understood English, either, but they were onto this one.

Then it became a chant, child and crowd speaking to each other responsively. "Pow'r! *Power!* Pow'r! *Power!*"

"The power of language!" I cried into the pickup, overriding the chant. "*Make* them teach you! Keep your own language, your own heritage—it is a fine one, no shame there—but know theirs, too, so you can do what I have done. It's a hard course, but it leads to victory. Power! Power! Power!"

The chant became deafening as they all joined in.

After a minute that shook the park I spoke again. "Remember this woman!" I cried. "My sister, Faith Hubris, flesh of my flesh! She will teach you! She will find more teachers, so all of you can learn! Those of you who are already bilingual, come to her and she will hire you to teach your people. This is the true beginning of power!"

They looked at Faith, who stood somewhat in awe of this cynosure. But she was a fine figure of a woman of that age, and her familial resemblance to me was evident, and these were definite assets.

"If you are unsatisfied, tell her, and she will tell me. She is my sister; I must listen to her!" And they laughed, knowing how it is with sisters. "She will do it the way I would do it. It will be as if I am among you. I am with you in my heart, but you know I must keep my eye on those Saxons in Hassee!"

They cheered. They liked the notion of a Hispanic governor supervising the Saxon legislature. They would accept my sister in lieu of me. They knew how strong the Hispanic family bonds are. I had given them the closest possible representative.

Spirit and I made ready to go. Faith remained, talking with those who spoke Spanish and English, proving that she knew both languages well. Already the bilingual Hispanics were approaching her. She was the center of attention, in a way she had not been since her years of youth and beauty.

As Spirit and I got into our car, waving good-bye to little Pedro, we heard the chant starting up again. Only this one sounded more like "Hubris! Hubris! Hubris!"

I may misremember, but I don't believe the Hispanic community of Ami ever rioted again while I was governor. Their problems remained, but now they were working on the solution. And Faith had found her mission in life.

Thorley, of course, had a different view:

And so the quixotic Hispanic, fresh into the problems of gubernatorial policy, has absconded with another coup: He has dazzled his folk of South Sunshine into quiescence with the proposition that their problems will somehow evanesce if only they learn to speak another tongue. In the process he has, with the legerdemain of the true politician, installed his sister on the state payroll and made the state like it. The man is certainly a master of his trade. One wonders what sleight of hand he will accomplish next. Without question he is a compelling orator; it has been mooted that the sound of the chant "Hubris! Hubris!" resounds throughout the Latin quarter of the city of Ami like the erstwhile refrain of "Heil! Heil!" in the Germanic segment of Uranus. If this man Hubris had ambition, he would be dangerous.

I can't say that I appreciate all of Thorley's notions, but I can appreciate his way with words. If I am, as he terms it, a compelling orator, he is a compelling journalist. He always knew what I was up to almost before I did, which surely facilitated his expertise. How prettily he remarked on my ambition!

The matter of Ami did not end here, for Faith led me into an event of greater consequence. She did her job well, and soon there were very few critics of my nepotism, for it was evident to most Saxons that Ami was quiet because the governor's sister was looking out for its minority interests, and not only those of the Hispanics. Faith made reports regularly from the ghotto, as she chose to put it, and it was manifest that the somewhat shallow and self-centered girl I had known as a child had become quite another person in the course of her travails in space. I soon got a composite picture of the true problems of Ami, ranging from petty discrimination to brutal murder. I did what I could to alleviate the problems, but it was only a token; the governor has less impact than the local authorities. But one matter did fall squarely into my bailiwick.

It seemed that during my absence from Jupiter, while I was ambassador to Ganymede, there had been a serious riot in Ami, this one in the Black community, where unemployment was chronically high. Police had charged a demonstration in a club-wielding phalanx; there had been an explosion, and several policemen had died. The due process of law had wended its tedious way, and now four Blacks were on death row, as it was called, their appeals denied, and they were due to be executed within a month. It was the prevailing sentiment of the Black community that the men were innocent or at least were guilty of a lesser crime than murder and that had they been Saxon they would have gotten off with lesser sentences or even have been freed for lack of evidence. There had been sporadic demonstrations; now, Faith assured me privately, if the executions proceeded as scheduled, there would be a blowout such as the city had not seen in a decade. I needed to act.

I investigated. I researched the literature of the case, consulted with legal experts, and went to death row to interview the four men directly. My conclusion was that they had indeed been condemned unfairly. Whether they were guilty or innocent I could not tell, but that was not the point; I was convinced that, based on the evidence presented at their trial, *no* one could have established either their guilt or innocence. Since, in a criminal case, it was necessary to establish guilt beyond a reasonable doubt, that meant they should have been acquitted. Why hadn't that happened? Because, apparently, the prosecutor had been savagely effective, a veritable tiger, while the counsel for the defense had been inadequate. The police had needed an example to prove their effectiveness as law enforcers; the state had wanted a demonstration of power to cow future rioters; and the men were Black. The specter of a dual system of justice loomed before me; these men would indeed have been acquitted had they been Saxon. This was clearly a miscarriage of justice.

So I exercised my prerogative as governor and pardoned the four men. Within hours of my decision they were free.

I had suspected that there would be mixed reaction to my act; Megan had warned me. But I had underestimated its ferocity. There was a storm of protest. The Saxon media condemned me with seeming unanimity. They claimed I was setting criminals loose on the street to pillage and kill again with impunity. None of them seemed to pay any attention to the facts of the case. I was amazed and chagrined; it seemed the Jupiter press really did not care about justice, whatever it might claim.

Furthermore, neither did the people. Regular polls were published; my popularity had been hovering at about seventy percent, but after the pardon it dropped to forty. Were I up for reelection at this point, I would lose.

I was shocked. It had never seriously occurred to me that the majority of the media and people could turn their attention away from the plain facts and policies of Jupiter and condemn a man on ignorance. Yet, as Spirit reminded me, they had done exactly that in condemning the accused bombers. I really should not have been surprised. But my disillusionment hurt.

"There is always a racist element," Megan said. "As a Hispanic person in power you are subject to suspicion. They do not like to be openly racist, so they focus on other issues. Had you been Saxon, the reaction would not have been this strong. Had you been Black, it would have been stronger. Now they have a pretext to condemn you, but the well-spring is deeper."

And, of course, Thorley had the last word:

Sometimes I despair for my profession. Governor Hubris has been widely praised in the past for being wrong. Now he is being condemned for being right. I do not for a moment condone the release of murderers, and I do not share the governor's predilection to leniency, and I do suspect that the four accused bombers were guilty as charged, but the case against them was not tight. That provided our liberal governor with the pretext to nullify the conviction. Don't blame him for being what he is; you knew that when you so foolishly elected him. Blame instead the inept authorities who could have made a tight case against the bombers, and should have, yet who carelessly flubbed it. Next time, do it properly. Don't provide the bleeding hearts with the tiniest crevice to insert their wedges for the overturning of justice.

Then the news of the hour moved on and the furor subsided. Slowly my popularity revived, until it nudged back above fifty percent, but it never recovered its former health. I had learned a cynical political lesson. Like a military commander who first experiences the carnage of battle, I had been blooded.

I stood for the things I stood for, but never again would I believe that the voters did. Their love was superficial. Perhaps they deserved the type of politician they usually got.

I had pardoned the four bombers, but I would not pardon the fickleness of the electorate.

Chapter 12

SATURN

When I was two years along in my governorship, President Kenson's second term expired and his party put up an inadequate candidate for the office. The precession of politics can tilt it into the promotion of imperfection, with the reaction seemingly at right angles to the force applied. The candidate favored by the party regulars is not necessarily the one favored by the majority of the electorate, and neither of these may be best for the actual office. As a result the opposition party won, and their standard-bearer was Tocsin, Megan's nemesis, who had lost to Kenson before. His second try, like mine for governor, had proved successful, and now he was president.

It did not take Jupiter long to feel his nature; the special interests were flourishing, and programs for the disadvantaged were being drastically cut back. Tocsin had railed against the bleeding-heart liberalism of his predecessor, equating it with Saturnism. He had promised to bring monetary discipline to the planet, along with good old-fashioned law and order. The results of these thrusts, which, of course, did not apply to the wealthy or the special interests, were increasing separation between the rich and the poor, erosion of the broad middle class, and various forms of rebellion. Violence had been increasing over the years, as my direct experience had shown; now it magnified. Strikes and demonstrations abounded, and there were more—and more savage—riots. Everywhere except the state of Sunshine. For reasons that remained somehow obscure to the conservative commentators of the planetary scene, the Hispanic and Black neighborhoods of Sunshine were comparatively quiet.

It was not coincidence, of course. We had bypassed irrelevant state requirements and certified more language teachers in the past two years than any state had ever done in a similar period before. We had freed more prisoners. There had been dire predictions of a wave of crime, but no such wave had manifested. We did not coddle true criminals; we just made sure of their nature before we put them away. The state of Sunshine also now had more female appointees than ever before; all we required for any office was competence, and Spirit handled the details. Thus Sunshine was becoming an island of quiet in a nation that was moving the other way.

Elsewhere in the Solar System, things were also intensifying. Tension was rising everywhere, so I realized that it could not be blamed simply on the policies of one government, tempting as that might be. Assassination was becoming a leading device for political change. Bombs were going off at embassies, and citizens of the southern nations of Jupiter were being "disappeared" at an alarming rate. I liked none of this, but there was little I could do about it.

Suddenly a portion of that situation changed. A small interplanetary passenger-ship line that operated between the moons of Jupiter and the moons of Saturn had had a problem: One of its ships that had been headed for Titan had somehow drifted off course and passed through restricted Saturn-space. The Saturnines had tracked it, fired on it, and holed it. All its crew and passengers were dead. It included fifty Jupiter citizens, eight of which were residents of Sunshine, and one of whom was a representative from a Sunshine district. That made it my business. The representative had been conservative, opposing my policies; it didn't matter. As governor I had a responsibility to all residents of Sunshine.

There was a national hullabaloo, of course: cries of outrage, angry denunciations, demands for action. "The Saturnines aren't like us!" pontificants exclaimed. "This proves it! Those beasts like to hole unarmed passenger ships!" I knew it couldn't be that simple, but I was angry, too. But what could I do? President Tocsin raged against Saturn in a special news conference and promised appropriate action but did nothing.

A message from Faith in Ami heightened my dilemma. "Two Sunshine Hispanics were on that ship. The folk of this community are asking when you will recover their bodies for proper burial."

Recover the bodies? A fantasy! The ship was in a decaying orbit around Saturn, and only the Saturnines could get at it. Yet my people expected me to act when the president could not.

"You know, Hope—" Spirit murmured thoughtfully.

"But it's crazy!" I protested, though she had not actually .oiced the thought.

"Yet, correctly played . . ."

I knew what she meant. There was a daring opportunity here. "Still, it could mean my life."

She put her hand on mine. "Our lives."

I sighed. It was time to be a hero again.

"You're crazy, sir," Shelia exclaimed when I told her what I wanted arranged. But she got to work on it.

"I cannot go there," Coral protested. "They would—"

"They would treat you the same way the authorities of Callisto would treat me if I went there," I agreed. "Don't worry; you will remain here with my staff, for this." I understood about the special problems of refugees, being one myself.

We chartered a yacht, a sleek and swift civilian ship with a competent crew. I made sure that her captain knew the nature of my project, so he could turn it down if he chose. He paled but accepted. "It's time someone did something like this, sir," he said.

I told Megan and Hopie, of course, expecting them to condemn this as idiocy. Indeed, Megan did: "You're going to Saturn? Hope, this is preposterous!"

"I want to go, too!" Hopie exclaimed, clapping her hands. She was eleven now, and already she reminded me hauntingly of Spirit at that age. Perhaps all little girls are somewhat alike, or maybe it's my foolish fancy.

"You will do nothing of the kind!" Megan exclaimed, horrified. "This thing is suicide!"

Hopie frowned. "You mean Daddy's supposed to go alone?"

Megan turned away, wounded. Children lack the subtlety of adults, and their innocent words can cut like lasers.

"Of course, she should stay with you," I told Megan quickly

Megan turned back to face me. "We'll both go," she said shortly.

Hopie jumped up and down. "Oh, goody! I'll do a school paper on it!"

Megan had decided that if I was determined to risk my death in space, she would accompany me. The stories on the entertainment holo imply that only young love is self-sacrificing; they err. I would give my life for Megan, and she for me. This is not to suggest that we don't have differences on occasion. This trip was an example of both unity and difference.

We wasted no time. We issued no public statement, but naturally Thorley knew. He phoned me.

"Governor, is this an official excursion?" he asked, his familiar face looking supremely relaxed on the screen. I have never been certain just how he manages that atmosphere; certainly he is most dangerous when seeming least attentive.

"It . . . will be," I answered guardedly. I didn't want any advance notice in the media but knew that what the governor did was, almost by definition, public business.

"Then you cannot bar the press."

I nodded grimly. I had not anticipated this. Even an innocent remark in the media, prematurely, could ruin the effort.

"I will be there in two hours," he said.

"*You?* Thorley, this may be dangerous!"

"And the supreme news event of the month," he said.

He had courage; I had never doubted that. "As you wish. But if that news gets out before we take off—"

"Credit this old conservative with some modicum of discretion, Governor," he said smoothly, and faded out.

Discretion? That, too, he possessed in considerable measure. He was my perpetual gadfly and annoyance, but he was no yellow journalist.

We set out for Saturn. When we were safely in space, my staff in Hassee issued the press release that announced my intention. I was going to Saturn to recover the bodies of Sunshine citizens, demand an apology, and obtain reparations.

The reaction, as it was relayed to us, was explosive. We had time to catch it all, as we were accelerating initially at 1.5 gee, then easing off to free-fall, spin-ship, and the settling in for a ten-day journey.

First, there was a cheer from the Hispanic community that we almost thought we could hear directly: *"Viva!"* Second, there was a media headline: HUBRIS DOES IT AGAIN! That meant that I was making another ass of myself, tilting at another windmill. Third, President Tocsin hit the phone.

We received his signal, coded for privacy. "What the hell do you think you're doing, Hubris?" he demanded, his jowls working. In that moment he sounded just like Kenson. Presidents of any party or philosophy cannot stand to have their prerogatives infringed. But what I owed Tocsin was rather different from what I owed Kenson.

"Mr. President, I am doing my duty by my constituents," I said, pleased to see him so angry. This was an incidental benefit.

"You have no business dabbling in interplanetary matters!" he exlaimed with some justice.

"When those whose business it is, renege on their responsibilities, it becomes necessary for others to take up the slack," I said smugly.

I had hoped to provoke him. I succeeded beyond my expectations. "You shithead spic," he swore. "Turn back or I'll blast your ass out of space!"

He was bluffing. He could indeed order my ship to be downed, but such an act would carry a horrendous political penalty, for the people of Jupiter were overwhelmingly with me on this matter. Presidents, like governors, are highly attuned to popular reaction. "You do your duty as you see fit, Mr. President," I said calmly. "I will do mine."

"I'm going to see you hung by the balls for treason, Hubris," he snarled, his face mottling red as he cut off.

"At least I've got them, Mr. President," I muttered under my breath to the blank screen, smiling. What a naughty pleasure this was! I had hated Tocsin since I learned of what he had done to Megan.

Megan stepped into the communications chamber. "I wish you hadn't done that, Hope."

I gazed at her levelly. "That man destroyed you politically. I will destroy him."

"And become just like him?"

That shook me. It wasn't that I believed it could happen, but I saw that she did. She really disliked hard-nosed politics. "I married you so that you could make sure I never go that route," I reminded her.

"I only hope I have the power." But she smiled, forgiving me, and I kissed her. She would never confess it openly, but she had to have felt some illicit satisfaction in my treatment of her nemesis Tocsin. That is about as much as I care to say on that. If I do not go into much detail on my private relations with Megan, it is not because they are unimportant to me. Rather, it is that I have no wish to perhaps demean them by setting them to crude paper. Megan was always a very private person, personally, and I respect that.

"I'll try not to bait Tocsin anymore," I promised her.

And, of course, Thorley sent his dispatch from the yacht. It was remarkably gentle to me, almost suggesting that the notorious Hubris might for once have done something of which he could approve. Certainly he would not have complimented me merely because I had permitted him to come on the major news scoop of the month.

Why all the fuss? One would almost suspect that the errant governor of the Great State of Sunshine had pardoned someone. Doesn't it make perfect sense to challenge the Saturnines on their home turf when they have done something slightly more than routinely reprehensible? *Somebody* has to, as it were, pick up the pieces.

Yet, of course, there was the chance that we would become pieces ourselves, for Saturn was no gentle power. Why was Thorley putting his own life on the line along with that of the governor, whose liberal policies he deplored? I didn't need to ask, for my talent brought me understanding. Thorley had a nose for significance; that was *his* talent. He liked to get close to the truth, whatever it might be, so that he could shape it into his image. Indeed, in his hands the truth could assume an entirely new aspect. He also knew well the value of publicity; his career could profit handsomely from this exploit.

And there was something else, deeper and more important than any other motivation, that would never be mentioned, that did him credit of a sort. But I think it is not my business to pass judgment on that. Thorley, like Megan, deserves the privacy of his deepest heart.

We ate and slept and ate again, and set the ship's time for Saturn time, which differed from Jupiter's by several hours. The days passed. No Jupiter ship came after us, and Tocsin made no public statement about my excursion. But he could not prevent the media from doing so, and they had a ball with it. An open planetary raffle was set up, to guess the day that Thorley would be put out the lock without a suit; naturally it was presumed that we were fighting tooth and nail. There were innovative and at times offcolor skits broadcast, in which the actors portrayed Critic and Governor and spewed out invective at each other while the ship headed for collision with a planetoid.

But Thorley, as I had learned early, was in person a most engaging companion; he kept his politics out of polite conversation. He joined us for meals and made a fourth for games of old-fashioned cards, teaming with Spirit against Megan and me, and his smooth wit made him a delight. He also taught Hopie to play chess, which he claimed was a game of royalty.

"You seem like such a nice man," Hopie told him. "Why are you always so mean to my father?"

Thorley laughed, as if this were rare wit. "It is my profession, child. I do to public figures metaphorically what your father does to them politically."

Megan and Spirit and I, theoretically engaged in our separate pursuits at that moment, paused to listen without interfering. There was more to this than was evident.

"Is it true you saved his life?" she asked with her typical directness.

Thorley smiled. "That might be an exaggeration. It is true there was an incident some time ago."

"And you got lasered instead of him?"

He shrugged. "It could be put that way. Actually I believe it was your mother the man was aiming at, as a target of opportunity."

"Back before I was born?"

"Prehistoric," he agreed wryly. "So the matter need not concern you Hopie, if I may address you so familiarly."

"So if it wasn't for you, I wouldn't exist."

Thorley knew what she had for the moment forgotten: that Hopie was an adopted child. But he did not remind her of that. "It is certainly possible."

"So I suppose I can't hate you, even if you deserve it."

"I would be distressed to have you hate me, Hopie, however deserving of the sentiment I may be."

"Then will you stop writing those mean things?"

Thorley spread his hands. "I can no more change my nature than your father can change his."

Surprisingly she smiled. "Well, at least you are honest."

He smiled back. "I fear I may not merit such an accolade. Let's just say I am consistent."

"Okay." She returned her attention to the chess game. She was doing well, there, for Thorley had spotted her the queen, both castles, a bishop, and a knight. There seemed to be a savage battle among pawns in progress.

I glanced about and caught Spirit and Megan exchanging a glance. It was as if a necessary hurdle had been navigated.

In due course we approached Saturn. This planet has, of course, always been known for its phenomenal ring system; indeed, there was a period in the history of man when it was believed that Saturn was the only planet to possess rings. Now it is known that all planets and a number of moons possess rings, albeit sometimes of insignificant scope. But those of Saturn are truly in a class by themselves, and all of us were fascinated as the details became clearer. First the eye perceived the archaically named A, B, C, and D rings, with the Encke, Cassini, and Guerin divisions. Then the rest of it came clear, for the total ring system is enormous, extending out some eight times the radius of the planet, and fading only as a matter of diminishing returns. We knew that the rings were inhabited by refugees from the former government of South Saturn, who had had to exchange embassies when Jupiter did the same with Ganymede. That gave me a certain feeling of identity, irrelevant as it was. We also knew that on one tiny moonlet, hardly more than a large ring-particle, was an isolated colony of Uranus' moon Titania, one of the diminishing vestiges of the Titanian Empire that had once spanned portions of the entire Solar System. Thus, in physics and politics, the rings of Saturn were a microcosm of System history.

As we came within local communication range—that is, close enough to allow conversation without significant pauses for transition—we were hailed by a cruiser of the Saturn Navy. "Jupiter ship, you are intruding on private space. Turn back immediately."

I took the screen. "I am Governor Hubris of the state of Sunshine of the United States of Jupiter Planet," I replied in English. "I am coming to claim what belongs to my state and my planet."

"You are intruding on Saturn space," the officer repeated firmly. "Turn back. We are giving adequate warning."

I stared him in the eye. "Please state your rank and identity. We are rebroadcasting this exchange to Jupiter for use by the uncensored news media and wish to give credit where it is due."

That did not seem to faze him. "If you do not turn we shall fire on you," the officer said.

"I am sure that will make excellent news," I said. "I am Governor Hope Hubris, and the members of my party are my wife Megan, my sister Spirit, my daughter Hopie, and the correspondent Thorley. The others are ship personnel who need not concern you; only we five will make planetfall at Saturn."

"We are firing one warning shot," the officer said.

Indeed, the in-ship report came immediately: "Laser beam at twelve o'clock."

"Saturn does seem to be competent at holing unarmed ships," I reminded the officer.

Suddenly the screen went blank. "Bluff successful," Thorley remarked laconically.

"Even the Saturnines do not knowingly shoot down a governor," I said.

"But they did hole that passenger ship."

I only smiled. The truth was, I was not completely certain of my position. Even a peaceful bear, when stung, can strike, and Saturn was not noticeably peaceful. But I believed the odds were strongly in my favor. The Saturnines had known we were coming from the time we left Jupiter; had they really intended to blast us, they would have done so well before this. We were indulging in a pose, a ritual confrontation. Meanwhile, our ship continued toward the planet unmolested.

Two hours later we were signaled again. "Governor Hubris," a new officer said. "Please adjust course for orbit at Ring Station; a shuttle will convey your party to Scow."

"Understood," I said. This was victory indeed, for Scow was the capital bubble of North Saturn, the seat of government for the Union of Saturnine Republics. They were now accepting our visit.

"If you will pardon the curiosity of a political innocent," Thorley said with his special brand of irony, "what guarantees do you have against arrest and execution as a spy?"

"The Governor of Sunshine, former ambassador to the Independent Satellite of Ganymede?" I asked with similar innocence. "Our esteemed president would be forced to make an issue."

"And you have placed Tocsin in the same bind you have placed Saturn," he said. "However much he detests your intestines in private, Tocsin can not undermine you in public. This could precipitate Solar War Three."

"Oh, I doubt it will come to that," I said in an offhand manner.

He laughed. "One must admire your finesse, Governor, if not your politics. To make the Eagle and the Bear waltz to your tune involuntarily."

"Finesse does have its compensations," I agreed.

"Still, I want to advise you in advance that I will be most perturbed if this leads to my obliteration in SW III."

"I will take your perturbation under advisement at that time."

"You characters would make light of Sol going nova tomorrow," Spirit muttered.

Thorley raised an eyebrow. "Indeed, there would be much light then!"

We decelerated and moved to the Ring Station, which was situated inside the orbit of the rings proper. We docked and our limited party transferred to the U.S.R. shuttle ship. The crew of our yacht would wait until we returned, confined to the ship. We were conducted by grim non-English-speaking troopers that made Hopie quite nervous; she stayed very close to Megan, hanging on to her hand. In due course we were in the giant bubble of Scow.

The adults were guarded about reactions, but now Hopie was thrilled. She had never before been to a city-bubble of this size. Of course, once we got into the internal labyrinth, it was difficult to distinguish it from any other, except for the Cyrillic printing on the signs.

We were ushered into a private chamber where three Saturnines sat behind a long table. One of them was Khukov. He stood up and leaned over the table to shake my hand. "Welcome to Saturn, Governor Hubris," he said in English.

"Good to meet you again, Admiral," I replied in the same language, noting his elevation in rank. His career was evidently proceeding apace.

"Please be seated, Governor Hubris—you and your party. We have much to discuss."

"Indeed we do, Admiral. Are you empowered to arrange for reparations?"

"What is he saying?" one of the others asked in Russian.

"He is demanding reparations," Khukov explained in that language.

"Reparations!" the man repeated indignantly. "Tell him we'll execute him and his disreputable party first!"

Khukov smiled at me graciously. "The Commissar wishes to reassure himself that your party is quite comfortable. He is eager to change your status if you are not."

I returned the smile. "Certainly, for the moment," I agreed. Then, in Spanish, I said to Spirit, "These characters haven't decided how to handle us."

"Then demand more than we can get, so we have a fallback position," she replied in Spanish.

"Now I am sure you are reasonable people," Khukov said in English. "You know we cannot make reparations!"

"Promise them a nice tour of the city," the Commissar muttered in Russian. "Him and his bastard child."

They didn't know that I knew Russian—or they were testing me. I was sure that Khukov had not told. I showed no comprehension. "Reparations and an apology—and the bodies," I said firmly in English.

"Everybody in the System knows his wife was already beyond bearing age when he married her," the third Saturnine remarked in Russian, chuckling. "She was a fool to adopt the spawn of his mistress."

"My companions are not sanguine about that," Khukov said. "You know it was a spy ship."

"You know your gunners got trigger-happy and shot down a civilian ship by accident," I retorted.

"And now the fools are locked into their error," Spirit said in Spanish.

Khukov glanced at her, nodding.

"He understands Spanish!" she hissed, alarmed.

"Now how could that be?" I asked her blandly.

She shook her head. "I don't know! But—"

"He speaks Spanish no more than I speak Russian," I told her, and turned to face Khukov. Thus did I advise him that I had not broken faith; I had not even informed my sister of our private deal.

I felt Spirit's eye on me. She was catching on now—to both parts of the deal. She made no further comment.

"Let us communicate as clearly as we can, in our circumstances," Khukov said to me in English. "Perhaps it is possible for planets as far apart as ours to achieve some compromise that will benefit both."

"One would hope so," I agreed.

"Naturally the loyal Saturn forces could not have made an error, even if the vessel did resemble in outline a type of Jupiter cruiser," he continued. "They holed a spy ship. It cannot be otherwise. Yet we concede the possibility that some civilians were aboard, and we bear no animosity toward those unfortunate victims of imperialist deceit."

"Then you will return our bodies to us," I said.

"As a gesture of goodwill by the magnanimous Union of Saturnine Republics—"

"And so forth," I agreed. "And the apology?"

"Apology!" the Commissar exclaimed in Russian, evidently picking up my meaning. "The foolish Jupiter lackey should apologize to us for smirching our space! Tell him to eat canine offal!"

"For abating the menace of the spy ship we should apologize?" Khukov asked me in English.

"Tell the Communist clown to go spy his own posterior,"

Spirit told me in Spanish, picking up the nature of this dialogue. Hopie stifled a giggle, and Megan frowned; she had learned enough of the language to grasp the insult.

"For mistaking a strayed civilian ship," I said in English, without hint of humor.

Khukov shrugged. "Suppose we apologize for underestimating the foolhardiness of your blundering attempt to spy on our planet?"

"Let's go on to reparations," I suggested.

"Reparations!" the Commissar exclaimed in Russian. "Let's just line the whole troupe up against the wall for trainee laser practice!"

"And trigger System War Three!" Khukov snapped back at him in Russian.

"Why? His own capitalist president ordered him to turn back, calling him a fecal-face!"

So they had intercepted that transmission, too. Tocsin's privacy coding had not been effective against the spy mechanism of the Saturnines.

"His president is the worst of the running dogs," Khukov replied. "Naturally he threw a fit when the governor refused to turn back, because it showed him up for the bumbling ass he is. We can best affront Tocsin by catering to Hubris."

Slowly the Commissar smiled. "True! True! It is the big poison we want to deal with, not the little one."

Poison—that was probably a play on the pronunciation of Tocsin as "toxin," though it could have derived from a confusion in translation. Certainly they didn't like Tocsin!

Khukov returned to me, in English, "The government of Saturn has deep concern for the common people of any planet. Perhaps we could provide funds to facilitate the proper burial of those who have been so far exploited by the capitalists that they lack the money to accomplish this themselves."

I nodded, accepting the pretext for the payment of money. This was more of a concession than I had expected; Khukov evidently had the real authority here. "For burial," I agreed.

He smiled grimly. "Your president will be pleased, no?"

Spirit, Megan, and even Hopie smiled, and Thorley coughed. The Commissar chuckled. All knew that Tocsin

would be privately furious at my success but would not
dare to disparage it openly.

Khukov and I shook hands formally, sealing the understanding. "And while we wait for the arrangements to be
complete, we shall give your party a welcome that will
please your president even more," he said.

Then I stood and shook hands with the Commissar.
"You are lucky, you imperialist cur," he said in Russian,
smiling broadly. "You should have been executed, and
your cuckolded wife and bastard child, too."

"And you irritate my penis, you ignorant double-dealing
pederastic Bolshevik," I returned in Spanish with just as
broad a smile.

Khukov almost visibly bit his tongue. "It is nice to over-
hear the exchange of such sincere remarks between supposed adversaries," he said in English. "I'm sure you hold
each other in similar esteem."

"Why do I get the feeling I'm missing something?"
Thorley murmured.

"You're not missing anything," Spirit returned darkly.

They gave us an official welcome that was more reminiscent of that accorded the head of a major planet than an
uninvited intruder. But, of course, they had to make it
seem as if this had been their idea; it was a matter of face.
There was a banquet with distinctly unproletarian trim-
mings. Megan and I were fêted at the head table with the
high-ranking dignitaries of the supposedly classless Saturn society, while Spirit and Thorley and Hopie had a
table with the ranking wives. There were translators to
render the remarks of the hosts into English. After that
there was—would you believe it?—a parade in our honor.
We rode under a massive, red, hammer-and-sickle banner
while the enormous crowd cheered. I was almost afraid
they would begin chanting "Hubris! Hubris!" but at least
we were spared that.

"Tocsin will be apoplectic," Spirit remarked, enjoying it.

"I fear I will never live this down," Thorley muttered,
but he didn't seem to be as unhappy as he might have
been. He would have an excellent story to write.

Hopie happily waved to the crowd.

In due course we returned to our yacht with a cargo of
four frozen Sunshine bodies that included the two Hispan-

ics and the representative. The rest would follow in a Saturn freighter. It would hardly have been possible to transport them all in proper condition in the yacht. We weighed anchor and put out to space with an escort of Saturnine Naval vessels.

Thorley got to work on his dispatches. Not eager to implicate himself in this ultraliberal connivance, he gave me all the discredit for this sally to Saturn. But, by whatever mischance, I had (he concluded) somehow managed to render my planet and president a signal service. It seemed that Thorley himself did not admire Tocsin personally and could not resist that particular needle.

Then the Saturn forces turned us loose for the long drift home. We played cards and board games to wile away the time, and debated the fine points of liberal versus conservative philosophy.

By the time we docked at Hassee I was notorious across the System, as the governor who had braved the Bear's jaws and won. For some reason there was little other than silence from the White Dome.

Chapter 13

IMPEACHMENT

But politics, even more than life, is a phenomenon of ups and downs. The day I set foot in Ybor after the Saturn excursion, I could perhaps have run for president and won. Six months later it was all I could do to avoid being lynched.

I should provide some background on my abrupt shift of status.

If there was one thing I intended to accomplish it was the elimination of the drug trade. Illicit, mind-modifying, addictive substances were pouring into the planet from the rest of the System and into the north from the south, and the state of Sunshine was perhaps the primary access point. The drugs were illegal, but that seemed only to make the trade more lucrative for the criminal element. In my time in the Navy I had acted to cut off the major middlemen of this trade, the Samoans pirate band, but like a hydra, the drug trade had sprouted new heads and seemed undiminished. Now I had opportunity to strike more directly, for the key to it was the market; cut off the market, and the supply will dwindle. A marketless product is doomed.

The prior efforts of the Sunshine enforcement agency had been sievelike, and it seemed to me that there had to be corruption. I intended to weed it out. I contacted Roulette Phist of the Belt—that is to say, Rue, my lovely onetime wife—and she used her connections to locate a crew of about fifty drug experts who were loaned to us. These were not the kind that pontificants on the physiology and psychology of addiction use as examples; these were men and women and children who could, in some cases, literally smell the drugs and who knew the sinister bypaths of distribution. I did not inquire how these folk had come by their expertise; I interviewed them only to verify that they intended to serve our interest faithfully. Some few I rejected, but in general Rue's selection was excellent; we quickly formed the most savvy drug-control team extant.

We put them to work first merely to identify the routes, not to close them. That was one reason why I seemed to have accomplished little in my first year in office; we were still in the developmental stage. I did not want another hydra experience; I wanted to kill the entire monster at one blow, when I finally did strike. The agents were instructed to accept any bribes offered and to report them privately, spending the money for themselves in ways that no ordinary enforcement agents would, so as to allay any suspicion. They enjoyed that part of it. For six months they infiltrated the delivery network of Sunshine, satisfying the professionals that business remained as usual; the new governor would not be any more effective at cutting the pipeline than any other had been.

Then we struck. We went after the personnel, not the drugs, and we got them. The line had been cut, and ninety percent of the drug flow ceased. Overnight.

Meanwhile, we had instituted another program: DeTox. This was intended to wean the clients away from the criminal sources. We had been confiscating illicit drug shipments all along, as we intercepted them; that was standard, but everyone knew that only twenty percent of the total flow was tapped that way, and the drug moguls simply increased the flow to compensate. In fact, news of the drug busts kept the consumers scared and therefore willing to pay higher prices. Thus the busts were actually good for business. The drug movers made more money than they lost, as a result of the busts; this was a fact that the law-enforcement agencies had taken centuries to catch on to. At any rate, we did not destroy the drugs we intercepted; we set up secret laboratories to test and refine them, and built up stores of high-quality stuff. We let it be known that this was available on the gray market; addicts could buy from us cheaper than from the criminal network.

We kept a legal crew operating full-time to cover our legal traces, knowing that others would not understand. Thorley, of course, got wind of it and blew the whistle;

there was an immediate fuss that died out after a few days, the net effect of which was to alert any addicts who had not yet gotten the news that this competitive source of supply was available. Thorley hammered away at us periodically, when other news was scarce, asking pointed questions we did not answer—and steadily our business increased. My political enemies, from Tocsin on down, were silent, hoping that all I needed was enough rope to hang myself. In that, perhaps, they were correct.

Then we cut the line, and abruptly there was very little available on the criminal circuit. Prices skyrocketed. Suddenly the addicts came to us in swarms. All a person had to do was identify himself, take his dose at our station, and pay for it. If he had no money we would trade for information. We were rapidly acquiring a comprehensive file of reasonably reliable tips to supplement what our other team was bringing in; we cross-referenced it constantly and cut off those who gave us false leads.

Naturally the hydra's heads sprouted again, but this time we were watching. Our moles traced the new lines as they developed. It was harder for the dealers, because now they had serious competition for clients and could not jack up their prices. Not only were Sunshine prices lower, but quality was higher and reliability much better. The greater part of the market was now ours. In due course we struck again at the illegals and wiped them out—again.

I had become a successful drug mogul, but my heart was pure. I knew it was necessary first to extirpate the criminal connection; then we could deal effectively with the problem of individual drug abuse. The cries of outrage sponsored by Thorley's exposés diminished; increasingly the authorities elsewhere on the planet were watching us. It seemed that we now had the most effective drug-control program on Jupiter. True, there were serious legal and ethical questions about our operation. But we obtained our merchandise free, by seizing it from the competition, and our operational costs were covered by the fees we charged our clients. Our books were on public record; our program cost the taxpayer nothing. Crime was dropping, partly because we now knew who the criminals were, and partly because they no longer had as much incentive to commit crime. About half of all crime in the state had been related to the drug trade; that was no longer so. Some dealers turned themselves in, plea-bargaining for their drugs; we imprisoned them for their crimes but provided them with their doses in prison. One might have thought that such people would consider that to be no bargain, but it seemed that they considered themselves better off than they had been outside. On the street illicit dealers were now killing each other for increased shares of the diminishing market; we offered safety.

We also did try to detoxify and rehabilitate them, with their consent (which was not forced), by shifting them to related drugs that were less addictive and/or damaging. It was not possible to cure a true addict, but he could be weaned to a milder, cheaper, and safer drug. Price, health, and legitimacy—these were powerful inducements.

All this took time, but in three years we had reduced crime in Sunshine to its lowest rate in the past century, and several other states were instituting similar programs. The legal complications were ameliorating; law does tend to become pragmatic about success. It was evident that we were winning the battle against drugs *and* crime. Obviously the criminal element had to do something about this or it would be finished. Therein lay our mistake: we underestimated the will and ability of the hydra to strike back.

Spirit and I should have known, for we had been combat officers in the Navy. But we had been seventeen years in civilian life, which was longer than our military tenure, and perhaps we had gotten soft. We were fighting pirates as savagely as we had in the Navy, but it didn't seem the same. One gets jaded, and reflexes relax. Maybe this was a lesson we needed, savage as it turned out to be.

Their strike was as swift and thorough as one of our drug-line cuts but had an element of subtlety that was a masterstroke. They did not go after the police or the program personnel; they went after me.

It started, for me, when one of our tame addicts blew the whistle—he claimed—on the biggest secret of my administration: a massive payoff by the drug moguls. "I was a courier for the money," he said. "I took it from the laundry in Ami and brought it to Hassee every week."

He was interviewed, live, anonymously, by a reporter

for *Post Times,* a major newsfax that did not favor us. "How much money?"

"A lot. Governors don't come cheap. Twenty-five super-gees a week."

"Twenty-five whats?"

"Super-grands."

"Oh. So this has nothing to do with gravity, other than being an extremely grave charge." The interviewer chuckled, but the whistle blower stared at him as if he were an idiot. "And a super-grand is—"

The courier adjusted visibly to the ignorance of the uninitiated. "A grand is a thousand dollars. A super-grand is a grand of grands."

"A thousand thousands? One million dollars?"

"You got it."

"A *week?*"

"Twenty-five a week," the courier explained patiently.

"Twenty-five million dollars a week?" The reporter seemed dazed.

"That's what I said."

"How could you even carry such an amount?"

"Well, it's in gees, mostly. Thousand dollar bills. That's how it comes out of the laundry. Packs of a hundred—two hundred and fifty packs, split between two cases. It's a load, but mostly I just ride the train with it."

"The laundry?"

"The fence-bank who launders the money, so it can't be traced easy. Got to have a good laundry or the tax boys'd be on it."

"I see. And where does this . . . this twenty-five million dollars a week . . . where does it come from, ultimately?"

"The big boys down south. The drug wholesalers."

"The big criminal suppliers?"

"Right. They put it in the pipeline to the laundry, and I pick it up in Ami."

"In two suitcases," the interviewer said, getting it straight. "And you take it where?"

"To Hassee."

"The state capital. By regular commuter train?"

"Yeah. So I can keep the bags with me. I don't want to check 'em into no cargo hold."

"I see your point. And to whom do you deliver them?"

"A guy called Sancho."

"Sancho!" I exclaimed as I watched. "That can't be!"

"Who is Sancho?" the interviewer asked.

"Some spic who works for the governor's sister. That's all I know. Always wears gloves, has a scarred face. I think he's an illegal. Small guy, talks in a whisper."

"Sancho works for Spirit Hubris?"

"Yeah. Or maybe for the governor direct. I don't know. He's the one who takes the money, anyway. I don't give it to nobody but him."

"Does he give you a receipt?"

The courier burst out laughing.

"No receipt for illicit business," the interviewer said, nettled. "How do your employers know you really deliver it?"

"I'm alive, ain't I?"

"Oh. I presume that if it doesn't arrive complete, there'd be a complaint?"

"There'd be a laser beam in one ear and out the other. I'd never dare cheat; those boys play for keeps."

"Then why are you talking to me now?"

"I'm out of a job."

"They fired you? But if you didn't cheat—"

"My face was getting familiar. A courier's shelf life is only a few weeks, then he's got to be replaced. Before the narcs catch on."

"Then you knew it was a temporary job."

"Yeah. But I was supposed to get a good settlement. All that money to the governor, and they couldn't spare a measly one s-gee for me."

"You expected a—a bonus for good performance? Of one super-grand? So you're blowing the whistle?"

"Yeah. It's risky, but it's a matter of principle."

"I see. What does this Sancho do with the money?"

"Takes it into a warehouse. After that, I don't know. I'd guess the gov's saving it, you know, for retirement."

"Twenty-five million dollars? Some retirement!"

"Yeah. I'd settle for that."

"And this is just one week's payment? How long has this been going on?"

"Ever since the big drug-bust program started. I've only been on it the past six weeks, but they've been coming to that warehouse maybe five, six months, and I don't know where else before that."

"But at twenty-five million dollars a week, for five months, that would be a good half a billion dollars!"

"Yeah. It's one sweet racket."

I shook my head. There was nothing to this, of course. I was not on the take. But why should someone broadcast such a claim, knowing it would almost immediately be refuted? One thing was certain: Sancho had taken no money from anyone, for anything. I didn't even need to ask Spirit about that; I *knew*.

But there was a considerable stir about the exposé. The State Senate demanded information, and the courier provided it. He solemnly led a newscrew to the warehouse where he said he had turned over the money.

By this time Spirit was with me. We sat back and watched the vid-cast. Our personnel had instructions to cooperate completely with the investigation; we had nothing to hide, and indeed were curious as to the outcome of this charade.

It was indeed one of our warehouses, used for storing campaign literature. Much of that literature would be useful again when I ran for reelection, so we had saved it, to keep our campaign budget as low as possible. Nothing incriminating there.

They opened the door, entered, and checked around inside. A search warrant was required for this, but I had waived it; I wanted them to search it.

There, hidden under piled campaign posters, was an enormous pile of money. Packs of thousand-dollar bills, hundreds of them, thousands of them!

The police took over the building, confiscating the money as evidence. In a few days the count was official: approximately half a billion dollars in used bills, there in my warehouse, just as the courier had said.

Too late we realized the truth; it was a frame. They had planted the money there, then planted the "courier," and suddenly I was in trouble. It *was* my warehouse, and the money *was* there.

Meanwhile, other reporters were seeking the other end of the chain, interviewing the drug moguls of the nations to the south. Surprisingly those hidden figures confirmed the payoffs: they claimed that I had put such a squeeze on their operations that they had had to come to terms to stay in business. True, very little of their commodity was sold in Sunshine now, so as to maintain appearances, but the state remained the major pipeline for delivery to other regions of North Jupiter. These deliveries were permitted to continue, as long as the graft was paid. "He's got a choke hold on us," one mogul admitted. "We've got to pay."

"But you can't market your product in Sunshine?"

"We make up the difference in the other states."

Thus, it seemed, Sunshine was simply passing its problem on to the other states. The crackdown was mostly for show.

That was enough for the State Legislature. A bill of impeachment was introduced and debated, and somehow it sailed through with phenomenal velocity. Objections were brushed aside or voted down by bloc—and therein was another pattern. A narrow majority was held by the members of a coalition formed of the more conservative members of my own party and those of President Tocsin's party. It was evident that Tocsin, perceiving an opportunity, had issued a private directive, and they were obeying with partisan discipline. This was his chance to, as he had put it during my trip to Saturn, see me hung by the balls. It hardly mattered what the facts were; the opposition was determined to see to my undoing. I, it seemed, had been fool enough to provide them an opening.

Megan seemed almost resigned. "I had just begun to believe that that man would not succeed in getting you as he got me," she said sadly. She meant Tocsin, of course. "It can be very hard for an honest person to anticipate the deviousness of one like him."

The Senate voted, and just like that, I was impeached, found guilty, and removed from office.

All this hurt, of course, but my attention was distracted by more immediate concerns. A grand jury had been formed to investigate me, with an eye to arranging for criminal prosecution. I could, all too soon, find myself in prison. But what really upset me was the demolition of my reputation. Why was no one ready to believe the truth? I had been a hero; now I was a criminal in the eyes of the public. I had been shaken and disgusted by the adverse reaction to the pardon earlier; now I was shaken and disgusted and angry. I was determined to do something about it.

I used my own connections to ferret out the agents of the plot against me. Specifically, I called QYV. That nefarious organization had caused me trouble in space, but was now more or less on my side.

I didn't even have to explain. My call was answered by Reba. She was older than she had been, her hair graying, but, of course, that could be camouflage. I got the impression that she had been rising through her echelons just as Khukov had been doing through his and I had through mine—until recently.

"It's about time you called," she said severely. "You made the perhaps fatal error of losing your paranoia and allowing the conspirators to catch you."

"I'll try to be more paranoid henceforth," I said humbly.

"It's a frame, of course," she continued. "Tocsin made a deal with the drug moguls to eliminate a mutual enemy. But you can still prevail if you get the truth before the public."

"The public will assume I'm just trying to cover up my guilt," I said dispiritedly.

She smiled. "You merely need to use the appropriate avenue."

"Avenue?"

She sighed. "I'm really not supposed to give you advice, you know."

"But your career is hitched to mine, isn't it?" I asked her, knowing it was true. She was good at concealing her reactions but not good enough. "You gained some of your own objective when I cracked down on the drug trade in Sunshine, and you will gain more if I get into a position to extend that crackdown. You don't want to throw me away."

She grimaced. "Just remember who helped you when, Hubris."

"I have never had a problem with my memory."

"Send Sancho to Thorley." She clicked off.

I pondered that, and indeed the avenue became apparent. I talked to Spirit, and she nodded. "Why didn't *we* think of that?"

"We have not been devious enough," I said. "I realize this is a sacrifice for you, however."

"Not as great a sacrifice as your career," she said. "It may be time to retire Sancho, anyway; he has become a liability."

In due course Thorley's response appeared. He had, it seemed, interviewed Sancho, that mysterious figure. The key portion went like this:

"What is your identity?"

"I am Sancho." The figure was exactly as described by the courier: small, scarred face, gloves, and the speech in a hoarse whisper. Obviously a fugitive Hispanic.

"The one who accepted the money for Governor Hubris?"

"No! I never accepted any money from anyone."

"But the money was found in the warehouse that you—"

"No, *señor*. I was not there. I was elsewhere."

"Elsewhere? Where?"

"I cannot say."

"Will you appear before a grand jury or legislative committee and tell your story under oath?"

"No, *señor.*"

"Why not?"

"Because I have no existence here."

"No legal papers? No citizenship?"

"Sancho—he does not exist."

"Oh, a pseudonym! And if the person you really are is discovered—"

"Much trouble, *señor!* I must be secret."

Thorley turned to speak to the audience directly. "I agreed to interview Sancho anonymously; that is, to honor his privacy of identity. I shall not violate that pledge. I shall just say that I have satisfied myself that this is indeed Sancho, and that he has convinced me that he was elsewhere at the time he was reported to be accepting the payments for Governor Hubris. I believe that this portion of the charge against Governor Hubris is false."

The report was a news sensation. Thorley was obviously no fan of mine, and his reputation for integrity was impeccable. A wedge had been driven into the case against me, and that case was beginning to split.

There was a flurry of investigation into the matter, none

of which succeeded in locating Sancho, who seemed to have vaporized after the interview. No evidence was produced that Sancho had been in the vicinity of the critical warehouse in the past six months but also none that he *hadn't* been there. The drug moguls had chosen well, in implicating Sancho, because of his inability to exonerate himself.

Still, the interview helped. Analyses were done of the recorded image and voice of Sancho, his scarred face and gloved hands, and it was established that this was indeed he. Sancho had always operated in deep privacy, but he was not a ghost. There were scattered pictures of him, and there were people who had met him in passing. Stress analysis of his voice indicated that he was not lying. Thus the challenges to Thorley's presentation came to nothing, and it rapidly assumed the status of fact.

This, however, did not establish my innocence. I could have used some other intermediary who resembled Sancho, though no such personage was in evidence. The drug moguls insisted that Sancho *had* accepted the money and could not be exonerated unless he was physically interrogated. The opposition had a vested interest in maintaining the case against me. The money *had* been delivered to that warehouse, after all. So Sancho seemed halfway innocent, but I still seemed guilty. It was a perplexing situation.

We sent Sancho to Thorley again. Two weeks after the interview, Thorley followed up with a written column on the subject. I quote it here entire, because in retrospect I perceive it as the pivotal point in my career.

LET JUSTICE BE DONE

Thorley

I dislike, on principle, to involve myself personally in the events I analyze professionally. Nevertheless, on occasion this becomes necessary, and this is one such.

My relationship with Hope Hubris extends back fourteen years. I covered his first political candidacy, in the course of which I intercepted an attack directed against him and his family. I have been asked, since that event, why I bothered. I can only answer that it is possible for honest men to differ, and I do differ philosophically with Hubris, but I do not espouse assassination as a mode of politics. I do not doubt that. Hubris would have done the same for me. One reacts to a given circumstance as one must, and situations are not always of our choosing.

During that encounter Hubris promised me that never would he interfere with the freedom of the press. One might consider this to be irrelevant to the issue, but it is as important to me as my life. I do not suggest that Hubris would have been inclined to suppress the media, merely that he was thereafter committed to uphold the free dissemination of news at all times. He has been scrupulous in this regard and has denied the press no information that pertained to its legitimate interests. The press, I might add, has not treated him kindly in return. Were Hubris not a man of honor, the press might have found itself in less comfortable circumstance in the state of Sunshine; certainly other governors have had little difficulty circumventing the Sunshine Law that keeps public affairs open to the public that both press and government supposedly serve. When, as governor, Hubris traveled to Saturn, I asked to accompany him, as a representative of the press; he acquiesced with perfect courtesy throughout, though this can hardly have been his preference. He has also seen to it that I have had direct access to information concerning his activities. I have considered such news carefully and published what I have deemed relevant, without regard to his preferences or opinions. It is standard policy for politicians to blacklist the purveyors of critical views, but never has Hubris practiced this; the flow of information has continued unabated. Hope Hubris, however wrongheaded his political and social views may be, is a man of his word. For this, if nothing else, he is to be respected.

Now he stands accused of the single charge I cannot credit. I simply do not believe that Hubris ever deceived the electorate about his positions or actions, or accepted a political bribe. If he had done so he would have released it as news. It is therefore my thesis that the charge on which he was impeached is false and that he was wrongfully removed from office as governor of the state of Sunshine. It would have been proper to remove him in protest to his open political policies; but it is an abomination to do so on the basis of a lie.

I have more specific evidence of falsification of the evidence against Governor Hubris. It was stated that approximately half a billion dollars was paid to him by the agency of an employee of his sister Spirit Hubris, a mystery man named Sancho. Sancho claims that he did not act in this capacity. However, Sancho is not considered to be a reliable witness, because of his lack of identity. He refused to testify under oath and therefore was deemed suspect.

Now I happen to believe in the right of the individual to be free of government coercion. Therefore I protected Sancho's true identity, as it is also the duty of the fourth estate to honor the anonymity of private sources. But now, perceiving that no less an action will enable justice to be served, I have prevailed upon Sancho to make the requisite testimony and to reveal his identity to the public. In fact, I shall do it for him, and allow others to follow up this revelation as they may elect.

Sancho is in fact a disguise used for convenience by Spirit Hubris herself. It is not necessarily appropriate, even in these enlightened times, for an attractive woman of any age to travel widely alone, particularly when she is closely related to a prominent politician whose life has been threatened more than once. Therefore Spirit Hubris has assumed masculine guise, donning gloves with a stuffed left finger to conceal her deformity and removing the makeup she normally employs to mask the abrasions on her face. In this guise, as "Sancho," she has had no difficulty and has required no cumbersome protection; her complete anonymity has been her safeguard. Naturally she preferred not to have this revealed, because a cover blown is a cover useless. This clarifies why Sancho was mysterious and had no formal identity. He was not an illicit immigrant, merely a fictive connivance.

In this guise Spirit has on occasion provided me directly with pertinent information about her brother's activities. It was she who informed me of the governor's planned venture to Saturn—an expedition that for obvious reasons could not be publicly advertised in advance. When such conflicts between principle and expediency arise, Hope Hubris has compromised by informing me in this direct and private manner, trusting my discretion not to nullify a particular thrust by premature exposure. At times the line between legitimate news and counterproductive exposure becomes extremely fine. In this instance I took advantage of the knowledge to force my attendance on the Saturn sally, in this manner amplifying my eventual report.

It happens that my records indicate that on two of the occasions in which Sancho is supposed to have accepted money at the warehouse, he—that is, she—was present at my office, delivering information to me. I can therefore vouch from direct personal experience that the charge against Sancho—and therefore against Governor Hubris—was on these occasions unfounded. I have also verified that on several other occasions Spirit, herself, was attending public or business functions in other cities, so could not have been at the Hassee warehouse when the courier claims.

Now, simple logic suggests that if part of a statement is demonstrably false, all of it becomes suspect. Certainly the courier's rationale is questionable; it is nonsensical to suppose that he could "go public" about the covert activities of the drug moguls without being promptly and nastily dispatched, unless he was, in fact, acting on their orders. I submit for public consideration the supposition that the entire charge against Governor Hubris is false, and I invite challenge by independent parties. But for the moment let us assume that my case has been validated and that an innocent man has been impeached. Let us now consider motives.

Governor Hubris is dedicated to the extirpation of the trade in illicit drugs in the state of Sunshine. His method may be questionable, but his thrust is not. This is consistent with his actions as a former military man, wherein he destroyed the power of the pirates of the Belt, a power that had seemed immune from compromise before. His motive is readily understood; his family and associates were ravaged by pirates. Pirates raped his older sister and cut off the finger of the younger sister. Captain Hubris became this century's worst scourge of piracy in space; now he is going after the planetary aspect.

The major roots of piracy on Jupiter are the drug trade, the gambling trade, and the sex trade. Now, one might quibble at the particular target and mechanism—certainly I do—but may not seriously challenge Governor Hubris's motive or the fact that, whatever its philosophical merits, his program was the most effective one seen in decades. A true military man, he did what he felt he had to do to get the job done. He reduced the flow of drugs through Sunshine to a tiny fraction of its prior level and saw a concurrent decline in crime. One may object to the method, but who could object to the result?

Who but the criminals! The nether grapevine has it that Governor Hubris has been Enemy Number One on the planetary drug empire's list for two years. Could they bribe him to desist? Hardly! On this issue especially, Hubris is not to be bribed. Certainly he has delivered nothing for the money. There has been no evidence, contrary to the courier's claim, that any drugs have been passing through Sunshine to reach other states; instead, the major pipeline has shifted to Lonestar—where they are about to implement a drug-control program similar to that of Sunshine. Why, then, would the drug moguls pay out such an enormous sum of money to the man who continued to stifle their operations?

I suggest that, unable to take Hubris out physically—the governor's female security force is remarkably loyal and efficient—the pirates at last devised a scheme to do it politically. The money was not to *bribe* him but to *frame* him. This was effective; he was promptly ushered out of office. It is evident that the drug business quickly reverted to normal, increasing in Sunshine to its former level. Recidivism is rampant among treated addicts, and crime in the streets is rebounding at a rate that has swamped the minions of the law. In a few brief weeks the halcyon days of Hubris's term have been eclipsed. Certainly this was a victory for the drug moguls, who thrive on political corruption, and for crime in general. At the present rate of activity, their parcel of half a billion dollars, surreptitiously planted in the governor's warehouse, should be redeemed within months. It was, it seems, a very sound investment. In addition I understand that much of that warehouse money has mysteriously disappeared from storage and that the proprietors are extremely reluctant to permit a recount by qualified parties. Perhaps the money was not an investment but a loan.

We come now to the question of the motive of those members of the State Senate that impeached Governor Hubris and removed him from office. It was evident throughout that these folk had very little interest in the facts of the case; they simply moved to get the job done. Why should they have committed such an atrocity? To that I have no answer, but as a sincere conservative I am appalled that the principles for which I stand should have been invoked for the likes of this. It was not conservatism that framed the governor, it was blind fanaticism. As a citizen of this great planet of Jupiter, I will not rest easy until the true answer to this question of motive is forthcoming. I would be doubly chagrined to think that we are governed not by law, of whatever persuasion, but by the kingpins of the criminal realm.

We have witnessed a rare perversion of due process. Now let justice be done.

If there had been furor following Thorley's interview with Sancho, there was absolute chaos this time. The details are a matter of public record; I'll only say that before it was over, approximately fifty percent of the state senators of Sunshine had resigned in disgrace, the White Dome itself had a political black eye because of its covert involvement, I was retroactively exonerated, my drug program was reinstated, a grand jury set out in pursuit of the mysteriously missing warehouse money, and I was launched into my candidacy for the office of the president of the United States of Jupiter. I now had a direct and personal score to settle with Tocsin, who had somehow evaded censure for his malign influence here, and I was about to bring him into combat, politically.

In the early days Thorley had interposed his body to protect one I loved from assassination by laser. This time he had interposed his literary talent—and lo! his pen was mightier than the sword. He had at one stroke laid waste the entire array against me. Historically it was to be known as "The Sunshine Massacre," but that hardly told the story.

With a foe like Thorley I hardly needed friends.

Chapter 14

FORFEIT

When I was released, Scar interviewed me. This time he was angry, but he couldn't tell me why without revealing that Dorian Gray was in fact a spy. But he made a good stab at it.

"You know we watch you now," he said gruffly.

"Yes, of course," I agreed innocently.

"We have infrared cameras on you constantly, and sensitive mikes, so that we can see and hear whatever you do."

"But I thought it was all right to—to have relations with Dorian, since you put her in my cell."

"As long as you both behaved," he growled.

"But haven't we cooperated perfectly?"

"You tried to keep a secret from us!"

"What secret is that?"

"Your restored memory!" he exclaimed with righteous indignation.

"My what?"

"You thought our pickup couldn't hear, if you cupped your hands and whispered in her ear," he said angrily. "But it *did* hear, and we got your secret. You have been punished for concealing it from us—and she for not telling us."

Of course, it was a lie, for I had whispered only gibberish in her ear. This was my confirmation that their pickup could *not* intercept such sound. But I allowed my face to be crestfallen. "Dorian . . . is supposed to tell?"

"What do you think cooperation is?" Scar demanded. "You must report on each other, anything you learn."

I spread my hands in defeat. "I thought I could get away with a secret memory."

"Where did you see the trigger word?"

I became canny. "If I tell you that you'll erase the others, and then I'll have nothing."

"Others?"

"There were several, but I haven't read them all yet."

He assimilated that. I could virtually read his thoughts: if there were other key terms, then I had not yet recovered all my memories, so his program was probably secure, so far. I would have to read the other terms, and he could pounce when I did so. All he had to do was watch me.

Naturally he didn't say that. He had to make it seem like another ploy. "You will not see that woman again until you tell," he said. "She will remain in the hole."

"Not the hole!" I cried.

"Then tell me!"

I was silent. So he returned me to my better cell, alone, to consider the matter.

I knew Dorian wasn't in the hole. She was locked away elsewhere in the sub. She was now serving in her other capacity: as a lever against my will.

I did miss her, despite my knowledge. It was not easy to be alone again. But I held out, knowing there was pressure on Scar, too. I could tell by his tension; he was almost out of time. He could neither mem-wash nor torture me; it was too late. He didn't even withhold the drug-beverage, so I didn't have to pretend pangs of deprivation. He had to have my cooperation. His own position depended on it.

I had another indoctrination session, and this one was strongly indicative. "You are going to give a speech," Scar told me.

"Why?"

"Because your girl friend will be killed if you don't."

That was no lie. The lever was now out in the open. Dorian might be their agent, but if it suited their purpose to torture and kill her in my presence, they would do so.

"And if I give the speech?" I asked, daunted.

"You both will be freed."

He was telling the truth, again. His job was done when I gave the required speech, and so was Dorian Gray's. They would pay her off with her baby, and she would retire to obscurity.

"If I agree to give the speech will you let me see Dorian?"

He waggled a reproving finger at me. "Your speech will win your freedom and save her life. If you want her company in the interim you will have to show me where those trigger words are."

Again he was serious. I knew I could not afford to lose my next key term, so I had to demur. Thus I was alone, and it did bother me. I felt guilt for being bothered, knowing that it compromised my love for Megan. My captors had intended to compromise me completely; they had succeeded partially.

I had to memorize the speech. It was an astonishing one. It was a promise to benefit all constituents, right all wrongs, and make the planet a better place instantly. All criminals were to be summarily sentenced and executed without appeal. The present tax structure would be replaced by a flat tax without exemptions. Welfare benefits for the poor would be enhanced, the military budget would be increased to make Jupiter preeminent in the System, and vast amounts would be allocated to research and development. The government budget would be adjusted to produce a substantial surplus, reducing the planetary debt. The membership of the Supreme Court would be increased to twenty-four, to alleviate the caseload. Minority problems would be redressed; Hispanics would be given all the most important posts on a preferential basis. Grants would be made to all churches and philanthropic organizations. Education would be sharply upgraded by the elevation of standards and pay scales for teachers and administrators. National medical insurance would be extended to cover every citizen at any age; no one would die because of poverty or neglect. There would be legal insurance, too; no person would be denied court redress because of lack of funds. And so on. This speech promised all things to all men, with a vengeance. Perhaps in my mem-washed state I might have thought this made sense; as it was, I knew it was nonsense.

"If I may ask," I said to Scar, "am I a candidate for planetary office?"

"You are, Hubris," he assured me. "You are running for president of the United States of Jupiter. But you head a minor ticket; there is no chance of your getting elected."

He was telling a half-truth, but I couldn't tell which half

was truth. My illicit memory suggested that I had been about to try for a major party nomination. Perhaps I had tried and failed, and splintered off into a minor party bid; such things had happened to others in the past. So it was possible that I had a minor party nomination that nevertheless had a fair chance to win, or a major party nomination with bad prospects. "Then why should I make a major speech?"

"To influence the election," he explained. "The two major parties are so evenly divided that the balance of power lies in the minorities. The Blacks and Hispanics, mainly. As the candidate of the Hispanic Party you influence a significant bloc of votes. You may be in a position to lever either major party into office."

"The Hispanic Party?" I asked, perplexed. "I know nothing of this."

"Because it was formed in that period you have forgotten. You, as a Hispanic refugee and former military hero, became its spokesman. Now you are going to do your best to increase its base, drawing in those Hispanics who have not yet expressed their support, together with sympathetic Blacks and liberal Saxons, to make it a significant third party. You will try to prevent either major party from winning a majority of the electoral votes. Then your power will be magnified enormously."

I looked again at the speech. "But doesn't this promise too much? I'm not sure it's possible to meet all those objectives."

"It isn't," he agreed. "Not right away, anyway. But you won't have to deliver; all you have to do is attract enough votes to deny either major party the victory. Then you will be in a position to bargain for whatever portions of your program are most important to you."

Still I was perplexed. "If my position is this, why was I mem-washed?"

"Because you had fallen into bad political advice and would not listen to reason. You were compromised, and that threatened to destroy everything that you and the party had worked for and miss the chance of the century. That had to be corrected, in time for the election. We had to erase it all and reeducate you in the basics while your mind was open. *Now* you are ready to do what must be done."

I did not trust this, but I seemed to have no choice. The programs of the speech seemed good, individually, and I agreed with most of them, and I did not think that this agreement was entirely a matter of reeducation. So I memorized the speech and rehearsed it, preparing myself.

Such preparation is not accomplished in a day. I returned to my cell, alone, for the night, and pondered what this signified. I was a candidate for planetary office; that much both memory and captors agreed on. My memories had caught up to what I judged to be about two years from the present. But to run as the Hispanic candidate—that did not make sense. I had never campaigned as a Hispanic; I had campaigned on a platform of competence and integrity. I had sought support from all segments of society and had tried to serve all segments while in office. It was true that the Hispanics had supported me massively, and that when I had first stepped beyond my Hispanic base to run for governor of Sunshine, I had been defeated. But the second time, with my Gany ambassadorship behind me, I had been successful, and I was satisfied that by the time I completed that gubernatorial term, the majority of the voters in the state of Sunshine had been with me, despite some bad times along the way. Why should I have thrown that away by returning to the narrower political base?

Could *that* be the "bad political advice" I had fallen into? The determination to represent all the people, not just one ethnic minority? If so, the mem-wash had not eradicated it!

My next—and probably final—memory should provide the answer. I had to read that key term. I knew there was some important element missing, and I had to know what it was before I gave that speech. But how could I get to read that word, without giving away its location to my captors?

Then I realized that it might not matter. Their deadline was close; I probably would not be here for any further terms, even if there should be a hundred of them. The next one would be the last, perforce, and discovery of the message location would no longer matter. But it probably *was* the last, for only seven spaces remained in the key sentence: "(space) HERE. (space)." I had read it up this far: ABANDON HOPE, ALL YE WHO ENTER

That clarified my course: I would show Scar where it was and call out the untranslated symbols to him, and remember them for myself. He would not then be able to stop my mental revelation.

But my thoughts were not finished. What would happen, here in the sub, if I did not give the speech I had rehearsed? Dorian would be revealed as a failure and would surely suffer. I could fetch her baby, but she, herself, might not survive to receive it. I had to find a way to protect her.

But, again—since this was a political operation—Scar would merely be a mercenary doing a job. The real person in charge would be elsewhere, and that person would not permit failure. The revelation of the sub and its business would be a serious political embarrassment. So there would be a way to eliminate that embarrassment.

My time in the Navy assured me what that way would be.

Under the guise of reading, I opened the text on Economics and made a penned note in the margin of page one hundred: "There is a bomb aboard. Defuse it before I speak." Then I riffed through other pages, read randomly, and in a bored manner closed the book. I doubted that my real action had been noted.

Then I paced the floor for a suitable time and finally spoke aloud. "Give me Dorian Gray tonight, and I will show you the place tomorrow."

There was no immediate response, but soon Scar came down the hall to my cell. "Show me now, and you can have her now."

Could I risk that? I didn't want my captors to have time to decipher my code. It was a good code but not perfect. I decided not to risk it. "No. Show me your good faith first. I need to know she is all right."

"No. You must trust me, because you have no choice. First the place."

"I do have a choice," I said. "I want her first."

He simply turned and walked away. I had lost the ploy.

Next day the bargaining resumed. "Show us now, and she joins you now."

That seemed to be the best I could do. "I will show her the place."

Scar shrugged. In a moment Dorian was brought to me. Her hair was in disarray and her hands were cuffed behind her. It hurt me to see her that way, but I had to play it through.

I went up to her and embraced her, though she could hardly respond. I kissed her on the lips, and then she did respond. I murmured in her ear, "Look in the economics text as soon as I go. It's important." The captors thought I was whispering an endearment. "Page one hundred."

Then I turned to Scar. "It's in the smell-cell. I will show you."

He took me there. Probably he knew he should check it himself, but he had no desire to get into that hole. What a joke, if I tricked him into fouling himself in my refuse—for nothing!

"Let me get down in there," I said as he hesitated. "I will locate the place."

He let me get down. I settled myself in a squatting position, heedless of the clothing, and felt under the muck with my fingers. I found the place immediately. I knew Scar wouldn't let me linger for more than a moment, so I feigned a continuing search, turning my head about, while I actually slid my fingers across the last seven symbols and committed them to memory. I did not try to translate them; I just remembered their configuration.

"Here," I said, as if just finding them. "Scratched beneath the muck, in the form of symbols."

"*Under* the—" Scar asked distastefully.

"That's right. In code symbols. I can read them off for you, if you give me time."

"No. Get out of there. I'll get it cleaned out and verify them for myself."

So I got out and retired to the shower and a change of clothes while a crew got to work on the pit. Scar had intended to prevent me from actually reading the key term, once he knew where it was, but I had it locked in my memory in code:

‖ Γ □ ⅃ □ ‖ ⅃ Seven symbols, fortunately easy to remember because three of them repeated. I concentrated, burning them more firmly into my memory so that they could not be lost. All I needed was time to myself and I would have my final memory.

When I emerged, Dorian was gone. Somehow I had expected that. She remained hostage for my performance on the speech, as did any further doses of the drug to which they thought they had addicted me.

Scar rehearsed me again, instructing me exactly where to pause for effect and where to raise my voice. "Do this well and we'll all benefit," he said, and he believed it.

He believed it, but I did not. His employer had to know that a sincere fanatic was much more effective than an insincere one. Yet I still didn't know the specific nature of the lie. So I perfected the speech, and indeed it was a splendid effort of its type.

Abruptly I faded out; they had zapped me with a knockout beam. I woke in free-fall; I was evidently in a shuttle ship descending to the Jupiter atmosphere. It was a good thing I had taken the precaution of preparing my message for Dorian in advance, for Scar had tried to prevent any last moment exchange of information by shipping me without warning.

I didn't know how much time I had before the speech, so I got right on my symbol translation. I visualized the seven symbols; the knockout had not dislodged those precious scratches from my brain. Scar had wanted no memory loss this time, lest it interfere with my prepared speech. What would this key term evoke in me?

L was 30, counted from the space between ENTER HERE in the open message. I counted methodically, as the knockout had not yet faded entirely. It came to S. I double- and triple-checked, to be quite sure; it was definitely S.

Γ was 9, from the H, and easier to count to P. □ was 5 from E, easier yet: I. ⅃ was one from R, which was itself. □, 5 from E, or I again. L, another 30 from the period; more tricky, but I got it: T. And ⅃, one from the space following the open-code sentence, another space. The word was done.

SPIRIT.

Chapter 15

SPIRIT

It was two years before the next presidential election for the United States of Jupiter, but that was barely time to do the job. Spirit was my campaign manager, of course; Megan was my strategist, and Shelia my coordinator. They worked together, organizing a complex political entity of publicity and fund-raising, hiring specialists for particular aspects, and dictating the very footsteps of my climb. I really had very little to do with this; I merely did as directed, much in the manner of Ebony, our gofer. In fact, sometimes when Ebony was overloaded, I helped her out; she promised not to tell on me. So if I seem to be glossing over much that is essential to a political campaign, it is not because it was neglected but because it wasn't in my department. The operation was somewhat like a military campaign—an analogy that would have appalled Megan—with every effort made to apply our maximum force to the key vulnerabilities of the enemy. The enemy in this case was the apathy of the public and the reputation of opposing politicians. Specifically Tocsin; somehow I had always known I would one day try my strength against him, to the political death.

I started with several considerable assets: I had a planetary reputation as the Hero of the Belt, now being refurbished by special ads and news releases. I had a national one as the "rescuer" of the bodies from Saturn and as the author of the first effective drug-control program of the twenty-seventh century. I had a sympathy vote as survivor of the fiasco of the impeachment and the Sunshine Massacre. I was also now the leading Hispanic candidate, with strong support among other minorities, too. My sister Faith had helped make such progress in the conversion of Hispanics to the language of English and the betterment

of their situation that they were now becoming a potent
nucleus of political force in that region, and they supported
me absolutely. I was credited by some and condemned by
others, with hiring a campaign staff calculated to appeal to
minorities, because I had a Hispanic, a Black, a disabled
person, and a Mongol, in addition to my Saxon wife. It
hardly passed unnoticed that all were female. All of this
was coincidental, as we had hired solely for convenience
and merit, but Megan strongly recommended that I not
use the word *coincidence* publicly.

These assets were basically raw material. They would
not win any campaigns for me. I had to do that myself, by
generating a great deal of new and favorable publicity.
Some of that was handled by advertising, but our funds remained limited, as the wealthy special interests, who were
not stupid, regarded me as their enemy. Most of it had to
be done by making provocative public appearances. That
is what I remember most clearly, rather than the many
quiet strategy sessions.

The other face of that coin was Tocsin's liabilities, which
I could exploit politically. He had catered shamelessly to
the special interests, alienating a large segment of the ordinary population. He had gone in for extensive deficit
spending, putting the government in dept at an extraordinary rate. To facilitate the printing of money to help cover
this, he had cut the last tie of the Jupiter dollar to tangible
value: gold. Now the paper money had nothing to halt its
erosion of purchasing power. Inflation was increasing, and
the common man was being squeezed between relatively
fixed wages and rising prices. Crime and suicide were becoming more popular, and bankruptcies proceeded at a
near-record rate. The economy was suffering a fundamental malaise that was to a significant extent traceable to the
insensitive and wrongheaded policies of this administration. I could orate on all of this and find a responsive audience anywhere in northern Jupiter.

But first there was the problem of transportation. In my
campaign for governor I had rented a car that hitched
rides on freight trains, but now I had to do national campaigning. My schedule was tighter, I had a larger entourage, and freights did not necessarily go where I was
going. The problem of expense remained; money is like

oxygen to a political candidate, and travel for a group is expensive. We had only been able to raise so much by solicitations, as I was considered to be a far-out candidate; no Hispanic had ever won a major party nomination for president of the U. S. of J., let alone won the office. Of course, neither had any Black, Mongol, or woman. North Jupiter, touted as the greatest nation in the System, was regressive in some great ways, too. So my campaign was, as the saying goes, climbing the gravity well without a shield. But I seemed to have a better chance than any minority candidate before me, and I intended to accelerate.

My staff huddled and concluded that the best and cheapest way to travel was still by train. Only this time we rented a whole train, locomotive and all. The days of passenger trains were fading on Jupiter, though not elsewhere in the System, so good equipment was now surplus and available for a fraction of its original value. The best bargains were in the older steam engines, with their matching antique cars, for these remained the most reliable heavy-duty items. I wondered why, suspecting that Jupiter's attention to quality was eroding in the modern day, but didn't argue. We wound up with a fine old luxury train, the *Spirit of Empire*, with seven ornate coaches. What significance there might be in that name I could not be sure; it is possible to put too much store in symbolism. Certainly my sister liked it, because of the coincidence of names, and perhaps it portended success.

Each coach was about eighty-five feet long and ten feet wide, and looked very much like its ancient terrestrial ancestor. The engine puffed clouds of dissipating smoke. All in all, I found it a highly satisfying vehicle, for reasons that surely derived from the genetic fascination of the species of man with size, power, and motion. Hopie was delighted; she was thirteen years old now and reminded me extraordinarily of Spirit at that age, though I had never known Spirit at that age. I had known her to age twelve, and from age sixteen. I had never seen her in transition from child to woman. Now, in a fashion, perhaps I would.

My term as governor of Sunshine was over; by the time Thorley's analysis had run its course and restored my honor to me, there was too little time remaining in my term to make it worthwhile. I was free to campaign full-

time. My secretary, Shelia, organized our office for porta-
bility, and the group of us presented ourselves at the station when our train came in. Of course, our baggage was
moved aboard separately, and Ebony had been back and
forth setting things up. We had other personnel who remained at my campaign headquarters in Ybor. We boarded,
officially, as a group: Megan, Spirit, Shelia in her wheelchair, Ebony, Coral, Mrs. Burton, Hopie, and me. There
was a small crowd of supporters to cheer us on, and, of
course, the train had its own staff of two engineers, cook,
maid, and porter. So we were to be a group of a dozen folk,
touring much of the planet. It promised to be interesting,
even if my quest for high office proved unsuccessful.

The railroad station was in the basement of Ybor, below
the residential section, where gee was slightly high. It
seemed cavernous, because it was mostly empty and
poorly lighted. Gee and illumination combined to provide
an illusion of great depth, though in fact we were now at
the outer rim of the bubble. The cars stood beside the long
loading platform, the tops of their wheels barely visible in
the crevice at its edge. The glassy windows reflected the
things of the station, making the whole scene seem
stranger yet.

"Ooo, I like it!" Hopie exclaimed, clinging tightly to my
hand. She was now almost as tall as Spirit, but she wavered back and forth between child and adolescent, and
this new experience put her at the younger range. "A real
old choo-choo train!"

I let the girls board first, then stepped on myself. I
turned at the entrance platform, before the lock closed,
and smiled and waved to the crowd, and they cheered.
Then the panel interrupted the view, and I turned again to
enter the coach.

It was like an elegant dayroom, with swiveling couch-
chairs and ornate pseudowood tables and fluffy curtains on
the windows. Light descended from hanging chandeliers.
The floor was lushly carpeted, with protective plastic over
the spots wear was likely to be greatest.

"Please take your seat, sir," the porter said. Originally a
porter had been a person to carry bags, but evidently the
job description had been amplified; he was making sure we

were properly installed. "If you dim the lights you can see out the windows better."

Hopie plumped into a seat next to mine and clasped her hands. "I want to see us pull out!"

We doused the light. Sure enough, the station outside now became more visible, because the light was brighter there. The people were still standing on the platform, watching the train.

There was a jolt; then the platform began to move. Correction: *We* began to move, ever so slowly, seeing the platform with its burden of people pass behind. Gradually we accelerated, so that the platform moved back at a walking, then at a running, pace. The vertical support pillars started to blur. Our weight increased because we were moving in the direction of the bubble's rotation, adding to the effective centrifugal force. Centrifugal force is, of course, nonexistent; we postulate it as a convenient way to perceive the constant acceleration that the vorticity of the rotating bubble generates in us. Every so often I bemuse myself by realizing how real that imagined force seems. There is no outward pull from the center, merely inertia, but since the moving bubble seems stationary to our perspective, we then assume that inertia is the force. Now, that pseudoforce was increasing because of our increased velocity of rotation.

"If you will buckle in, sir," the porter reminded me gently.

Oh, yes. I fastened the seat belt. I have always been a trifle absentminded when I'm thinking.

"I like this part," Hopie said, her hands holding tight to the arms of her couch-chair.

There was a warning whistle, a double note. Then the coach flung out of the station, going into free-fall, and simultaneously rotating a quarter turn to my right. The surface of the bubble had seemed to rise abruptly; now it descended again, and I saw that we were drifting parallel to Ybor's equator. My body was not entirely weightless, for now the engine was drawing the cars briskly forward, pressing us all back into our seats.

In a moment we were out of Ybor's gravity shield. Now we felt Jupiter's own gravity—diffused more than halfway by the train's own gee-shield, to reduce it to Earth-normal.

The city's centrifugal gee was at right angles to planetary gee; hence our need to rotate ninety degrees as we shifted from one to the other. We would suffer the same twist when we pulled in to the next city-station. It was a minor inconvenience, and for Hopie, no inconvenience at all.

We unbuckled and relaxed. We were on our way. Naturally Hopie and I set out on a tour of the train the moment Ybor city fell behind; this was a novelty for both of us.

First we saw the dining car. This was domed, with a restaurant in the dome that seated as many as eighteen people; they could peer out to either side and above, seeing the sights while they ate. Beneath it was a smaller restaurant for greater privacy, that I might use when entertaining some important supporter or local figure. There was also the sleeping car, with neat cubicles containing wall-to-wall beds; we agreed that we could hardly wait for evening to come so we could try it out. There was a conference car, with an officelike section and equipment; Shelia's files were already ensconced. There was a playroom car, set up for games and entertainments ranging from pool to commercial holovision; Hopie's mouth fairly watered at that. There was a baggage car, used also for supplies. And there was the caboose. This was where the train's own staff resided; they ate and slept there when not on duty, staying out of the way of the paying clientele. Naturally Hopie found it the most fascinating one of all, perhaps because it was tacitly forbidden; we were not supposed to intrude on the crew's privacy. We had rented their services, not their lives.

At the other end was the engine. This was my own principal interest, for I knew that the welfare of the train depended on it. We were not drifting, we were traveling; this meant that each unit had normal Earth gee and would plummet down into the prohibitive depths if not hauled along fast enough for the plane surfaces to grip the atmosphere. Of course, if we lost velocity, the individual gee-shields would automatically compensate, bringing our weight down to the point of flotation, but then we would all be drifting in air inside the cars, because there was no spin-gee here. We would be stranded in nowhere and have to signal for a tow.

The engine was steam, but, of course, not exactly the ancient style. There was no wood or coal or oil to fire its boiler—not here in the Jupiter atmosphere! Its heat source was the same as for spaceships: CT iron.

The problem with pumping CT iron in atmosphere was that it reacted as avidly with gas as with metal, and the interference of terrene hydrogen atoms caused the detonation to be unstable, and some CT molecules could be thrown out in the drive jet. So CT was severely restricted on-planet, permitted only in the heavily protected units of large cities or in special laboratories. CT was definitely not a do-it-yourself power supply. But in the heyday of the railroads, political clout had been brought to bear to permit CT in special locomotives. Thus the classic steam engine came to be a phenomenally heavy-duty apparatus whose firebox was a miniature seetee plant, sealed and buttressed to prevent any leakage, whose inordinate captive heat was used to produce the steam that ran the propeller wheels that urged it forward. Steam, being gaseous water, was too valuable to waste, so it was conserved. In the ancient steam engines of Earth, the steam pressure drove the cylinders and was then released into the atmosphere; this led to a constant depletion of water, which had to be periodically replaced. The steam engines of Jupiter funneled the expended steam into a condensation chamber, returning it to the form of water, which was then recycled into the CT firebox. Thus it was not steam but surplus heat that was radiated into the atmosphere, in the form of fast-moving hydrogen coolant. The process might seem cumbersome, but it worked. A steam engine was a huge, hot, powerful thing, a veritable dragon in the sky, which held a natural fascination for most people, me included.

The chief engineer was Casey, a grizzled veteran of the old days. Not merely of the period of the heyday of the Jupiter rails but of the spirit of the Earthly railroads, too. He chewed mock tobacco—the real stuff, once used primarily for sneezing and smoke inhalation had been outlawed for centuries because of the savage cost it extracted in human health—and periodically expectorated it into a genuine imitation brass spittoon. The first time she saw him do that, Hopie jumped, then laughed at herself. Casey was like a page from history. He had his song, too, "Casey Jones," which he sang lustily in the manner of the migrant labor-ers with their own songs. I liked him immediately.

The *Spirit of Empire* was more than a name to Casey; as he watched the dials, he saw in his fancy the coal going into the firebox and the steam puffing from the wheel cyl-inders. The engine itself was impressive enough, with its puffs of gray "smoke" from the exhaust of the heat exchan-ger; it was mostly coloring matter, to provide a visual con-firmation of the volume of hydrogen passing through. Any failure of the condensation chamber or the heat dissipa-tion system would be a serious matter, but the smoke also replicated as closely as feasible the appearance of the ancestral terrestrial engines. There was an enormous amount of nostalgia in the railroad, and it showed in many ways.

The propellers themselves resembled wheels only when the engine was in the station; here in the atmosphere they were extended to the sides, bottom, and top, to form a hexa-gon, blasting six columns of gas at great velocity. Those propellers hurled the engine forward much as the turning wheels had once impelled the terrestrial locomotives. This mighty engine hauled the seven cars along behind. In the cars the vibration was damped, but here in the cab the brute force of it was manifest, shaking every part. Hopie clutched my arm with gleeful apprehension; certainly this was an impressive monster!

We admired the quivering dials that told a story only the engineer could understand, and we watched the smoke pluming from the tall stack. It came out in powerful puffs and billowed voluminously as it carried back, and eddy currents from the nearest propeller curved it into interest-ing configurations as it passed.

From here we could also see the railroad tracks ahead. These were actually two beams of light, used to guide the train on its course; as long as the engineer kept it between those tracks, all was well. The tracks glowed into the dis-tance until they seemed to merge, seeming quite straight though they could be gradually curved by angling the gen-erating units, causing the route to shift to avoid inclement turbulence. We were hurtling along between them at a ve-locity that only became apparent as we watched the track markers click rapidly by.

Satisfied with our tour, we returned to the dining car, where the cook was serving lunch. For this first meal aboard the train, all eight of us gathered in the dome restaurant where we could further admire the distant smoke through the curving ceiling. Theoretically I was the leader and Megan was my consort, and Ebony, Shelia, Coral, and Mrs. Burton were mere employees, but we had long since abandoned pretense in private; we were more like a family. Hopie excitedly told the others about the wonders of the engine, and they listened with suitable expressions of interest. At first the cook and waitress (in other cars she became the maid) evinced muted disapproval of this unhierarchical camaraderie, but slowly they relaxed, perceiving that it was genuine. A long train journey, like a space voyage, is a great leveler; social pretensions tend to fade, biding their time until the ride is over.

After the meal, the ladies took turns in the powder room (as a former military man I was tempted to call it an ammunition dump but managed to keep my humor to myself), and I looked for the male lavatory (the head, in civilian parlance), which, of course, I had all to myself; the cook did not use the passenger facilities. Unfortunately I wasn't sure where it was, and Hopie, who naturally knew everything about the layout of the train already, was with the ladies, so could not direct me. I was at a minor loss. I didn't want to blunder randomly about, though there was no one to perceive my awkwardness aside from myself. We tend to be captive to our social foibles, however much our intellects deride this.

Fortunately Casey came along the passage, evidently having turned over the helm to his assistant engineer. "Glad to see you!" I said.

"Got to get to the caboose to take a leak," he muttered apologetically.

This gave me pause. "You have to proceed the entire length of the train, from engine to caboose, bypassing all the facilities of the cars, just to—"

"Yeah, they should've put one in the cab," he agreed. "Some engineers keep a li'l piss pot for emergencies, but that's a nuisance to clean."

"Well, use the one in this car," I suggested.

"Oh, no, sir, that wouldn't be right," he protested. "The help don't use the—"

I clapped him on the shoulder. "Casey, when the train's in the station, I'm the candidate and you're the engineer. But out here in transit there's no one to know. Use the damn facilities."

He looked at me to make sure I meant it, then acquiesced. "Sure thank you, sir, if you're sure. It's over this way." He led me to a door I should have spotted before; it was plainly marked with the silhouette of a gentleman in a top hat. We entered, and there was a spacious chamber with three sinks, two toilets, and a genuine archaic urinal. That was what we both needed at the moment.

Casey approached it first, as I was standing, looking about at the elegant fixtures: tiled floor, separate stalls around the toilets, mirrors by the sinks, and even small, paper-wrapped bars of old-fashioned soap waiting to be used. No sonic cleansers here! Such conspicuous waste was awesome—and intriguing. We really were living in a by-path of primitive luxury.

Casey hawked his mouthful of juice and spat. The globule sailed in a beautiful arc to score on the urinal. Just before it struck, there was a zapping flash.

He stopped dead in his tracks. "What was that?"

"A spark," I said. "Are these devices electrically cleaned?"

"Naw. They flush with water, recycled. No current in 'em."

Strange. A little mental claxon sounded. "Let's hold off on this a moment, Casey. It's probably foolish, but I'd like my technical manager to look into this."

"Sure, bring him in. You rented the train."

"It's Mrs. Burton. She's my stage manager, but she's handy with everything."

"Oh." He seemed disgruntled.

I returned to the restaurant and found Ebony. "Send Mrs. Burton down to the men's room," I told her.

She raised a dark eyebrow but went in search of Mrs. Burton. Soon the latter appeared, flanked by Coral. "Boss, I can help you with a lot, but some things you've just got to manage by yourself," she said with a smile.

"There's a complication," I said.

"Something broken in the john?"

"There was a spark in the urinal. Maybe just static charge, but—"

"Not here," she assured me. "All these fixtures are decharged." She forged ahead, pausing at the door. "No one's on?"

"None we know of," I said, and Casey grimaced, still not liking a woman poking about this room.

She went in and approached the urinal. She held an all-purpose detector in her hand. As she got close she whistled. "Look at that needle jump! That thing's wired!"

"Electrified?" I asked.

"Like an execution chair! And look at the floor—see those wire bands that hold the tiles? Perfect ground. Field so strong it flickers even when a nongrounded object approaches. You know what would have happened if you'd used that thing?"

I worked it out. "High voltage—traveling along the stream—grounding through my body."

"You'd have been fried from the crotch down," she said. "If you didn't die outright from shock, you'd have wished you had. What a booby trap!"

"I was about to use that thing!" Casey said, looking faint.

"You'd only have used it once, sonny," she said. Casey was no youngster; he was in his fifties, but she still had twenty years on him and exploited it.

Coral touched my elbow. "Only a man would use a urinal, sir," she said. "You're the only male passenger aboard. It was rigged for you."

My knees felt weak. In the Navy I had been somewhat hardened to the prospect of sudden extinction, but that had been some time ago. "Casey, let's get down to your caboose," I said. "Mrs. Burton will see to this." Indeed she was already using her detector to trace the wiring, preparatory to nullifying and dismantling the system. I knew there would be no further danger, once she was done.

We traipsed to the caboose. "I don't know how it happened, gov'nor," Casey said, still shaken. "We don't run that sort of train!"

"Of course, you don't," I agreed. "But has this coach been in your train all along?"

"No, sir. The old one was in for refurbishing, so we picked this one up in Ybor. We sure thought it was okay."

"And it *was* okay," I agreed. "Until someone got in and booby-trapped it."

"Looks like somebody's out to get you, sir," he said.

"Looks as if somebody's out to get me," I agreed grimly.

"Why is that, if you don't mind my asking?"

"I conjecture that there are parties who fear my campaign to be president will be successful, and they do not want me in that office."

"So they try to kill you, just for that?" he asked incredulously.

"It is only a conjecture. I do have enemies from my past."

"Say, yeah! You're the one who cleaned up the Belt. Those druggies sure must be mad at you!"

So he was aware of my Naval record but not of my gubernatorial record. This was probably an insight into the way the average man outside the state of Sunshine perceived me. "It is true that I have always worked to eliminate crime, and the drug trade is perhaps the main source of criminal income."

"Yeah, they're bad customers, all right," he agreed. "I had a friend, got hooked on comet dust; they bled him dry, and when he couldn't pay anymore—" He grimaced. "I never saw a man so torn up. He looked like a damn zombie. He's dead now and better off for it. They say his suit popped a leak when he was working outside, but I know he holed it himself. He was a good engineer, too, before." He shook his head. "Think there's any more traps aboard, sir?"

"It seems likely," I said. "I regret this matter has put you at risk, too."

"Hell, man, if you hadn't of been a decent chap, you'd be dead now, and I'd be out of a job. If I hadn't of spit in that—" He broke off, the closeness of his own brush with electrocution catching up with him again. Casey had not been in Navy combat, and so did not have the background experience of violent death that I did. He was severely shaken, and I knew it would take him some time to adjust.

"Now we are warned," I said. "We'll rout out all the other traps."

We got on it. Mrs. Burton dismantled the urinal trap and discussed its details with Coral, my bodyguard. They agreed that this was a sophisticated device, requiring special expertise and no mean expense, and that it was surely only one of a number of traps. They would have to check the entire train before any of us could relax. "Meanwhile," Coral told me firmly, "you stay with me, close, Governor. I will taste your food first; I will use your facilities."

"But the sanitary—"

"You want privacy at risk of life?"

I looked helplessly at Megan, but she only nodded agreement. "Coral is only doing her job," she said. She was pale, not from the notion of another woman staying so close to me but because of the immediate threat of death. She had taken a tranquilizer but remained tense, and I could not honestly reassure her. For her sake, as much as my own, I had to abate this menace swiftly.

"Good luck using the urinal," I murmured to Coral.

Actually she didn't have to go that far, for Mrs. Burton was on that job. She checked them all out. No other urinals were pied, and no other electrical traps were found, but this did not alleviate our suspicion. "It means the other traps are different," Coral said tersely.

We elected to retire early. This first leg of the tour was a long one, by design; we had wanted to have several days to become acclimatized to the train, so my tour was starting in the state of Evergreen, with speeches scheduled in Attle and Kane. Thereafter we were scheduled for Ortland in Beaver, and on south to Langel and Cisco in Golden, where Megan's reputation guaranteed good reception. We were not speeding, so we had a good four days' travel. Thereafter we would have stops separated by no more than hours.

We were traveling above the residential zone of Jupiter, so were not intersecting any bubbles on the way out, but our route was taking us past the states of Dixie, Magnolia, Opportunity, Show Me, Sunflower, Cornhusk, Equality, Treasure, Gem, and perhaps others, their very names evoking marvelous images. Physically, the atmosphere of Jupiter in this band was fairly dull, for we were clear of the great turbulences of the south, but evocatively this was very special. I think every human being, in his deep psyche, really longs for the old planet and finds comfort in its figurative recreation. Our dreams survive our changing reality, and that is no bad thing.

Coral took the whole bed apart, remade it, then stripped and climbed in herself. "Now, wait . . ." I began, for I was standing beside it with Megan the whole time.

Coral smiled. "No seduction, sir," she reassured me. "Maybe chemical on sheets, or radiation; I know if I feel."

She was right, of course; some powder in the sheets could be toxic, and if I innocently lay in it—

"But that wouldn't be selective," I pointed out. "Obviously the traps are for me alone, if only because if any woman is taken out, I will be warned. They had no way of anticipating which bed I might be using."

She climbed out and stood for a moment, nude, considering. I had not before appreciated how well formed she was; her Saturnine skin was silken, her torso slender and extremely well toned, her breasts not large but perfectly shaped, her waist so small that her hips and posterior became pronounced. Coral was every bit as pretty in her fashion as her reptilian namesake, and as lithe, and her face was of matching quality. She certainly had not had to go into this sort of work; any man of any planet would have been glad to marry and support her. But she was her own woman, and I certainly respected that in her.

"Good point," she said. "Still, I check the rest." She proceeded to do just that, getting in each bed in the sleeping car. All were clean.

"You have a taste for young flesh?" Megan inquired when we were safely in bed together.

"Not any more," I mumbled, embarrassed.

"Your eyes bulged only from fatigue?" she teased me. She knew that I noticed and appreciated all flesh, but also that I touched none but hers. There was no jealousy in her.

"That must have been it," I agreed, reaching for hers.

"I cannot offer you the like of that," she continued. "Coral is a plum; I am a prune."

"I'm an old man; give me some prune juice," I said, and she laughed. She knew, as I did, that youth is only one aspect of sexuality, and a lesser one than love. Megan, as she was at the age of fifty-four, was all that I ever desired. A glimpse at a body like Coral's was, for me, passing fancy;

Megan was reality. I kissed her almost savagely and had at her as if we were teenagers who would be forever separated on the morrow. Certainly there was some of that in it, after the death scare. Flattered, she responded in kind, and it was desperately good. Her adaptation to this side of marriage had been gradual but complete; she was now capable of passion approaching my own, when she knew it would please me. On this occasion it did indeed please me.

Next day the quest for traps resumed. Coral stayed so close to me, she often touched, suspicious of everything. But it was not only that. "I am jealous of Megan," she confided when I looked askance.

She had stayed in the adjacent bed-cell overnight. Her duty required her to be as close to me as possible. She surely had overheard our lovemaking. She was not being coquettish; she was stating a fact we both understood. If I notice flesh so does the flesh also notice me; this is a situation I have lived with all my adult life. In this, Coral was no different from any of the girls of my staff. It was one of the things we all lived with and accepted. Perhaps this is typical of all politicians; I have never inquired.

Still no traps turned up, and that was bad because we were sure they existed. All of us felt the tension, especially Hopie. "I don't want anything to happen to you, Daddy!" she cried, hugging me tightly.

"Or to you," I said, kissing her on the forehead. Indeed, she was my only child, and my universe would have darkened without her.

"Her, too," Coral muttered. That was a corollary aspect: If Megan had my love as wife, Hopie had it as daughter, and the others were excluded. They suffered an amicable jealousy of any such attachment.

"Actually you're young enough," I reminded Coral, for she was eighteen years my junior and looked younger.

She quirked a smile. "I suppose I can't keep both jealousies, logically. But I do."

Jealousy is considered to be an ugly emotion. Somehow it never struck me that way. To me it seems more like a compliment.

I spent the morning reviewing my campaign material. It was important that I come across lucidly and powerfully from the outset, making no missteps. A single small-seeming error can ruin a year's political groundwork. So I rehearsed with Hopie, my willing audience; she had heard it all before but seemed never to tire of political themes. "Are you going to be Jupiter's first female president?" I asked her teasingly, to which she replied, "Maybe."

At noon I went to the lavatory to wash my hands. Normally I use the sonic cleaner, but this train was equipped only with the archaic basins, faucets, and wrapped bars of soap, and they intrigued me. I picked up a bar and began to unwrap it.

"Me first," Coral said, taking it from my hand.

"Harpy," I muttered. The harpies of mythology were ugly half-birds noted for snatching things from others. She ignored that. She wet her hands and squeezed the bar through them, pausing to smell it.

Nothing happened. "No poison," she concluded, satisfied.

"Unless it's just male poison," Hopie put in, laughing. She had followed us in; there was no longer any such thing as privacy for me.

It was a joke, but Coral stiffened. "Sex-differentiated enzymes—it just could be!" She took the bar and hurried away, leaving me to make do with unadorned water.

Soon she was back. "It was, sir. I ran it through my chem-kit. Affects only Y chromosome, so no effect on female. But you—if not death in hours, brain damage in days."

Hopie seemed about to faint. "I thought it was humor," she whispered.

"That enemy not laughing," Coral said grimly.

Not funny, indeed! Again I had survived largely by luck. Had Hopie not made her facetious remark . . .

Coral sent Ebony to check all the soap on board. Only one type was bad: the fancy-wrapped passenger-intended bars. The kind that a potential president might use, rather than one of the train crew. The differentiation remained; I was the only target.

"Bound to be something else," Coral muttered. "But this enemy clever, very clever. Not sure I'll catch the next."

I did not like the sound of that. I wondered again exactly

who my enemy was. Such cunning; the drug moguls were normally not that subtle.

We discussed it during lunch. We made no effort to conceal what had happened; we were all in this together, with Hopie sharing the risk. We had to make a team effort to win through.

Mrs. Burton summed it up: "One electric trap, one chemical trap. Third one must be something else. Something only the boss will encounter."

"Electric, chemical, physical," Coral said. "Maybe physical trap just for him. Spring-loaded knife where only he goes. But where that?" She had learned to speak almost perfect English during her years with me but tended to revert when concentrating on something.

"I have no plans to go anywhere alone," I said.

"See that you don't," Mrs. Burton said.

The porter met us after lunch. "Phone for you, sir."

It turned out to be an appeal from the city of Phis, in Volunteer. It seemed I had support there, and the mayor was begging me to make at least a whistle-stop in passing.

Such an appeal is hard for a politician to turn down. We consulted and agreed; we would pause at Phis for half an hour, no more, and I would speak a few words of encouragement from the campaign train. It seemed an excellent way to break in, and it might alleviate the tension of the death threat.

Casey brought the train about and followed a spur-track to the bubble. They were really eager to see us in Phis; their station was packed with cheering people. This was extremely gratifying but probably a fluke. I would be playing to sparsely filled houses on my regular tour.

As we passed through the maneuvers for entry to the station, Hopie was at my elbow, trying to tell me something. I'm afraid I was distracted and not paying attention; this really was not the occasion for the indulgence of childish prattle. This was, after all, to be my first campaign speech as a candidate for president of the United States of Jupiter. There were so many issues to develop, and there was so little time, and the manner of my delivery was so vital.

We were gliding to a halt in the station. "You'll have to

let me go now, honey," I told Hopie gently. "I have a campaign address to give."

"Daddy, you aren't *listening!*" she exclaimed, and I saw with surprise that she was crying. Suddenly I realized how frustrating it must be for a child to be ignored. What did it matter if I won over the people at Phis if I alienated my own daughter?

"I'm sorry," I said sincerely. "I'm listening now."

"Daddy, I had a dream, sort of," she said, her tears abating. Sunshine follows rain very quickly, with teenagers.

"A dream," I agreed.

"Sort of. I don't think I was exactly asleep, so—"

"A vision," I said. "I have them sometimes. Maybe it runs in the family."

She smiled gratefully. "Maybe." It was a running joke: How could an adoptive child inherit a genetic trait? We maintained, for the sake of companionship, that it was possible. Indeed, Hopie's blood type matched mine, further evidence. "But this was a bad one."

"Sometimes they are. But often there is truth in them."

"Daddy, I saw you start to talk to the crowd, and then . . ."

"Don't keep me in suspense," I said, smiling.

"Then it all blew up. Daddy, I'm terrified!"

"Premonition of disaster? Hardly surprising, after what's happened on the *Spirit of Empire.* But you know that we detect and analyze all metals in my vicinity; if anyone brings a bomb, we'll know."

"Are bombs metal?"

"Well, no. Usually they are cased in metal, though, and have metal detonation wires, that sort of thing. It's hard to avoid metal entirely."

She seemed reassured. "So no one can bomb you when you speak?"

"Nothing is impossible, honey. But it does seem unlikely. For one thing I'll be inside the train, talking to them via loudspeaker. This is standard practice for politicians who are whistle-stopping; the train is kept sealed, so there's no foolishness about carrying in any disease or forgetting to close a port before going back out on the track. Fast and neat and sanitary. No one outside can throw anything inside, which is just as well, because some nuts may try to."

"Okay," she agreed. "I guess I'll let you talk. But if you see anything like a bomb—"

"I'll back off," I agreed. "This may be news to you, but I'm not really partial to explosions, up close."

She laughed, relieved.

Now I approached the mike. "This thing turned on?" I asked Mrs. Burton.

"Oops," she said, touching a switch. "Now it's on."

There was a rippling chuckle in the crowd outside. Her words had just been sent out to them.

I took the mike, opened my mouth, and paused, remembering Hopie's vision. Of course, it probably had been an animation of apprehension—that would soon be dissipated by reality—but as I had told her there was often truth in visions. I see no supernatural agency in this; a vision may be merely a form of intuition, a conjecture based on a collection of impressions assimilated on a subconscious level. Our brains are marvelous things and often know more than our conscious minds choose to realize. Just as I had not paid attention to Hopie before, so the conscious can ignore the unconscious. When the matter is important, sometimes the unconscious breaks through with a vision. It is an attention-getter of last resort. Or so I conjecture; I'm not expert on the matter.

Hopie had seen me start to talk to the crowd, and then everything had blown up.

A booby-trapped mike? But it was already on, and Mrs. Burton had used it. Some things were voice-activated, but obviously this was not.

Voice-activated? How about voice-coded?

I shut my mouth tight and backed away, signaling Mrs. Burton to turn off the mike. Coral started forward, concerned. "Sir, is something—"

Mrs. Burton switched off the mike. "What's on your mind, Governor? Surely not stage fright!"

"Let's try a test record," I whispered. "One with my voice."

"Sure." We had made several recordings of single-issue spot discussions for backup use in case my voice got strained; that's another standard precaution. She put one on and turned on the mike, while the crowd outside looked on curiously. We retreated to another chamber.

"Hello, friends," my voice said on the loudspeaker. "My name is—"

The mike console exploded. Metal shrapnel blasted into the wall and cracked the shatterproof pseudoglass window. Hopie screamed.

In a moment there was silence. The broadcast chamber was a shambles; anybody in it would have been damaged beyond repair.

Coral nodded ruefully. "Voice-activated bomb, coded to your voice only," she said. "Sir, I failed you. I did not anticipate that."

"Fortunately Hopie did," I said, putting my arm around my daughter's heaving shoulders. I squeezed her. "I think you saved my life, cutesy."

"Oh, Daddy," she said, sobbing and turning into me.

In due course Mrs. Burton rigged another mike, one not booby-trapped, and I gave my address from the shambled chamber. I kept Hopie with me, holding her left hand with my right. "Someone tried to assassinate me," I told my audience firmly. "Don't worry; it wasn't anyone from Phis. My daughter anticipated it and saved my life; but for her I would have had trouble addressing you now. I think she deserves to participate." And I lifted her hand in a kind of victory gesture.

The crowd cheered so hard that the train vibrated, and Hopie blushed. No one had ever cheered her before.

My first presidential campaign address was a great success.

Chapter 16

VISION

We moved back out on the track, resuming our scheduled route. Our group was somewhat sobered, for that last trap had been a close thing. No one had thought to check the public address system for bombs; Mrs. Burton had tested it routinely and found it in good working order, so had let it be. I could not blame either her or Coral for the oversight; it had been a fiendishly subtle trap. The explosive had been plastic, not registering on the metal detector, and the current that detonated it had been part of the regular mike system. Only if someone had delved into the console would the explosive have been evident, and since there had been no malfunction, there had been no reason to do that. But both Coral and Mrs. Burton blamed themselves.

Megan, distraught, refused to take any more tranquilizers. "If you are in danger, Hope," she said nervously, "I don't want to ignore it, when perhaps I could do something—"

Here she broke down, and I could not completely comfort her. I saw that I was inadvertently leading her into a life that was not to her liking. She had retired from the stress of politics and now was back in it—with the added element of personal, physical danger. This campaign had become akin to a military operation; it was too much for her.

"If my campaign hurts you I will give it up," I told her. Indeed, my love for her was such that this was true. I had started to tune out my daughter in the press of preparations; I did not want to do worse to my wife.

She patted my hand. "No, Hope. You must follow your destiny. You are of sterner stuff than I. It is not my prerogative to interfere."

That was the way it stood. She was afraid for me, desperately so, and this fear was taking its toll on her, but she would not let me deviate from my chosen course. She was a great woman, and it showed in ways like this.

Coral and Mrs. Burton restricted me to the "safe" sections of the train while they checked out everything else they could think of, armed with electronic detectors and recordings of my voice. I doubted they would find anything; three traps seemed to be enough. But during those long hours we had to have a distraction, as much for Megan's and Hopie's benefit as mine, so we played cards. There were all manner of computerized games available, of course, but none of us had any present taste for these. They had been checked safe, but it was too easy to imagine a unit blowing up when a certain configuration was achieved, such as the code word *Hubris*. And, despite all the advances in game-craft, the old-fashioned physical cards still represented an excellent all-around repertoire of diversion. We taught Hopie how to play partnership canasta, and she and I tromped Megan and Spirit. But after a few hours the adults tired of this, leaving only Hopie and me. Shelia and Ebony were busy assisting in the booby-trap search, so we could draft no further foursome. We played Old Maid, War, and Concentration, but even these palled in time, perhaps because Hopie, with the wit and luck of the young, kept beating me. In the afternoon we were at the point of staring out into the Jupiter atmosphere, watching the cloud formations just above us, as they were augmented by the drifting column of train smoke. We fancied we saw shapes and pictures there—goblin heads, potatoes, dragons' tails, and such. Imagination is wonderful stuff, and Hopie's was akin to mine.

Then Casey passed through. "Them dames is tearing up the whole damn train," he grumbled.

"Women are like that," I agreed, skillfully moving my leg before Hopie could kick it. She identified with women the moment they were criticized. "Happens every spring and sometimes in the fall. Are you off-duty now? Sit down and watch clouds with us."

"Don't mind if I do," he agreed, taking a seat. "But why watch clouds when you can see the real scenery going by?"

"Real scenery?" Hopie asked alertly.

"Sure. See, we're passing through Centennial now, near

the great Continental Divide. We been rising for hours, having to make the grade, so's to get over the Rockies."

Hopie exchanged a glance with me. "The rocks?" she asked.

"The Rockies. The Rocky Mountains, greatest range of the west. Got fourteen-thousand-foot peaks hereabouts—quite a change from them flat marshes down in your country. Headwaters of the Rio Grande *and* the Arkansas *and* the Colorado Rivers are hereabout, girl; you know the Colorado, don't you? Ever see the Grand Canyon?"

"I . . ." Hopie said hesitantly. "Uh, not yet."

"Well, you won't see it this time, neither; we're too far north. But they're sights enough on this track. You like mountains—well, look at 'em! Fir trees thick like a carpet right up to the snowline."

We looked where he pointed, and as I concentrated on the jagged fringe of a cloud formation, color developed, and the white became snow, the gray was rock, and below was the green line of fir trees.

"You can still see the old molybdenum mine, there by the cattle herd; it's reclaimed land now, converted to pasture."

"Brown cows," Hopie said. "With white faces."

I saw them now, grazing on the slope near the railroad tracks that wound up and up, tracks that were striving to cross the high ridge of the Divide: the place where one drop of water flows forever east, the other west.

"Oh, see the flowers!" Hopie exclaimed. "Pretty yellow—"

"Yeah, they got golden pea here, Indian paintbrush—wild flowers galore, in summer. We'll be passing nigh Enver real soon now; see, we're crossing the South Platte River now; got to follow the river channels to find the best passes."

Indeed, I saw the river now; the tracks paralleled it for a while, then crossed on a trestle bridge, winding on into the mountain range. I saw the old Earth that Casey described; I had, in fact, slipped into a vision.

"I wish I could get out and splash in that water!" Hopie exclaimed.

"Naw—it's ice-cold, even in summer," Casey said knowledgeably.

I realized that Hopie was seeing the same scenery I was, guided by Casey's nostalgic description. She was sharing my vision. Did that mean that she truly had the same capacity I did? How gratifying that would be!

Hopie peered ahead. "Those mountains look awful tall," she said. "Can we really get over them?"

"Don't have to," Casey said grandly. "Got us a bridge—and a tunnel."

"A bridge *and* tunnel?" she asked.

"There's a chasm just before the face of the last peak," he explained. "Train has to go level, or at least stay within a three percent grade. Can't yo-yo up and down the jagged edges. So the track bridges across the valley and bores right through the peak. You'll see."

And we did see. The train rounded a turn, and there before us was a phenomenal cleft of a valley, dropping away from the mountain we were on, and the much higher mountain beyond. The tracks were mounted on a bridge that seemed to have no support; it was, in fact, a "hanging bridge" anchored in the rock at either side, and it looked precarious. Beyond it was the mouth of the tunnel through the mountain, seeming too small to hold the train, but, of course, that was just perspective.

We moved out on the bridge. Hopie peered down, made a little moan, and grabbed my hand tightly. Indeed, as the ground dropped precipitously away from us, it seemed we were flying. We feared the weight of the train would snap the cords of the bridge and send us hurtling to doom below. But the bridge held, and soon we were steaming into the tunnel, which expanded to take us in.

Inside, lights showed not the smooth, rounded walls I had anticipated, but rough-hewn rock—what remained after the tunnel had been irregularly blasted from the layers of the mountain. It was, in fact, a cave—a man-made cave without stalactites, crudely rounded at top and sides, just wide enough for the train. It seemed delightfully interminable, the spaced lights going by in blurs of brilliance. I was fascinated, and so was Hopie, who continued to squeeze my hand tightly. "I hope we don't run out of steam *here,*" she whispered.

At last we shot out into the light again, and into a wooden tunnel. The beams rose vertically above the height of the train, then across the top, braced by substantial corner boards set at a forty-five-degree angle. "What—" Hopie asked, startled.

"Protective snowshed," Casey explained nonchalantly. "Set up where the drifts get bad. Without those, the trains could not move in winter, 'cause the pile-up gets too heavy for the snowplows."

"Gee . . ." Hopie said, staring raptly out.

We chugged on across the state line into Equality, seeing the sheep grazing the slopes. "You can still see some of the old ruts where the wagons of the Oregon trail passed," Casey said. It was evident that he knew every bit of scenery along this track. "Further along we'll see Grant Teton National Park, about as pretty a spot as exists, and then Yellowstone. You ever see a geyser, girl?"

"Daddy, can we stop and see a geyser?" she demanded immediately of me. She was really excited.

I was about to answer when Shelia rolled up. The vision extended only to the exterior view; inside remained mundane. "Train approaching, boss," she said.

"Passing from the other direction? We've seen those before."

"Overtaking us from behind," she said grimly.

"Hey, there's no train scheduled now," Casey said.

"We know," she said. "That's why we're suspicious."

"Notify Coral," I said. Then, to Casey: "Can this train take evasive action?"

"She can leave the tracks, sure," he said. "But she's liable to get lost if she does. If that other train means trouble, she can follow us, anyway."

"Can we outrun her?"

"We're already doing max; the *Spirit*'s a tourist train, not a racer. That other's got a heavier engine or a lighter load, or she wouldn't be overhauling us. You figure trouble?"

"It's a distinct possibility," I said. "Our enemy knew he had failed to kill me when the Phis blast missed me. It seems logical that he would try something more direct."

"I never heard of no train robbery from another train," he said, scratching his head. "Usually it's horse-mounted men who board and—"

"My enemy didn't happen to have any horses handy in

this area," I said, smiling briefly. "It must have been easier to rent a spare train in Yenne, hustle some thugs aboard with their weapons, and take out after us in this isolated stretch where help will be slow arriving. It may be a jury-rigged effort, but we can be sure they believe they can do the job. Let's assume the worst and plan our defense accordingly. Suppose we turn up the gee-shields and rise quickly?"

"They can do the same," he said. "Can't get away that way."

"Suppose we drop lower?"

He shook his head. "I wouldn't, sir. We're at five bars now; this old train was built to take as high as eight, but I wouldn't trust her beyond seven now, and I'd feel nervous much beyond six. You'd be asking for implosion."

"So we could escape then but die in the process?"

"Yes, sir."

"I regret getting you folk of the train crew into this," I said.

"Just you figure out how to get us *out* of it!"

I held a quick council of war with Spirit and Coral. Spirit and I had both had battle training and experience in the Navy, and Coral was generally knowledgeable about inclose violence. Together we decided on our strategy for defense. We knew we didn't have much time, but we thought we could manage it.

There was a lot of work for Mrs. Burton to do in a hurry. First she had to go over the nether restaurant of the dining car, borrowing the train's supply of emergency sealant to shore up the car's interior doors, rendering it into a kind of space capsule. Then she rigged a temporary remote control system for the engine; it was crude, but it would enable a person inside the restaurant to trigger an unusual event. Then she went to the engine to set up that event, while the rest of us retreated to the restaurant. The windows were limited here, but we had an in-train video system that enabled us to view the rest of it or to peer out the dome windows of the restaurant above. We were all there, with the remaining personnel of the train, united by the common threat.

Hopie and Casey and I peered back, and now as the track curved we saw the pursuing train, steaming up the grade, definitely closing on us. "We'll pick up speed as we start down the other side of the Divide," Casey said. "But so will she. The grade don't make no difference for this. She'll catch us, sure."

"Grade?" Shelia asked.

Hopie glanced at me and winked. "Come here, Shel," she said. "Look out the window. See the mountains out there? The snow? We're crossing the Great Divide, and it's been an awful climb, but now we're almost at the top, about to start down the other side. We old railroad hands call the slope the grade."

"Oh," Shelia said, nonplussed. It was evident that she did not see the mountains or the snow outside.

Casey smiled. "Most folks are mundane," he murmured. "That's their curse. They don't even know what they're missing. You and your little girl're the first real folk I've met in a long time, Gov'nor."

"We're very rare species," I agreed.

"She sure favors you. I'd a known she was your kid right away, even if you hid her in a crowd. Bloodlines run true."

"That must be so," I agreed. I decided it would not be politic to inform him that Hopie was adopted.

The enemy train heaved within a train length of us. "Mrs. Burton," I said into the com, "is it ready yet?"

"Not yet, boss," she replied, sounding harried. "This monster's safety-cocked every which way, and I don't have the tools for a simple bypass. It'll be chancy."

"Do what you can. How much time do you need?"

"A good half-hour yet, boss, and then it's not sure."

"Very well. We'll try to get you that half-hour. Engineer?"

"Sir?" the other engineer responded. His name, naturally, was Jones.

"Start putting out that smoke—all you have left—in the next half-hour."

"Gotcha, sir," he agreed. Mrs. Burton had explained the reason to him.

We peered forward and watched the smoke. It started pouring out thickly, the volume seeming much greater than before. Because it was merely a coloring agent it could be intensified at will, but there was only so much color available. Jones was now dumping it in, expending the trip's supply in a short time. The cloud of smoke thinned as it carried to the rear but was now so thick at the start that this merely expanded it. Soon it was larger than the train, drifting just above us and slightly to the side.

"Okay, Casey," I said. "Put us in it."

Casey got on the com. "Okay, mate; damp her down and up the nulls; guide her in steady."

"I wisht someone was watching this," Jones muttered back.

"Someone *is,*" I pointed out. "The enemy train."

"Hang on," Casey said. "Reality's 'bout to take a beating."

Hopie and I smiled and took firm hold on the anchored furniture, as did the others in the chamber.

The big propulsion-wheel fans damped down. The train slowed immediately and began to fall, as it depended on forward velocity to maintain its elevation. Then the gee-shields increased their effect, and we lost weight. Soon we were in free-fall, dead in the atmosphere and moving up toward our own voluminous cloud of smoke. It was a perfectly simple maneuver in the atmosphere of Jupiter, but to those of us who were watching it through the vision of old Earth, it was fantastic.

First our train slowed on the track, and the enemy train overhauled us rapidly. Then, just as the other was drawing up beside us, its passenger cars illuminated from inside so that we could see the armed men peering out at us, aiming their lasers, we left the track and floated into the sky. Hopie gave a little sigh of amazement, locked into the vision, and I was startled myself though I had known exactly what to expect. As it was, one laser beam angled in through the window, but after passing through the thick, glassy panes of each car, it lacked its originally punishing force. Glass may pass a laser beam through, but it tends to diffuse and deregister it, causing it to become more like ordinary light. Which is not to say a person can't be hurt by a laser through a window, just that he will be hurt less.

We left the other train below. We maneuvered on the small wheel fans of the cars, angling them down to provide propulsion. Slowly we ascended into our great cloud of smoke. I took a last look at the snowy mountains beneath, bidding adieu to the remnant of my vision. I saw the enemy train blundering on ahead, caught by surprise by our maneuver. It had no special equipment, such as a flatcar-mounted cannon, fortunately. Such weapons existed, and they could be devastating, but they were hardly available to illicit assassination squads on short notice in the outlying districts. So this enemy could not simply blast us out of the atmosphere, and, in fact, could not fire any solid projectile at us, because any attempt to do so through the windows would cause the cars of that train to leak and perhaps implode. The men inside were confined to lasers which, as we had seen, were relatively ineffective in this situation.

Then the cloud enveloped us, and darkness reigned outside. We had disappeared into our smoke.

"We got away from them!" Hopie exclaimed happily.

"Not exactly," I said. "We have smoke for only half an hour, and when it dissipates, we'll still be out here, and so will they."

"What will they do then?" she asked, worried.

"They'll board us. We're like spaceships; the locks can be mated and used anytime the pressure is equal on both sides."

"Maybe we'd better phone for help, then."

We had already checked that. "They're jamming the broadcast."

"Can't we stop them?" She didn't have to ask what they would do once they got aboard our train.

"We could laser them down as they entered," I said. "If we could guard every lock. But they'll mate the whole train and could cross through any of a dozen locks. They're bound to get in sooner or later." I was answering her questions seriously, because at thirteen she was old enough to understand, and I didn't want her to be exposed to combat conditions without being prepared.

She was taking it well enough so far. "So we're holed up in here, in this sealed chamber, where they can't reach us, anyway?"

"That's part of it."

"But won't they just pry open the door and—"

"Yes. That will take them a little while, however, because they won't have heavy-duty equipment."

"But after that little while—"

"They would be in," I concluded. I suffered a momentary

vision of one of the times in my own youth when pirates had boarded our refugee bubble, when Spirit and I had bracketed Hopie's present age. Violence, rape, and murder had ensued. This was not a vision I cared to share with my daughter, and I intended to protect her from ever experiencing it.

She glanced at me cannily. "But you're cooking something, aren't you?"

"I think you'd rather not know, honey."

"I think I'd rather *not* not know, Daddy," she countered. "I'm scared."

She spoke for those other than herself. It seemed better to reassure them all, especially Megan, who was sitting pale and tight-lipped. Again I was reminded that these were not combat personnel. Only Spirit and I had been toughened to this sort of thing, and Coral could handle it. The others were in trouble. "Mrs. Burton is arranging to shunt some steam inside," I said.

"Steam?" She didn't grasp the relevance.

"It will make them uncomfortable," I explained.

"Oh." She still didn't get it but did not pursue the matter further, and the others who did comprehend did not comment.

Our time passed. The other train could not connect to us because it could not see us. To enter the cloud blind would be to risk a collision that could cause both trains to implode, and obviously they didn't want to perish with us. But we knew they were outside, waiting.

Our smoke thinned. "Are you ready, Mrs. Burton?" I asked on the com.

"Not yet, boss. This thing's tough!"

"But our smoke is dissipating."

"Don't I know it!" she retorted. "But this baby's a stinker. I've got to have more time."

The enemy train was coming into view as the smoke continued to fade. "Casey, how sure are you about the implosion resistance of this train?"

Casey shook his head. "Not sure at all, Gov'nor. She's pretty old."

"Then the other train won't be sure, either."

"For sure. We all get nervous about going down."

"So if we go down, they may not."

Casey swallowed. "I'd sure rather go *up,* Gov'nor!"

I angled my head, peering up. "That contrail—isn't that a high-velocity plane?"

Spirit glanced up, nodding. "Navy surplus dual element fighter," she said. "I've been watching it."

I raised an eyebrow. "It was there before the smoke?" "Dual-element" meant that it functioned in either space or thin atmosphere.

"Affirmative. Circling above us."

"So if we rise, we'll get strafed."

"Seems likely," she agreed. "And one bullet through our seal—"

"I got the message," Casey said. "They figured to drive us up, then hole us. We can't go up."

"We can't go up," I agreed. "They can't come down this deep, but they don't need to, as long as that other train's here. We must go down—until Mrs. Burton's ready."

"I hope she's ready soon," he said fervently. Casey was no coward, but the notion of implosion had him green about the gills. I suppose those who travel in atmosphere all their lives feel about implosion the way we who have traveled much in space feel about sudden depressurization. We all have our peculiar horrors. Still, I remembered the way that city-bubble had gone down during the storm a dozen years before, and I knew I was not immune to that fear.

The enemy train drew alongside us again, ready to lock on. We dropped suddenly as our gee-shields moved to quarter-gee. It took the enemy a moment to reorient; then it dropped, too, but we dropped faster. It took them another period to phase in on our rate; then they closed again.

The alarm klaxon went off on our train: pressure had reached six bars. Everybody jumped, and Casey stiffened. "God, I'm not a praying man, but if they don't stop soon, we'll have to."

The enemy train slowed its descent, evidently similarly wary of the pressure. We slowed, not going any deeper than we needed to. But then they tried to close again, and we had to drop farther. Six point five bars. Six point six. We were all getting uncomfortable.

"Resume forward motion," I ordered the engineer.

"Gotcha, Gov'nor." He sounded just like Casey. The

train commenced forward motion, and as the vanes took hold, the gee-shields eased, allowing trace gravity to return. That was a comfort.

But the enemy matched velocity and closed again. We had gee but not freedom. "Ready yet, Mrs. Burton?" I inquired, keeping my voice calm.

"Almost," she replied. "I've got the bypass, but I don't have the stuff I need for the release. I'll have to rig a mechanical release, and that'll take time."

"We're down about as far as we dare go," I said. "If we go too far—"

"I know, boss. But without a remote-control unit—"

"Well, rig your chain," I said. "Then get over here as fast as you can—you and Jones. They're about to lock on and board."

"We can let them board at the tail end," Spirit pointed out. "There are five cars back there we won't be using. One guard at the back of the diner can hold them off for a while."

"And we can concentrate our force at engine, travel car, and diner," I agreed. "Between us we have six lasers; two lasers per person, one person guarding the rear, one the engine, and one the travel car—"

"Three, right," Coral said. "But you not one of them."

"But I'm trained," I protested.

"You the king. You die, all dead."

She was right. My life could not be risked any more than that of the king in a chess game. It was the single nonexpendable piece.

The locks were four-way affairs, actually almost separate units, which clamped to the ends of the connected cars to provide access from either side and/or an open passage between cars. They could be closed, but we had the car access open for our own convenience. This meant that the enemy train could connect by one lock between each two cars, for, of course, it could only tie in on one side of us or the other. We had, in effect, a series of T-connectors to guard, with the enemy coming through the stem of the *T*.

Spirit went to the rear of the diner to guard the access from the back of the train; she would retreat to the home chamber when she had to. Coral went to the front, guarding the entrances to both diner and passenger car—a difficult position but one for which she was most competent. Ebony was ready to go to the engine, but Casey protested. "Can't send a little gal into that," he said. "That's a man's job. I'll do it."

"This isn't your quarrel," I reminded him. "You just come with the train."

"And it's my train they're raiding," he said. "And my pal Jones up there in the cab. Gimme that laser."

I had to acquiesce; he surely would be more effective than Ebony. I gave him two lasers and let him go. "But when I call you in, you and Mrs. Burton and Jones come in here fast," I told him. "You know what we're planning."

"Sure do," he said, and headed grimly out.

The enemy train closed the moment we stopped maneuvering. We tried to confuse it by jogging up and down, but they flung magnetic grapples, normally used for moving individual cars about, and captured us. Now we could see that the enemy cars were packed with armed men; there must have been fifty of them. This was going to be rough, indeed.

Still, a single person with a laser could hold off an army at a narrow aperture, and all the locks were narrow. As long as the laser charges held out we could hold on, and we hoped that would be long enough for Mrs. Burton to complete her job.

We closed off the restaurant chamber, but the com kept us in touch with the rest of the train. We could see Spirit's post, overlooking the entrance to the sleeping car; she had good coverage of the locks there. Coral had similar coverage of the passenger car, but her job was more difficult because she could not risk firing toward the engine unless she was sure that Jones and Mrs. Burton were clear. Casey had the easiest post, backed by our own people, but it was also farthest from the security of the diner. When we contracted, Coral would have to protect the retreat from the engine; then she and Spirit would follow, leaving the rest of the train to the raiders.

The enemy connected with a series of clanks as each car lock mated with its opposite. These things were largely automatic; with five bars pressure outside, or more, it was foolish to risk the unreliability of human beings for the multiple couplings. It made sense, but I was struck by the similarity of this situation to the one we had faced as refugees in a bubble-ship in space, unable to prevent the entry of pirates. Surely these were pirates here!

They did not come cautiously; they came with the abandon of grossly superior numbers, seeking to overwhelm us in an instant. Every lock opened simultaneously, and men came through each, holding their lasers ready.

They were met by the fire of our own lasers. One beam from Spirit, one from Coral, and two men fell, each holed efficiently in the throat. Casey, untrained in this, hesitated, but when a beam coruscated into the frame of the lock beside him, he fired back, winging an enemy. The man fell but fired again, and a second man appeared behind him.

"Shoot for the face," I told Casey. "One beam per man, no more; they outnumber us." Of course, the enemy could hear the com speaking, but that couldn't be helped.

Casey gulped and did it, taking out the second man and then the first. Casey was no killer, but it was his train he was defending, and he knew he was in a desperate situation.

After that initial round the enemy paused; no man came into our range. But they were boarding all along the rear of the train, and now they knew exactly where we were.

"Progress, Mrs. Burton?" I asked, still keeping my voice calm. I knew that our time was running short—very short.

"Close enough," she said. "I'm rigging a line; I can pull the cork from the diner; I think it'll work."

"Then unroll your line, Mrs. Burton," I said. "Get back here quickly—you and the engineers."

She strung her line, and the three of them retreated from the engine, entering the passenger car. But, as they reached the center, more men burst in at the now-unguarded engine lock, threw themselves into the crannies of the cab, and began firing into the passenger car. Casey whirled to face them but too slowly; a beam seared into his leg, and he cried out and fell, dropping his own weapon. Coral aimed her laser but could not fire at the enemy without striking our own people.

"Get under cover!" Coral screamed at them. "Behind the seats!"

Belatedly they obeyed. But now the enemy men had a direct line of fire down the center aisle of the car, making further retreat hazardous.

"Cover your heads," Coral called. Then she hurled something. It skidded along the floor, then rolled, fetched up at the far end, and exploded. A small grenade. "Now get into the diner—fast!" Coral ordered.

Jones and Mrs. Burton scrambled up, but Casey could not regain his feet. Jones grabbed him by the shoulders and started hauling him along.

Mrs. Burton lifted her spool of line. "It's been severed!" she exclaimed, horrified. "I've got to reconnect it!"

But already more men were piling into the cab and into the front of the diner. I saw that Coral could not hold off both groups simultaneously. "I'm going out there!" I cried. "Otherwise we're lost! Shelia, take over coordination." Then I wrenched open the lock and dived out. I had no laser, but I was combat-trained, and the old reflexes guided me.

Now I could not see what the others were doing, for the com was a spot-address system, but I knew Shelia would be advising Coral of my approach. Accordingly I did not concern myself about her; I assumed she would cover the far side of the passenger car and leave the near side to me.

I was right. I burst into the lock area between cars and plowed into two men. I clubbed one on the side of the neck hard enough to send him reeling into the wall and dived low at the other. I caught him by the knees and lifted, sending him to the floor. Thank God for gee; that maneuver would not have worked in free-fall.

The first man was not completely stunned. He started to bring his laser about. I grabbed his arm, straightened it against my body, and broke his elbow with a strike of the heel of my left hand. This isn't sanitary fighting, but it is effective. I took the laser from him, set it at his ear, and fired a half-second beam.

Steam boiled out of his ear, and he fell. I beamed the other in the throat, and he ceased operation. The messy throat shot is the one that holes the jugular vein; the neat shot merely cooks the spinal nerve. I had done it neatly. Then I moved on to check the passenger car.

To my surprise our people weren't moving; they were huddled in dialogue. "Get into the diner!" I yelled.

Without turning, Coral answered me. "Her line was severed by my grenade, but we can't restring it. Enemy's got the engine."

I saw the problem. We had to have that line intact or our retreat was pointless. "Jones, get your friend to cover," I snapped. "I'll take care of this."

Without a word Jones heaved Casey up on his shoulders and staggered toward the diner. It wasn't the weight that gave him trouble, for gee was fractional, but the lack of it; he had been braced for a much heavier load.

A pirate face showed above a seat. Coral skated a metal star at it, and it disappeared.

I joined her. "I'll cover you. Toss another grenade."

She ran on to the cab while I watched, laser poised. When she was beside the lock, I moved up. There were two bodies there, but a laser beam speared out from the cab. I fired back, forcing the man to duck away, and fired again as Coral readied her grenade. Then she hurled it in.

We were shielded from the direct blast, but the concussion rocked me. We jumped into the lock, guarding it from approach from the other train, while Mrs. Burton stepped through.

"No good," she said as soon as she saw the cab. "My attachment's been broken off. Can't use the line now."

"Can't set it off?" I asked, dismayed. The enemy force, numerous as it was, was spread throughout the train; four men dead had depleted this region, but I heard more charging forward in the other train. We could close the lock, but they would just open it again. Without that device of hers, we would be finished.

"I'll set it off," she said. "You scoot back to the diner. I'll give you thirty seconds."

"But—"

"Better do it, boss," Shelia said on the com. "They're moving against Spirit; she'll have to retreat in a moment. Another's in the lock behind you; he doesn't know where you are yet, but—"

I had a hard decision to make in a hurry. "You want it this way, Mrs. Burton?"

"I'm old, boss," she said. "You gave me a good retirement. Now *move!*"

"Move," I echoed, knowing it was the only way. We

closed the lock to the other train, which I hoped would delay entry for thirty seconds. Coral preceded me down the length of the passenger car, running fleetly.

A beam speared out from the next lock. Coral returned the fire, but then she stumbled. I knew she had been hit. I vaulted over her body, landed beside the lock, started my beam, and poked my hand around the corner, spraying the entire chamber without looking. I heard the noise of someone falling. Then I jumped back to Coral, heaved her up, and careened on through, stepping over the bodies. Gummy blood adhered to my soles; one of those killings had been messy. Our thirty seconds was up, and we weren't safe yet.

I heard a loud hissing from the cab. I knew what it meant. "Farewell, Mrs. Burton!" I gasped as I launched myself at the door to our chamber. It opened as I reached it; I stumbled in, and it closed behind me. I saw that Hopie was operating it; she had been alert and timed it perfectly.

Now we watched what happened beyond our sanctuary. The screen showed it clearly. A great rush of steam was pouring from the cab, billowing out, funneling through the locks from car to car in both trains, spreading throughout the length of both. We heard the screams of the men being burned. They could not escape; the steam quickly permeated every crevice of both trains, and it was super-hot. It was the steam that normally drove the propulsion propellers; Mrs. Burton had tapped into one of its lines, routing it into the passenger section. This was, of course, an abuse of valuable water, but a necessary device on this occasion.

I checked Coral. She had been burned through the abdomen. She was alive but unconscious. We gave her a sedative to keep her that way; she would live but would only be in pain while conscious, until we got her to a competent medical facility.

"She did her job," Spirit murmured.

Indeed, she had. Coral had taken the shot that might otherwise have caught me.

After a few minutes the trains were quiet. We waited for the steam to cool; in due course it condensed to water. No more came from the engine; we had exhausted its limited supply.

Spirit and I emerged to find globules of water floating

about the cars; naturally we had returned to null-gee when the drive power of the engine was sabotaged by the loss of steam pressure. Such was my distraction, I hadn't even noticed. We could no longer use this engine, but fortunately we had another available, from the other train.

There were dead men everywhere; the steam had suffocated them all. I exchanged a glance with Spirit. Yes, we remembered the bubble in space! We had been attacked once too often by relentless pirates and had killed them all by depressurizing the ships. Had anything really changed?

Mrs. Burton was dead, too, of course—and that also echoed the past. "Helse," I murmured. There was no similarity between the young, beautiful girl of my past and the old woman of the present, except this: each had knowingly sacrificed her life in horrible fashion to save mine.

I leaned against Spirit and cried.

Chapter 17

REBA

We limped on to Slake in the state of Beehive and made our report. This wasn't on our planned route, but we knew we needed to stop in a city of sufficient size to handle our problems: two wounded, some fifty or so dead, and badly battered equipment. Hereafter we would carry a jamproof broadcast unit on the train, so as to be able to summon the police promptly.

Megan was in a state bordering on shock, and Hopie, despite her good performance under pressure, was not much better off. They had never been exposed to savagery of this intensity and personal nature before. I think a significant portion of their horror was from the fact that Spirit and I had actively participated in the killing. Had we not done so, all of us would have died, and our train might have disappeared without trace, scuttled in the atmosphere: the perfect crime. But the necessities of combat are seldom intelligible to civilians. Shelia and Ebony came through it fairly well, however; it seemed that they each had had prior exposure to savagery.

I had not scheduled a campaign speech in Slake, but my news conference there became very like one. I described what had happened, suitably edited, and concluded that one of my earliest priorities as president would be the restoration of true law and order in Jupiter society. "Especially along the railroad tracks," I concluded with a smile. And do you know, the applause lasted several minutes. The general tide of violence had been rising throughout the nation, because of governmental policies that simply did not address the needs of the people and a rate of monetary inflation and unemployment that was accelerating. There was a deepening unrest, and now I had, almost inadvertently, tapped into it as a campaign issue.

Then some idiot began chanting "Hubris! Hubris!" and the conference dissolved into a rather delightful anarchy.

The police launched their investigation, of course, but I knew that our attackers would simply turn out to be hired thugs, paid anonymously. I knew that true professional assassins would have come prepared to do the job properly, and we would have had no chance to resist. A single missile to destroy our power source, which was the engine, and cause implosion; then a suited technician to board and deactivate the gee-shields and send the train to the deeps. No evidence of foul play; it would have been listed as an unfortunate accident.

However, it was now imperative for us to locate our specific enemy. I just did not believe it was the drug moguls, though they would certainly be amenable to my extinction. After the reversal of their bribe ploy in Sunshine they were disorganized, and the police everywhere were monitoring their activities closely; they simply couldn't have arranged this sort of action. I had a very strong suspicion who it was but hesitated to voice it until Megan, emerging from her emotional stasis, voiced it for me.

"Tocsin," she said. "He knows how dangerous you have become to him. You can martial the Hispanic vote, which would otherwise have gone to him, and the female vote, and a fair share of the general vote: enough to destroy him. He will stop at nothing to nullify you as an opponent."

"But we can't accuse him," I said. "There is no proof."

"He never provides proof," she said. "How well I know!"

Yes, Tocsin was a cunning one. But with Megan's confirmation of my suspicion I was ready to proceed to the offense. It was obvious that we could no longer afford to be strictly defensive or to live and let live; the political war had become a physical one.

However, with what irony only he knew, President Tocsin now officially deplored the violence and designated me as a candidate of stature, entitled to government protection. The Secret Service moved in to take over my bodyguarding, and this extended to my family. This was just as well, for Coral had been grievously wounded; she would recover but required surgery and a prolonged convalescence before she could return to duty. I made it a point to interview the key Secret Service men assigned to us and found them to be professionals who had no concern for party or personality; they were dedicated to the proposition that no body they protected would be damaged, and they had an excellent record. There was no deception here.

Still, there were occasions when it was not possible to safeguard me perfectly. One such occurred in Firebird, in the state of Canyon, well along on my campaign tour. I had played to increasing audiences; news of my train ordeal had generated an immense groundswell of sympathy that was translating into support as folk thronged to hear me talk. Never would I have gone into that train attack voluntarily or brought my family and staff into such risk; but it had become a considerable asset to my campaign. Instead of being a long-shot candidate, I was now advancing into Serious Candidate status.

Curiosity brought many folk, but once they heard me speak, it became more than that. If there was one thing I could do well, it was move a crowd. It seemed to be an extension of my talent. I treated the crowd as an individual and responded to its signals, using the information to amplify the things that made it respond. It is often said that a man is learning nothing while he is talking, but that is not necessarily true; his speech can be like radar, bouncing off the audience and educating him by the response. There can be a very positive feedback. I suspect that this is the root of the success of every truly effective campaign. What I actually said hardly mattered, and pundits—notably Thorley—roundly panned my positions in print. But the people were becoming mine. Yet I needed more, so had an eye for the spectacular, for something that would tie more directly in to the malaise of the times and enable me to dramatize my position positively.

In this instance a desperate man had taken an employment office hostage; he demanded a job or he would blow up the place. They thought he was bluffing but weren't sure. Police surrounded the region but did not dare enter. This event was typical of the times; there had been a number recently, as the notion spread about the planet, and some bombs had indeed been detonated. Terrorism was becoming more popular in the United States of Jupiter and bringing in its wake a deep disquiet among people who had never known such violence before. I had only to look at Megan to understand how they felt.

"Hubris!" the man exclaimed suddenly to the holo-news pickup. Evidently they had a remote-controlled unit there in the office with his permission. "He's in town, isn't he? Let me talk to him! He's for the common man!"

I glanced at Spirit when that news reached me, then at my secretary, who already had details flashing on her newscreen for me: the man was called Booker, and he had lost his job when an injury made him lame. He was running out of unemployment compensation but had been unable to get any other job despite being declared technically fit by the welfare office. Standards for unfitness had become ludicrous in some instances, as the government tried to cut down on expenses. I saw my opportunity.

"Are you ready for this?" I asked Shelia.

"Anything you say, boss," she said bravely.

"I'll handle it," I told the local authorities.

"Not on your life, sir!" my SS guard protested. "We can't let you march into a bomb-wielding maniac!"

"I'm sure he won't let you into the office," I said. "But this is a thing I must do; I am, after all, a politician, and this is a potentially newsworthy event."

"Sir, you won't need any news if you're dead! We can't let you expose yourself to such hazard."

"Let me explain what I have in mind," I said. And I explained. "Okay with you?" I concluded.

The man was amazed. "Let me clear it with my superior, sir." He did so, and we proceeded to the site of the event.

A huge crowd was forming, cordoned off by the police, and more folk were coming in, attracted as much by my involvement as by the situation. I made my way through and approached the office. It overlooked a street-size mall that was now clear of pedestrians. "*Señor* Booker," I called, naming him in Hispanic fashion to help identify myself. "I am Hope Hubris." The camera was on me, which was exactly where I wanted it.

"Come in, Governor!" he called.

"I must bring my secretary," I said.

"No way! It's you alone!"

I stood my ground. "It is very important that my secre-

tary be able to do her job," I said. "Surely you would not
deny her that."

"Deny her that!" he repeated. "Listen, Hubris, they denied me *my* job! What do I care for—"

But I had signaled Shelia, and now she rolled down to
join me. "Here is my secretary, *Señor.*"

There was a pause as the lame man peered at the crippled woman. It would have been difficult indeed for him to
deny her in this circumstance. "Okay," he said, realizing
that on this front, at least, he had been outmaneuvered.

We entered the office, Shelia's wheelchair preceding me.
Three office workers were seated on the floor, leaning
against one wall; Booker stood with his bomb by the opposite wall. Shelia and I came to a halt in the middle. Her
eyes were on the miniature viewscreen mounted on her
left armrest. She glanced briefly up at me and nodded
slightly.

"Señor, let's sit down and work this out," I said heartily.
"Why did you ask for me?"

"Because you're the only politician on the planet a regular man can trust," Booker said. "You get things done
when they can't be done."

I smiled. "You know the camera is on us; you are helping my campaign."

"I think your campaign's fine, Hubris; I hope you make
president. We've got to get *somebody* in there to clean up
this mess. But right now you've got to help me. I need a
job."

I frowned. "You know you cannot get a job by blowing up
the employment agency. You have committed a crime, and
for that they will make you pay. Surely you knew that before you decided to do this."

He nodded. "Guess I wasn't thinking straight. I realized
too late. I said to myself, Booker, you've dug yourself a
hole. A black hole! But then I thought, Hubris is in town.
He can help me if anyone can. So I asked for you; never
really thought you'd come."

"My guards tried to stop me," I admitted. "It is their job
to see that I don't get myself blown up before election day."

"Yeah. Well, I don't want to blow anybody up, but my
wife, she's sick, and my little boy needs surgery, and the

money's gone. What's a man to do? If they'd just give me a job!"

Things began to add up. "Your son . . . when did the need for surgery develop?"

"Last year. He had a medical exam, and this irregularity in his heartbeat showed up on their graph. Said he'd have to have it operated on when he got older; something about a valve not closing right, so the blood didn't always go right. Then I hurt my leg, and—"

"And they had a pretext to fire you," I finished.

"Yeah. Said I couldn't do the work well enough anymore. Hell, Hubris, I could do it okay; I'm no pro track runner, anyway! Then the welfare folk said I wasn't sick enough for them, but I still couldn't get a job."

"That's called falling through the crack," I remarked.

"Yeah. Too sick to work, too fit not to. So what the hell'm I supposed to do—starve and let my family die?"

I resisted the impulse to editorialize on the unfairness of the system; that was self-evident. Meanwhile, I had spied a key that might unlock this situation. "Don't you realize, Mr. Booker, that it wasn't your leg that did it? It was your son."

The bomb wavered in his arms. "What?"

"Your company had comprehensive medical insurance for all employees and their families, didn't it? That would have covered the surgery on your son when it was time for it. But your company gets a rebate if the insurance claims are low; that's standard practice. They knew your son's surgery was coming and that it would be a large claim, so they acted to minimize it. That, too, is standard practice."

"They—they fired me so they wouldn't have to pay on my boy?" he asked, appalled.

"And the other companies declined to hire you for the same reason," I said. "The welfare folk are right; you *are* fit enough to work. And you are willing. But your son is a serious liability."

"But—"

"Of course, we can't prove that," I cautioned him, just as if this wasn't being picked up by the camera for what would, with luck, be planetary news. "But it does make business sense."

"But my boy'll maybe *die* without that operation!"

"Señor, that is one problem with the present system of private insurance," I told him, knowing that this was as fine a campaign issue as any. Tocsin had led the crackdown on supposed waste in welfare and medical insurance; now the consequence of applying business ethics to medicine was coming clear. "They seek, naturally enough, to minimize claims. They are interested in saving money. I believe that system should be reformed so that no children have to die for the sake of a company's balance sheet. I can't promise to get that changed right away, but I will certainly work on it."

"All this—these months out of work, my wife taking it so hard that she lost her health—just to get out of paying for my boy?" He was still struggling with the enormity of it.

"Mr. Booker—" I was having trouble sticking to "señor," but it's hard to be letter-perfect in an extemporaneous situation. "You have been wronged, the way a great many workers are wronged. But you are no killer. You don't want to hurt these people here at the employment office who have done you no injury and would have helped you if they could have. They can't *make* a company assume the burden of your family's medical expenses. But perhaps we can help your son. You need to get legal aid to institute a proceding against your former employer on the grounds that he terminated you wrongfully. Win that case, and not only will they be liable for the expense of your son's surgery, they also may be required to restore your job and pay punitive damages. It is certainly worth a try."

"But—"

"But you have committed a crime. For that you will have to pay the penalty. But perhaps not a prohibitive one. If it were, for example, to turn out that your bomb was not real, then you would be guilty only of the *threat* of mayhem, not the reality. I believe any reasonable judge would take into consideration the provocation that drove you to an act of desperation. You might have to serve some time in prison, but not long, and meanwhile, your own legal initiative would be working its way through the system—"

Booker grabbed the top of his box with his left hand and lifted it off. "It's just an empty box," he said, showing it to the camera. "I couldn't afford the makings of a real bomb."

I turned to the camera. "The siege is over," I announced.

"Please have an attorney come with the police, to represent Mr. Booker. One competent in medical law."

Booker looked at me. "You knew it was a bluff!"

I approached him, bringing Shelia forward with me. "See her screen, *señor?* Beneath her chair she carries a metal detector with a computerized image alignment. It told her you had no bomb in there. But I didn't come to give away your secret; I came to help you decide what was best for you. I think you will receive justice now, *señor.*"

We shook hands. "I knew I could trust you, Hubris."

Needless to say, that incident made a good many more headlines than one of my routine campaign speeches would have. I had gambled and won—again. I cannot claim that there was not a healthy element of luck in this, but this is the nature of winning politics. Unlucky politicians lose.

So it went. There were no more direct attempts on my life, or at least none that could be demonstrated to be the result of organized malevolence, but we knew that Tocsin was not about to let me challenge him for his office with impunity. It was not a purely personal thing with him; he simply worked to see that *no* serious threats to his power developed. There were other candidates for the nomination, and awkward or embarrassing things happened to them with suspicious frequency, but nothing was ever traceable to the source. I had survived most successfully, partly because I had planned well—Megan remained invaluable for that—and partly because I worked hard and had several formidable assets. Spirit was matchless on supervising the nuts-and-bolts details of the campaign, and my staff was competent and dedicated. I made good progress.

Then we came to the hurdles of the primaries. Over the centuries there had been attempts to reform the confused primary system, but each state fought for its right to have its own, so nothing was ever done. The first was in the small state of Granite, and it generally had a disproportionate effect on the remaining campaign season. The polls favored me to come in third, but I suspected that I had more support than that, because, though my political base was not great and I lacked the money for much advertising, my voters should be highly motivated. If not, I would be in trouble, so it was nervous business, and I spent as much time in the bubbles of Granite as any candidate.

I did not win it. But I came in second, significantly stronger than predicted. That, in the legerdemain of politics, translated into an apparent win. Suddenly I was a much stronger candidate than I had seemed before, and the media commentators were paying much more attention to me. In their eyes I had become viable. They had much fun with the Hispanic candidate, but my issues were sound, the unrest of the populace continued to grow, and the aspirations of those who were sick of the existing situation focused increasingly on me. I showed up more strongly in the next primary, becoming a rallying point for the disaffected, and the third one I won. Then I was really on my way.

The party hierarchy did not endorse my candidacy, but I came in due course to the nominating convention with significant bloc support, and former President Kenson made a gracious speech on my behalf. The polls of the moment suggested that I had a better chance than the other candidates to unseat President Tocsin, because of my strong appeal to women and minorities, and that was a thing we all wished to accomplish. There was the customary interaction of overlapping interests, but Megan and Spirit and my staff handled that, so I won't go into detail here. The hard-nosed essence was that though the party regulars were not thrilled with me, I had the most solid grass-roots support, and my ability to take the sizable Hispanic vote away from Tocsin without alienating the general populace was decisive. We did not make an issue of my female staff, but every woman was aware of it; I did not have to make promises to women any more than I did to Hispanics or Blacks, because they knew I would do right by them. I also picked up strong union support. As the convention proceeded a powerful groundswell of public sentiment buoyed my candidacy. The handwriting was written rather plainly on the wall: If the party regulars opposed me openly, they were liable to become irregulars, and the nomination would still be mine after a divisive battle. That could cost us all the election. It was to their interest to move graciously with the tide and to accept the first Hispanic nominee.

And so it came to pass. I chose as my running mate my

sister Spirit, and there was massive applause from the distaff contingent for this innovation, and stifled apoplexy elsewhere. It was not the first time a woman had been selected for this office, but it was the first for a sibling of the presidential candidate. Oh, I knew the party regulars preferred a ticket balanced geographically and philosophically, but my argument was this: It was pointless to have a vice-presidential candidate whose major recommendation was that he did not match the locale or philosophy of the president. I wanted a running mate who understood and endorsed my positions exactly, so that in the event of my death in office my program would be carried out without deviation.

No person, male or female, fitted this definition better than did Spirit. There was grumbling in the back rooms, but this was my will, and it would not be denied. Many of the wives of delegates made their will known unmistakably to their spouses; what might seem a liability with male voters was an enormous asset with female voters. We seemed to have, on balance, a stronger ticket than the conventional system would have provided. There was one half-serious complaint: a delegate from Ami muttered that I had chosen the wrong sister. Faith was in attendance, of course; she demurred, blushing, looking prettier than she had in years. The Ami contingent, of course, had been absolutely solid for me from the outset of the campaign.

Now I was the official nominee, going into territory where no Hispanic had gone before. Now I had comprehensive party support, financial and organizational. I addressed monstrous and enthusiastic crowds. But the popularity polls were sobering; though my chances were indeed significantly better than those of any other nominee would have been, I remained six percentage points behind Tocsin. He was, after all, the incumbent, and had a secure base of power, seemingly unlimited funds provided by the special interests, and the name recognition and power over events of a sitting president. These were truly formidable assets. In addition, I knew, there remained sizable conservative and racist elements—the two by no means synonymous, as Thorley had shown me—that did not take to the halls to demonstrate but would never vote for a liberal Hispanic. Six points might not seem like much, out of a hundred, but when it meant that Tocsin was supported by forty-five percent of the responding population, and I by thirty-nine percent, it meant deep trouble. I had to campaign hard enough to make up the difference.

I did. I continued to use the campaign train; it had become a symbol. Now it had many more cars, for the Secret Service men, the big party supporters, and the media reporters. They all seemed to take pleasure in riding the same train with the candidate, and perhaps, to a degree, they shared the fascination with trains. On occasion Thorley was present, shuttling between my campaign and Tocsin, trenchantly torpedoing me at every turn. But I couldn't help it: I liked the man, and I did owe him for two significant services. When I could discreetly do so, I had him in to the family car for a meal and chat; Megan, Spirit, and Hopie liked him also. He never commented on this in the media, though he now had the leverage to put anything into print he wished. It is possible for people to be personal friends but political adversaries, and very few others realized the full nature of our friendship or adversity. Spirit continued to provide him full information on our campaign, honoring my agreement; we kept no secrets from the press.

Indeed, this agreement was to prove fundamentally important and open the way for Thorley's third significant service to me. One matter occurred that did have to be secret, and so we had to trust Thorley and even ask his cooperation. I do not claim that this was the proper interaction of politician and journalist, but it was necessary. I owed Thorley for a life and a reputation; now my career itself was to be put into his hands.

It happened in this manner. In the course of two months my campaign succeeded in drawing me up almost even with Tocsin despite his advantages, forty-two percent to forty-three percent. The election was now rated a dead heat; no one was certain which of us would win. It was my magnetic presence on stage that did it, my talent relating to ever-larger audiences, turning them on. As I gained, Tocsin pulled out all the nether stops, as was his wont when pressed. In addition to a phenomenal barrage of hostile advertising, there were anonymous charges against me, each with just enough substance to give it a semblance of credibility: I was a mass murderer (that is, I had killed a shipful of attacking pirates), I was a notorious womanizer (I had known many women sexually, as was required by Navy policy), I had been charged with mutiny as a Naval officer (but exonerated), and I had adopted a child who resembled me suspiciously. All these were subject to detoxification by clarification of the circumstances; I ignored them except when directly challenged, and then I answered briefly. With one exception: the last. That one I addressed by means of a challenge: "Show me the mother of this child."

Would you believe it, three different Saxon women came forward, each claiming to have been my paramour fifteen years before and to have conceived by me and to have given up the baby for adoption by me because I had paid her to do so. But none could produce evidence of such payment, and when we had them blood-typed, two were shown to be impossible as parents of Hopie. The third was possible, but a search of her employment record showed that she had not missed a day in the critical period, and an old photograph of her in a bathing suit showed her definitely unpregnant when she would have had to be in the eighth month. Medical records concurred: no baby had been delivered of her in that year. "It is evident," Thorley commented wryly, "that the girl's mother has sufficient discretion to avoid publicity." This was, I believe, the only period he remarked publicly on my family situation, because it had for the moment become legitimate news.

"But what does it matter?" I asked, bringing fifteen-year-old Hopie to a news conference and putting my arm around her. "She is my daughter *now,* and I will never deny her." Indeed, the blood tests showed I could have been her natural father, and her resemblance to me in intellect as well as the physical was startling. I was so obviously pleased by this that the effort to smear me by this avenue came to nothing. Perhaps it was that every man has his secrets, and this was the kind that anyone can understand. What really finished it was Thorley's interview with Megan, in which he asked her point-blank why she had agreed to adopt this child, who could not have been her own.

"I love her; she is mine now," she said, echoing my own response.

"But surely you have wondered about her origin—"

"I know her origin. That's why I adopted her."

"And yet you have no misgivings about your husband?"

"None. I married him for convenience, but I came to love him absolutely."

"Yet if—"

"I love him for what he is," she said firmly. "That has never faltered."

Thorley shook his head eloquently. "Mrs. Hubris, you are a great human being."

And that closing compliment, so evidently sincere, coming as it did from my leading political critic, effectively closed the issue. The public seemed to feel that if my wife could so graciously accept the situation, no one else had the authority to condemn me. Certainly I had done right by Hopie.

So Tocsin's most insidious efforts had been insufficient to blunt my progress; perhaps they had even facilitated it. But we knew that he would not allow me to gain any more without drastic reprisal; there was no way he would voluntarily leave office. It was rumored that he had even commissioned a private survey to ascertain public reaction should the upcoming election be canceled; evidently such action had proven unfeasible, or maybe he had concluded that he could win without such a measure. But we did not know precisely how he would strike. I was now just about assassination-proof; there was no way he could arrange for that without betraying himself. He had to be more subtle, and he was the master of subtle evil. We were all concerned.

The first signal of trouble was the Navy. A formidable task force approached the planet Jupiter for extensive maneuvers, with battleships and carriers hanging over individual cities as if targeting them. The public was assured that it was only a routine exercise, but it was a massive and persistent one.

I talked to my old Navy wife Emerald, who was now in easy communication range because she commanded one of the wings. She was an admiral now, her brilliance as a strategist, proven in my day, having enabled her to rise impressively.

"What's going on up there, Rising Moon?" I asked forthrightly. This was a private channel, but there really could be no secrets between us now; certainly Tocsin would know. I called her by her nickname, taken from her personal song, "The Rising of the Moon." "As a candidate for the office of commander-in-chief, I believe I should be advised if the Navy has any problems."

Her dusky face cracked into a smile. She was a Saxon/Black crossbreed, once routinely discriminated against in the Saxon-officered Navy, but that was a thing of the past. I knew that she remembered the details of our term marriage as well as I did. She had always been a sexual delight, not because of any phenomenal body—she had been well constructed but relatively spare—but because of her determination, energy, and enterprise. She had regarded sex as a challenge; to make love to her was to ride a roller coaster around a planteoid. She was older now—forty-nine, like me—and had put on weight, but still I saw in her the seed of our savage romance of a quarter century before. I was otherwise married now, and so was she, but I knew that were things otherwise we could still step into bed together and enjoy it immensely. It did not detract one whit from her subsequent marriage, to an admiral now retired, to know that she still loved me.

"Hope, you know there's been increasing civil unrest recently," she said. "There is concern that the election itself could be disrupted. So the Navy is on standby alert, ready to keep the planetary peace if that should prove necessary."

A form answer—with teeth in it. The Navy was under the ultimate command of the civilian president, Tocsin. Was he preparing for a military coup in the event he lost the election? That seemed incredible, but if several civil disturbances were incited, the president could invoke martial law to restore order. How far would such temporary discipline go? Military coups were common in the republics of southern Jupiter but unthinkable in northern Jupiter. So far.

"It is good to have that reassurance," I said. "We know how important it is to preserve order." Which was another

formal statement. "Give my regards to your husband."
And there was the hidden one: her husband, Admiral
Mondy, was the arch-conspirator of our once tightly knit
group within the Navy. He prized out all secrets and fathomed all strategies; he liked to know where everybody was
hidden. I was telling her that something was up and to
alert Mondy if he was not already aware. He might be retired, but I knew he kept his hand in. That sort of thing
was in his blood.

"Have no fear, sir," she responded, and faded out. That
concluding "sir" was significant, too; it meant she was
thinking of the time when I had been the commander of
our Navy task force that cleared up the Belt. That team
still existed in spirit, if not in form; my officers had spread
throughout the Navy and now wielded considerable power.
I still had friends in the Navy, excellent friends—more so
than perhaps Tocsin realized.

After that call I pondered the implications. Was Tocsin
merely setting up a threat, as in a chess game, to intimi-
date those who might vote for me? Or was he really getting
ready to preserve his power militarily? What use would it
be to me to win the election, if it was only to be set aside by
a military takeover?

My misgivings were enhanced by a second development.
I wrapped up a rousing campaign speech in Delphi, Key-
stone, and retired to my quarters to discover Spirit there
with a visitor: Reba of QYV.

"Hubris, this is off the record," Reba said immediately.

"This car is secure," I assured her. "But I have a covenant with the media—"

"It could mean my position—and your life," she said
grimly. "The press must not know."

This put me on the spot. I knew she was serious; only an
extraordinary matter would have caused her to risk her career to visit me personally to confide a secret. But I had
made a commitment to Thorley.

I risked a compromise. "Let me bring one member of the
press here, now, while I hear what you have to say. If he
agrees to keep it secret—"

Reba sighed. "Thorley."

I nodded. "He happens to be aboard now."

"You always did drive an uncomfortable bargain," she said.

Spirit left us and we chatted about inconsequentials for a few minutes, until my sister returned with Thorley. Evidently she had explained the situation on the way, for he evinced no confusion. He sat down and waited.

"I am . . . an anonymous source," Reba told him.

"Understood." That was a convention of many centuries' standing. If he published anything he learned from her, it would not be directly attributed.

"I represent an anonymous organization." Again Thorley agreed; it was obvious that he recognized her, for he had sources of his own, and he knew of my prior association with her.

"This woman knows me as well as any," I said.

Thorley raised an eyebrow but made no other comment. There had been a chronic run of conjecture in the media about the other women supposedly in my life, but Thorley knew that this was not one of those. He was surprised that any woman should know me as well as my wife or sister did. He would pay very close attention to what Reba said. I had just given her a potent recommendation.

"I am in a position to know that a plan is afoot to kidnap Hope Hubris," Reba said carefully. "To mem-wash him and destroy his credibility as a candidate for the presidency."

News indeed! Trust QYV to be the first to fathom Tocsin's mischief.

"This is not a plot to keep secret," Thorley remarked. "I differ with Candidate Hubris on numerous and sundry issues, but I do not endorse foul play."

"Some secrets must be kept until they can be proven," Reba said. "If this is published now the plot will fold without trace, and an alternate one invoked—one I may not be in a position to fathom in advance."

"Ah, now I see," Thorley said. "This fish you have hooked but not necessarily others. From this one the candidate may be protected, if the perpetrator does not realize that the subject knows."

"Exactly," she agreed. "The perpetrator is playing for high stakes and will not stop at murder as a last resort."

"Yet surely the Secret Service protection—"

"Could not stop a city-destroying bolt from space."

Thorley glanced at her shrewdly. He pursed his lips in a soundless whistle. We all knew that only one person on Jupiter had the authority to order such an action—and the will to do it, if pressed. "Certain mischief has been done, and hidden, the details accessible only to the president. Revelation of that mischief could put a number of rather high officials in prison and utterly destroy certain careers."

"You seem to grasp the situtation," Reba agreed.

"And it seems that the details of that hidden mischief could no longer be concealed, if a new and opposing person assumed the presidential office at this time."

Reba nodded. "That office will not be yielded gracefully."

Thorley smiled. "Perhaps you assume that one conservative must necessarily support another. This is not the case. Some support issues, not men, and their private feelings may reflect some seeming inversions. I might even venture to imply that there could be some liberals I would prefer on a personal basis to some conservatives. Strictly off the record, of course." He smiled again, and so did Spirit. Thorley was an honest man, with a sense of humor and a rigorous conscience.

"Then you will withhold your pen?" Reba asked.

"In the interest of fairness—and a better eventual story—I am prepared to do more than that. I prefer to see to the excision of iniquity, branch and root, wherever it occurs."

"Then perhaps you will be interested in one particular detail of the plot," she said grimly. "Candidate Hubris is to receive a message, purportedly from you, advising him that you have urgent news that you must impart to him secretly, in person, without the presence of any other party. When he slips his SS security net and goes to meet you, he will be captured by the agents of the plotters, taken off-planet, mem-washed, addicted to a potent drug, sexually compromised, reeducated, and returned to his campaign on the eve of the election armed with a speech of such nonsense as to discredit him as a potential president. He will be finished politically."

Thorley blew out his cheeks as if airing a mouthful of

hot pepper. "This abruptly becomes more personal. As it happens, I have no need to summon the candidate to any personal encounter; I have another contact."

"So you have said," Reba agreed, glancing at Spirit, who smiled. "I know that Hope Hubris would not fall for such a scheme, though it seems that the other party neglected to research that far. Some suprisingly elementary errors have been made. But it occurred to me that, considering the alternative—"

Now I caught her drift. "That I might choose to!"

"Choose to!" Thorley exclaimed, horrified.

Reba looked at me. "Tell him," I said.

She returned to Thorley. "Hope Hubris is immune to drug addiction," she said. "His system apparently forms antibodies against any mind-affecting agent. This takes time but is effective. We believe that he cannot be permanently affected by the program they propose. His memory will return far more rapidly than is normal, and he soon will throw off the addiction to the drug. Which means—"

"That the attempt is apt to backfire," Thorley finished.

"Particularly if the candidate is forewarned and properly prepared," she agreed.

"And we would finally establish our direct link to the guilty party," I said. "Which would at last put him out of commission. No fifty-fifty gambling on the election; no waiting for a bolt from space. At one stroke, victory!"

Chapter 18

COUNTERSTROKE

I stood at the podium, addressing a small, select group of reporters in this chamber, and the holo-cameras for a vastly greater audience. It was time for me to give my prepared speech.

I had been so absorbed in my final flashback revelation that I really couldn't remember how I had gotten here. It hardly mattered; I knew that I was back on Jupiter, in a major city—probably New Wash—and that I had a meticulously crafted script to deliver. I also knew, now, that it represented disaster to my campaign, for it promised so much that no one would believe it. I was no minor party candidate; I was the leading challenger, with an even chance of winning the election—if I did not throw it away here. But if I repudiated the script, Dorian Gray would suffer, and, of course, I myself would be summarily whisked away and doomed, for I remained in the power of the enemy. They did not realize that my system had fought off the addiction, the mem-wash, and the reeducation program. I was no robot to do their bidding, but they still had some power over me. Not the city-blasting threat—not here!—but still the power of individual murder.

A man stood at my elbow, theoretically to assist me, but as I hesitated, he touched something in a pocket, and I felt a dread twinge of discomfort in my gut. He had a pain-box there—tuned to me! They had buttressed their program in the professional manner, giving me positive and negative incentives to perform. Tocsin really wanted me out of the race! How could I get out of this?

Then I spied a familiar face in the group before me: Thorley. Suddenly I knew it was all right. If he was here, then QYV knew my location; indeed, QYV would have tracked me all along. Spirit would have the situation in hand.

Except for that pain-box. I literally could not act independently, as long as that was tuned to me.

I had no time to ponder. The broadcast signal came on, and I started my prepared speech. I had no other, and I could not risk what would happen if the enemy caught on to my awareness before we gained control of that sub and nullified the pain-box.

Actually the text began moderately enough; it was the cumulative effect of it that would be devastating. While I spoke, I watched my audience—especially Thorley. He knew that I had been abducted; I was sure that fact had been concealed from the public, but Thorley had been, as it were, in on the conspiracy. He would let me know when it was safe for me to break free. But did he know about the pain-box, which would cripple me the moment I tried?

Then the signal came: Thorley's thumbs-up. That meant that our people had completed the nullification of my captors, working quietly behind the scenes. The enemy administrators, elsewhere in the city, would not know. Tocsin would not know. I was free to pursue my own course.

Except for that man beside me with the pain-box. They couldn't approach him without alerting him, and that would be bad for me. He could screw the agony up to the fatal point, if he saw I would otherwise escape. I would have to take him out myself.

Easier decided than accomplished. A pain-box could not simply be grabbed or smashed; the victim could be holding it, and still be helpless. The thing had to be detuned or retuned; only then would I be truly free.

I paused, looking about . Part of the takeover had to be of the broadcast facilities, so that I could not be abruptly cut off. This was, after all, a campaign speech, after a long hiatus; my silence would be almost as damaging as my wrongheaded speech. Now I could speak plainly, and to good effect, assuming that the man beside me was a hireling who did not know my specific script. But what should I say? What could I afford to reveal that would not alert him or alert someone in touch with him and bring immediate cutoff by pain?

Then I got a notion. Thorley's thumbs-up meant more than success elsewhere; it meant he had the solution to my immediate problem. Pain-boxes are easy enough to defeat, because of the particular impulses they generate; my people had to know my predicament. They would have a damper or detuner, if it could be brought within range. I had to get it here.

"Now, I have been making promises," I said. "I realize that some of you are doubtful. You don't believe I can or will fulfill these promises as president. I would like to reassure you specifically." I glanced about again. "I see that some of my most effective critics are in attendance. You, sir . . . " I pointed at Thorley. "Do you doubt?"

Thorley smiled with that relaxed-tiger way he had. "I confess I do, Candidate."

"Well, I shall refute your doubt!" I declaimed. "Come up here if you have the nerve! Debate me face-to-face, and I shall destroy your silly points!"

The others in the small audience smiled now; this was more like my old form. "You are a glutton for punishment, my liberal Candidate," Thorley responded, rising huffily. "I came here ostensibly to report the event; however—"

"Report the event!" I exclaimed indignantly. "When did you ever do that, you sly provocateur? You have been sniping at me from the safety of your wretched column for years."

Thorley puffed visibly with indignity and marched up to the podium, carrying his briefcase. "Since you have seen fit to fling the gauntlet at my veracity, sir, I must advise you that in this valise I carry complete refutation to all your foolishly liberal postures."

And more than that, I thought. "Well, Sir Conservative, let's see you refute this: my position on tax reform. Do you oppose elimination of the nefarious loopholes that favor the rich?"

"Allow me to bring forth my armament," Thorley said, lifting his briefcase and twiddling with the latch. My guard, now right next to him, seemed amused by this development; obviously this display of pique would not establish me as a presidential candidate. "A moment, if you please; it seems to have jammed."

"The way all your positions jam when challenged!" I retorted, and a ripple of mirth traveled through the audience. It was not that they were taking sides; they were merely enjoying the repartee, as they might the sight of two pugilists scoring on each other.

Thorley grimaced. "If you believe yourself to be so clever, perhaps you can operate the latch more effectively than I can," he muttered.

"Certainly I can, you conservative incompetent," I agreed, taking the briefcase from him. I put my fingers to the fastening—and felt a jolt of pain.

But the guard had not done it. His hands were out of his pockets as he followed the mock quarrel. The latch had done it.

It was the control to the pain-box tuner inside the briefcase. I adjusted it the other way, and the pain abated. Now it was damping out the pain-box.

I damped it down to zero. Then I reached across, casually, and placed my hand on the back of the guard's neck. Suddenly my fingers dug into a nerve. I gave him a moment to operate the pain-box in his pocket and realize that it was no longer operative; then I increased my pressure while still arguing with Thorley, letting the guard know that the control had changed over. When I was sure he understood, I released my grip. He stood unmoving; he knew it was the price of his health.

I handed the briefcase back to Thorley. "It will open now, Journalist," I said. Of course, the case was not intended for opening; it contained no papers, merely the damper.

"Upon reconsideration, I believe I can do this barehanded," Thorley said, setting down the briefcase. The audience was not aware of the true nature of our interaction. "As I understand your position on taxes, it is to play Robin Hood to our society, taking from the affluent and redistributing the wealth among the poor. Now the fallacy of penalizing our most productive element while rewarding indolence is—"

"On the contrary," I broke in. "I subscribe to the so-called flat tax."

Thorley paused, genuinely surprised. "You do?"

"Actually, I suspect that taxation itself may be a form of theft from the population," I said. "I would like to find some other way to raise money for government operations. One of my first acts as president will be to seek some feasible way to reduce or abolish taxation entirely."

There was a kind of collective gasp from the audience. These were seasoned journalists, seldom surprised, but I had just lobbed a bombshell. No candidate spoke like that!

"If you can do that," Thorley said slowly, "you will prove yourself to be a magician." He shook his head and laid a small sheet of paper on my podium. "I have changed my mind, Candidate. I don't believe I am ready to debate you at this juncture. I prefer to hear first what other changes your position may have undergone." He returned slowly to his place.

While the cameras followed Thorley, I read the paper. It was another bombshell: "One week past, Tocsin broke relations with Ganymede on suspicious pretext. Candidate cannot afford to ignore issue."

A virtual election-eve ploy, and I had been told nothing of it! My planned speech did indeed ignore it and left me a patsy for a pointed question. I *had* to address this issue, for I had been the first ambassador there. Even if I had revised my speech extemporaneously to cause it to make sense, this trap would have caught me. I almost had to admire this aspect of Tocsin's cunning.

I thought fast and decided on an approach. "I know you are waiting for me to address the issue of the hour. As you know, I was at one time Jupiter's ambassador to Ganymede. Naturally I regret what has happened. But before I commit myself, I would like to be sure I have the facts." I glanced directly at the camera. "Please establish a connection directly to Ganymede and ask the premier to do me the kindness of speaking with me now."

There was another ripple of surprise. This was an extraordinarily risky undertaking for a candidate on the eve of the election. The angry premier could torpedo me.

But few people were aware how close I had been to the premier of Ganymede, despite our differing politics. In our fashion we understood and trusted each other. It was not to his interest to torpedo me; it was Tocsin he would be after.

They put through the call, of course. Formal relations might have been severed, but a public call from a candidate for president of Jupiter was too dramatic a move to deny. In a moment the premier responded. His familiar face came on our monitor screen. "Where have you been, Ambassador?" he asked.

"That is a special story, Premier," I said. "As you may have heard, there is a local election tomorrow, and I am to participate. If I win, I would like to act on the basis of full information. I would appreciate it if you would tell me—and our Jupiter audience—as concisely as you can what happened to alienate our two planets."

There was a delay of about seven seconds' travel time for the signals, for Ganymede is three and a half light-seconds out from Jupiter. Complications of our rotation and the Gany orbit make for variations, and, of course, the premier needed time to assimilate my words and formulate his response. But the public understands about this sort of thing. We waited patiently for his response.

The premier was amazed. "This is being broadcast? Alive?"

"Yes. You can verify it on your monitors." We waited another seven-plus seconds.

He had evidently done so. *"Señor,* all we know is that our ship left our port carrying a cargo of sugar bound for south Jupiter. Then these pirates board it and claim it carried Saturnine arms, and diplomatic relations are broken."

"Did it carry Saturnine arms?" I asked, nailing this down.

"Not when it left Ganymede, *señor."*

"But then how did the arms get aboard?"

"They were put there."

"By whom?" This might have been tedious, with the delay between each response, but my audience was rapt.

"By your Navy, *señor!* Who else had access to our ship?"

"But why should the Jupiter Navy do that?"

"That I would like to know, *señor!* We have been selling sugar to your ships, and we have gotten along until this."

I could think of a reason: to make big headlines the week before the election, arousing popular indignation against an external government, and showing how tough the incumbent president could be against the dread Communist menace. A pure grandstand play, an ancient formula. Such activity always rallies the electorate around the existing leader. Vintage Tocsin. The nice touch was that it implicated me; as Jupiter's first ambassador to the revolutionary regime of Ganymede, I was tainted by that association. I had been there, I had hobnobbed with the premier who had now seemingly reneged on the covenant he had made with Jupiter. By implication it was my fault. Tocsin was very good at implication.

I could see that the premier, canny political in-fighter that he was, had come to a similar conclusion. His protestation of ignorance was merely for show. I decided to play the game out; it seemed promising. "So you say that Ganymede did not break the agreement; it was framed?"

The premier shrugged. "Now, why would anyone want to do that?" He had reversed my question. I saw some of the journalists nodding; they understood political maneuvers as well as anyone.

"You say those weapons were planted on your ship," I said. "Do you expect us to believe that? How can we know you aren't violating the covenant?"

The premier smiled, knowing the opening I had given him. "Señor, we made that covenant in 2643, six years ago. Ganymede has shipped no Saturnine arms since then, and there is no other route from Saturn to Jupiter for this sort of merchandise. If the arms aboard that ship have dates of manufacture after that, then we must be guilty. But if they do not—"

"But couldn't you have shipped old weapons?" I asked.

"Why should we? We have access to new ones." He paused, considering. "But I see your point, señor. We cannot prove we did not, but you can prove we did—if you find recent weapons there. It is like a paternity test, is it not?"

I smiled. "Not quite, Premier. That test shows only who could not be the parent but cannot say who was."

"A half-proof may be better than none. Let an independent agency of the United Planets inspect those weapons."

"You recommend this, Premier, though this could only prove you guilty, not innocent?"

"I am innocent, therefore I recommend it. Let the UP trace the serial numbers of those weapons and see where they lead." He grinned, as if knowing the lead would not be to Ganymede.

"Thank you, Premier," I said. "I'm sure the United

Planets will pursue this matter vigorously, being concerned only with the truth. If the charge against you turns
out to be false, I may be in a position to restore diplomatic
relations."

We broke the connection. "As I said, I prefer to have the
facts before I commit myself," I reminded my audience. "I
regret that the election will be past before the facts are in,
but I have my suspicion." The tally on the monitor indicated that my audience had been expanding geometrically
as my address continued, and was now being carried
planet-wide and broadcast-system-wide, despite the time
delays for the more distant planets. I now had one of the
largest audiences ever, for a mere political candidate, and
I was making it count.

Tocsin had set me up to destroy my candidacy, but I did
not intend to cooperate. I had just defused another potential disaster and perhaps turned it to my advantage. Now
it was time to take the offense.

I addressed the camera. "You may have wondered
where I have been these past two months," I said grimly.
"I'm sure my campaign staff made excuses for my absence,
but it has been a mystery, hasn't it? Well, I was in space—
held aboard a sub. Let's see whether we can raise that sub
now."

There was another ripple of surprise. If my enemy had
suspected I was free of control before, now he had confirmation, but it was too late for him to cut me off. I had control and a monstrous audience. My immunity to drugs had
enabled me to turn the tables, and I intended to make the
most of the opportunity.

"Please get me Admiral Mondy," I said, and the technicians hastened to comply. The original Admiral Mondy
had retired five years before, as the Navy disapproved of
officers beyond the age of sixty. The present Admiral
Mondy was his younger wife.

Indeed, her face came on. "Hello, President Hubris."

"Not yet, Emerald," I said. "There is a formality tomorrow that—"

"Sure enough, Hope," she said, her white smile flashing
in her dark face. She knew that this was being widely
broadcast, and she enjoyed the exposure. She had always
been a feisty woman, and power had not changed her. "Are

they still giving you a hard time about your daughter? They never asked me if *I* was the mother."

I laughed, and so did several of the reporters. They knew that Emerald had once been my wife, Navy-fashion, but not at the time of Hopie's birth, and, of course, Emerald was not Saxon. Racism still existed on Jupiter, and Emerald loved to bait it. "Sorry they neglected you," I said. "Emerald, there's a sub near Jupiter that—"

"We've got it spotted," she said. "We did that automatically when we moved in close to Jupiter. It's not on our registry."

"Oh? Does the Jupiter Navy tolerate alien subs in Jupe space?"

"Not by a damn sight!" she snapped. "But when we set out to challenge this one, we got a leave-alone signal down the chain of command. So we kept a quiet fix on it—"

"A leave-alone order from above?" I asked. "How high?"

"Hope, I can't speak for the civilian sector!"

But the implication was plain enough: This sub was being protected by someone very close to the White Dome. I saw the reporters nodding. Another arrow was pointing toward Tocsin.

"Please establish communication with that sub," I said. "I want to speak directly with its skipper."

"I'll just bet you do," she agreed, flashing her teeth again. "We're raising it now, but it's not acknowledging."

"You know how to deal with that, don't you, Admiral?"

"Sure do! But without orders—"

"Admiral, that's an unidentified sub that has not been specifically cleared with you. It is your duty to identify it. I believe Navy protocol is quite clear on that sort of thing. So, unless you receive a specific and identified order to desist . . ."

She paused a moment in thought, catching the tip of her tongue between her teeth, then decided to go with me. "We'll bracket her with lasers, and if she still won't open up—"

"Don't blast her yet," I said. "I want her captured and brought into port."

"We're working on it," she said.

I addressed my audience again. "You see, I was abducted and held aboard that sub, where they attempted to brainwash me. As you can see, they did not succeed, but I am most interested in ascertaining exactly who hired that sub. I can, offhand, think of only one party who would benefit by the elimination of Hope Hubris as a candidate on the eve of the election, but I hesitate to make an accusation without proof." Again the reporters nodded, and I saw the audience tally nudge up further. This little mystery was playing to an enormous house!

"Got the sub," Emerald announced.

"Ah, the laser-bracketing must have made them see the light," I said. A ship that was bracketed could be destroyed; only the boldest or most desperate captain would ignore it long. "Have them put Dorian Gray on." To my audience I explained, "That is another captive; I fear she will come to harm unless we watch her."

"Not available," Emerald reported.

"So?" I inquired challengingly. "Tell the sub you will blast it out of space unless she is put on screen within sixty seconds."

A pause. Then: "Message conveyed. No response."

"Then put me on that line," I said grimly.

In a moment I was looking into the sub, and so was my planetary audience. My interrogator, Scar, sat there, not speaking. "Listen, *señor*," I said. "Your reprogramming did not work. I remember everything and am addicted to nothing. I am giving my own speech, not yours. Dorian Gray helped me, and now I will help her. Admiral Mondy answers to me now, and will act on my directive unless directly countermanded by the Commander-in-Chief, President Tocsin. Do you suppose he will tip his hand to protect you?" I paused. The man still bluffed it out, not responding. "Emerald, hit him with a laser, just enough to make him feel it."

The screen split to show the interior on the left, and the sub in space on the right. Its black-hole effect made it fuzzy, but now the Navy had a pinpoint fix on it, making it visible by electronic enhancement. Suddenly it glowed, and simultaneously the man on the left jumped; he had felt the strike of the laser. Still he did not speak.

"Give them a harder jolt," I said.

Again the ship glowed, and suddenly the fuzziness dissipated and it came into sharp focus. The defensive circuit had been overloaded, and the sub was now fully visible.

"Your employer has deserted you, and the Navy hierarchy is afraid to interfere without his order," I told him. "I have no legal power here, but I am about to destroy you while the whole Solar System watches. Only Dorian Gray can save you—if she intercedes with me. Now I'm giving you that one minute to put her on screen. If you do not I will conclude that she is dead and that there is nothing worth saving on your vessel, and I will destroy it. I have more nerve than your employer does, and I have no love for you, brainwasher."

He cracked, as I had known he would. I had screwed up the pressure to his threshold. In a moment Dorain Gray appeared. She did not appear to be in discomfort.

"I have come for you, Dorian," I told her. "Did you heed my message?"

"Hope, they found the bomb," she said. "But they can not disarm it."

That was bad news! It meant they were still hostage to the bomb. It surely could be detonated by remote control.

But *would* it? That would be the open murder of one's own hirelings and no good sign for others who did the bidding of this party. Would Tocsin sacrifice the sub and such goodwill as his hirelings had, merely to protect his secret?

"Ask them to whom they answer," I said to Dorian. "Who hired the sub?"

She asked but got no answer. "It is anonymous," she reported. "They do not know."

That, too, was to be expected. No direct connection to identify the criminal with his crime. "Then provide us the channel through which the orders come, so that we can trace it to its source. In return we shall see that you are granted immunity from prosecution."

"*You* guarantee this, Hope?" she asked.

"*I* guarantee this," I agreed. I now had the leverage to ensure this; the Jupiter court system would not renege, knowing that I would soon be coming to presidential power. In fact, the case probably would not come to court before I assumed the office.

"Then he will tell," she said after consultation.

And the screen went blank. The view shifted, showing the sub from space, and it was a fragmenting fireball.

The bomb had been detonated, destroying the sub and killing all aboard.

It seemed that Tocsin would indeed sacrifice his associates in order to save his own skin a little longer. Suddenly the most tangible evidence of his complicity was gone; we had no direct lead to him. But for the moment I was aware of only one thing: Dorian Gray was dead. She, who had helped me escape, had paid for it with her life. How could I keep my commitment to her now?

I knew how. "Get me the premier of Ganymede again," I said.

In a moment the premier was back on screen. "Unfortunate you lost your evidence, *señor*," he said.

"The woman," I said. "She has a baby boy, taken to Ganymede by the father to spite her. I promised to recover that boy for her."

"I do not think she wants that baby anymore," the premier said wryly.

"Yet I promised. Will you fetch that baby and deliver him to me? You surely can ascertain the one I mean."

He nodded. "You will have him, *señor*. I do not know what he will cost you." He faded out.

I returned to my audience. "The woman helped me recover my memory, after they mem-washed me. I owe her more than ever, now that my act has cost her her life." I paused, trying to fend off the tears that threatened to overwhelm me, and succeeded partially.

Then I got down to political business. "We know who is responsible for this outrage," I said savagely. "Only one person plainly profits from my failure as a candidate. He would have been revealed, had those on the sub survived to give their information. So he destroyed them. *But we know!* We know he is completely unscrupulous, that he will stop at nothing, not even kidnapping and murder, to secure his reelection. Is this the man you wish to preserve in office?"

It was, of course, a rhetorical question, and my true audience could not respond directly. But even some of the reporters, shaken by the destruction of the sub, reacted. "No!" one murmured.

"It is time that this sort of criminal corruption was rooted out from the government of Jupiter!" I proclaimed. "This great planet must restore its reputation in the System for truth, justice, and equality!" And the reporters were nodding affirmatively.

"The government of Jupiter has turned away from the needs of the citizens," I continued. "Children go hungry, education declines, and there is a rising tide of crime, so that today no citizen is safe—not even a candidate for president!" And someone among the journalists forgot himself so far as to murmur "Amen!"

"It is time to put an end to all this," I repeated. "It is time for the great planet of Jupiter to return to the greatness it has known. It is time for the restoration of decency, honor, and joy!" Pure rhetoric, but my cynical local audience was swept up in it, and I knew that at this point even the citizens of Saturn would have voted for me. My magic had taken hold.

"Tomorrow is the election!" I thundered. "You now know how to vote!" And in pure rhetorical style I worked my audience up to a righteous fever, ready to march to the polling places. There would be very few against me at this moment. In the hours before the election sanity would return to a great many, but still I should have a clear advantage.

As I finished, the technicians played back a news item showing the reaction in the great cities of Jupiter. Massive crowds were gathered in the parks, chanting, "Hubris! Hubris!" They were not just Hispanics.

The trap Tocsin had so carefully laid for me had been reversed because of my special talents, because Dorian Gray had helped me regain my memory, because Thorley had helped me regain my freedom, because my friends on Ganymede and in the Navy had supported me, and because I had seized the moment. Now at last I could relax.

I took a deep breath—and fainted.

Chapter 19

WIVES

I woke in a hospital in Ybor. It seemed I had suffered more during my captivity than I had realized. By the time my body threw off the sedation they had loaded me with, the election was over and I was the president-elect. But I remained disoriented, and Spirit decided that I should spend a month or so in private recuperation. I was glad to do so; for one thing, it gave me leisure to write this narrative of my political experiences.

In fact, this has been a vital occupation. My system does develop immunity to drugs of all types, but it cannot act retroactively to cancel all the damage they may have done. I could no longer be memory-washed, but that first wash really had obliterated many years of memories for a time, and I was concerned that some parts would never return unless I made a special effort to recover them now. My life through my Navy experience has been covered in my prior diaries, but not the past twenty years, so it was important that I get on this before the distractions of the presidency overwhelmed my attention. I don't know how others feel, but to me, memory is almost as important as the present or the future; I value *all* my life and want no part of it lost, not even the painful portions.

Just as the key words I had planted for myself in the slop-cell had triggered major segments of my missing memory, so now my effort to record that experience amplified those segments of my memory. I cannot honestly say that I relived those parts of my life in the manner I have described; my memory returned in complex flashes rather than in an orderly, narrative, holo-type format suitably edited for relevance. Still, those flashes did the job; they made me aware of what I needed to know in order to restore my perspective and enable me to foil the plot against my candidacy. But it was the writing of the manuscript that made my life real again. In a sense, my life formed as I recorded it; the effort of searching out the details and feelings I had, had made them substantial. It took me a month to write them out, but when that job was done, I was satisfied that I knew where I had been and what I had been doing.

In that month exterior events did not cease, of course. There were some matters that couldn't wait on my literary convenience. In a manner my life consisted only of these scenes and my manuscript memories.

There was the evening I was home with Megan and Hopie. My daughter flung herself into my arms and sobbed; she had feared I was dead, and now at last she could relax. She was close to fifteen years old now, but at this moment resembled a tiny, frightened child. Spirit had explained to me, on the way from somewhere to somewhere, that she had put out word that I had retired from active campaigning for a time to organize coming responsibilities such as researching the best appointments and preparing a major address. She had, in effect, covered for Tocsin's crime, knowing that my life would be forfeit if she did not. We had taken an enormous chance—to reap an enormous gain. She had carried on in my stead, giving my speeches and in general showing that she was indeed competent to stand in lieu of me, never showing her natural concern for me. So my campaign had proceeded without visible falter, and at the time of my reappearance the odds remained fifty-fifty. My concluding address had been critical indeed.

"If Tocsin had been smarter," I told her, "he would have kidnapped you instead of me!" It was not really a joke; Spirit was competent at all the necessary details I ignored. She had been running my campaign throughout, based on Megan's strategy, and this had not changed during my absence. The campaign had survived my absence; it could not have survived her absence.

Then I was alone with Megan, and it was difficult. "About Dorian Gray—" I began.

"I understand," she said quietly.

"No, I mean—"

"You were memory-washed," she said firmly. "Your system fights off drugs, but it takes time to develop specific antibodies, and so at first you remembered nothing, not even your marriage. They put you with a comely young woman—"

"I remembered you," I said. Another person might have found it expedient to deceive her on this point, but there was no way I would lie to Megan. "But—"

"But you realized that if your captors realized that, they would have killed you," she said. "So you had to do what they wanted. Hope, it isn't as though you have never had a relationship with another woman. You had four wives before me."

Four wives. She was counting Helse, who had died on the verge of our marriage, and Juana, my first Navy roommate, and my two formal term-wives. It was true I had had enduring and loving relationships with those four, and sexual liaisons in the Navy fashion with many others. "You are very understanding," I said.

"Hope, I love you," she said, as if making a point.

I took her in my arms and kissed her, and she was all my desire. I was just shy of fifty years old, and she was in her mid-fifties, but what I felt for her would have been completely comprehensible to folk in their twenties. Or their teens. But when I thought to go further, she demurred.

I let her go immediately, knowing that despite her intellectual understanding, she had been hurt emotionally. I could not step lightly from the arms of one woman to the arms of another. Not when the other was Megan. In a way I found that reassuring; I loved Megan in part because her love was no casual thing. If her condemnation did not come readily, neither did her forgiveness. Our relationship had suffered two major blows during the campaign: the horror of the siege of our train, which had exposed her to a level of violence that gave her post-traumatic nightmares; and now the horror of my separation from her, including a relationship with another woman. Yes, I understood.

But then she turned back to me, and her face was washed in tears. "Oh, Hope!" she cried, and fell back into my embrace. She gave me everything, then, forgiveness and all, with a kind of desperation reminiscent of that of our daughter, though on a distinctly different plane. Her love had overwhelmed her reserve.

Still, I knew those two strikes remained, and I knew I could not afford a third one. I loved Megan and she loved me, and because it was no casual relation we had, any damage to it was not casual, either. Forgiveness and forgetting may come most readily to those whose real feelings are only lightly committed.

I swept to victory on election day; it was evident before the polls closed that I had a planetslide. I was tuned out at the time, of course, but it interested me when I learned of it later. Analysis indicated that I had ninety-seven percent of the Hispanic vote, with a record turnout; ninety-two percent of the Black vote; seventy percent of the Saxon female vote; and thirty percent of the Saxon male vote. Overall it came to fifty-five percent, a very comfortable margin.

But Tocsin refused to concede defeat. In fact, he acted as if he had won. The arrogance of the man was amazing.

Then I found out that the campaign was not yet over. The United States of Jupiter, almost alone among contemporary republics, retains what is termed the Electoral College. Over the past six centuries or so, one variant after another had been tried, but the dynamics of politics generally interfered with the simple ratio of one citizen, one vote. At present each state was allocated a block of electoral votes in proportion to its population, and that entire block went to whatever candidate had a plurality in that state. This tended to leverage the voting, giving the large states a disproportionate weight in the Electoral College. Indeed, it was possible for a candidate to win the national popular vote and lose the electoral vote. In addition, in a number of states, the electors aren't technically committed to the candidate who won the state. They were expected to vote as the ordinary voters had, and normally they did, but they didn't actually have to. Now it became apparent that special pressure was being brought to bear on some electors to break ranks and vote for the wrong candidate: Tocsin. His campaign had a staggering amount of money available, and it seemed that bribes were being proffered that were quite substantial, as well as promises of political patronage.

In addition, the results were being challenged in several key states. A sophisticated kind of gerrymandering was systematically excluding Hispanics and Blacks from important aspects of the recounts, so that the results were bound to shift to my disfavor. Somehow my strong supporters were being shunted to regions that were already solidly in my camp, leaving the borderline regions to tilt marginally the other way. A margin was as good as a mile for this purpose; I could lose whole states, and all their electoral votes. This process was illegal, of course, but private money does talk, and evidently it was talking persuasively. We really had to scramble to keep abreast of it, challenging the challenges, and forcing re-recounts, lest we forfeit states we had actually won. Had Tocsin had his way unchallenged, he would have shifted enough electoral votes to achieve a scant majority in the College. As it was, he did abscond with some but not enough. Our dyke held, and I was confirmed. I felt as if I had won a second election, and in a way I had.

Then a bill appeared in Congress, concerning something routine—in my scramble to plug the leaks in the dyke (though really Spirit was doing it, and my staff; I was merely watching nervously) I never really ascertained what—bearing an obscure amendment relating to the political process. The bill passed shortly before the turn of the year, and the nature of the amendment became belatedly clear. It was a "clarification" of the requirement for holding major office in Jupiter. Above a certain level it was now illegal for any foreign-born citizen to hold office.

Spirit and I were foreign-born, technically, as we had come from the independent satellite of Callisto and had been naturalized as full Jupiter citizens when we left the Navy. Suddenly we were barred from taking the offices to which we had just been elected.

Naturally we challenged this bit of skullduggery on several grounds. We pressed for a rehearing and revote in Congress but were stonewalled; by the time we got through that, the day of taking office would be past. So we sued and got an expedited hearing before the Supreme Court itself, a week before the deadline of January 20, 2650. This was highly unusual, but the entire situation was extraordinary. Only direct access to the highest court could settle this in time.

The technical question was whether Congress had the right to pass ex post facto legislation affecting a candidate already elected. We argued that this was inequitable at best, and a mockery of the entire election process at worst. The opposition argued that this was not properly considered as new legislation but was merely a clarification of existing policy and therefore was valid. They succeeded in obfuscating the real issue—that of who was to be president—to the point that it became a question of my fitness for the office. I actually was required to summon character references on my behalf. Naturally Tocsin summoned character-assassination witnesses.

So while the twelve Supreme Court Justices listened in seeming passivity, Spirit and I suffered through the ordeal of being publicly judged as persons. All manner of innuendo was brought out in an evident effort to make us lose our tempers. We survived that—our Naval combat experience helped—but we were almost torpedoed by our friends.

My first Navy roommate, Juana, now a master sergeant, testified to my excellent character and confessed that she and I had met in the tail—i.e., Navy institution of sex, the complement to the head—and had subsequently lived together as de facto man and wife for two years before moving on to other assignments. Cross-examination established other partners in sex that I had had. It was, of course, the Navy way, neither right nor wrong, but it was a way that was not generally understood in civilian life. Emerald gave similar evidence, except that she had actually married me, until it became expedient for her to go to another officer in order to obtain his expertise for the benefit of our unit. Again it was the Navy way; again it was damaging in the present context, as was the fact that Emerald had obvious Black ancestry. The Navy strove to extirpate racism from its midst by civilian directive, and mixed marriages were accepted without question, as were interracial liaisons in the Tail. But the civilian sector had not applied similar discipline as strenuously to itself; interracial marriages, though legal, were socially problematical. Twelve old Saxon men were listening; were they free of the taint of covert racism themselves? I had to pray that it was so, but I doubted it. Three of them had been appointed by Tocsin himself, and they were recognized as ideological rather than quality selections; no hope that they would rule against him. Three others had been appointed by his predecessor Kenson, who were of superior merit. The six remaining were similarly divided, so that there was an even conservative/liberal split and no great certainty that merit would be the deciding aspect of any particular case.

Then we came to the last of my Navy liaisons. Admiral Phist (Retired) and his wife Roulette, Ambassador from the Belt, were brought to Jupiter, to the court in the bubble of New Wash. They were cross-examined like criminals by the lawyer from the other side. "And isn't it true that you are a pirate wench?" the lawyer demanded of Roulette.

Roulette was now a striking woman of thirty-nine, retaining fiery hair and a figure that caused even the venerable heads of the Supreme Court Justices to turn. She had been in her youth the most beautiful woman, physically, I-had known, the veritable incarnation of man's desire. She had also been the daughter of a prominent pirate. I had married her, in the pirate fashion, and we had loved each other in our private fashion. This detracts in no way from my love of Megan. Roulette had been an extraordinarily fetching passing fancy; Megan was the true love of my life. Yet I cannot deny that my pulse accelerated somewhat when I saw her here in person, hourglass figure intact.

"Objection!" our attorney protested, but Roulette waved him away.

"I can answer for myself," she said. She turned disdainfully to the interrogator and fixed him with a gaze that actually made him step back. "Yes, I was a pirate wench—until Captain Hubris made a woman of me."

"And how did he do that?"

"He beat me and raped me," she said with pride.

The attorney straightened up with overdramatic shock. Obviously he had been fishing for exactly this response. "He *what?*"

Some character witness! The twelve Justices seemed somewhat less sleepy now. But Roulette was not about to let this drop. "Same thing you'd like to do, if you had the chance," she informed the man, shifting the angle of her sculptured bosom.

The attorney was speechless for a moment; evidently

she had scored. But he quickly recovered himself. "And did you press charges?"

"For what?" she inquired archly.

"For abuse!" he said with relish. "For . . . rape."

She laughed. "That gentle man? He never abused me!"

"But you said—"

"Of course. But he didn't really want to rape me. We made him do it."

The lawyer knew he was losing the thread. "We?"

"My father and I."

"Your father—and you—made Hope Hubris rape you?"

"And his staff. We really worked on him. And finally he did it. I had a knife. I stabbed him in the shoulder. But he—"

"You love him yet!" the lawyer accused her.

"I have always loved him, ever since he mastered me. I always will."

The lawyer pounced. "And what does your husband make of this?"

Admiral Phist smiled. "I understand completely."

"Your wife loves Hope Hubris, and you *understand?*"

"Of course. I love Spirit Hubris." He made a nod in my sister's direction, and Spirit smiled.

The Justices sat stonily. How was this affecting them?

The lawyer's gaze cast about the chamber as if he were looking for something to hang on to. They fixed on Hopie. Suddenly they widened in wild surmise. "A Saxon woman," he said. "Still in love with her former husband, free to travel where she wishes, without objection by her present husband—" He whirled on Roulette. "*Where were you*, Roulette Phist, fifteen years ago?"

Roulette straightened. She glanced at Hopie. "Why, I don't remember. But—"

"Will you submit to a maternity blood-typing test?"

Roulette frowned. "You'll have none of my blood, mate!"

"Do you deny that you are the mother of that child?" And he pointed dramatically at Hopie, who seemed equally startled.

Roulette considered. "Where *was* I, that year, dear?" she asked her husband, her lovely brow furrowing in seeming concentration.

Admiral Phist grinned. "You have certainly traveled widely, Rue."

"This is no laughing matter!" the attorney snapped. "As you, Admiral, should be the first to recognize!"

Roulette studied Hopie openly. "She certainly is a pretty one," she said, turning once more to her husband. "She does favor Hope. Do you think I could have . . . ?"

Phist had been looking at Spirit. Slowly he nodded, as if coming to a conclusion. "It does seem possible ," he agreed.

"But if I claim her she would have to leave Jupiter—"

"True," he agreed soberly. "It had better remain secret."

The lawyer was flushing, aware that he was being mocked. One of the Justices was quirking half a smile. "Madam, your blood type is surely on record. We can verify—"

"Lots of luck, shithead," she said sweetly. "I'm not a Jupe citizen. I came here only for the chance to see the man I love."

There was a muffled chortle from another Justice; I couldn't tell which one. Evidently he understood about lovely women coming to see powerful men. But I knew that none of this was doing my case much good. The executive and legislative branches of the government were already against me; where would the judicial be when its limited mirth abated?

There was a brief recess following this interview. Admiral Phist and Roulette approached the section where I sat with Megan, Spirit, and Shelia. "Maybe we?" Roulette asked Megan.

Megan smiled with a certain gentle resignation, then swung her chair around so as to face away. Spirit and I stood up, and Admiral Phist took Spirit into his arms and kissed her, and Roulette did the same to me. Hopie's eyes widened, as did those of a number of the other folk present.

Then we separated. "You are still a creature to madden a man's mind," I murmured to Roulette. "Your thyme has not yet been stolen."

"I know it," she agreed. "But you would not need to steal it, Hope. It has always been yours for the asking."

They departed. Megan turned around again, ending her

symbolic ignorance. "She's beautiful," she said. "She does still love you."

"I gave her up for you," I reminded her.

"I can't think why." But she was nevertheless flattered.

Next day the news arrived: the decision of the Supreme Court, by a vote of six to five, with one abstention, was in favor of the legislation. The interpretation stood, and Spirit and I were barred from assuming the offices we had been elected to. All three branches of the government were against us, and we had lost.

But it wasn't over. We might have lost, but Tocsin hadn't won. He had not been reelected. There would have to be a special election, and in the period from January 20 to the emplacement of the winner of that election, the speaker of the house would serve as president. The speaker was of my party and had supported my candidacy; it was entirely possible that he would use his leverage to reverse the legislation that had cut me out. Tocsin was scrambling to get a ruling that would permit him to remain in office for the interim, but he lacked the leverage to secure that. Meanwhile, more ships of the Jupiter Navy were converging on the planet; what did this portend?

Spirit, oddly, seemed unworried. "The game has not yet been played out," she said. "Tocsin has been concentrating on controlling the branches of the government; we have been concentrating on the will of the people. Ultimately that will must prevail."

"What do you mean?" I asked. But she only smiled and went about her business. Evidently she had not limited her endeavors to the normal campaign during my absence.

There was certainly a reaction from the people! Demonstrations erupted in all the major cities, from Nyork to Langels, so fervent that they overwhelmed the police, who, it seemed, were not unduly committed to their suppression. The Brotherhood of Policemen had supported my candidacy from the outset. All across the land the chant sounded: "Hubris! Hubris!" I had been elected, and the popular mandate was being thwarted by a technicality, and even some pretty solid conservatives, such as Thorley, questioned the basis of that technicality. The common man was angry. In state after state martial law was declared, but it did little good, for the National Guard was sympathetic to my candidacy, too. The migrant workers of the agricultural orbit rioted, doing no damage to the crops but hardly bothering to conceal the threat—in the event I did not take office. They regarded me as one of their own, with some reason. Likewise, women of every walk of life made a more subtle demonstration, as even some opposing legislators confessed ruefully; and those men who sought relief at establishments of ill repute discovered that the girls there were boycotting any man who did not support my candidacy. Something very like a revolution was building.

A spot popularity poll showed that my general support had increased to sixty-six percent, evidently augmented by sympathy. Mail was pouring in, much of it from those who had become my supporters only after the election had been set aside. Outrage was the emotion of the hour.

The great ships of the Navy moved closer yet, and I realized that Tocsin had anticipated trouble like this. If he declared a national emergency he would assume extraordinary powers—and would not use them to benefit me.

"I think you had better pacify the animals," Megan told me grimly. "Don't give Tocsin a pretext to go on a war footing."

So I pacified the animals. I sought and got planetary video time; Tocsin did not interfere with this, because if I tried to foment revolution openly, he could use that as a pretext to have me arrested and could put the entire nation under military control. If he succeeded in that maneuver it might be a long time before he relinquished his office, if ever.

I addressed my supporters, in their separate categories, pleading with the Hispanics to keep the peace so as not to reflect unfavorably on their kind, which included myself and my sisters and my daughter; I assured the Blacks that I was doing everything in my power to see that justice would be done; I begged the women to wait a few days more, for something good might come of our various appeals on technical grounds, or from the upcoming special election.

"I did not come to Jupiter to generate strife, " I concluded. "I believe in law and peace. Be patient; show the people of the Solar System that you support the same goals I do."

It worked. The tide of violence receded, and life returned to an approximation of normal. But it did not recede far; everyone knew that phenomenal activity could break out almost instantly if triggered. The Navy ships orbited very close, ready and ominous.

There was unusual silence from the other planets of the System. Even Saturn made no comment. But North Jupiter was the object of the cynosure of all mankind, at the moment. It was as if some critical sporting event was now in the closing stage of an extremely tight contest for the championship, and every breath was held while the outcome remained in doubt.

Naturally Thorley commented. He pointed out something few people had noticed: There was one of the perennial movements afoot for a constitutional convention to balance the budget. Now the constitutional convention, he explained, was a truly venerable device; it rose directly from the people, by way of the several state legislatures, and once it passed certain hurdles, it could not be denied. This one was now only two states shy of the necessary two-thirds majority of state approvals to become viable, and once it became established, it could not be dissolved by any power other than itself. Our present system of government, he reminded us, had been instituted by the first constitutional convention, close to nine hundred years ago, and could conceivably be overturned by another. Such a convention might be brought into being for a specific purpose, but it was under no binding directive to stick to that purpose. "You may suppose this is a simple matter of balancing the chronically unbalanced planetary budget," he concluded, "but it could conceivably be the route to tyranny. A fire, once started, may spread beyond the original site."

The measure was currently up for consideration in five states, and two of them were Golden and Sunshine. Spirit had been shuttling her attention back and forth between them, and suddenly I realized why. She was working to get them to vote to establish the constitutional convention!

And it happened. We had strong support in both states, for one was where Megan had been a representative, and the other was my own political base. On January 18 Sunshine ratified the bill, and on the nineteenth Golden followed suit. I strongly suspected they could have done it earlier, but Spirit had arranged for the delay in order to keep this from being a public issue before it had to be. Timing was vital—and now was the time.

On the twentieth, the day the presidency was supposed to change, the constitutional convention convened. Now it was evident how carefully Spirit had orchestrated this, for a clear majority of the delegates were my supporters. The whole time I had been captive, Spirit had been touring the planet in my stead, giving public speeches and privately seeing to the selection of the delegates for this convention, so that there would be no confusion or delay at the critical moment. The skids had been greased, and the whole thing came into being with amazing ease, fully formed. Tocsin's forces, supposing they had victory in hand as long as they held me captive, had not been aware of this. They had been blinded by their own connivance, not recognizing Spirit for what she was: the mistress of their undoing.

Now the constitutional convention, governed by our majority, acted with extraordinary dispatch. First it declared that the budget should be balanced. Then it declared that, inasmuch as neither executive, legislative, nor judicial branches of the government had proved able or willing to do this in the past century, all were to be disbanded forthwith. Then its spokesman addressed me publicly:

"Hope Hubris, do you pledge to balance the budget without delay or compromise, if granted the power to do so?"

"I do," I replied. It really was not a difficult answer.

"Then this convention hereby declares Hope Hubris, the evident preference of the people of the United States of Jupiter, to be the new government of this nation, effective immediately."

Ex-President Tocsin acted instantly. He renounced the validity of the constitutional convention, declared planetary martial law, and postponed the date of the changeover of the office of the presidency, to preserve, as he put it, "the present constitutional system of Jupiter." In the name of this preservation he directed the Jupiter Navy to enforce his edicts. He was, in fact, assuming dictatorial powers himself, as Thorley recognized.

"We are hoist between Scylla and Charybdis," Thorley said when the news service was scrambling for precedents and comment. "Faced with a choice between a tyrant of the left or of the right."

"But which side is correct?" the interviewer persisted.

Thorley grimaced. "Appalling as I find the situation, I have to say that technically the constitutional convention is correct. This is a horrendous abuse of its office, but it does have the power to void our entire system of government."

"But the Navy—"

"Ah, yes, the Navy," he agreed. "If the Navy answers to President Tocsin, then perhaps might will make right. We are in an unprecedented pass—"

The interview was interrupted for more pressing action. Tocsin was on again. "I declare Hope Hubris to be a traitor to Jupiter, and I order his immediate arrest. I am directing the Navy to dispatch a ship for this purpose."

The picture shifted to the representative of the Navy. Emerald's dusky face came on. At that moment I knew I had won, for there was no way Emerald would arrest me. "The Jupiter Navy recognizes the authority of the legally constituted government of the United States of Jupiter," she said. "This authority, as we understand it, now lies with the constitutional convention. The convention has appointed Hope Hubris. Accordingly, the Navy answers to Hope Hubris." She paused, her gaze seeking me out—and quickly the news cameras shifted to me. "What is your will, sir?" There was a certain relish in the way she accented that last word. She was in effect challenging me to accept.

Megan was with me now. "Hope, you can't take power by force!" she protested.

"I can't take power any other way," I pointed out. "Tocsin has refused to abide by the decision of the constitutional convention and has tried to have the Navy overturn it by force."

"But he is evil!" she said. "You are not! You can't do things his way!"

I pondered that while the planet waited. My relationship with her was the most important thing in my life.

"What would you have me do, Megan? If I do not assume command, Tocsin will."

She seemed to shrink, turning away from a horrible reality. Then she firmed. "It is true. You told me that at the outset. Things have gone too far; the republic has already been overthrown, and a tyrant will rule." She swallowed. "It is a choice between evils, and the lesser evil must be chosen. Do what you must, Hope; I shall not deny you your destiny."

She was giving me leave, but I would have known even without my talent that there was a dreadful price to pay. I reached for her and brought her to me while the planet beyond the camera watched. "Megan, I must have you with me!"

Her eyes were bright with tears. "No, Hope. I cannot go there. You must go alone."

"Megan, I'll turn it down."

"You cannot, Hope. You must do what you must do, or all the planet will suffer worse. You—must be—the Tyrant."

"Not without you!"

"No!" she flared, jerking away from me. "Do it, Hope! Do it!"

Do it! Suddenly I saw Helse, my first love, lying in her wedding dress, entangled on the deck of the space-bubble, crying out those words to me, knowing they would destroy her. The love of my life, sacrificing herself for the good of our group. Megan, in my heart, was the reincarnation of that girl, and in this respect she was the same. *Do it!*

With the tears standing on my own cheeks, I turned to the camera to give my first order to the Jupiter Navy. I had indeed assumed the mantle of a tyrant, by taking power outside the framework of the prior government, but I feared I had lost as much as I had gained. This was the third and final strike against my relationship with Megan.

Editorial Epilog

The separation of my parents when I was fifteen was the traumatic event of my early life. It took me a long time to understand it or the necessity for it. Megan simply could not associate with the Tyrant, however necessary she knew his office to be. She was a creature of the old system, dedicated to its preservation. But she recognized that the society of Jupiter had come to such a pass that the old system could no longer function, as it had thousands of years before with Rome. She knew that Hope Hubris, like Julius Caesar, represented the only hope for the restoration of order. Hope was of the people, and the people would follow him. The alternative was anarchy and disaster. She compromised by leaving him, though she loved him, even as his prior wives had. In so doing, she freed him from the restraint exercised by her association, permitting him to exercise his power completely. There was no divorce, but the separation was permanent.

I was not required to choose between them; I had complete freedom to be with either or neither. Thus I became the most tangible link between them, and every time I went from one to the other I experienced a resurgence of that private tragedy. But I learned to live with it because I had no choice. After all, my father had suffered the brutal loss of all his family at this same age; how little my loss seemed in comparison! Neither Hope nor Megan ever spoke ill of the other to me; in fact, the first concern of each was for the welfare of the other. He always had to be reassured that she was well cared for and had enough money, and she would fret that he was too busy to take proper care of himself. It was as if they were apart only temporarily, and indeed, they longed to be together. But we all knew it was over.

I found considerable solace with Aunt Spirit, who seemed to have extraordinary empathy. She, of course, hardly left her brother's side, and devoted her life to him; I honestly believe that the one separation he could not have survived would have been from her. If she was Sancho, he was Don Quixote—with a dream become treacherously real. Spirit had a will of CT iron; any who opposed it were destroyed, and she was the true strength of the Tyrancy. But she was not a cold woman, despite her reputation; she was always gentle and loving to me. Perhaps she remembered her own separation from her husband in the Navy, Admiral Phist, though as it turned out, that separation was temporary. I just don't know. But that, by a chain of association, reminds me of my father's interaction with Admiral Phist's wife, Roulette. Could she indeed have been my natural mother? I cannot imagine Hope Hubris being untrue to Megan during their years together, yet Roulette loved him and, even in middle age, was the most beautiful woman I have ever seen. If she had come to him in those early years, before he was intimate with Megan, and pleaded for some token—no, of course not! Definitely not! I just can't accept the notion that he would do such a thing or that Megan would knowingly accept the situation—and, of course, he would not have deceived her.

But for weeks I dreamed of being a pirate lass, living in a ship in the Belt, earning my livelihood in some nefarious manner. It was romantic nonsense but fun at the time. Remember, I was fifteen. It ended about the time I remembered the way pirate women married: by getting brutally raped, if they did not manage to kill their suitors. Roulette had killed two before being overcome by my father in one of the legendary encounters of the Belt. No, I did not care to marry that way! But still I wondered, Where *had* Roulette been that year? The next few years would see me age at an extraordinary rate, for there were deep shocks coming, but then I had romantic notions. My father never commented, either to con-

firm or deny; he could be quite aggravating that
way.

Meanwhile, Jupiter was perforce embarked on the
period of the Tyrancy, as it was popularly known. It
was probably the most significant decade in the history of the planet and had no parallels to the politics
of prior ages. The Hispanic refugee had finally
achieved ultimate power, and he used it. Oh, did he
use it! We have seen the signals of his increasing
cynicism about politics and the use of power, in such
episodes as the Pardon; we should not have been surprised or dismayed by its fruition. He set out to cure
every ailment of the society—simultaneously. Such
an attempt could only have been made by an absolute dictator or a total fool or the Tyrant of Space.

But to me he was just my father, with the virtues
and frailties of the office, and I loved him dearly.
That made my own course as difficult in its way as
his. But I must let him speak for himself, in the following manuscript.

Hopie Megan Hubris
May 28, 2671

BIO OF A SPACE TYRANT
Piers Anthony

"Brilliant...a thoroughly original thinker and storyteller with
unique ability to posit really *alien* alien life, humanize it, ar
make it come out alive on the page." *The Los Angeles Time*

Widely celebrated science fiction novelist Piers Anthony ha
written a colossal new five volume space thriller—**BIO OF
SPACE TYRANT:** *The Epic Adventures and Galactic Conques*
of Hope Hubris.

VOLUME I: REFUGEE   84194-0/$2.95 US /$3.50 CA
Hubris and his family embark upon an ill-fated voyage throuc
space, searching for sanctuary, after pirates blast them fro
their home on Callisto.

VOLUME II: MERCENARY   87221-8/$2.95 US /$3.50 CA
Hubris joins the Navy of Jupiter and commands a squadrc
loyal to the death and sworn to war against the pirate warlorc
of the Jupiter Ecliptic.

VOLUME III: POLITICIAN   89685-0/$2.95 US /$3.50 CA
Fueled by his own fury, Hubris rose to triumph obliteratir
his enemies and blazing a path of glory across the face
Jupiter. Military legend...people's champion...promisir
political candidate...he now awoke to find himself tr
prisoner of a nightmare that knew no past.

Also by Piers Anthony:
The brilliant Cluster Series—
sexy, savage interplanetary adventures.

CLUSTER, CLUSTER I	01755-5/$2.95 US/$3.75 CA
CHAINING THE LADY, CLUSTER II	01779-2/$2.95 US/$3.75 CA
KIRLIAN QUEST, CLUSTER III	01778-4/$2.95 US/$3.75 CA
THOUSANDSTAR, CLUSTER IV	75556-4/$2.95 US/$3.75 CA
VISCOUS CIRCLE, CLUSTER V	79897-2/$2.95 US/$3.75 CA

AVON Paperbacks

Buy these books at your local bookstore or use this coupon for ordering:

CAN—Avon Books of Canada, 210-2061 McCowan Rd., Scarborough, Ont. M1S 3Y6
US—Avon Books, Dept BP, Box 767, Rte 2, Dresden, TN 38225

Please send me the book(s) I have checked above. I am enclosing $_____
(please add $1.00 to cover postage and handling for each book ordered to a maximum of
three dollars). Send check or money order—no cash or C.O.D.'s please. Prices and num
bers are subject to change without notice. Please allow six to eight weeks for delivery.

Name _____

Address _____

City _____ State/Zip _____

ANTHONY 5-8